UNRELENTING
PERIL

Gary D. McGugan

Unrelenting Peril
Copyright © 2019 by Gary D. McGugan
Reprinted April 2020

Cover and book design by Castelane.

No part of this publication may be reproduced, distributed, or transmitted in any form or by any means, including photocopying, recording, or other electronic or mechanical methods, without the prior written permission of the author, except in the case of brief quotations embodied in critical reviews and certain other non-commercial uses permitted by copyright law.

This book is a work of fiction. Names, characters, businesses, organizations, places, events, and incidents are the product of the author's imagination or are used fictitiously. Any resemblance to actual persons, living or dead, events or locales are entirely coincidental.

ISBN
978-1-9995656-0-2 (Paperback)
978-1-9995656-1-9 (eBook)

1. FICTION, THRILLERS

Printed in Canada

Also by Gary D. McGugan

Fiction

Three Weeks Less a Day
The Multima Scheme
Pernicious Pursuit

Non-Fiction

NEEDS Selling Solutions
(Co-authored with Jeff F. Allen)

What People are Saying About Books by Gary D. McGugan

"Thoroughly enjoyed *Unrelenting Peril*, the third installment in the story of the Multima Corporation. It is definitely the best of the three books! I was so absorbed in the story it was difficult to put the book down. The author's writing style, which was excellent already, keeps getting better which each book. I can't wait to read the next one!!"
– *GoodReads Reviewer, Mary*

"One thing is clear - Gary D. McGugan knows how to write top caliber stories. Some authors write predominately character-driven books, while others drive their stories through enticing plotlines. McGugan does both, and with equal excellence – no small feat, especially in keeping a series exciting and suspenseful with escalating intensity."
– *Sheri Hoyte, Reader Views*

"As is the case with McGugan's two previous novels, *Three Weeks Less A Day* and *The Multima Scheme*, the plot of *Unrelenting Peril* is tight and complex. McGugan has a gift for well-paced, well-blocked flurries of nail-biting action that all lead up to a surprising finale."
– *Norm Goldman, Bookpleasures.com*

"*Unrelenting Peril*, is an enthralling story about corporate intrigue. The characters and exotic locales, add to the engaging story. *Unrelenting Peril* will keep you on the edge of your seat until you finish the last page." – *GoodReads Reviewer, Cathy*

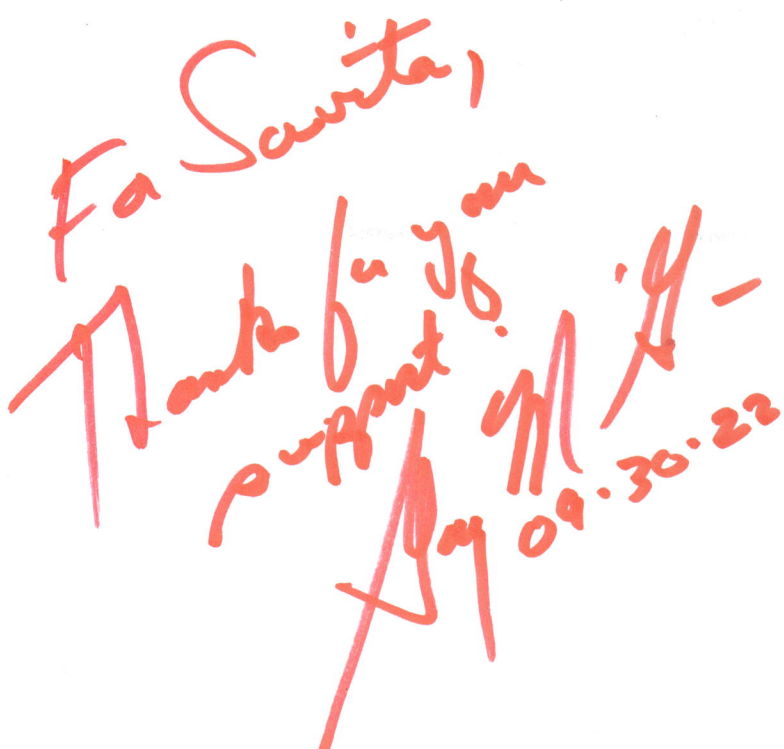

For all family and friends who provide unwavering encouragement.
You know who you are.

NE

Friday January 6, 2017

"You win," the sweating visitor said. "The guys who run this outfit accepted your offer."

Howard Knight stared, unbelieving. Was it possible they were really planning to let him out of this hellhole?

"My boss thinks they're all idiots at the top. He refused to meet you again and forced me to come instead. I'll tell you up front, this whole thing turns my stomach, but like a good boy scout, I'll follow orders."

The much younger man paused and glared at Howard, who remained silent. Now wasn't the time to vent his considerable anger and frustration.

"Sit down." The agent jabbed his thumb toward a chair facing a makeshift desk before he took the other seat. Without looking up, he shuffled several previously organized sheets of paper.

"You need to complete some paperwork," he said. "Going forward, you'll be Eduardo Fortuna, a successful former business guy. Like you, he's more than middle-aged. A retired Italian. After you sign the documents, I'll give you a European passport. It has stamps showing you traveled to Belize recently with a stop in Miami."

Although he glanced toward the papers, the agent still didn't share them. Instead, he pointed at two oversized backpacks. "Inside those bags, you'll find your million dollars. Count them if you want, but I can assure you there are ten thousand hundred-dollar bills."

Howard kept his mouth shut, taking care to project neutral impassivity. This bureaucrat was just a kid. Let him sweat a bit and babble on as long as he wanted.

"There are clothes for you in this bag. Change out of that prison garb before you get on a jet that will take you to Panama," he continued, his tone matter-of-fact and decidedly cool. "One of our local guys will meet you inside the Panama City terminal. Here's a map showing where you'll find the first small boat moored, and this is a key for it. They took out the GPS and tracking equipment just as you so adamantly insisted. The fuel tank is full, and there are two portable containers in the hold with enough gas to get you to Belize."

Apparently, the inexperienced agent found his task distasteful and didn't wait for questions or comment. Howard didn't care. It was his survival the guy was talking about, so he was content just to listen.

"Your new Carver yacht will leave Miami once you sign the paperwork. Here's a photo of the vessel and the original documents. They registered it to a numbered company. Two other agents will set sail on that Carver from the Florida Keys at the same time you arrive in Panama. They'll head to Belize and anchor two miles off San Pedro. They'll stay there until you're within a mile of the ship. When you signal you're there, the agents will call for a helicopter to fetch them and leave the yacht anchored," he recited, glancing twice at his notes to be sure he delivered the correct information.

"You'll be entirely responsible for the yacht after that and will also be responsible for getting rid of the first small boat you use. Any questions before you sign the paperwork?" the FBI official asked as he handed over a file.

A few questions surfaced as Howard read through the extensive document. The fellow sounded more like an attorney than an FBI agent as he answered each question perfunctorily. The paperwork confirmed Howard was waiving all rights to any legal action for his incarceration. He acknowledged the government of the United States of America had provided him with all requested compensation plus a new identity to start over his life. Finally, he agreed never to disclose any details of either his illegal imprisonment or subsequent financial settlement to anyone.

What more could he say? They'd given him everything he asked. There seemed no benefit to prolonging the exercise. This unfeeling agent would have no interest in how badly the FBI had disrupted his life. The guy would have no interest in the hundreds of hours his superiors had spent grilling Howard for information. He likely wouldn't have any idea about the trove of names, dates, and events his interrogation provided, or the personal risk Howard took revealing that damning information.

Nor would the agent care that release without Fidelia at his side left him feeling only hollow and sad. Why bother trying to explain it? When he finished reading the document and listened to the few clarifications his questions required, he signed the papers and handed them back to the bureaucrat without another word.

Immediately after the official stashed the completed paperwork in his bag, he instructed the armed guards to prepare their prisoner for release and travel. A jet would arrive from Miami in less than an hour.

Amazed at how quickly things were now moving, Howard showered, shaved, and changed his clothes as instructed. Then, two guards escorted him to the canteen for a tasteless and unmemorable meal. When he finished eating, they led him back into the same dreary interrogation room to wait. After only a few minutes, a roar of jet engines and the screech of brakes announced the arrival of a plane nearby.

He grabbed his two bulging sacks of money as one guard motioned it was time to go. Outdoors again in the searing, humid Cuban weather, a third guard joined the procession toward the aircraft carrying the backpack they had confiscated when the Argentinian police seized him. No one said farewell, and one guard used the opportunity to deliver a final shove of disgust. The stairs to the jet lowered slowly, offering a tentative invitation to board before Howard climbed the steps gingerly with the weight of the bags balancing him.

Inside the cabin, the co-pilot instructed him to take any seat and buckle up for immediate departure. Howard stowed the bags of money in a small nearby closet and kept the well-worn backpack in his lap. Seatbelt secured, he opened the bag to check its contents and was amazed to see they had returned it all. The other false passports, the night vision goggles, and his few bits of clothing were all still in the grungy knapsack. Remarkably, even the same neatly sealed Ziploc bags held the crucial components of his treasured handgun.

Howard drew in a deep breath to slow his rapid heartbeat, and his thoughts darted involuntarily back to the beginning.

It started with a bizarre kidnapping. Howard Knight and his love, Fidelia Morales, had spent several weeks and thousands of dollars undergoing cosmetic surgery to alter their appearance when Argentinian police thugs snatched them from the streets of Buenos Aires and unceremoniously turned them over to the FBI. Rather than taking them to the United States for a trial, the rogue Feds instead delivered them to Guantanamo Bay— that notorious offshore facility usually reserved for suspected terrorists.

Their captors treated them only slightly better than the other detainees. They dressed alike, ate the same bland food, and bunked next to a handful of desperate and dejected foreigners. Then, the FBI threatened and cajoled them into divulging information about the criminal organization to which both belonged before their escape. Fidelia called their bluff. Refusing to betray her criminal masters, the FBI acted on their vicious threat and heartlessly shipped her back to Argentina where she was wanted for her role in human trafficking activities.

Howard eventually capitulated and provided his captors with extensive and detailed information about The Organization and its key leaders around the world. He did it with the promise of a new identity under the FBI's well-known witness protection program. They guaranteed him a new name and appearance, with life in a new location, all in return for testimony leading to convictions of major players in the organized crime outfit.

Then—right after the US presidential election—they informed him the FBI director was no longer prepared to indict the named criminals. There was no chance of conviction under the new administration. At that point, Howard immediately and dramatically changed his demands. However, there had been no response or communication since. Until today.

After flying about two hours, the aircraft descended sharply as it swooped in for a landing at Marcos A. Gelabert Albrook International Airport in Panama. A former US Air Force base now used for civil aviation, there was no inspection of documents or other immigration formalities. As Howard walked away from the aircraft, a hum signaled the staircase already rising. A few seconds later he felt a powerful, hot backdraft from the jet as it prepared to taxi for take-off. The plane was gone before he reached the entrance to the airport.

Inside, he spotted a local person holding a piece of cardboard with "Fortuna" scrawled in black ink. With a nod, Howard and the short, compact man holding the card connected. Both walked toward a white SUV in the corner of an almost vacant parking lot.

With a shrug of his shoulders and shake of his head, Howard refused the man's offer to help carry the bags. They might be bulky and uncomfortable to lug in the heat, but there was no way those bags would leave his grip even for an instant. It was bad enough he had to ride in a car with the guy.

After a less than ten-minute drive, they arrived at a commercial shipyard. The promised twenty-one-foot Boston Whaler bobbed against a high cement dock, nestled between two massive ocean-going vessels under repair. After the driver helped him down a rope ladder, enormous twin two-hundred-horsepower outboard engines caught Howard's attention. That power would be more than adequate for the trip to Belize. Closer inspection confirmed the craft had been used previously, but it appeared to be seaworthy. The FBI had held up its end of the deal so far.

With a hearty thumbs-up, Howard dismissed the driver and quickly stowed his backpack and money bags in the storage compartment below the steering wheel—well out of sight of any curious eyes working on vessels high above. The promised supplies of food and water and a waterproof sleeping bag were under the console as well. Within minutes, he started the engine, gingerly guided the boat toward open water, and sighed heavily.

That nightmare with the FBI was over. Now, he could focus on the more menacing threat. The Organization.

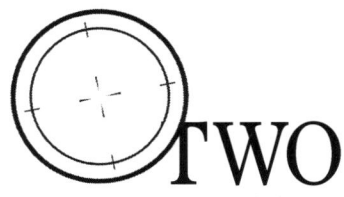

Two

An office tower on Wall Street, New York, NY
Saturday January 7, 2017

"You'll have to leave now," the powerful head of The Organization announced just seconds after Douglas Whitfield sat down in a plain leather chair next to his long-time friend, Earnest Gottingham III.

Douglas had been summoned to Gottingham's office at the headquarters of Venture Capital Inc. It was a weekend, and he could only imagine the anxiety his friend must feel seeing Giancarlo Mareno occupying the chair of authority behind the desk while the two younger men sat like supplicants before him. It didn't look good at all. Equally worrisome, burly thugs stood with hands behind their backs on either side of Mareno, weapons unmistakably bulging beneath their jackets.

It was terrifying for Douglas and he figured the scenario would be even more so for Gottingham. Mareno's towering mass dominated the space around the desk in a most intimidating manner. His scowl of anger added to Douglas's discomfort and spoke far louder than the giant's calm tone. "You'll have to leave now" could have several meanings. No one spoke.

The leader of The Organization remained silent for several seconds. Then he looked each directly in the eye and said, "The billion dollars you boys cost me is just the beginning. The loss of that much money irritates me, but I have more. I won't feel too much pain financially. But my reputation will suffer miserably."

Again, he paused to reinforce the intensity of his concern. "Your flawed scheme to buy that division of Multima Corporation has caused angst among our partners. Do you college-educated boys know the meaning of that word angst? They were pissed. When that special computer software you persuaded us to buy for a billion dollars blew up, I had to give all our partners their money back. But it also caused our associates to question my judgment. And that bothers me far more than the money lost."

Douglas Whitfield remained silent but risked a glance at Gottingham who squirmed uncomfortably in the chair beside him. Mareno glared at both, shifting his head and gaze dramatically from one to the other to reinforce his message. The veins on his neck bulged and pulsated hypnotically as the man hesitated. The pause extended for many seconds—a minute maybe—before he continued.

"You see, a billion dollars has great value, but it's a finite amount. In my line of work, respect has infinite value," Mareno emphasized. "So, my real losses in this debacle can't be measured. Our partners will remember how easily Multima Corporation swindled us out of the money. Now, they'll question or second guess every suggestion I make. I have to do something to reassure them. I need to show 'em I'm still in control, send a message that I don't suffer fools lightly. Then people will understand they can't take advantage of Giancarlo Mareno."

With a pained expression on his face and dark eyes slinging daggers of accusation at both men, Mareno waited. Neither defendant spoke, but another sideward glance showed Gottingham was now visibly shaken.

Mareno resumed. "Earnest, you no longer work here. You'll go with Luigi and Carlo now to discuss your termination and severance package."

As though on cue, both thugs swiftly circled the cowering Gottingham, and lifted him from his chair. Gottingham yelped in terror and wet himself as he twisted back and forth, futilely resisting the iron grip of the huge thugs. Douglas's friend screamed "No! No! No!" while the burly ruffians dragged their struggling victim across the floor and out the door.

For several moments, Mareno stared at Douglas without so much as a blink. Undoubtedly, he wanted the shock and horror to have maximum effect. The look he gave was different, even haunting. It looked so melancholy that Douglas pondered if Mareno might be wondering whether he should preserve his investment or not.

Everything Douglas had he owed to Mareno. The elite private school education. The business degrees. The job that paid millions with bonuses. All became possible only because of the powerful hulk ominously staring at him.

Was there a trace of racism in those burning eyes? Before, Mareno never seemed to care about the color of Douglas's skin. But the current intimidating look had an edge and hardness that Douglas was accustomed to seeing. It happened often when your skin was the light brown result of a mixed-race relationship.

Mareno appeared to relax and leaned back in his chair gazing skyward as though deep in thought. Finally, he stood up, walked around from behind the desk and hovered over Douglas, looking down with pursed lips and an expression of fierce determination.

"Your friend Earnest is about to have an accident, but you probably already know that. He's going to take a fall from a bridge. Later today or tomorrow, his body will turn up in the Hudson. The police will advise the media, and they'll report his death appeared targeted. Our partners will read about that, and they'll be reminded that I take quick action to correct my mistakes," he said in a clear, quiet voice just above a whisper.

"And your fate in this mess really should be the same as Gottingham's. But two things save you. First, I admit I find it hard to give an order to kill you. You're my son, after all. But make no mistake. I'm prepared to give that order if there's ever another screwup.

"Second, I need you to get revenge. I need you to devise a plan to get total control of Multima Corporation. So, here's what's going to happen. You're going to disappear for a while. I want you to leave immediately after our little talk. Here's enough cash for a year or so living in Costa Rica or Guatemala or some such out-of-the-way place." He gestured toward a large, brown leather briefcase looking out of place on the corner of the bare mahogany desk.

"You're going to lie low," he continued. "No communication with anyone back here. We'll plant a tip in the media that you probably met the same unfortunate fate as your friend and your body will likely show up sometime soon. That story should buy you some time.

"While you're hiding out in the tropics, you'll develop a plan to steal Multima Corporation from the bitch who's now running it. We know it was Suzanne Simpson who crafted that clever idea to turn their software into a self-destructing bomb and cheat us out of our billion-dollar investment. I'll only regain my stature with our partners when I pull all the strings at that fucking company.

"Forget her old man. He's not worth wasting any time on. He's already got his punishment coming with cancer and won't be around much longer. Take whatever time you need to devise the plan and come back only when you're sure you've covered every eventuality and are ready to explain it to me. Then we'll act.

"And, Douglas. Don't screw this up," Mareno whispered menacingly.

With that admonition, he hoisted his son from the chair with one burly hand and gave him a token bear-hug of farewell, then turned to stroll back toward the chair behind the desk.

"I won't let you down," Douglas replied to Mareno's back.

Wordlessly, he snatched the large leather briefcase and scurried from the office not even daring to breathe. Only after he was in the elevator and sure no one was following him did he exhale. It was really too bad about Gottingham. He was a good friend, but survival was always more important than emotion. Time to start plotting. His unforgiving father would never again have confidence in him if he didn't find a way to steal Multima, and soon.

THREE

The Mucky Duck restaurant, Captiva, FL
Saturday February 3, 2017

Suzanne Simpson, the new chief executive officer of Multima Corporation, was delighted when her assistant buzzed to let her know Michelle Sauvignon, president of Farefour Stores China, was on the line. They were long-time friends from their days in the MBA program at Stanford University, but Suzanne hadn't talked with her since a business trip to China a couple years earlier. She took the call immediately.

"I'm visiting Southwest Florida for the next few days," Michelle explained when their pleasantries were finished. "Are you in the area?"

Suzanne was in Fort Myers, only a forty-minute drive away. They compared schedules and settled on dinner Saturday evening at The Mucky Duck, a one-of-a-kind restaurant on the tip of Captiva near Michelle's hotel. It was a favorite spot of Suzanne's—not for the food—but for the outstanding view of the Gulf of Mexico and its laid-back, easy-going atmosphere.

When Suzanne arrived, Michelle already sat at an outdoor table, gazing at the white-sand beach and sipping something cold. As always, the French woman appeared fashionably stylish, wearing a casual short sundress and sandals. The broad, floppy hat was a crowning touch, Suzanne decided as she rushed toward her table.

They greeted each other in French with enthusiasm and cries of welcome, hugging several times and planting kisses on both cheeks in the European tradition. They'd started that ritual at Stanford when they realized they were among a minuscule group of francophones at the prestigious California university.

They were not only in the same MBA program but also housemates and the closest of friends. Some mistook them for sisters. Both were taller than average. Both had long brunette hair in those days, and their dark brown eyes looked almost identical. To further confuse people, they often wore each other's clothes.

After graduation they both accepted positions with large supermarket chains—Michelle with her father's company in France and Suzanne with a Canadian company eventually acquired by Multima Corporation. Throughout the years their bond of friendship grew. Contact was infrequent and unpredictable, but every time they met, it was like they had just seen each other the day before. However, both were also serious and ambitious executives so it didn't take long for their conversation to drift into business.

"They made you CEO," Michelle gushed. "Congratulations! How does it feel to run one of the biggest companies in America?"

"It's only been a month, so I'm still settling into the job," Suzanne replied. "There's more to learn than I expected, but I have a great management team around me. We'll muddle through."

"I heard John George Mortimer is battling cancer," Michelle said tactfully. "Is he still involved as Chair of the board?"

"Yes, he's still alive, still the Chair. In fact, his health has recently improved a bit," Suzanne added before a short pause as she considered whether she wanted to continue in that direction. In deference to their long friendship, she decided she would. "You know he is more than just the Chair of Multima, don't you?"

"Am I aware he also recently revealed that he's your father?" Michelle peeked coyly over her sunglasses as she sipped her drink. "It must have been a real shock to you."

"Yeah, shock is a good way to describe it. A surprise. A shock. A revelation. A life-altering development. Any of those descriptions would work fine," Suzanne replied as she felt her smile slowly fading. "And that totally unexpected bit of news was only one factor that made last year hell. Coping with all that happened in the past few months was far more taxing than the challenges of the CEO role."

"How so?"

"Well, you can imagine the emotions it triggered when he let me know. Just the bit that I was his daughter from a casual sexual relationship was a huge shock. Then, he revealed that he discovered our connection over a decade earlier. In fact, he bought the Canadian supermarket chain I led and made me president of Multima Supermarkets knowing he was my father. And he kept it a secret for years!"

"Wow." Michelle slowly shook her head in disbelief. "Why?"

"Who knows? He gave me a cockamamie story about not wanting my peers to think I was advancing only because of our relationship. For months, I was devastated. I couldn't grasp how someone having such vital information kept it to himself for so long."

"Have things improved?" Michelle probed.

"Yeah. Over time and more talking with him, I gradually came around. I started to think a little more from his perspective and eventually began to like the situation. I always looked up to John George and respected him almost like a father-figure, I guess. What we went through with the company last year brought us closer together, too."

"I heard you guys sold off the Multima Solutions business. Is that what you're talking about?" Michelle asked.

"Well, the selling off was probably the easiest part of the whole escapade with Solutions," Suzanne started while she decided just how much she should reveal to her friend. "I know I can trust you not to share this with anyone, Michelle, but I need to hear you say it. I need to talk with somebody, but there's just too much at stake."

"You know my lips are sealed." Michelle looked directly into Suzanne's eyes while she put her hand over her heart. "It will stay with me."

"The whole debacle started with John George's ambition to dramatically grow and diversify the company. He was a corporate wizard when he created the Financial Services business that became so successful. A lot of people thought he made another brilliant decision to acquire that small technology company he made into Multima Solutions. And for a few years, it worked well with Supermarkets, Financial Services, and Solutions all reporting to him here at headquarters in Southwest Florida. Then, that idiot he put in charge of Solutions went off the deep end."

"What happened?"

"Wendal Randall was the guy's name. He was a technology geek, but the business world thought he was a genius. And his people really did help the Supermarkets division a lot. I really appreciated their expertise. They gave us some really slick systems to manage inventory and logistics. It made us the best in the business. But, for some reason, the moron decided to hack our mainframe and steal a bunch of sensitive data about our personnel!"

"What?" exclaimed Michelle. "He hacked into another system at the same company he worked for? Why would he ever do that?"

"He asked me for the files, and I refused for privacy and policy reasons. Of course, we didn't know who did it right away, so we called Homeland Security. We have to do that in the USA. They sent the FBI to investigate. Within days they found the culprit in Solutions and traced his involvement directly back to Randall. While the FBI was investigating his role in the whole thing, they learned he was also harboring a European woman, a fugitive wanted by Interpol. They arrested the woman and Randall. John George fired him immediately, and we haven't heard anything about the guy since."

"This is all just incredible," Michelle murmured.

"But that wasn't the end of it," Suzanne hurried to reply. There was much more to her story, and she felt compelled to share it. "At precisely the same time the FBI was investigating Randall, we learned an influential member of the board of directors was secretly plotting to overthrow John George and install Wendal Randall as the new CEO. His plan failed for two reasons. First, Randall acted like a fool and got himself arrested. But that outside director also made a fatal miscalculation in the amount of support he was able to muster for his coup. It turned out John George had far more voting rights than Knight was able to cobble together."

"Who's Knight again?" Michelle inquired.

"Howard Knight, a director. He's the former president of Venture Capital Inc., a big private capital outfit in New York. Sorry, that's another bit I left out. When John George wanted to buy the company that became Multima Solutions, he didn't have enough cash available to do it. So, he granted preferred shares to Venture Capital Inc. Later, he found out that VCI is really a front company for a rather shady criminal entity known as The Organization."

"This is all unbelievable!" Michelle leaned toward Suzanne with her face expressing total fascination, virtually begging for more detail. "What happened next?"

"During the meeting of the board where Randall's arrest and termination of employment at Multima were announced, it also became apparent Knight couldn't complete the overthrow of John George Mortimer, and he left. Just like that, he walked out of the meeting and hasn't been heard from since."

"He just got up from the boardroom table and disappeared?"

"Yes. There have been lots of rumors. Some thought he may have committed suicide. Others suggested he may have fled the USA to escape the wrath and retribution of The Organization. After all, he put a billion dollars of their money at risk with his foolishness," Suzanne said.

"That is really scary stuff."

"No kidding. And that's why I have these guys with me all the time," Suzanne whispered, nodding her head toward the couple at the next table.

"The massive brute who looks like he should be playing football with the woman who looks like she lifts weights for fun?" Michelle asked in an equally low tone.

"Yeah. They're the ones. Corporate security decided I need them all the time since our store in Kissimmee was bombed last year," Suzanne replied with no smile or ambiguity about her concern. "That's when John George finally told me about Knight, the preferred shares, and The Organization."

"Doesn't that connection to organized crime worry you?" Michelle asked.

"It worried me then, and it worries me still," Suzanne said hesitantly. "We might be rid of them now, but that was when I first wondered if John George might be starting to lose it. I had great respect for the guy. He accomplished so much in his career. Whether it was the effects of cancer, or his treatments, or his advancing age, or everything combined, he didn't seem as infallible as he had for much of his career. And learning about all his vulnerabilities somehow drew me closer to him. Our business rapport was shifting, evolving to more resemble a father-daughter relationship."

"Aww, that's sweet." A broad smile spread across Michelle's face. "Is that when he decided to make you CEO?"

"Not right away. He let me know that was his goal, but he gave no indication of timing or anything like that. I decided we needed to act and get rid of both Multima Solutions and The Organization. We found a way we could do both and successfully divested Solutions by selling it to Venture Capital Inc. for the equity they held in Multima Corporation. An elegant solution, we thought."

"Then your father's cancer returned," Michelle said.

"Yes. Cancer returned, and he knew he had to relinquish control of the company."

Suzanne took a deep breath to contain her sudden gloom. She'd recounted all she was willing to share, so she nibbled at the remnants of her veggie burger. Michelle had already finished her meal but appeared to have trouble processing so many details and the gravity of her friend's circumstance. She refilled both glasses of wine before speaking.

"I understand why my father asked me to meet with you," Michelle said. "He thought Multima Corporation was going through a lot of upheaval right now and was he ever right!"

"I think the upheaval, as you call it, is finished—more or less. I haven't heard from Randall, Knight, VCI, or The Organization in several months. I'm curious why your father would think there's upheaval now and even more curious about why he asked you to come."

"You're right," Michelle quickly conceded. "He mentioned the upheaval in the context of recent events because, at Farefour, we're going through some tough times ourselves. You probably know my father is no longer actively involved in the company. He's still the largest individual shareholder though, so he pulls a lot of strings in the background. We've got a new CEO, and my father's uncomfortable with him. Our operating results over the past couple years have been abysmal. To make matters worse, even in Europe, the supposed threat of the Amazon Effect fascinates the business media. And the value of our shares has plunged. My father thinks this might create an opportunity for both of our companies."

"How so?"

"Both corporations need some unexpected and dramatic good news to appease shareholders, and my father thinks he found a way for both of us to win big. He also feels he can engineer a promotion for me to replace the current guy if the deal is big enough," Michelle explained.

"Let me hear what you're thinking, sister," Suzanne said with a giggle. If Michelle's father was plotting a scheme, it should be entertaining at least and also might have potential.

"Multima Corporation's balance sheet is the envy of the industry. Your father may have made some recent mistakes in judgment, but the rest of us in the supermarket business would kill for your financial strength. Acquisitions must be on your mind. Recently, my father heard rumors you might be looking to divest your financial services business to raise capital for some potential takeovers. He thinks it would be a mistake to sell Multima Financial Services. In his view, this is precisely the direction all your competitors will need to go if they hope to compete with Amazon. To just sell food and dry goods in supermarkets won't be enough to survive in the future."

"I'm not so sure I agree, but I understand the rationale," Suzanne allowed, leaning in and tilting her head. "What does he have in mind?"

"He thinks you need to outflank Amazon geographically rather than waging battle with them only in the US. He suggests you consider buying Farefour's operations in China—the division I manage. I cleaned up the culture of bribery and payoffs I told you about when you visited. Our sales are growing double digits every year, and the bottom line is growing just as fast. I'll open a new store every two weeks for the next year. But we're stretched too thin. China needs deeper pockets to maintain the pace of growth. You have the financial heft to do it. We don't."

"I'm a long way from even thinking about your asking price, but are you contemplating an outright sale or something a little more creative?" Suzanne asked.

Neither watched the sunset, and they only noticed the darkness when a chill set in hours later. In the interim, neither ate nor drank anything. Instead, they were engrossed in the complex but brilliant plan Michelle's father had conceived which they probed and dissected from every perspective Suzanne could imagine. Clearly, no concrete decision was possible; nor did Suzanne's old friend seek one. Instead, they ended their discussion with an understanding both needed to give the matter some careful thought and see how events might evolve in the coming weeks.

Suzanne sensed their meeting needed to end at that point and Michelle appeared ready to finish their discussion. They had shared more business confidences than ever before. It seemed both were intrigued with the possibilities. Yet neither could identify a clear way forward.

Before the idea went anywhere, Suzanne needed to get corporate security involved. Was there more to Michelle's father's idea?

FOUR

A small cottage near Colonia del Sacramento, Uruguay
Friday March 2, 2018

Howard Knight's first impression of the neighborhood was tainted by a derelict property that caught his eye as he gazed out the window of a little red taxi. The unsightly relic was right there on the corner as they turned onto the street of what would be his new home for the next month or so.

As the driver veered onto the street, the sedan jolted, scraping its bottom on a deep rut in the poorly maintained dirt road. The momentary pause of the vehicle gave Howard time to better look at the dilapidated structure. It was in tatters with piles of broken rock scattered around the yard. To his amazement, he could see directly inside the ugly, crumbling stone building and picked out the forms of at least five people.

On his right stood a magnificent home, meticulously maintained and landscaped.

What an odd neighborhood.

This pattern of alternating unkept buildings unfit for habitation immediately adjacent to beautifully designed homes of significant worth continued almost to the end of the street where the driver eased to a stop in front of the address highlighted on his phone.

The house was tiny—a cottage, really. However, from the outside, it looked satisfactory. The yard in front was neat and well-trimmed. The swimming pool appeared to be acceptably clean and inviting. A large sliding wood fence enclosed the yard and blocked the view of curious passersby. Large picture windows along the front of the home implied a bright interior. Howard couldn't resist a smile as he noted the hammock outside the front door. He'd never tried one of those things before.

Relaxing in a hammock might fit perfectly with the orders Howard had just received from a doctor at *Mutualista Hospital Evangélico*.

"You have a severe case of parotiditis," the emergency room doctor explained after completing his examination of Howard's severely swollen right gland. "You'll need lots of water and rest for the coming few weeks while the swelling abates. You should also take ibuprofen for the next two weeks. Moreover, be careful. With people your age, if you don't drink enough water, infection can set in, and it becomes even more painful."

Unrelenting Peril

Dismissed, Howard immediately googled the word parotiditis because he didn't know its meaning in English. Even that didn't quite work because Google explained the translated English word was 'parotitis' and he didn't know the meaning of that word either. One more Google inquiry and he got an explanation of the disease. He learned that somewhere in his travels he had contracted a disease virtually eradicated in the US: the mumps.

So, he searched Airbnb, found this available cottage, paid for a month's stay with a prepaid credit card, and only minutes later arrived by taxi to inspect his new surroundings. It would work. He didn't need a lot of luxury and wouldn't have much contact with neighbors.

He didn't bother checking inside right away. Through the picture window, it looked adequate and his pain was severe. He popped two of the ibuprofen the doctor prescribed, washed them down with a gulp from a bottle of water, then slid awkwardly into the hammock. There, he waited for the pills to bring relief from the persistent throbbing pain as he thought about those eventful months since the FBI released him from that hellhole in Guantanamo.

A thirty-four-foot Carver yacht—even one with twin 250-horsepower stern drive engines—is not an ideal boat to cruise in an ocean. Howard realized that when he made his demand from the lead FBI negotiator, but he had given the matter considerable thought.

The top echelon of the FBI had proven too queasy to arrest any leaders of The Organization despite all the juicy information he gave them. Even with the promised relocation and new identity in their witness protection program, his life would soon be over if they didn't incarcerate the top people. Even from prison, The Organization might get to him. But if the hooligans were free to roam throughout the United States, he didn't like his chances of survival at all.

They had infiltrated several federal and state government agencies. That was well-known. Their methods would be thorough and exhaustive. And the resources they could draw on were extensive. Regardless, Howard had no intention of staying in Guantanamo for any longer than necessary.

Instead, he hatched the scheme to negotiate a million dollars, a modest boat, and a new identity. He planned to live on the Caribbean Sea for as long as possible, touching ports only as often as absolutely necessary and living with the barest of essentials.

His demands needed to be fairly reasonable for the FBI to buy into them. So, he asked for a small Carver yacht. He knew the brand's performance at sea was extraordinary for a small craft, and reports he read in the past gave him enough confidence to tackle the stormy seas and inclement weather for which the Caribbean is known.

When the FBI accepted every one of his demands and delivered a boat to a cove off the coast of San Pedro, Belize, Howard changed direction abruptly and set sail for the Cayman Islands. The trip was about five hundred miles and the seas were reportedly calm, so he decided to make the trip in one long day to avoid anchoring far offshore the first night. Twenty hours after he set out, he had safely secured his vessel in the Port of Grand Cayman.

After registering and paying his dockage fees, Howard made the two-minute walk from the port to The Harbor Center only a few hundred yards up the street. There, he entered a modern building covered by gleaming glass and climbed steep stairs to the second-floor offices of TBV Bank. In its lobby, he presented the fake passport he had used to open several accounts years earlier and asked to speak with his usual contact, Mr. Fernando.

"How nice to see you again, Mr. Smith," the banker opened with a knowing smile.

"Good to see you again, Mr. Fernando," Howard Knight replied. "The stock market has been good to me again. I'd like to make a deposit to my account, prepay my credit cards, and leave some documents in my safety deposit box."

"Certainly, Mr. Smith. Where would you like to start?"

"Let's put five hundred into my account first," Howard replied as he passed one of the backpacks to the banker. "And while your people are verifying the amount, perhaps you can load one hundred thousand onto each of these credit cards."

Howard reached into the second backpack and pulled out four large bundles of cash with a different credit card bound to each pile by an elastic band. Each of the credit cards bore different names, but Mr. Fernando didn't pose any questions.

While Fernando and his staff checked and processed the small mountain of cash in a private and secure room on one side of the bank, another employee escorted him to a safety deposit box on the other side. There, they both entered digital codes so Howard could insert the remaining one hundred thousand dollars in cash. It all took less than thirty minutes, and they parted with hearty handshakes and broad smiles.

His next stop was a marine electronics store. There, he spent about thirty-thousand dollars from one of the cards to buy state-of-the-art electronic equipment for the yacht and arranged for its installation the same afternoon. While the technicians installed the electronic gizmos, Howard shopped in nearby stores.

He bought cartons of packaged foods, cases of bottled water and several bags of tinned fruit and vegetables—enough to eat and drink adequately for about a month. He found a bookstore and bought a dozen interesting-looking novels. All were delivered to the boat and carefully stored in secure hatches. As the day came to an end, Howard drove the boat around to the marina entrance and filled the main tank and seven portable containers with fuel.

By nightfall, Howard set off from the port in a southerly direction, confident about his finances for the next year or more. He felt comfortable sailing or anchoring anywhere in the Caribbean by day or night and was ready to stay afloat for about a month before refueling or restocking. That night—and for a further few weeks—he slept comfortably.

During January, Howard traveled by night at low speeds to conserve fuel, using electronic navigational aids. By day, he read or slept after his daily regimen of aerobic calisthenics. He studied the boat's operating manual to learn everything possible about the care and maintenance of both the engine and boat and ate or took in water only when he was hungry or thirsty. He lost about ten pounds that first month.

At the end of January, as supplies dwindled and fuel became perilously low, Howard stopped in the tiny Port of Macaé on Brazil's east coast. Located in the heart of Brazil's petroleum industry, this city was a convenient place to refuel all seven gas tanks and restock with supplies and fresh vegetables. All were available a short distance from the harbor and stores again willingly delivered to the boat.

Through February, Howard repeated his pattern of night travel with his electronic aids and night vision goggles, then rested by day as he worked his way toward Montevideo, Uruguay. His goal was to store his boat in some obscure harbor and eventually find a place to live on land in a small village or out-of-the-way location. However, he chose to stop first in Montevideo to better research his options. It was probably there he caught the mumps.

The woman surely didn't show any symptoms of illness. He remembered inspecting her carefully as he tugged his condom into place. She appeared healthy, fit, and happy. However, in her line of work, who knows with what sorts of individuals she came into contact. It had been the first time in years he had paid for sex, and his judgment that night was no doubt clouded by many months without relief and more than a bottle of wine with dinner.

For that night of folly, he now had a throbbing pain on the right side of his face. His ear ached. His throat was continuously dry and irritated. The glands below his ear swelled to a grotesque size that made swallowing painful. To make matters worse, the damned ibuprofen was having little effect, but the doctor had refused to provide an antibiotic because the disease was viral. "You simply have to let it run its course," he claimed with a shrug and a smile of sympathy.

Howard decided to wait in the hammock for nightfall. It would arouse less curiosity with the neighbors if he called a taxi later and made a couple trips to bring food and supplies from his docked boat to the little cottage. At least things would be ready when he eventually felt like eating or drinking again.

However, this cursed illness might take some time.

FIVE

Miami, FL
Friday March 30, 2018

Douglas Whitfield immediately followed his father's advice to get lost, but it took a while to leave the country. First, he needed new identification for international travel. Using his current passport wasn't an option because any number of government people could track his movements outside the US, and he had no doubt Giancarlo Mareno's enemies could easily penetrate federal government systems and influence its people.

But he couldn't contact the typical resources of The Organization either. Any paper trail left with its usual criminal elements could become lethal if someone decided to track him down. So, he chose first to hunker down over the festive holidays in Miami. His rationale was simple. Sometimes the most effective way to be invisible was to hide right out in the open. If people suspected he'd run away, the last place they would anticipate him going would be Miami where he lived and worked.

Naturally, he couldn't go anywhere near his home or office, but the city of over five million people provided lots of places to lie low while he sorted out details and found documentation to meet his needs. Considered America's gateway to Latin America, the city also sheltered plenty of Cuban elements that operated in their own isolated underworld cocoon—quite removed from The Organization but equally adept at forgery and entirely able to penetrate the State Department's stash of passports.

Douglas rented a car and drove from New York to Miami in one twenty-five-hour period, stopping only for fuel, food, and breaks to stretch. Two days before Christmas he checked into The Jefferson Miami at South West 9th Avenue at the Calle Ocho Walk of Fame. His brown skin color wouldn't attract undue attention in the neighborhood, he'd be able to practice Spanish for a few days, and—most important—he could find a source for his fake documents.

His small room in the two-star hotel was cheap, clean, and surprisingly charming. However, he spent little time there. Instead, he visited the coffee houses that dotted the area surrounding the hotel. It would be only a matter of time before a casual conversation turned to more serious issues and a new acquaintance proved helpful.

Christmas Day, Douglas met a guy who could do the job discretely and quickly. He'd make three separate passports, with three different identities but all using the same photographs Douglas provided. Douglas paid the one-thousand-dollar cash deposit demanded and then waited.

In the meantime, Douglas stayed busy with his laptop and Wi-Fi at nearby cafes. He found a place in Costa Rica he could rent for several months and paid for it by Western Union using one of the invented names from the promised passports. He found a bank that would issue a prepaid Visa credit card and loaded it with a fifty-thousand-dollar balance. He had to pay sixty thousand dollars in cash for the card but saw little alternative.

Three days after Christmas, the contact delivered new, authentic-looking passports issued by Canada, Barbados, and Belize. They'd all pass electronic document readers flawlessly, and all carried the same picture of Douglas Whitfield with different names. He was satisfied with the results and paid the remaining thousand-dollar balance with new twenty-dollar bills as instructed. He booked a flight for early January to Costa Rica.

With all the small details resolved, he had one last pressing issue to address. He needed to get that fox Janet Weissel up in Chicago onside with his plans.

Last fall, he had dumped her rather unceremoniously when it looked like his ascendency to the CEO position at Multima Corporation was on track. Candidly, she was trouble. The best lay he ever had, she also came with a lot of baggage and eventually began talking about a longer-term relationship. The divorce proceedings with his wife were scheduled to start then too so he didn't need a woman with her background and reputation dragged into any settlement with his ex. That was going to be expensive and nasty enough on its own.

Sometime later, Mareno had instructed him to get back in the woman's good books, but with all the hectic activity around Multima Solutions, the new software app, and their billion-dollar loss to Multima, he hadn't found a good time to do that. Now he needed her.

This time it was for more than great sex. Instead, Janet Weissel might be the key to a scheme brewing in the deep recesses of his brain for an eventual plan to take over Multima and be rid of its troublesome CEO once and for all. That was Mareno's prerequisite to restoring his role in The Organization. It was likely also the key to his survival.

So, he hacked Janet Weissel's Facebook and email accounts to learn she was spending the week between Christmas and New Year's Day at a swank resort in Hawaii. Discrete telephone inquiries with the front desk of the Sheraton Waikiki determined she was traveling alone. A bit later, with a combination of trickery and charm, he learned she was in room 716. But he didn't dare call. After the way he broke up with her, she'd abruptly hang up, doing longer-term damage. Instead, he booked a flight from Miami to Honolulu. With arrival three days before the end of her planned vacation, he was confident his charm would carry the day. He'd have her onside before they both left Hawaii.

When Douglas found Janet sitting alone by the pool, soaking up the sun as only northerners on vacation can, he thought a lighthearted approach might be the best way to start. "Hey, good lookin'. Where've you been these past few months?" He put on the most disarming grin he could muster.

"I've been managing just fine without you," Janet Weissel replied coldly. "And let's keep it that way." Her tone was louder than necessary.

"I get it. I acted like a total jerk, and I apologize," he said as contritely as his acting skills allowed. "I made a big mistake. Now, I realize that and want to make amends. Can we talk about it?"

"You can take your apologies and amends and shove them both up your ass," she said louder than before.

Before Douglas could reply, he felt a firm hand grip his shoulder. "Is everything all right, ma'am?" a deep voice inquired.

"Yes. Yes, everything's okay," Janet purred with her most inviting smile. "Except I don't think this man is a guest in the hotel and I'd really rather keep my pool time private."

Douglas had to respect the physical strength of the large Hawaiian man and the authority his uniform implied. He graciously apologized for interrupting her tanning session and bid farewell as casually as possible. Then, he chatted amiably with the pool custodian as the big fellow escorted his unwanted visitor from the pool area and off the grounds. To show there were no hard feelings, he slipped a fifty-dollar bill into the man's hand, apologizing at the same time for any inconvenience his too-ardent love for the woman caused.

Next, Douglas arranged delivery of an extravagant flower arrangement to Janet's room. A few hours later, room-service delivered a bottle of champagne. While she had dinner in the dining room that night, he sent an expensive bottle of French red wine to her table and a dessert she would love. Then, with a master key stolen from the unattended bag of a cleaning woman working on another floor, he let himself into her room and waited.

She was neither alarmed nor angry when she discovered him lying on her bed.

"You're so predictable." A tiny smile formed on her lips despite her best efforts. "With your over-the-top courting techniques, I knew it was only a question of time before I'd open the door to see you lying right there as though nothing had happened since you dumped me in Miami."

It was better to make no immediate comment. Instead, he fashioned his expression as contrite as possible and waited for Janet to continue.

"Three months ago, I wished you dead. I hated you for the way you treated me. You're the only guy I've ever felt something for, and you treated me like shit. But I've moved on. So, it's better now for you to move on." She pointed toward the door.

"I will," Douglas said, "as soon as I explain to you why I'm here. It's not to seduce you. It's not to hurt you or open old wounds. I truly feel bad about the way I treated you and apologize unequivocally. However, I'm here to discuss business—The Organization's business."

Fear glimmered in her eyes before she quickly recovered and asked, "And what organization would you be talking about?"

"It's okay, Janet. I know all about you and your background. I know about your seedy video that incriminated Wendal Randall—the one with the bastard choking you while he was having an orgasm. I know about the support you got from The Organization in college. I know about The Organization assigning you to infiltrate the corporate communications group at Multima. I know that management suspected you were a mole and shuffled you off to Chicago to get you out of the way in Multima's Financial Services division. Moreover, I also know how well you have performed as the perfectly dressed, well-behaved young corporate rung-climber since I broke up with you." He gauged her reaction.

She showed no surprise, no emotion. She faced him directly with cold, unwavering eyes and waited for Douglas to continue.

"You're probably wondering how I know all that," he whispered. "You're smart. So, you've likely already deduced that I too am part of The Organization. You've also figured out that I must be well-connected to senior leadership to know all those details. Now, I'll take a major leap of trust and share something with you that you must never pass on to anyone."

He mentally counted five full seconds before he said, "Giancarlo Mareno is my father."

She sagged slowly into a chair across from Douglas as though weakened, her mouth agape, as she processed the revelation. Sure, he was taking a huge chance. If she ever shared the information, it might put Mareno's life in danger as well as his own. But his intuition told him she would quickly do the calculations assess the potential for personal gain, and decide to cooperate with him for mutual benefit. She didn't disappoint. Within just a few seconds, she responded in a voice as soft as his own.

"What do you propose?"

Douglas ordered their favorite bottle of Pinot Noir from room service and made himself comfortable in the swivel chair in the room's workspace. Janet sat on the sofa with her legs crossed, propped up by a couple oversized cushions, as he explained his idea over the next hour or so.

He watched her reaction intently as he revealed each step of the scheme he had developed so far. He particularly watched her body language while he described her anticipated role and the eventual outcomes. As skillful as she might be camouflaging her emotions, it became clear she was engrossed in the plan he outlined. With a final nod of her head, she told him she was in. She'd do it all. As they finished their talk, she rose from the sofa, approached him, and wrapped her arms around his shoulders, her gorgeous breasts inches from his face.

"Since we're going to be working so closely together for the next few months, shall we carry on like before?" She teased him with her most seductive smile.

And they did carry on. Until it was time to leave on New Year's morning, they made love with the same passion and intensity they had months earlier. Douglas lost count of the number of times he brought her to a climax. But he made sure their final deep and passionate farewell kiss offered enough potential for the future to keep the woman well-focused on their new mission.

SIX

An office tower, Hoffman Estates, IL
Friday March 30, 2018

They didn't celebrate Good Friday at Multima Corporation. Like many American companies, personal days had gradually replaced mandated holidays to deliver better customer service while respecting religious tolerance and cultural sensitivities. That was just fine with Janet Weissel because today was her last day in her current job. When she returned to her office on Monday, she would start a fantastic new job.

Even before Douglas Whitfield outlined the steps she needed to take to help execute his plan to control Multima, Janet had vowed to become a star performer and win promotions to higher levels of management at Multima Financial Services. This good news just sped things along, and she couldn't wait to tell him the exciting news.

"I know you told me not to call," Janet blurted out. "But I just couldn't send an impersonal email to tell you that Monday morning I start my new job as a vice president."

"Great news! But are you sure this line is secure?"

"Yeah. I'm on an encrypted line from that office I rented. They guaranteed one hundred percent security."

"Okay, tell me all about it."

"Fitzgerald is creating a new position. I'll be vice president of quality assurance just like we planned," she enthused.

"So, you managed to get your black belt in Six Sigma?"

"Yeah. It was a grind, though. I studied five or six hours online at home every night for the past three months since we met in Hawaii. Luckily, math and statistics come easily. I received my Black Belt certification two weeks ago," Janet explained.

"Impressive. That's a huge accomplishment. I remember you didn't even know what Lean Six Sigma was when I asked you to get the certification," Douglas replied with a guffaw. "Now you're a guru in statistical process improvement. You did in a few weeks what some spend months to achieve. Nice work."

"Fortunately, I got my certificate the week before the annual performance review conducted by HR. So, I highlighted my certification to my boss, then the personnel manager, and ultimately to James Fitzgerald.

But it really helped that you used to work in Financial Services," Janet added. "That knowledge you shared with me about all the players—and how to influence them—really helped me push the right buttons at every stage."

"It looks like you used it well. How long did it take to get to Fitzgerald?"

"Only about two weeks. HR set up a meeting for me to pitch the idea to the senior management team in the big conference room right next to his office," she replied.

"And the rest of the plan? Give me all the juicy details."

"Well, two days after the meeting, Fitzgerald invited me to his office. Your predictions were right. I detected the sadness in his eyes as soon as he asked me to sit down. His speech pattern was slightly lethargic. I sensed he was a little distracted or depressed. But after a few minutes, he responded well to my suggestive smiles and fake shy demeanor. I think you're right. He's really affected by the death of his son and he never once mentioned his wife."

"So, were you able to make any progress on the hook?"

"Yeah. I got him to invite me for a drink that evening. Believe it or not, it was quicker and even easier than you thought," Janet teased. "I had him in bed that first night. For such a normally reserved guy, he sure had some rather enjoyable staying power."

"Okay, spare me the juicy parts, then."

Is that a tinge of jealousy showing?

"By the time he left that first night, I had him hooked. I could tell by his body language that going home to his wife was about the last thing he wanted to do. The next morning, I sent him an email asking if he'd considered the merits of my proposal to create a Lean Six Sigma program. He asked me back for another meeting in his office and offered me the new job, with an excellent increase in salary, by the way. It becomes official Monday."

"It was that easy?" Douglas asked.

"It was that easy. I made a video of our night in bed like we discussed but didn't need to mention it. He decided all on his own," Janet affirmed.

"Great job. But continue sleeping with him once or twice a week. We need to keep him nice and compliant while you do your work. Keep me posted by email," Douglas said before abruptly hanging up.

In the coming days, she'd have an opportunity to discuss, review, record and perhaps change every process Multima Financial Services used to administer the billions of dollars the division financed every year. This new role would allow her to know more about the internal workings of Financial Services than any other individual—including James Fitzgerald.

Of course, she'd also follow orders and continue sleeping with him once or twice a week. She'd even treat it as one of the perks of her new assignment.

SEVEN

Multima Corporation Headquarters, Fort Myers, FL
Friday March 30, 2018

A company director living in San Francisco thoughtfully sent her an email with a news headline of "First Victims Fall in the Grocery Wars." He tactfully added the question, "Do you think this might merit a formal statement from Multima?" Suzanne Simpson wished the other directors who'd called and emailed her that morning had been as sanguine about the announced collapse of competitors Top Markets and Southeastern Grocers.

Sure, both companies were major players and their failures big news, but both had been on her radar for years as probable casualties in the hyper-competitive supermarket business. Her team had scrutinized both as possible acquisitions but concluded there was too much rot within their balance sheets to salvage them profitably. However, the media had a fascination with technology stocks and the "Amazon Effect" that seemed to turn every negative development in the business into an Amazon-induced disruption.

No, the news didn't merit a formal response from Multima, but she would direct the public relations team to draft one just the same. For almost a year now, the stock markets had lived on a precarious ledge. Stock values soared to unrealistic and unsustainable highs. Everyone knew that. Equities were priced to perfection, the analysts liked to say. As a result, as soon as some background market noise occurred, or a company missed performance expectations, the market would pummel the share prices of the offending company.

Suzanne couldn't allow that to happen to Multima shares. Their value was already well below other competitors when compared to profits because of Howard Knight's shenanigans in his quest to overthrow John George Mortimer as CEO and replace him with Wendal Randall. That absurd scheme had spooked shareholders and analysts. So, the value of Multima shares had not soared in recent months like most other major American corporations. That concerned her board of directors.

She buzzed the office of Edward Hadley—her director of corporate and public affairs—and asked him to join her for a fifteen-minute conference. While she waited for him to make his way from the other side of the building, Suzanne quickly compiled a mental checklist of the items on her current wall of worry.

Foremost was the news that John George Mortimer's condition had worsened. His cancer was incurable, but the medical specialists still held out hope his otherwise good health and excellent fitness might cooperate with the immunology therapy experiment they were conducting. Delivery of medicines to stimulate John George's own immune system had been successful for the first three months. In fact, the tumors had not increased in size at all until they measured them again just two weeks ago. The results of the MRI disappointed everyone. Some tumors had doubled in size over the period, and all had shown growth.

As expected, John George took the news in his usual stoic manner, pronouncing, "It is what it is." The doctors encouraged him not to give up hope but admitted few options remained. They persuaded him to accept another round of massive doses of chemotherapy in a desperate attempt to slow the growths while they searched for other immunology solutions or treatments. They maintained the hope that researchers were discovering new solutions so quickly that maybe even within a month there might be some new treatment to try.

However, John George's worsening health weighed heavily on Suzanne. Since learning she was his daughter only a few months earlier, she anxiously hoped to see him live as long as possible. Her professional admiration for him remained constant, but a feeling she could describe only as love prevailed. She respected his great intellect. She laughed at his stories. She marveled at his wisdom and depth of experience in all facets of life. But most powerful of all was an affection that flourished over the past few months as they spent more time together, learned more about each other, and savored the time they shared.

The business needed John George around longer, too. The media, investment analysts, and the board of directors had all accepted her promotion to Chief Executive Officer with a clear expectation that Mortimer would hover in the background for some time to support her learning curve in the onerous new role and keep her in check should she veer in the wrong direction.

Already, bits of news occasionally surfaced from unexpected sources about John George's setbacks with cancer and speculation about the impact these developments might have on Multima's management stewardship and financial health. The whispers grew louder, and Suzanne knew she had to manage expectations delicately to maintain the value of the company's shares. It was a heavy responsibility. So, Multima was forced to make a formal response to mollify any lingering concerns about those issues.

Suzanne valued Edward Hadley's expertise. He sensed the mood of the general public and business journalists with uncanny accuracy. And his creativity was legendary.

"What do you think we should say about the Tops and Southeastern Grocers news reports this morning?" Suzanne asked.

"I've talked to my team about that. We think we should launch an all-out offensive rather than simply issue a statement," Hadley replied.

"An all-out offensive? That's intriguing. Go on."

"We guess every supermarket in the USA will feel compelled to issue a statement about those business failures and assure their shareholders, suppliers, and customers that they're better equipped to deal with the Amazon threat than the two failures," Edward Hadley explained. "We think the media will find that all somewhat predictable and boring. We doubt they'll even bother to publish most of the communiques.

"Instead, let's do a full-court press with Fitzgerald's announcement of a Six Sigma initiative. My people think it's an outstanding story that can get us lots of mileage. The woman he appointed to lead the initiative, Janet Weissel, used to report to me. She's great with the media, very telegenic, and her success story is inspiring," Hadley enthused.

"I know. I met her at a meeting once. She handled herself well," Suzanne replied as she thought about the recommendation.

"And the optics could be great. Doing interviews with James Fitzgerald and Janet Weissel together, we'll project the professionalism and stability of his maturity with her youth, energy, and innovation. I think we can build a spin that Six Sigma is just one more way Multima continues to innovate to solidify its relationship with customers. At the same time, we can get some great coverage for Fitzgerald's home mortgage program." Hadley could barely contain his excitement.

Suzanne nodded, then paused to think more about it, a powerful example of her father's positive influence over the last few months. John George had taught her to become comfortable with silence. She first realized it only a few months earlier, but John George never felt pressured to fill space with his words. If it took a few minutes to process something he'd just heard, to consider the implications and ramifications, so be it. She was learning to do the same.

The idea sounded interesting. The Financial Services division's success story with the home mortgage program was truly a great one and investors needed to hear about it. The plan to use Six Sigma as a process improvement initiative seemed sound. Surely, a company working to improve the quality of its services by examining ways to enhance every process would reinforce the Multima brand. Moreover, the heart-warming story of Janet Weissel studying every night for months to get certified, then selling her concept to her entire senior management team, had a certain appeal for women and their advancement in the workplace.

Unrelenting Peril

"But what could go wrong?" she wondered out loud.

"Very little from our perspective," Edward replied. "Janet graduated from Columbia, has undergone extensive media training, and handled herself extremely well with our unit. She oozes charm and enthusiasm. With James, we've got a rock. I don't know anybody more respected in the financial community, and he always conducts himself well during interviews. Furthermore, we have CBNN ready to do an interview at the beginning of its top-rated eight o'clock hour Monday."

"I like the idea in principle," said Suzanne. "But is the timing right? As I understand it, James just announced this woman's promotion a few days ago. Should we wait until she's actually made progress with Six Sigma at Financial Services before we tell the story?"

"We could," Hadley countered. "But that would leave us with just a run-of-the-mill press release to put out today for the media to ignore."

"Okay, Edward. I'll buy your recommendation," Suzanne said with a laugh of resignation. "It's a great idea, and I'm sure you're reading the broadcast angle better than I. Let's go with it. Do you need me to give James a call for his buy-in?"

EIGHT

A comfortable home in a Chicago, IL, suburb
Sunday April 1, 2018

At two o'clock in the morning, James Fitzgerald couldn't sleep. He had tossed and turned in his bed long after he shut off his reading light and tried to sleep. But he gave up and quietly moved to the leather reclining chairs in their home theater and put the television on with very low volume. He certainly didn't want to wake Dianne. That could be disastrous.

His wife was not the cause of his current angst, but she was undoubtedly a central player in it all. The other key figure was that woman Janet Weissel and her meteoric climb up the corporate ladder over the past few weeks. It was all moving far too fast. He felt intense discomfort.

She deserved the new job. Human resources offered a glowing recommendation. Her story of dedication and extraordinary hard work to complete her Six Sigma black belt certification in just seven weeks was remarkable. Her near perfect scores on the tests and exams were exemplary. Even Natalia Tenaz, her current manager, fully supported her promotion to the new role.

He'd checked all the appropriate boxes. In a private conversation with John George Mortimer, James had casually let the ailing chairman know about his plans. John George reminded him of her possible connection to The Organization. But he offered no rebuttal when James countered that they hadn't found a single link after months of monitoring all her conversations and emails—company and private.

James's heads-up to Suzanne Simpson a couple weeks before was equally uneventful. His new CEO loved the idea of proactively seeking new ways to improve quality processes and seemed delighted he planned to make the role a high-profile one. She particularly complimented his decision to fill the position with a young woman and seemed intrigued by Janet's story of dedication and perseverance to win the sought-after Six Sigma certification.

However, he was caught off-guard when Suzanne called to share the plans Edward Hadley and his team in corporate and investor communications had hatched. The whole scenario made him wary. Janet Weissel had just completed her quality training. She would only start the new job on Monday. They planned to put her on national TV her first day in the new role. Moreover, he had never seen her handle either a media interview or perform in a situation fraught with pressure.

When Suzanne positioned her request as an ideal opportunity to gain investor awareness about the great work he was doing in Financial Services and a chance to plug the new mortgage program to a national audience, he felt trapped. How could he make any reluctance sound credible? So, he had agreed and embraced the request with feigned enthusiasm.

He had little doubt the woman was remarkable. She impressed him as Hadley and his team briefed and coached her during their three-hour video conference Saturday morning. The corporate communications team had done their homework and bombarded her with information.

They started with the proposed questions planted with the show's producer. Typically, interview questions were submitted in advance, and an appropriate on-air personality who had little time to either research or become familiar with the subject matter would merely read the questions from a teleprompter. The team coached both Janet and James on ideal responses to those questions, and he was amazed to see the woman required no rehearsal or second attempts. For each issue, she not only churned out the precise responses they suggested but also used perfectly appropriate voice inflections and facial expressions.

The team briefed them about other scheduled guests that day and their areas of expertise, just in case their stories might tempt an interviewer to digress somewhat. They suggested impromptu questions an interviewer might ask should he or she forget the one planned or stray from the script. They warned about interviewers' habits or possible attempts at entrapment to make their interview more newsworthy. They even reviewed the height of the chairs James and Janet would sit on and the number of camera angles to expect.

Janet Weissel understood the significance immediately. She correctly proposed the type of dress she should wear, with the most advantageous style and length to attractively feature her legs. Her understanding of what was the most visually desirable attire delighted Hadley's team, and they gave her just a couple makeup tips.

Then, they told James the studio staff would take care of his makeup. He only needed to wear his most expensive dark suit and a pale-colored shirt with a plain necktie.

James had never been so well briefed and prepared for a media interview, so why was sleep so elusive tonight?

He couldn't kid himself. It was all about his extra-curricular activities with Janet regardless of how qualified she might be for the job. He still couldn't explain why he had allowed their sexual relationship to develop.

It was complicated. He knew it was dangerous. And he knew he would never have done it at any previous time in his career.

Why had his judgment altered so dramatically? There were many factors. However, none seemed completely satisfactory. Yes, the loss of their son Alistair the previous autumn had been horrific. Even now, a violent chill shuddered down his spine as he thought about that call from the police up there in Canada. The despair he felt as the detective told him their only son died that night from a drug overdose on a dark, cold street in Toronto came back again.

That loss had changed him. Things previously important were much less critical now. Money meant little. Success seemed a foreign concept. Hard work and discipline that characterized his almost forty-year career now had been replaced by a feeling he was mechanically going through the motions of his job, doing only what he was supposed to do.

Except for that one significant lapse in judgment with Janet Weissel, he had practiced and preached John George Mortimer's notorious dictate to all management that they must never dip their pen in the company ink. Despite hundreds, perhaps even thousands of possible temptations in his work, until Janet Weissel he had never once considered becoming involved with a colleague whether a subordinate or a peer. Or anyone else for that matter.

What had changed with this astonishing woman? Was it just a question of time and place?

Admittedly, things had changed much with Dianne since Alistair's death. Her sense of loss seemed even greater than his, if that was possible. The therapy she started at the beginning of the year seemed to be helping her cope with the depression, but a huge void remained in their relationship.

After forty years of marriage, it appeared they had remarkably little left in common. Alistair had been the essential link between them, and his death meant they now had little to share with each other.

Over the span of his career, the business success of Multima Financial Services had sapped his time and energy to such an extent they had constructed separate lives with Alistair their sole common denominator. Dianne had her circle of friends and enjoyed their company and common interests. James's friends were mainly those people with whom he did business and his time with them was often at baseball, hockey, or football games that held no interest for Dianne.

This gulf between the two had existed for years, papered over by their love for Alistair and parental desire to see him succeed with his life in every way possible. When he died, parts of James and Dianne died as well. Maybe this fascination with Janet Weissel was a subconscious attempt to fill that void.

So far, his affair with the woman had been sensational. He found her extraordinarily beautiful. Her youthful exuberance when they talked or made love stimulated him in a way he could not recall ever experiencing with Dianne. Her smile could be both mischievous and innocent, while her touch did things to him that were almost magical.

But it was stupid. During a period when an entire women's movement passionately rallied around the slogan #MeToo and accused embarrassed men of sexual harassment and assault, he now found himself embroiled in an affair with a subordinate. Janet's promotion to vice president could easily be construed as a reward for sexual favors.

Should she become disenchanted with their relationship, Janet could threaten to make it public or try to gain leverage in return for keeping it quiet. It didn't take much effort to imagine a parade of other scenarios that might all turn out badly. Moreover, none of those scenarios considered the possibility that Janet Weissel may indeed be The Organization's plant in his company as John George Mortimer suspected.

It was folly, he concluded. It all made no sense. Logically, he must find a path to elegantly end this affair in a way that avoided unraveling his career in the fog and malaise of an extra-marital affair. But how?

NINE

Hospital Evangélico, Montevideo, Uruguay
Monday April 2, 2018

His throat dry and aching from the mumps, Howard woke in the middle of the night and wandered into the kitchen for another couple ibuprofen to ease the pain. Swallowing was so uncomfortable the tiny pill felt more like a golf ball squeezing through his esophagus. But he forced it down before reaching into the refrigerator to put back the pitcher of chilled water.

As he closed the door and twisted away from the refrigerator, Howard suddenly felt lightheaded. His legs wobbled, and his body tilted to the left. He reached out with his right arm for a counter or something to maintain his balance. Instead, for just an instant, he felt like a floating character falling in a dream before everything suddenly went black.

It was light when he opened his eyes and discovered he was lying face down on the floor with his head throbbing terribly. A drop or two of blood on the floor caught his eye, and he reached for his face. He had difficulty moving because his arms were lodged under his body. His left arm and back hurt as he shifted his weight.

One hand freed, Howard touched his forehead and found a small cut just below his hairline. The wound was no longer bleeding so the cut couldn't be too serious, but he'd probably need a doctor to check for a concussion. Slowly, he tested to see if his hands, arms, and legs worked. Every part was stiff and slow to respond but nothing seemed broken or paralyzed. He arched his back, rising until he rested on hands and knees.

Body parts all seemed functional, so he pulled on a nearby countertop and hoisted his body up to a standing position. Upright, he was dizzy again. Fearing damage to his brain from the fall, he decided to call an ambulance.

He found the phone and dialed 9-1-1. There was no response. He tried several more times but no one answered. Then, it occurred to him that Uruguay might not use 9-1-1 for its emergency services. A quick check with Google revealed he should dial 1-1-2, and that number brought an immediate response. Less than a half hour later, Howard arrived at Hospital Evangélico in Colonia del Sacramento where, after asking several questions and taking an extended look at Howard's head, the doctor displayed alarm.

"We'll take an x-ray to be sure there's no fracture," the young *doctora* explained to him slowly in Spanish. "But I see no signs of a concussion, and I think you survived the fall without major damage. I'm more concerned about the cause of your fall. You have a nasty infection in your ear and several abscesses in your mouth—three at least. This ear infection probably caused you to lose your balance and fall. I'll talk to my colleagues at our main hospital in Montevideo after we see the x-ray results. If they agree, I recommend you go there for more comprehensive treatment—like a CAT Scan—to see if there are any internal blockages inside your ear or around the parotid gland."

He followed her advice and five hours later, Howard rested on a stretcher in the emergency area of the Hospital *Evangélico* in Montevideo with intravenous connections protruding from his right arm. A more mature *doctora* had just arrived and started to probe in his mouth, throat, and ears. It took only minutes before she concluded a CAT scan was indeed required and scheduled one for the next morning.

There was no permanent room with a bed available, but the friendly and professional staff of nurses and doctors made him as comfortable as possible in the emergency area after he made a ten-thousand-dollar deposit for his care with a prepaid credit card. "Uruguay has universal health care," one sympathetic nurse explained, "but only for residents. Foreigners have to pay."

Howard managed to sleep fitfully through the night with the aid of more powerful pain medication before staff wheeled his stretcher down several long corridors for a CAT scan early the following morning. Immediately after Howard returned to the emergency area, the *doctora* specializing in ear, nose, and throat matters arrived to deliver more bad news.

"We'll wait for the results of the CAT scan to be sure there are no other complications, but your most recent blood tests are very worrisome. Your white blood cell count is dangerously high. We'll need to do a surgical procedure to install a small drain on the side of your face to allow the infectious secretion to escape rather than spread through your body."

"What alternatives do I have?" Howard wanted to know.

"None. Untreated, your life is at risk. We don't yet know the precise cause of your infection, but we need to drain it before it spreads throughout your bloodstream and creates new complications," the *doctora* insisted.

There was no argument. It needed to be done. She patiently explained the procedure in detail and informed him he'd need to stay in the hospital for a few days after the surgery to frequently clean the incision and monitor the infection. Once they were confident the antibiotics were doing their job and the infection cleared, they'd help him get back to Colonia del Sacramento and his boat.

The surgery went just fine, the *doctora* reported. However, the infection persisted, and they couldn't isolate its cause. The medical team tried different antibiotics. They consulted infectious disease experts, but nothing seemed to work. Hours in the hospital turned into days and the days soon became almost a week. Finally, an infectiology specialist isolated a rare and often lethal strain of tuberculosis they were able to cure with a powerful antibiotic.

When the *doctora* informed Howard his white blood cell count had at last returned to acceptable levels, the nursing staff cheered. Even the fellow who delivered those annoying little evangelical Christian brochures each morning seemed delighted to learn Howard would leave soon.

There was just one matter to resolve. The hospital financial controller entered his room carrying an electronic credit card reader just before the scheduled arrival of a taxi to transport him back to Colonia del Sacramento. Mechanically, the fellow requested Howard's credit card and entered an amount slightly more than fifty thousand dollars. He was free to go.

As Howard walked toward his ride, he did some quick mental calculations. That payment to the hospital would leave a balance of fewer than five hundred dollars available before he would need to start using a new prepaid credit card—and with that change, his identity would also need to change. That thought prompted him to consider one other complication. There were a lot of cameras in that hospital.

TEN

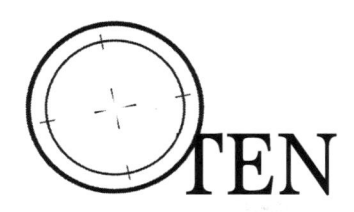

A small condo complex, Quepos, Costa Rica
Monday April 9, 2018

The rented condo was only a mile or so from the heart of Quepos at the southwest tip of Costa Rica. There, about twenty neatly maintained units nestled against the base of a mountain, well back from the road to the hospital. Douglas created a low-profile persona for his temporary neighbors and visitors. He tried to act like a Canadian, just one of thousands visiting the country. He modestly told them he was a lucky investment banker, living off the fruits of his past efforts and looking for the next golden opportunity. He was careful never to volunteer more, and he never divulged the full name on his fake Canadian passport.

He wanted folks to think of him only as Duke, a happy-go-lucky guy who spent a lot of time on his computer. Or a fellow who walked the eight-mile circumference of the quaint little city for two hours every morning wearing a Blue Jays cap and large dark sunglasses. The quiet dude who dutifully swam his twenty laps in the pool every afternoon just before the dinner hour and never voiced an opinion.

There remained many details to sort out before he could deliver to Giancarlo Mareno a final blueprint to seize control of Multima Corporation. There was little time for distraction or disruption.

After his morning walk, he scrolled through the videos, browsed newspaper clippings, and clicked on electronic links that Janet Weissel had attached to the email she'd sent late last night. His smile grew increasingly broad and his spirit soared to almost giddy heights.

She'd aced the assignment. She not only had won the Six Sigma quality certification that would let her peer into the deep recesses of Financial Services, but she'd also snared James Fitzgerald in her bed. Then, she finagled a promotion to vice president. On top of those impressive accomplishments, she scored a prime-time interview on CBNN that the wire services subsequently covered. Overnight, it seemed, she had become an American business celebrity.

His old mentor James Fitzgerald was the weak link they needed to exploit at Multima. Before he first outlined his germinating scheme to Janet in Hawaii, he was confident James Fitzgerald was vulnerable psychologically. Douglas and his deceased friend Earnest Gottingham had discovered that while they'd plotted to create a gigantic swindle using the deficient software inherited by Multima Solutions.

Gottingham covertly ordered up-to-date psychological profiles on Multima's senior management team. He thought such deep intelligence might give them an upper hand in negotiations when it came time to take Multima Solutions public. Unfortunately, Mortimer pulled the rug out from under them and forced a decision to buy the division earlier than they'd originally planned. They couldn't get the psychological reports they'd commissioned in time, and that misfortune may have cost Gottingham his life.

The Organization had secret compartments. One controlled a high-profile psychology practice in New York. Just days before Earnest Gottingham met his demise, the covert unit delivered psychological profiles on Multima's senior leaders. Douglas still felt terrible about the loss of his friend, but at least the quality research the psychologists provided would now be useful.

The profiles for John George Mortimer and Suzanne Simpson were unsurprising in every respect. Behaviors and tendencies summarized by the psychologists seemed to be consistent with Douglas's personal observations and suspicions. General Counsel Alberto Ferer and Chief Financial Officer Wilma Willingsworth also showed little variance from what he experienced in his day-to-day activities with each.

James Fitzgerald, though, showed a dramatic change from the personality Douglas had worked closely with for almost a decade. The image they painted was one of a man in emotional turmoil.

The sedate and reliably logical James Fitzgerald had evolved into a depressed and somewhat erratic person since the death of his son Alistair. The report highlighted that his eating, exercise, and work habits had all changed dramatically over the past few months. The psychologists specifically highlighted James Fitzgerald as an extremely weak link in the management team—mainly because his colleagues had come to rely on his superb judgment and advice over a thirty-year period and might be slow to realize just how much change he had undergone.

Based on that report, Douglas saw an opportunity to get his revenge. When Giancarlo Mareno gave him a chance to redeem himself, Douglas started to sketch a plan to penetrate Multima through Fitzgerald.

Janet Weissel was the key. He had always seen something special in her, something bigger than the spectacular sex that had first attracted him. The psychologists gave him some information about her as well. Several years earlier, The Organization had already paid the firm to assess her. The results of those tests were the reason they planted Janet at Multima in the first place. The woman scored in the range of Mensa candidates when they tested her IQ, demonstrated unusually honed interpersonal and social interaction skills, and had no moral compass at all.

Her ability to entrap James Fitzgerald into a sexual relationship during his current vulnerable state was never in question. Douglas also had no doubts about her ability to excel in the Six Sigma certification. She was a brilliant woman. However, it had all happened far more quickly than he'd expected. When plans materialize too rapidly, sometimes it's best to reassess them.

Before sending an email with next steps and priorities to Janet, he poured a glass of iced tea, went outside into the bright, eighty-degree sunshine, and sidled into the hammock strung between two wood poles on his patio.

From there, he looked out at the pool and lush tropical landscaping to plot his next moves. He thought about additional information he needed from Janet and pondered whether he should recruit other players or renew contact with his network. The pieces of the puzzle were not yet coming together as precisely as he would like, but the outline looked solid.

When he finished his hammock session, Douglas went inside and opened his laptop. Until sundown, he pounded out instructions on his keyboard, connecting with contacts around the world. This flurry of activity lasted well into the evening until he finally pressed the 'send' button to set in motion his latest instructions to Janet. Pointedly, he ignored one specific question from her last email.

When can we meet up somewhere?

It was much too early for that. It would be better to just ignore her question than possibly irritate her with an answer she might not like. She needed to be entirely focused on the mission for at least the next several months.

Satisfied with his day's output, Douglas poured a glass of chilled Chablis and ordered in dinner. Soon after arrival in Costa Rica, he had discovered a delightful restaurant in downtown Quepos that prepared great local food, delivered it, and even allowed the charming delivery girl to park her motorcycle and stay the night. Conveniently, he could arrange that package with one telephone call and a remarkably modest charge to his prepaid credit card.

ELEVEN

A large, luxurious executive home, Fort Myers, FL
Sunday April 22, 2018

John George Mortimer still found it challenging to step back from the business he'd founded and nurtured into one of America's largest and most successful. He had formally transferred all operating and decision-making authority to his daughter, Suzanne Simpson, at the start of the new year. But he held on to the title of Chairman.

Suzanne handled her new role well. He talked with her for a few minutes almost every day, and it was clear she did what prudent leaders do early in their tenure: she listened. Sometimes he marveled at just how powerfully she listened. At her age, he was still developing skills that encouraged people to share their knowledge and deftly let them know he valued their counsel. It was a complex skill to hone, but she was probably already more capable than he'd been in his prime.

That was a good thing for both Multima Corporation and the gradual development of its new CEO. However, there were slight nuances apparent to him that Suzanne might miss, and he was torn between the wisdom of letting her discover and cope with those issues on her own or giving her a heads up that she might interpret as unwanted interference.

James Fitzgerald's situation was the most critical. John George appreciated his weekly calls to touch base, check on the latest cancer treatments, and keep his former mentor positive through the challenging experience. However, John George noticed some troubling indicators the Financial Services division president was undergoing significant changes in his own life.

Their conversation about the promotion of that Weissel woman was a good example. Throughout his entire career, James had studiously cultivated new ideas and used John George as a confidential sounding board before he took them anywhere. It was smart leadership and served him well. So, he was surprised when his protégé shared his intention to focus his operating division on Six Sigma quality improvement and appoint Janet Weissel to lead the charge.

James hadn't floated the idea for feedback. He merely stated it as a fait accompli. He wasn't requesting an opinion. Instead, his tone implied her promotion was essentially a done deal. However, John George withheld comment about James's decision despite his lingering concerns about the woman's reputed links to The Organization and his overall negative impressions of her.

Then, there was that interview with CBNN a few days earlier. James had acted like a different man. He let the young woman answer almost all the questions and seemed like a cheerleader for her when he talked about his reasons for creating the role and appointing her to lead the initiative. It's important to be positive in televised interviews, but it looked almost like they were going to hold hands at one point! Added to that were James's evasive answers when John George had inquired about Dianne.

Might there just be something else in play?

James and Dianne had both suffered a traumatic blow when their only son died of a drug overdose. At first, John George expected they might only need time to adjust and cope with the profound loss. He even thought the death would eventually draw them closer together, but it now appeared their relationship might be suffering.

More crucial was the change in James's appearance. The amount of weight he had gained was shocking—at least forty pounds. The only other time James had become bulky rather than lean was decades earlier when the Fitzgeralds were grieving a series of miscarriages. Back then, his young subordinate realized the effect stress was having on his health, and he'd acted to lose the weight and kept it off until now.

There wasn't enough information yet to raise the subject with Suzanne, but this week's confidential call from his friend, the vice-chairman of investment banker Goldman Sachs fueled his concerns. They'd been getting inquiries from odd sources about Multima Financial Services. Was there any possibility Multima was considering a divestment?

Suzanne hadn't mentioned anything, and John George was sure she'd consult with him about such a significant issue if it truly was on her radar. But the conversation reminded him that he ought to chat with Suzanne about the fragile legal structure of Financial Services and the corporation. She needed to know that any attempt to sell or make an initial public offering for Financial Services might weaken Multima's balance sheet and leave the company vulnerable to a takeover.

Without adequate attention to those details, the corporation could all fall apart.

TWELVE

A spacious apartment, Montevideo, Uruguay
Wednesday July 4, 2018

Howard Knight felt stronger every day. That nasty bout with the mumps and resulting surgery deflated him but recovery was underway. In April, he'd returned from the hospital in Montevideo to the small rented cottage in Colonia del Sacramento only long enough to collect his belongings and food supplies. He crammed everything into a cab and retreated to his boat moored in the port of the small, historic town.

He regretted leaving so quickly and losing his chance to explore the UNESCO heritage site more thoroughly. When he'd visited Hospital *Evangélico* for the initial diagnosis of mumps, Howard saw a bit of the downtown, but sightseeing was clearly low on his list of priorities while he struggled with the painful illness.

Now, the trail of images he'd left over the past weeks became an obsession. Payments with his prepaid credit cards weren't a major worry, and his forged passport hadn't created any curiosity or interest with authorities. But the panic of possible detection consumed him. It was just as powerful as the fear he and Fidelia Morales experienced in Bolivia when they realized facial recognition software might have detected them.

In fact, a fear that it might be as life-altering as their decision to have cosmetic surgery in Buenos Aires continued to haunt Howard. That decision led to their eventual capture by the FBI and incarceration at Guantanamo Bay. Tragically, it also led to his companion's decision to abandon him there. Fidelia Morales had been the love of his life for over a decade. However, she chose to take her chances with the secret police in Argentina over a life with Howard in the FBI witness protection program.

Of course, that was all before the FBI director chickened out on prosecuting all the villains Howard had named. Fidelia had probably died in the custody of those Argentinian thugs. But her fate may have been no worse than what he should expect if The Organization ever tracked him down. Despite his surgery in Argentina, the FBI now knew what he looked like, so he should assume The Organization did too.

There had been cameras everywhere in both hospitals—mounted in the corners near the ceiling in the emergency departments. Others were obvious when he went for the CAT scan and in both rooms where he stayed for treatments. They made and retained copies of his passport at every stage. Should The Organization access any of the hospital records, facial recognition software could quickly pinpoint his general whereabouts. They could muster all the resources they'd need to find him on land or at sea if they knew where to look.

While he was out on the water, motoring slowly and anchoring often in the broad Rio de la Plata estuary between Uruguay and Argentina, Howard felt comfortable. When he periodically tucked into a tiny port to replenish fuel and supplies, he became apprehensive.

For hours at a time, those damned security video files dominated his thoughts. There must be a way to delete them, but his technology skills were limited. He needed some help, and he'd only find such expertise in a larger city. It would probably be best to try someone in a sizeable Uruguayan city, someone who would know how the health system worked and might even be connected to a hospital.

Howard found an apartment to rent for a month in the capital, Montevideo. He booked it for all of July. Right after settling in, he set off from the apartment for a walk about the old city. He loved the location of his temporary home, across from Plaza Zabala where there always seemed to be children playing, and just around the corner from Peatonal Sarandi. From that pedestrian walkway, he wandered down alleys and side streets identifying prospective business partners for his illegal but crucial technology adventure.

He frequented coffee shops, bars, and restaurants, making new friends and establishing trust. It was only a question of time before he found someone with the necessary equipment and expertise. More important, his candidate needed to be hungry enough to find a large cash payment adequate inducement to discretely circumvent Uruguayan privacy laws to hack the system of the Hospital *Evangélico*.

It might take time to pinpoint the particular personality, but he'd eventually find the right guy. Every city had one. Montevideo appeared to be a progressive city with an established, well-educated middle class. Still, someone in a substratum of society could always be motivated to accept his challenge by the right blend of curiosity and financial need. But where was he?

THIRTEEN

Late at night in a tiny office, Hoffman Estates, IL
Sunday July 15, 2018

Janet Weissel exhaled a deep breath as her shoulders slumped forward in exhaustion. It was nearing midnight and she couldn't wait to escape the barren little room she rented for her Douglas mission. He'd instructed her to rent an office away from Financial Services where she could carry out her subterfuge.

The guy was unbelievably friggin' smart! He alerted her to the probable surveillance.

"Don't trust Fitzgerald for a moment," he cautioned. "Even if you're sleeping with him, he'll probably have you monitored continuously. He has a secret 'Business Intelligence' unit buried in the marketing department of Financial Services. They monitor everything—computers, phones, email. You name it, they're probably surveilling it."

He was right. When Janet dug deeper into his monitoring concerns, she learned her former boss Natalia Tenaz—the one she liked to call the bitch—was actually Fitzgerald's closest confidant. Even now, with the new promotion and all, it seemed they monitored every conversation she had and every email she sent or received. So, they needed this ugly little square cubicle on the fourth floor of an equally ugly office tower where she could work away from prying eyes and ears.

Douglas wanted data. He coached her on the best ways to use her new Six Sigma training and elevated stature in the business division to ferret out all the details. He told her about the three main cost-drivers in the lending business and instructed her to focus on them.

Most important of all was the cost of funding. Mortgage or credit card lenders all charged whatever the prevailing rate of interest was. They might be able to vary their rate by a fraction of a percent, but there was little wiggle room to stay competitive. The secret was in the funding.

"Learn everything you can about all the levers Multima uses to raise the billions in funds they need to loan out on mortgages and credit cards. Analyze every method they currently use and feed that info to me," he commanded.

James Fitzgerald immediately agreed to start their quality initiative with funding and instructed the section leader responsible to make available all the information and resources Janet needed to analyze processes and make recommendations for improvements. Throughout May and June, she had worked studiously every day with the team of ace analysts the funding director provided.

Together, they mapped out every process used to source working capital, building multi-paged PowerPoint charts that described every minute detail including timing, sources, and costs. They calculated the expenses of each step in every process and modeled possible improvements or cost savings. They analyzed every conceivable alternative to make individual processes quicker, better, and less expensive for the company.

It was a tribute to the operating expertise of Multima that her funding task force could recommend only five relatively minor improvements to the hundreds of individual processes after almost two months of continuous study. When she sent the files off to Douglas on July fourth, he immediately assigned her the next targeted priority.

Once again, James Fitzgerald agreed loss prevention would be a tremendous second area for improvement and asked his chief risk officer to provide a similar team of experts to help Janet find ways to improve. In an aside to Janet before she left his office that day, he quietly counseled that he was hoping for much more output from this exercise than the inadequate harvest from funding.

The newly assembled team was a great one, and they had worked studiously over the past two weeks to identify more than a dozen areas where they could better prevent losses from either credit cards or mortgages. It was that analysis Janet had just finished summarizing and sent to Douglas over the secure virtual private network they had added to the laptop she used in her secret rental office.

But there was no time to relax. Tomorrow, she needed to be ready for an interview and photo shoot with *Chicago Woman* magazine. They wanted to feature her on the front cover of their fall edition and had asked her to set aside the whole day. It was exciting!

Edward Hadley had been so thrilled by her first interview—the one she did with James Fitzgerald—that he instructed his team to get exposure for her everywhere possible. This latest feature in a business publication followed a two-minute story CBNN did about her new Six Sigma job, as well as an interview with Harvard Business Review about Six Sigma and the ways quality processes were changing in the digital age. After those, there had been three shorter features on CNN, ABC, and NBC morning shows.

Not only had she successfully squeezed that critical image-building exposure into her grueling pace with the Financial Services task forces, but she'd also successfully kept James Fitzgerald interested.

Surprisingly, that had become more challenging than she'd first expected. There was no doubt he enjoyed their regular love-making sessions at the Marriott in Hoffman Estates. Even so, since about the time of their interview with CBNN, she had sensed an unease. She couldn't put her finger on precisely what was causing his discomfort, but it was always there just below the surface.

Even after an exhausting session in bed, with both breathing hard, giggling, and enjoying their romp, she still felt a touch of reticence in his manner. She worried he might suddenly suggest they take a break or use the old excuse that he needed some time apart. Whenever that feeling enveloped her, she doubled down and showed him more love or a new sexual favor.

From her point of view, they really didn't need her to sleep with James anymore. He had already established an expectation of cooperation from his management team. Edward Hadley also continued to promote her with the media and Suzanne Simpson at every opportunity. In fact, the CEO had just invited Janet to speak at the Multima annual general meeting in Toronto next month.

But Douglas insisted she keep sleeping with James. They'd need him in the longer term. So, Janet was resigned to be a good soldier, follow orders, and enjoy some reasonably good sex—even if it wasn't the same mind-blowing kind she enjoyed with Douglas. That thought immediately brought a smile to her face and a sudden surge of energy to her tired body.

In his email last night, Douglas had finally responded to her repeated questions about when they could meet up again:

Plan to escape for the Labor Day weekend. I've booked a hotel in Panama City.

Fourteen

John George Mortimer's home, Fort Myers, FL
Monday July 16, 2018

Just as he'd suggested, Suzanne brought her list of things to discuss while they enjoyed dinner at his place. Apparently, his appetite had returned in the past few days, so Lana prepared an excellent fish bouillabaisse. Suzanne chatted with John George about his health while his housekeeper served wine and her delicious seafood broth.

It was increasingly hard for her to remain positive though she knew she must. Her father's pallor projected the extent of his decline. His skin tone was the color of the clam shells in the bouillabaisse—gray, dull and lifeless. Worry lines were now deeply etched into his forehead, and his graying hair had receded even more. Where he used to have charming dimples, he now had limp skin that looked much too large for his face.

His eyes still showed some of their usual sparkle. Suzanne could see he enjoyed the opportunity to meet and talk, but his smile appeared a little more strained than usual, and he frequently covered his mouth to camouflage a yawn or, more likely, a grimace of pain.

"They grew again last month," John George said abruptly. "The oncologist called this morning. The latest MRI was not encouraging, and she wants me to try a new concoction of chemicals. I'll do it. However, at this stage, I feel I'm doing it for those who come along later. Hopefully, they'll learn something with me that can prolong someone else's life at some stage."

Despite her best efforts, Suzanne felt a sense of melancholy as the pressure behind her eyes suddenly welled into tears. She forced the best smile she could manage as she swallowed hard, fought back tears, and calmly replied, "I'm sure you were hoping for better news."

"Yes, hope is a good word to use," he said softly. "Our former president used hope to win two election campaigns, didn't he? Hope is what helps millions of people get out of bed every day. Moreover, when the experts say there is no known cure, we still try to dig deep and hope they're wrong. And when we know they're right, we still hope some brilliant young researcher toiling away in an obscure lab somewhere will miraculously discover something. Maybe not a cure, but something that can extend the inevitable a little longer."

He paused. Suzanne wasn't sure if he was running short of breath or generously giving her time to strengthen her resolve and maintain control of her emotions. His voice was unexpectedly soft, his demeanor resigned. Still, she seized on his theme to introduce a subject they needed to discuss.

"Speaking of hope, I know people are hoping you'll be able to attend the annual general meeting next month. How do you feel about that?"

"Nice segue, Suzanne," he replied, his eyes more animated and his smile wider. "I didn't mean to sound too morbid, and you probably have a lot to cover tonight. The short answer is I plan to be there. The oncologist wants me to start the new treatment Wednesday. They'll poke holes in me every day for two weeks to inject the treatments. They'll monitor the side effects. If they're all manageable, I'll have a couple weeks of recovery just before the meeting. I should be able to go."

"Are you planning to speak?" Suzanne asked.

"How skillful you are!" he laughed and clapped his hands together. "We both know the ultimate end-point to that question is, really, if I'm planning to announce my retirement."

Suzanne laughed with him and reached across to gently place her hand on his forearm and hold it there while she replied. "You know me too well. No doubt we will eventually have to talk about that, but when we do, it'll be entirely up to you. I'm certainly in no hurry, and I really mean it when I tell you I value every piece of advice you give me."

"I know. I'm just trying to lighten the mood here," John George said with a more serious demeanor. "I'm trying to stay out of your way as much as I can. You're doing a great job. However, I think the stock markets might get a little spooked if I make an announcement now. You probably know better than I that the current market indexes are unsustainable. Apart from Multima, many companies on the Dow or S&P indexes are trading at multiples far too high. There will be a collapse at some point. That's when I'd like to announce my retirement.

"In the meantime, if we can keep my health out of the news as much as possible, Multima shares might increase in value for a while and drop less than most when the correction occurs."

It was a relief to see their thoughts were aligned. It had been hard for her to think through all the possible scenarios that could occur over the coming months from the perspective of Multima's financial health. There was no doubt. The longer John George Mortimer stayed alive and involved in the company the better it was for everyone. But the question remained: would he speak at the meeting?

"How do we best achieve that goal? If you're not at the meeting, there will certainly be speculation in the business media. To be candid, if you make an appearance your physical appearance might not instill the level of confidence we'd both like to see," she said, laughing at the incongruity of both the comment and the situation.

John George shared her laughter before he sipped from a glass of water and said, "That's the dilemma, isn't it? How do I make an appearance without causing alarm? I may have an idea."

For the following several minutes he outlined—in carefully considered detail—a possible scenario that involved the prime minister of Canada, Multima's upcoming announcement about a new facility in the Toronto area, and a clever use of optics to show him actively involved in the company's progress without attending the crucial annual general meeting in person. Suzanne loved the idea and promised to make a call to the prime minister and then get Edward Hadley working on making the event happen.

Their moods gradually shifted and considerably lightened over the hours that followed. Both Suzanne and John George let their attention drift to more pleasant subjects. Suzanne first regaled him about the enjoyable week she had just spent in France's Provence region. She carefully avoided any mention of business, her research, or the discrete private meeting with her college friend.

Instead, in meticulous detail, she described each of the unique villages she'd visited and portrayed their appeal to her senses, for John George had never been in the south of France and now was likely never to have such an opportunity.

He peppered her with questions that showed keen interest as she passionately described the architecture, people, food, and customs in towns that had existed for hundreds of years before Columbus arrived in America. Their shared enthusiasm fueled conversation well into the night and Suzanne parted reluctantly only when she noticed John George was obviously exhausted. The number of days they would be together might be limited, but she remained determined to treasure every hour that remained.

FIFTEEN

A comfortable condo apartment, Montevideo, Uruguay
Tuesday July 31, 2018

She was about thirty, Howard guessed. Taller than average, with a dozen or more tattoos decorating both arms and legs. That first day, she wore blue cut-off jeans, a loose-fitting yellow tank top, and chunky shoes with heels about four inches high. She was immersed in something on her phone when he arrived at the coffee shop just around the corner from his newly rented apartment in the historic district of Montevideo.

He sipped his cup of black coffee, sneaking glances her way when the opportunity presented itself. He sat at a tiny round table in the corner with his back to the wall. She was right at the front of the small café, alone at a table large enough for four with her backpack slumped over one of the other chairs. Her short hair particularly caught his eye. One half of her head sported neatly trimmed hair to a length just below her ear. The other half was a buzz cut as short as he had ever seen on a woman's head. The side with hair was a translucent shade of green with four other colors interspersed.

Her body piercings were innovative too. There were two in her nose—one dangling from each nostril—but of two different styles and sizes. Her lip ornaments sported three rings in a neat row at the front, but again in odd shapes. As Howard expected, when she turned sideways, he noticed the loose-fitting top was cut short in front, and there were more piercings on her belly button as well.

Howard was never judgmental about these things. He was from New York, after all, and had seen almost everything at some time or other. So, the way the woman dressed or groomed herself wasn't at all what struck him as particularly odd. Instead, what caught his attention was the frantic, almost manic activity of the woman pummeling screens of three different telephones—seemingly all at the same time.

Intermittently, she showed spurts of feverish, almost violent, activity. With her head lowered and tilting from side to side while scanning the phones, it appeared she made an entry or two on the first device, then repeated the process on the next, then either reverted to the first or moved on to a third. There appeared to be no distinctive pattern to it all, but her facial expressions showed the intensity of a stock trader desperately trading shares in a period of hyper-volatility.

It all intrigued Howard, and he ordered another coffee to justify continuing to watch the strange young woman in action with her three phones. For at least two hours she barely lifted her head and continued entering something onto her handsets until he heard a squeal of delight as the woman jumped from her chair, thrust her arms high in the air and yelled in Spanish, "We did it!"

He was curious but waited until the woman was calmer and more composed at her table. When he concluded the time was right, he walked over and asked if he might join her for a moment. She didn't mind.

"Excuse my curiosity," he started in Spanish, "but I couldn't help noticing you working very hard for a while before you appeared to achieve some sort of success. What were you doing that was so exciting?"

"Just playing with some friends," she answered obliquely. "Who's asking?"

"Forgive me. I should have introduced myself. I'm Michael Henderson. I'm from Canada, visiting Montevideo for the first time," he lied.

"I'm Luisa. You speak Spanish very well. Are you here on business?"

"No, I'm a retired businessman just traveling to enjoy life while I'm still able. I try to learn new languages. I'm also intrigued by games people play on their phones." He refocused her attention.

"Cool. Are you going to school in Montevideo?"

"No. Just practicing as often as possible. But I'm really curious about your obvious excitement a few moments ago. Was it something with your phone?"

"I find lots of things interesting, sometimes even curious men. Where do you live in Canada?"

For about another hour, the young woman playfully twisted every question Howard asked into a non-reply, then asked him something in return. He thought he detected a pattern to her method, so he was patient. Of course, every answer he provided was a lie, but Howard enjoyed their interchange. He studiously kept all his misinformation straight. Sure enough, just as she was casually packing up her phones to leave, she asked him a question for the second time.

Taking care to show no hesitation, he answered Luisa's question with precisely the same untruth he gave her earlier. It worked. She finally divulged her game: she liked to crack computer codes. She did it all the time she said as she casually swung her bag over her shoulder and left the shop.

He had to visit the café four more times and invest several hours in conversation with Luisa before she divulged that the computer codes she liked to crack were passwords. Then, she offered to show him. She asked him to pick a name of any company in Uruguay. He chose a well-known Canadian bank with a major presence throughout Latin America.

After her hands skimmed over three different telephone screens at frantic speed for about thirty minutes, she announced she had entered the bank. Was there a specific account Howard might like to see? When Howard shook his head no, she immediately shut down her phones and packed them in her bag to leave. He asked if he could walk with her for a while and she consented.

As they sauntered along the *Peatonal Sarandi,* Howard carefully outlined his mission. He told her the truth, more or less. The thought that some recent images of him might fall into the wrong hands terrified him. He recounted his experiences at the Hospitals *Evangélico*, in Montevideo and Colonia del Sacramento. He let her know his life might depend on retrieving and destroying those images. And, he would pay handsomely should someone help him out.

Luisa agreed only to think about it. In fact, they briefly encountered each other in the coffee shop twice after that initial probe before she was willing to talk about his inquiry again.

"Your mission is dangerous," she said as they prepared to leave the coffee shop that day. "I checked the law about stealing health-related data in Uruguay. It's severe. Someone might spend a long time in prison for hacking hospital records."

"I realize that," Howard replied. "But I need your help to find someone ready to take that risk, someone who is extraordinarily good at what they do and won't get caught. I'll pay that person fifty-thousand US dollars."

"Wow!" Luisa replied. "That's more than I've made in my entire life. You'll probably find someone. When would you be able to pay that person?"

"I would give them half that amount immediately, the other half when they delete all my records and images from the Hospital *Evangélico* system," Howard said slowly, making sure the timing and amounts were clear.

"Someone would need a new computer and a place with secure Wi-Fi that couldn't be traced back to her," Luisa mentioned casually. She was swallowing the bait.

"If you found someone willing to help me with this, I could buy that person a new computer and let her work from an apartment I've rented under an untraceable false name," Howard said temptingly.

"Let me talk to my friends," she said. "I'll meet you for coffee again tomorrow. Come with money—enough for both the half payment and a good new computer, maybe an extra two thousand American dollars or so."

The suspense ended the next afternoon when Luisa consented to give it a try and went with him to buy a new Asus laptop computer. It was their top-of-the-line model loved by gamers for its extraordinary processing speed.

She pretended to be Howard's consultant for the purchase, convincing the sales clerk her role was merely to help Howard excel with his newly acquired passion for video games.

After their purchase, they walked back to his apartment where Luisa immediately checked every crevice for video or audio monitoring equipment—precisely as Howard did every time he returned from an outing. Then, she asked for the twenty-five-thousand-dollar deposit. She counted the money twice before she was satisfied, jammed it into a vinyl backpack, and strapped it over her shoulders.

Then he pointed her toward the small desk area overlooking *Plaza Zabala* and took a more comfortable chair for himself looking out another large window. From there he watched an impromptu but highly competitive soccer game among several young boys until dark.

Luisa didn't speak for hours. With her head down and bobbing in rhythm to the frenetic pace of her hands speeding expertly across the keyboard, she seemed almost like a musical prodigy creating a new symphony. He brought her a bottle of water after a few hours, but she barely glanced up and didn't drink a sip.

Approaching midnight, Howard became hungry and imagined she might be as well. From some advertising flyers he found tucked in one of the kitchen drawers, he learned about a pizza delivery service that operated until three in the morning. He ordered a large one, then settled in for the promised half-hour delivery.

Louisa finally took a short break when the doorbell rang. She gulped down two slices of the pizza without saying a word, guzzled a bottle of water to polish it off, and asked if she could use the bathroom. Then she abruptly returned to her intense preoccupation with the new computer. About an hour later, with the same joyous squeal she used that first day at the coffee shop, she pumped her arms in triumph and danced around the room. She was in!

When she calmed down again, Howard joined her at the keyboard. He watched as she checked all the related files—admission, emergency department records from both locations, all his blood tests and imaging results. Then, she navigated to the data file for the hospital floor of his stay in a room, where she first copied—then removed—all evidence of his stay. Finally, she located the security camera records in a completely different database.

They checked those files for each day of a meticulously maintained list of dates tracking Howard's visits to the *Evangélico* facilities in either Colonia del Sacramento or Montevideo. Carefully, Luisa inserted a computer virus that corrupted the security videos. She didn't steal the files. That would attract too much unwanted attention and might alert someone immediately. Instead, the planted virus would gradually creep through the video file like a worm, distorting every image. Anyone could open any of them, but the only images they would see would be fuzzy and the faces impossible to discern. Facial recognition software would be useless.

It was dawn before they finished copying, deleting, and destroying files. However, about fifteen hours after Luisa first began her quest, they were confident she had scrubbed all evidence of Howard's visits from the Hospital *Evangélico* servers—both those at its headquarters and on every other computer server used to deliver care.

While he'd watched the boys across the street play soccer several hours earlier, his interest in the game really provided cover for some deep thought and calculated analysis. What should he do with Luisa?

He knew his former cohorts in The Organization would have no doubts. After using her to perform such a delicate task, one of them would take her for a walk to some dangerous part of town—like the port only a mile or so from this apartment. She'd have an accident or mysteriously disappear. There would be no connections for anyone to explore.

Howard struggled with that idea. He'd killed previously. It was a basic requirement to be trusted within The Organization. However, that was many years ago and an experience he had no desire to repeat. He remembered how he threw up immediately after he'd watched the victim's brain explode from the close-range gunshot. The horrible nightmares lingered for months, and he felt such intense remorse he could barely eat or sleep for weeks.

But Luisa was a significant risk. If apprehended, would she talk? If tracked down by The Organization, would she cooperate? Was there any chance she might ultimately be an operative for the very criminal element he was trying to avoid? For those exhausting hours she worked diligently to penetrate the hospital system, little did she realize Howard felt trapped in painful internal turmoil.

Should she share information with The Organization or any of the authorities, there would be no trace of him at the apartment address in Montevideo. She didn't know about his boat. And the only information he'd given her was false. He laboriously weighed his alternatives. In the end, he felt secure enough with all the circumstances. He'd let the woman live.

Although her fee was significant, it was still a small amount in the scheme of things—equal to about a month's interest from the account in Grand Cayman. Moreover, he had other accounts with even more substantial amounts of cash in the same bank.

As a precaution, he kept the computer. She wouldn't have any of the evidence buried deep in its memory bank. Then, immediately after he handed her another envelope, he vacated the apartment and returned to his boat. On the way, he checked over his shoulder five times to be sure no one followed him. He refueled in the harbor, then set out to sea. Before noon, he crossed back into Argentinian waters. It was much safer there.

SIXTEEN

Shangri-La Hotel, Toronto, Canada
Thursday August 16, 2018

Suzanne saw the merits of John George's scheme for the meeting immediately and made two necessary calls to set the wheels in motion. She called in Edward Hadley to outline what she wanted to do and the general reasons why. Then, she called the prime minister of Canada and shared with him two pieces of information. First, she confirmed Multima planned to build a massive new distribution warehouse in a Toronto suburb, exactly as he'd asked her father to consider about a year earlier.

She also told him she'd like to make the big announcement at the same time as Multima's annual general meeting, which they were holding for the first time in Toronto. Might they work together to make a big media splash?

The youthful prime minister was elated. The past months had been challenging for him while some nasty conflict-of-interest scandals swirled around his office, withering trade negotiations dragged on, and a brutal election decimated the Ontario wing of his political party. Major end-of-summer good news was just the thing he and his elite team of communicators craved.

Hadley's team followed up directly with the prime minister's office, which resulted in today's phenomenal virtual reality event in Mississauga, Ontario. It was all coordinated to coincide with the wind-up of Multima's elaborate annual meeting with investors, lenders, and the media in the ballroom of the glitzy Shangri-La Hotel in downtown Toronto.

John George didn't attend the meeting. They had all agreed that would be most prudent. But his creative scheme left Suzanne with butterflies in her stomach from the time she woke that morning. Despite their careful attention to the script and the minute-by-minute activities designed to inform investors, assure lenders, and tantalize the media, a dreaded fear lingered that something might go awry.

Early in the event, Suzanne teasingly announced that John George Mortimer would not attend the meeting. Instead, he had other momentous responsibilities. She'd promised to share more later in the session.

All her senior management leaders made polished, high-energy, presentations. There were videos. A sixteen-piece ensemble pulled together from the Toronto Symphony Orchestra broke up the presentations with inspiring music. The speakers kept teasing the audience about an upcoming major announcement.

As the session appeared to be wrapping up, Suzanne took the stage again as the ensemble raised the energy intensity further. To highlight her bright red outfit, a flashing white spotlight followed her every step from a seat in the front row of the audience, along the length of the massive stage, and finally up the seven steps to the stage where she looked out over the crowd. The cramp of anxiety in her stomach intensified.

When she reached center stage, there was no podium or teleprompter, nor any prop to accompany her speech. She silently prayed it would all work. Suzanne looked out at the crowd with a mischievous smile and shouted out, "Ladies and Gentlemen, please welcome the prime minister of Canada!"

At that precise instant, a giant fifty-foot-wide screen instantly lit up high above her head to show the smiling and photogenic face of Canada's prime minister. Standing just to his left, and one step behind, was John George Mortimer.

He looks okay.

"Thank you, Suzanne Simpson," the prime minister roared into a microphone, with an enthusiastic pump of his arm high above his head. Applause of delight broke out simultaneously in both the crowded hotel ballroom and among the several hundred party supporters surrounding the politician at the outdoor location.

"This is a wonderful day for Multima, and it's an equally wonderful day for the people of Mississauga, the people of Ontario, and the people of Canada," he shouted before pointing to John George. "This iconic business leader has asked me to announce to the world that Multima Corporation has chosen this exact location to build its massive new warehouse that will span more than one million square feet, be entirely energy self-sufficient, and use more than three hundred fifty advanced robots. Plus, Canadians will design and manufacture all those robots right here in Canada."

"Let's give Mr. Mortimer a rousing welcome," the enthusiastic leader called out as a TV camera followed his gesture toward a smiling John George. Suzanne scrutinized his image on the screen with continued apprehension.

Edward Hadley had negotiated with the Canadian TV networks that one of them would control the feed and then share it with the others. He also took care to arrange the camera angle and close-up distance. Each was tightly controlled to portray John George in the best light possible. As one last precaution, before the event, Hadley's team had spent thirty minutes skillfully making up John George's haggard face to appear as healthy and youthful as possible.

Thankfully, the magnitude of the occasion and the need to project the most positive image possible motivated John George to flash a smile as energetic as Suzanne had ever seen. As he basked in the spotlight, John George managed not only to grin and wave to the fawning crowd but also to step forward and shake the prime minister's hand—with strength and enthusiasm—as the applause from the crowd in the surrounding field continued.

The prime minister respectfully waited for the applause to subside before he waved his arm and said, "Now, let's put on these goggles we gave you earlier to see just how impressive this project will be!"

Suzanne held her breath again. At that moment, massive screens in both the Shangri-La ballroom and the field at the site of the new Multima warehouse came alive with an image of a building taking form—a structure that seemed to stretch as far as the eye could see. What followed was technology mastering art as a one-million-square-foot building took shape digitally.

Virtual workers installed hundreds of solar panels across the roof and erected massive aluminum windmills on the four corners of the property to generate more electricity than the warehouse would need. The video narrative described plans to install all the extra insulation necessary to keep out Ontario's cold winters and help the high-efficiency heat pumps cool or heat the massive facility from power generated right there on the multi-acre site.

The crowd oohed and aahed as though they watched fireworks while the virtual reality presentation created robots before their eyes, then showed the robots moving vast quantities of groceries and other merchandise on massive tracks to load dozens of trucks parked along an entire wall of the building. No humans appeared in the footage.

Suzanne paid particular attention to the crowds. Their reactions were critical to the entire effort. To see them enthralled with the virtual reality technology meant their diversionary tactic was a success. Edward Hadley had it right. He'd confidently predicted that people would be so caught up in the theatrics they would forget all about the fact John George didn't speak at the event. Elated, their corporate communications guru pointed out later there was no need for John George to speak at the meeting. He narrated the entire virtual reality show.

Any skeptic could easily go back and check the soundtrack. They'd discover the voice was indeed John George's, although the recording took place in a sophisticated studio where they could alter intensity and volume as needed to compensate for his current vocal fragility. Hadley was confident their charade offset any lingering doubts among shareholders and quelled any curiosity of the media. Everyone agreed.

Their elaborate charade bought Suzanne a little more time.

SEVENTEEN

Hyatt Place, Panama City, Panama
Monday September 3, 2018

When he left Costa Rica, Douglas Whitfield had three options to get to Panama City to meet up with Janet Weissel. He could rent a car and drive about ten hours south on paved but less than ideal roads. He might drive two-and-a-half hours north to the capital San José, then take a one-hour flight south. Or, he could take off from a dirt runway near Quepos for an eighteen-minute flight over Costa Rica's rugged mountain ranges to San José's international airport, then fly to Panama.

Without hesitation, Douglas selected the dirt runway of a local skydiving club. It was on loan to Sansa Airlines because the regular Quepos airport was closed indefinitely. Apparently, local politicians wanted to expand the length of the runway to accommodate larger aircraft, and this field was the only remaining option.

Despite the unpaved surface, departure was not nearly as bumpy as expected, and the view quickly became spectacular. African Palm fields extended for miles along the coastline and well into the interior, producing the fruit and seeds that become millions of gallons of palm oil for export around the world.

Lush, green vegetation covered even the peaks of mountains—unlike the more barren summits of the Rockies or Alps—and seemed to color the horizon in every direction. Several consecutive months of daily rain had produced the flourishing greenery but was also the primary reason for Douglas's depression and desperate need to escape for a few days. What a stark contrast to the sunny, hot, and dry weather during his first months in Costa Rica. This break from the rain and a few days romping with that helpful fox Janet Weissel seemed a perfect antidote.

The second flight was on a Copa Airlines large, comfortable Boeing jet to Panama City. Unfortunately, his cab ride from Tocumen International Airport to the Hyatt Place Panama took almost as long as the flight. Traffic was horrible. At times there was total gridlock, with no movement in any direction for several minutes. During other parts of the trip, the car crept along at speeds slightly faster than walking with sprinkles of rain, insufferable heat, and punishing humidity. To make matters worse, the car had no air conditioning.

The hotel was mediocre. Not luxurious, but comfortable. It offered limited services but was close to the downtown core and anything they might want. From Douglas's perspective, they shouldn't need much because he planned to spend most of the weekend in bed with Janet Weissel.

He had a couple hours before she was scheduled to arrive and make her way to the hotel by taxi, so he walked to a nearby convenience store and returned carrying two bulging plastic bags full of champagne, red wine, beer, and a half-dozen sacks of unhealthy but delectable snacks.

Janet arrived late in the evening and in less than optimal humor. A thunderstorm had delayed her flight from Chicago. She found her connection in Miami compressed from ninety minutes to less than thirty, and her connecting gate was almost at the opposite end of the massive terminal. No food was served on either flight. Then her journey in from the Panama airport took just as long as his. She recounted this in exasperated detail to explain she absolutely needed a decent meal before she could even think about sex.

At a good, late-night restaurant, they had drinks as they ate, then more drinks in the room. Later than Douglas had initially hoped, they were engaged in the same torrid sex he recalled from their escapade in Hawaii. And it seemed even better. Janet was even more confident, relaxed, and hungry. Her rapid climb up the corporate ladder seemed to induce an even more adventurous spirit and a complete abandon of any inhibitions.

They woke late Saturday morning. He suggested a day of sightseeing before they got down to business and they spent a few agreeable hours visiting Panama City on the hop-on-hop-off tour. It was a nice way to get a taste of their surroundings quickly. Again, the painfully slow traffic detracted from the experience, but they both agreed it was a fun day.

At dinner, he encouraged her to talk more about the goings-on at his former company.

"I'm genuinely interested in learning about your most recent challenges with the Six Sigma project. I didn't create that arduous exercise just to accelerate your career, you know. I need every morsel of information about the company's current business practices."

"I'm still astonished by how few significant initiatives I've been able to drag out of the exercise," Janet replied. "With every program, I end up making only a few lame recommendations for improvement. The friggin' company is already operating unbelievably well!"

"Are the teams Fitzgerald provided working with you to find opportunities to improve?" Douglas wondered.

"I really think so. They were enthusiastic. They answered all my questions. One or two seemed mainly interested in my breasts, but most worked hard to find better ways to do things. Unfortunately, we found woefully few areas to improve."

"How has Fitzgerald reacted?"

"Honestly, I feel he's already questioning the value of my role. After I presented the latest findings, he appeared less than impressed," she said.

As they rode the elevator back to their room, Douglas reassured Janet the information she had accumulated precisely matched what he wanted, her concern was legitimate, and they'd tweak their strategy before she left.

"We've got someone in the corporate offices again," Douglas said as he opened a bottle of Chilean red wine back at the Hyatt. "Suzanne Simpson has met secretly with high-powered investment bankers from both New York and Los Angeles. It looks as if she's planned some grand new strategy to sell or spin-off Financial Services then go on a buying spree for other supermarket companies. Our source thinks she intends to make Multima exclusively a supermarket company, but she has designs on making it the biggest chain in the world. The whole thing is very hush-hush."

"Are you wasting your time then, with all this stuff I'm collecting through Six Sigma?" Janet asked a little more plaintively than he expected.

"Not at all. Once we know which investment bankers she chooses for the initial public offering, we'll penetrate their team. I'll know which levers to pull to influence the deal structure and initial listing price. You've given me more than enough information. Add in those factors to what I already know about the company and I'll influence the spin-off of the company. It will leave Multima vulnerable to financial collapse. Your great info will help me destroy the fucking company rather than replenish its coffers as Suzanne Simpson naively expects," he added derisively.

Douglas watched her reaction to that claim intently. As expected, she didn't reply right away. Instead, she actively processed the implications, weighed alternatives to see if his contention made sense, and computed it all before she revealed any formal reaction. He liked watching that kind of intellect at work.

"I don't expect you to show me all your cards," she coyly replied after a moment. "But I'm enjoying the poker-like aspect of this senior management thing. Where do I fit in the longer-term?"

"Great question!" He let out a loud laugh and took a long sip from his wine glass. "As long as you keep up the good work, you'll have my support and the support of Giancarlo Mareno. He kind of likes you."

"And you? Do you kind of like me? Or is this to remain solely a business relationship?" Her tone had a slight edge.

Douglas caught the undercurrent and saw where they were headed. He paused and took a deep breath. The last time a woman asked such a loaded question he fluffed the answer, and the result was miserable. It cost him a marriage to a decent woman and a lot of money. He'd learned from that experience and took several seconds to choose his words tactfully.

"From my perspective, we've never been just about business. You're a beautiful woman. You're probably the most intelligent person I've ever met. Our sexual compatibility is extraordinary. I not only like you, I think what we have together has the potential to blossom into something much more lasting." He hoped his feeble effort at poetic imaging might do the trick.

"Yeah. Good try." Janet smiled warmly, wrapping her arms around his neck. "My bullshit detector alarm just activated but your charm disarmed my defenses ... as usual."

After only a few more passionate kisses and a couple sips from their glasses of red wine, both undressed each other with more desperation than the night before. Their haste surprised him, but the rollicking until the wee hours of the morning attested to their lust for each other and their incredible staying power. His last thought before sleeping was unspoken amazement about the ways women respond when there is even a hint of love in a conversation.

Before Janet woke up about noon on Sunday, Douglas was again all business. In fact, he had been hard at work for several hours, studying the USB file Janet had carried to Panama. It contained data revealing the results of her last Six Sigma exercise with the Financial Services operations team. It also revealed vital information about the area of the company he knew best. After all, oversight of credit card operations was his direct responsibility when he worked there.

It intrigued him to see the company had already improved several processes after he left—even before Janet's Six Sigma deep dive. Financial Services had embraced artificial intelligence to a far greater extent than he'd imagined and at a far quicker pace. Employee productivity had increased almost thirty-five percent in the year or so since his promotion to lead the Solutions division. That gain was attributed entirely to digitizing processes. The reduction in errors was staggering. Clearly, computers were not only taking over but were also doing a far better job than the humans they replaced.

Just before noon, he made a quick run downstairs to the snack bar in the lobby to get breakfast and have hot coffee ready when Janet eventually woke. She actually found it a nice romantic gesture, and he was tempted to have another round with her right away, but he maintained focus on the task at hand.

Throughout the afternoon, Douglas outlined the next steps. He followed a project management program on his laptop populated with data, organization charts, and action bubbles showing the progression he envisaged. He coached her on the Financial Services balance sheet and operating statements to be sure she understood the significance of every entry and the implication of every trend.

As dusk approached, they took a fifteen-minute cab ride to the Waldorf Astoria Panama despite Google Maps' contention that it was an eleven-minute walk. It was safer that way. They found the restaurant's decor ordinary, but their meals were delicious, and the bottle of fine Chilean wine was exquisite. He used time during the meal to refine their afternoon discussions, clarify ambiguities, and anticipate potential challenges.

They risked the walk back to the Hyatt despite the late hour. The streets were busy with sidewalks full of pedestrians, and the temperate evening weather was pleasing. He took her hand as they went outside and held it casually for the few minutes it took to walk to the Hyatt. She seemed to enjoy the gesture and walked nonchalantly, smiled often, and chattered about how great it was to spend time together.

They made love again as soon as they returned to the room, knowing they'd part early the next day. Janet seemed just a little more desperate, a little more urgent as she coaxed him to bring her to orgasm. As they dozed, her last murmur was that she'd be okay for a while.

Mid-morning, they left together for the airport and completed her check-in formalities first. He'd promised to see her off before he checked in for his return flight to Costa Rica and he embraced her with passion before parting at immigration. He looked into her eyes and whispered that he hoped to see her again soon and asked her to keep up her great work.

In return, Janet murmured something about more time together. He should have ignored the comment but instead, he asked her what she meant.

"I think I'm falling in love with you," she whispered, tilting her head upwards with her large brown eyes slightly moist. It took his quickest thinking for a response.

"Be careful what you wish for," he blurted, trying for levity. It didn't work. She spun on one heel and walked purposefully toward security. He gave a friendly wave of farewell, but it was in vain. She didn't look back.

EIGHTEEN

Hoffman Estates, IL
Friday September 7, 2018

For the first time in months, James Fitzgerald started his day with a vigorous jog. Running had been a part of his life for years, and the brisk autumn morning air felt stimulating and inviting at the same time. As his heart rate increased and breathing became more labored, he started to think with greater clarity than he had for weeks.

It was time to act. He was fed up with his inability to sleep properly, and his constant sense of guilt was affecting every aspect of his life. The whole circumstance had become intolerable. He had never dreamed he'd be saddled with this kind of dilemma less than a year before he retired. He needed to bring the matter to an end.

His most senior direct reports grumbled openly about the ridiculous amounts of time their subordinates were devoting to Janet Weissel's infernal meetings about Six Sigma. Clearly, their people were expending wholly disproportionate amounts of time and energy for pitifully little benefit.

The last report she'd delivered, just after the Labor Day long weekend, was the worst yet. It included only five modest recommendations, three of which were part of the latest artificial intelligence learning update already scheduled for testing and release. Moreover, last week, two more subordinates expressed a strong preference that she not spend any time at all with their teams.

To compound the simmering issue, she wanted to veer off in yet another direction with her Six Sigma venture. It was important to head off a coming directive from the Federal Reserve to address gender compensation equity. She wanted to refocus the statistical power of Six Sigma to ensure Multima Financial Services compliance with the concept of equal pay for equal work. Apparently, only Six Sigma had the methodology and expertise to effectively channel that vital information. He couldn't imagine a messier can of worms to open than that one!

Things were also worse with Dianne. She had easily detected his transparent pattern of 'being out' Wednesday evenings and now had her own night out to match his schedule. The difference was that he returned home after a few hours with Janet Weissel. His wife didn't return until sometime the next day. He never knew when, of course, because he was at the office. Questioned, she would only volunteer that she stayed with a friend.

Suzanne still had not responded to his formal request to retire at the end of June, in 2019. In fact, she never officially acknowledged it. When he casually inquired during a phone conversation, she said she meant to get together with him about it. But with other pressing issues she hadn't yet been able to either prepare for that conversation or schedule time to meet. Could it wait another month or two?

Another even more ominous cloud lurked on the horizon. Yesterday's conversation with his former favorite resource in business intelligence confirmed it when they had lunch.

He'd been remiss the past several months with his star performer, Natalia Tenaz. While Janet Weissel was complicating his life uncomfortably, the young woman he promoted to liaise with the Supermarkets division performed spectacularly. It was her job to assure the newly introduced home mortgage program linked to the Multima credit card and Supermarkets rewards programs achieved optimum success.

To date, mortgages were a company home run. Every month the mortgage loan balances soared. Penetration among Multima employees approached eighty percent, and their overwhelming satisfaction encouraged hundreds of new credit card customers to sign on. In turn, those new customers usually refinanced their current mortgages with Multima to benefit from the savings of weekly repayments plus bonus points to redeem for gifts, travel, or grocery purchases.

It was a resounding achievement, and Natalia Tenaz deserved much of the credit. He told her exactly that at lunch. He also told her she'd see a twenty-five-thousand-dollar bonus added to her next paycheck. She was grateful, but her manner remained oddly aloof and her usual enthusiasm muted.

He got her talking more as he posed a series of questions about her project. The job still thrilled her, she loved what she was doing, and she suggested her relationship with the new president of Supermarkets was even better than the one she'd enjoyed with Suzanne Simpson. Gordon Goodfellow, who'd replaced Suzanne when she became CEO, was a joy for Natalia to work with.

She raved about his openness to new ideas and collaborative approach. His relaxed demeanor was equal to Suzanne's but with a better sense of humor. Natalia loved the way he encouraged his team and all those he interacted with to laugh and enjoy themselves—even when dealing with critical issues. She thought it was a marvelous way to stimulate creative solutions under challenging circumstances.

They talked for almost an hour before he realized they both had meetings to attend and needed to return to the office. As they drove the short distance back, he asked if anything troubled her.

"No," she replied, almost too quickly. "Everything is fine. I love my job. Everything will be okay."

James detected the unease and too pat reassurance. "I think I hear a big 'but' somewhere in there." He waited several seconds until she responded.

"There is. I'm not sure how I should handle the electronic monitoring of Janet Weissel you assigned to me last year. With her promotion and all the attention she's getting in the media, do you still really want me to monitor her every conversation?"

James understood immediately. The relationship with Janet he had tried to keep discretely covert must have triggered an alert. Natalia probably knew there was something amiss and might be uncomfortable about her position. However, he stayed wary as he drove, his eyes fixed firmly on the road.

"Is there anything in particular that's come up?" he asked as casually as he could manage.

"Lots. I wouldn't even know where to begin," Natalia said with her rapid-fire delivery. "And I think we need to talk about it when you have some time."

He saw a driveway to a small shopping plaza just ahead, turned in and stopped the car.

"Let me call to delay my 2:00 o'clock." He reached for his cell. "Then, I'll have all the time you need."

Natalia quickly dispatched a text, apparently postponing her meeting as well.

It was like he had opened a floodgate when she started, and he didn't interrupt her to ask a question or clarify a comment for over an hour as his protégé rattled off a litany of observations. Her usual source at headquarters—the one with the special software like the CIA used—had seen or heard about some troubling incidents at headquarters in Florida. Several untoward incidents recently occurred with that same person. And now that friend felt some additional pressure to divulge highly sensitive company information to someone new.

She lamented secret meetings Suzanne Simpson was having with investment bankers, and the nasty rumors Financial Services was about to be sold or disposed of in some other way.

Finally, she came to Janet Weissel and her trip to Hawaii, which was followed by another jaunt just last week to Panama. Her friend's facial recognition software indicated Douglas Whitfield might still be alive, and a picture they found on Janet's phone suggested the woman might have been with Whitfield in Panama.

Then she told him about the secret office Janet rented close to the Financial Services headquarters, about halfway to her home. Natalia had followed her to that office on more than one occasion. In fact, she thought Janet went there almost every evening. Why would it be necessary for any employee of Multima to rent an outside office at her own expense?

James sat aghast and listened. He instantly regretted his failure to keep in touch with this unusual woman with her seemingly unlimited amount of information. When she finished, he thanked her for sharing it.

"I want to dig deeper into this to better understand it," he said. "I realize it's important for me to address the issues and I will. But let me ask you one question. Why have you kept all this bottled up when it's obviously of such concern to you?"

"What else would you expect me to do?" she spat out. "We're talking about the woman you're sleeping with!"

NINETEEN

Office of Multima's CEO, Fort Myers, FL
Sunday September 9, 2018

"There is nothing lower on the food chain than an investment banker," Suzanne complained to Alberto Ferer and Wilma Willingsworth in a tone of total exasperation. "Both firms signed non-disclosure agreements before we met, and it looks like both leaked info about our discussions to the media."

"The agreements are watertight, Suzanne," Alberto said. "Do you want to launch legal action against them?"

"That wouldn't solve much," Suzanne conceded. "The damage is done, and any action we take would only draw more unwanted attention."

CFO Wilma Willingsworth remained silent. She probably thought she'd gain little by reminding her colleagues she had strongly advised them it was too early for any discussions with investment bankers. Tactfully, the cautious woman now appeared to be thinking about ways to control the damage instead and would surely share those thoughts at an appropriate time.

"Have you given John George a heads-up yet?" Multima's general counsel wondered.

"Yeah, we had dinner last night. I didn't want to burden him with the news, but I think he was already aware. He took it calmly and told me to remind him to review the capital structure of Financial Services with him when I come to visit the next time. He said he was too tired to talk about it last night. He had a few tough days last week. Again, I had a hard time getting out of there with dry eyes. He looks awful. I think he's down to about a hundred and twenty-five pounds now and talking seems painful for him. We spend much of our time just holding hands and looking out at the Caloosahatchee River from his lanai."

"I'm glad the AGM went so well for him," Wilma offered. "He'll get real enjoyment from his memories announcing the new distribution center with the Canadian prime minister. He looked truly animated that day, and to think it was less than a month ago. It's tough to grasp that his condition has worsened dramatically in a matter of weeks."

"Is he still okay to receive visitors?" Alberto asked.

"Yes, John George asks about both of you every time we meet, and he remains stoic about it all. At least once in every conversation, he repeats his mantra that he won't let cancer define his life. He'd welcome you any time. Just call Lana in advance to be sure he's dressed and ready. She stays most of the day now to help with things like that. But we must move on despite John George's circumstance. Wilma, I thank you for not reminding us you told us so, but you did. Now, do you have any advice on how we can contain the damage from the leaks?"

"I have some thoughts, but I really don't think we should beat ourselves up too much." Wilma straightened in her seat and organized her thoughts one final time before expressing them delicately. "I recommended those two firms as the best of a bad bunch. Alberto did everything he could to bind them legally, and you eloquently beseeched them to respect our confidence again when we spoke with them. My first suggestion would be to cut them out of any action when we decide to make a deal."

Suzanne nodded and pursed her lips in appreciation of Wilma's face-saving diplomacy. Both she and Alberto waited for the CFO to continue.

"There's little merit in denying our interest in an IPO or pretending the exploratory talks never took place. Now that the rumor mill is running, anything we say to quash the rumors will only add fuel to the fire," Wilma continued in a calm, reasonable tone. "I suggest you have Hadley create a media release that says Multima doesn't comment on rumors about its business, but regularly undertakes assessments of strategic options and consults with a variety of expert resources. The release should remind investors not to read any significance into any speculation."

"I agree," Alberto added. "I think it's important for us to comment but not confirm or deny. Hadley's people can put a good positive spin on both the release and any background information they share with opinion-makers."

"Fair enough," Suzanne said. "I see the merits of damage control and agree we have to be truthful. So, where should we go from here with the assessment of our options?"

"To be candid, I think you must deal with one major factor before we spend too much time on an assessment," Wilma started. "To get maximum value from an initial public offering for Financial Services, we need to demonstrate to the market a strong and profitable path to growth in the coming five to ten years. We'll also need to show we have an experienced and resilient management team in place to do the job."

"Is your concern primarily with the question of James Fitzgerald's plans?" Suzanne asked with an arched brow.

"Exactly. I think we'll be able to make the profitable and sustained growth story in just a few more months. That home mortgage program they introduced is generating phenomenal activity and looks like it's building momentum. But if James follows through on his intention to retire, our story weakens considerably. There are few executives in America more respected in the financial world. Frankly, I don't see anybody on his team who can fill those big shoes."

"No argument from me," the general counsel added. "Financial Services has generated some great publicity over the past few months with James's promotion of Janet Weissel and her Six Sigma initiative. That's good. However, I don't think anyone considers Janet or anyone else on James's team a probable successor. Douglas Whitfield was the last real superstar with the potential to lead over there. Unfortunately, we all know how badly that turned out."

"I agree with you both. Hopefully, we'll find that we already have a strong internal leader or two who could fill James Fitzgerald's shoes," Suzanne said. "Let me think about the leadership issue more. There are a couple folks in Supermarkets who we might groom quickly. Think too about top performers in your own areas of responsibility who might have enough potential to assume leadership. I'll also get input from the HR folks. Let me know about anybody that comes to mind by Friday."

With that appeal, Suzanne moved on to more immediate issues on the agenda of their weekly review meeting. The executives worked through the list of pressing issues methodically and efficiently. By noon they had discussed all fifteen items that demanded attention, had developed an action plan for each, and made three decisions on subjects to add to the board of directors meeting scheduled for the following week.

As her two most trusted advisors left her office, Suzanne called James Fitzgerald to invite him for dinner the evening before the board meeting. She wanted to talk with him about his retirement request. After that call, Suzanne leaned back in her plush leather chair and gazed out over the Caloosahatchee River for a while, deep in thought. During those crucial moments, she made her decisions.

TWENTY

A tiny rented office, Hoffman Estates, IL
Saturday September 22, 2018

Their plan started to unravel. Just look at the past few weeks. James Fitzgerald had not requested an evening with Janet since her return from Panama. There had been opportunities. Two of their interactions were private meetings in his office. And both meetings went badly despite her best efforts.

It started with that damned report on operational improvements from her Six Sigma sessions in August. She knew the recommendations were weak, but they were the best she could do. God knows she tried to find weaknesses they could correct with that operations team, but it was already functioning too smoothly.

Then, James poured water on the idea to focus on equal pay for equal work. Naturally, she didn't present it as Douglas Whitfield's idea. She carefully researched the subject and thought she made a compelling case for both the legal and moral imperative. They urgently needed to be sure Financial Services was complying with the Fed's requirements.

James thought it needed a little more study. He'd consider it. In the meantime, maybe she could prepare a nice statistical synopsis of her past six months with Six Sigma. Present a concise summary of the projects she handled, the outcomes, the person-hours involved, her best estimates of both the cost of doing the Six Sigma deep dives, and the probable financial benefits. She should try to quantify everything.

Well, she wasn't born yesterday. That whole thing sounded awfully close to a justification for holding onto her job. And that could not be a good thing.

Meanwhile, Douglas was pressing for more information. In addition to all the payroll information the investigation on gender pay equality was supposed to generate, he was looking for copies of documents. He wanted things like the Multima Financial Services articles of incorporation, inter-company agreements with Multima Corporation, and even James Fitzgerald's current employment contract.

All that information now seemed beyond her reach. The only way she could get the payroll information and the other documents would be to hack the Financial Services central server. But she knew that data was protected by the same clever software app that caused all the misery for Multima Solutions before Mortimer sold the division. Natalia Tenaz made that abundantly clear the day Janet started at Financial Services. The app would track every instance of the data being hacked, copied, or transferred, the bitch had emphasized. If anyone tried to penetrate their system, management would know precisely which computer was used to steal the data. It was far too risky for Janet to try.

Only one way remained to get at all the information Douglas needed. She'd have to dream up a way to get her secret relationship with James Fitzgerald back on track. Only with his support and unambiguous authority could she access the data Douglas wanted.

But that avenue also presented obstacles. Last month, James had invited her to attend the September board of directors meeting in Fort Myers and implied they might be able to arrange a romantic night on Sanibel Island before they returned. Yesterday, he sent her a text canceling that invitation. Suzanne Simpson required him to attend a private meeting. Further, she had also altered the meeting agenda. There would be no time available for a Six Sigma presentation.

The other disturbing hindrance related to her old nemesis, the bitch. At first, Janet thought she was just being a little paranoid. Two or three times during the past few weeks, she'd had a strange feeling that someone was following her car. Each time she checked the rear-view mirror but nothing seemed unusual. Until tonight.

She felt the sensation once again just a few blocks before her turn for the office complex where she rented her tiny secret work area. She looked in the mirror and was shocked to see Natalia Tenaz's SUV following a block back behind. Just as Janet noticed this, the bitch signaled, pulled out around her, and then waved as she passed. It could be coincidental. The woman lived in this direction, but unease about that situation remained.

She'd just tell Douglas the straight goods. She was bumping up against a solid wall of resistance with James Fitzgerald. What cards should she play?

TWENTY-ONE

John George Mortimer's home, Fort Myers, FL
Sunday September 23, 2018

Five weeks had passed since his performance at the announcement of Multima's decision to build a massive new warehouse in Canada. It had been fun, John George thought as he looked back on the day with a feeble smile. Now, it felt as if months had gone by.

The decline—as he privately referred to it—had started right around Labor Day. For no apparent reason, he vomited every few minutes during the night until he voided his system some hours later. He tried to drink water but couldn't keep it down. He nibbled on some snacks, but almost immediately threw them back up.

When Lana returned from running errands mid-morning, the sight of him alarmed her. He told her the number of times he had been physically ill during the night and she dialed 9-1-1. He would be severely dehydrated if nothing else. He was too weak to protest, so an ambulance came and carted him away to the same hospital where he'd had his surgery last year.

They fed him intravenously to replenish his fluids and called his oncologist. The specialist ordered a series of urgent blood and imaging tests. When the doctor returned several hours later, she brought two other people with her. Colleagues she respected, she said.

They prodded, poked, and peered into his eyes, ears, nose, and throat. They spoke quietly, and occasionally asked him questions or consulted each other. After a short while they left, and sometime later, the oncologist returned to see him.

"You always tell me to be straight and direct with you, John George," she said. "We'll release you today because there's nothing more we can do right now. Your body is rejecting the immunotherapy, and cancer cells are metastasizing quickly. I already told you we have no other options at this point. It will take some time yet. Except for the malignant tumors, your body has remarkable strength and resiliency. We'll keep searching the globe for viable treatments that might slow the process, but I recommend you get full-time care at home."

Suzanne suggested Lana move in to oversee his care, and that helped. She was a wonderful woman who continuously offered support and encouragement and reminded him often of his instructions to her: Never let him feel sorry for himself. Never let him complain. Keep smiling. As the pain intensified, it became increasingly hard to do.

Suzanne helped considerably as well. She came for short visits almost every day or called if she was out of town. Her dedication and the love she expressed were the same, he supposed, as a daughter who had lived an entire life with her father. Thankfully, she no longer showed anger or disappointment about the years they had been apart and had apparently forgiven his poor judgment about withholding his knowledge of their relationship for so long.

She still sought his advice every day although John George was sure she did it more for his benefit than hers. She didn't need his counsel any longer. Her intellect and judgment were without equal. He'd never met another executive who could analyze a situation as quickly or devise a solution more appropriately. Suzanne was even better than James Fitzgerald at his peak. He was leaving the company in excellent hands.

Tonight's discussion was a case in point. Suzanne told him what she would propose in her coming discussion with James and why she'd made that decision. She knew how close he and James were and how much respect John George had for his long-time subordinate. She sought his affirmation that she had correctly assessed the situation and looked for validation of her strategy. Her thought process was correct in every respect.

Then she listened while John George explained the possible pitfalls with an initial public offering for Multima Financial Services. She listened, but he was still not entirely sure she got it. In fact, she seemed uncharacteristically distracted. Within a few minutes, she glanced at her watch and told him she'd pay attention to his concerns but needed to dash away for a conference call.

She wanted to cover one more subject before she left. "Everyone on the board will want to know how you're doing. How do you want me to handle their questions?"

"Because we worked closely for so many years, I suppose they're probably curious and concerned," John George started. "Honesty is best. Let them know I'm not doing well. Tell them I may not last much longer."

"I certainly won't tell them that," she replied. "You're not a quitter. Things might look grave at the moment, but it might just be temporary. Researchers might still find something to slow the cancer down. With your determination, it's too early to count you out."

Suzanne said the words with the right tone and facial expression. Her voice may have wavered slightly, but he wouldn't make it more difficult for her.

"You're right. We can never give up hope, and I don't want your colleagues unduly alarmed. We need to keep them focused on business," he said with a short laugh. Her face relaxed with his attempt at humor. "But let's tell them visits should be suspended right now. Guests are just too difficult for me at this stage."

"I get it," she replied. "I'll let them know."

Was that a tear she wiped quickly from her eye?

It was time for her to leave. With a massive heave from both arms, John George raised himself upright and extended a hand toward her. Suzanne gripped it tightly as they walked to the front door.

"I'll see you tomorrow," she managed before turning quickly to make her exit.

Maybe. The pain he felt caused him to wonder if there really would be a tomorrow. The heavy burden he carried was becoming onerous. A final relief might not be an entirely bad thing.

TWENTY-TWO

A small cottage, Colonia del Sacramento, Uruguay
Monday September 24, 2018

Howard Knight bolted completely upright in bed from a restless sleep to find the muzzle of his own gun pointing at his head. The brown face in the darkness behind the weapon was familiar, but he still recoiled involuntarily when Douglas Whitfield spoke.

"Easy now, Howard," he said with a sinister smirk. "Don't do anything we'll both regret. Don't make a sound. Don't make any sudden moves. Don't even think about overpowering me. Just relax and ease out of the bed."

Whitfield continued to point the handgun directly at Howard's face. It was just out of arm's reach and Douglas pre-emptively stepped back a pace as his quarry rose naked and trembling from the bed.

"I don't want you pissing or shitting all over the floor here." He pointed to a small lavatory just a few steps down the hall. "Go into the bathroom and sit on the toilet."

He did as directed. Immediately, Whitfield lashed out at Howard's legs with some sort of whip. In reaction to the sharp pain, Howard reached to protect his ankles, and within a second or two found himself bound hands to ankles. Whitfield's motion was so swift and his strength so great that Howard had no time to react. He could only sit on the toilet, nude and uncomfortably bent forward toward the floor.

"You should have killed her," Whitfield said with a taunting grin. "Or, at the very least, destroyed the computer. Did you already forget everything The Organization taught you?"

Whitfield didn't really expect an answer. Protest or argument would gain nothing. It would be better just to see where this was headed. How on earth did the bastards find him?

"It seems she found you kinda weird. She liked your fifty K all right. But she couldn't quite understand why you were that paranoid about someone recognizing your face. It seems your young friend is quite a smart cookie. She programmed a few keywords into that new computer you bought that informed her of your physical location from the laptop IP address every time you connected to Wi-Fi. Then she got to thinking. If you were willing to pay fifty, might someone else out there pay more?"

Again, Whitfield paused several seconds to let his message fully sink in. He was enjoying the drama and in no hurry to get to his point.

"You were very careless, Howard," he sneered. "Careless and stupid. Of course, she did what any enterprising young technology genius would do. She poked around on the dark web for a few days until she came across your picture. In fact, she found three pictures. One the way you looked last year as a director of Multima Corporation. Another as you looked on at least one forged passport. And another one as you look right now. I heard that last one was picked right from the files of fortress FBI after they captured you in Argentina."

Howard did his best to remain stoic. There was no benefit in showing the fear that almost paralyzed him, and he had no idea how he should respond to this recitation of his mistakes even if he were so inclined.

"Fortunately, she called the right people and negotiated a fee far greater than you paid. They called me. Now here we are. Howard Knight, the victim of his own repeated carelessness. And me, the guy you tried to shut out of the Multima CEO sweepstakes. Yeah, everyone realizes your haste to install Wendal Randall in Mortimer's chair was the gaffe that caused your whole scheme to implode.

"You were so confident you could make your mark in The Organization. You persuaded the Miami interests to help you win Mareno's support to charge forward with your ill-advised scheme. But you didn't have anything close to the entire picture, did you?" he taunted.

Whitfield spat on the floor to emphasize his disdain, then reached for his telephone.

"Let's get a photo of the genius Howard Knight celebrating his successes." He chuckled as he snapped his phone camera. Its flash momentarily lit up the deathly dark bathroom. "You knew nothing about Suzanne Simpson and her relationship to Mortimer, did you? Or the clean-up I had to do to deflect attention after you ran away with your tail between your legs?"

"Listen, Douglas," Howard interjected as Whitfield made another dramatic pause. "I think you may have this wrong."

"Shut up!" Whitfield commanded. "I'll tell you when it's okay to open your mouth. I understand the situation perfectly. Giancarlo Mareno will pay me a reward of five hundred thousand if I simply slash off those tiny balls, jam them in your mouth, and pull this trigger to blow apart your brains and testicles. But he'll give me a million to package you up alive and cart you back to New York so he can do his own artwork on your body before the end."

Apparently, Whitfield's strategy was to add humiliation to whatever else he'd planned. To underscore his menace, Whitfield reached for a butcher-sized knife he had placed nearby in advance, then loudly clicked off the safety latch of Howard's gun.

"I remember all the training The Organization gave me," he threatened, changing his tack. "Unfortunately, your young friend had a fatal accident shortly after I handed her the exorbitant fee she negotiated with Mareno. Now, I need to decide which option I should choose to dispense with you. Might it be quick and tidy? Or should I be patient and get you back to Mareno and his friends for the much larger payoff? Don't move while you think about that."

Douglas left Howard sitting there, bound on the toilet while he walked around the small cottage closing windows and drawing curtains and shades. The cabin became even darker with the moonlight blocked. The only sound was the incessant barking of dogs—the curse of this neighborhood where threatening howls filled the nights while days were tranquil as surly canines slept.

Douglas returned, carrying a chair in one hand and Howard's gun in the other, still pointing it menacingly toward Howard's head.

"But it's all a little more complicated than that," he said as he sat down on the chair and lowered the gun's aim slightly. "You see, I'm in a bit of a spot with some of the boys in The Organization as well. Your carelessness might be a little contagious. Gottingham and I made a big miscalculation too. You probably don't know the name, but Earnest Gottingham was named to replace you at VCI. Poor guy later showed up floating in the Hudson. Luckily, I got a temporary reprieve."

Howard again chose silence and struggled to process his circumstances. Meanwhile, his captor appeared moved by the recollection of his friend and his demise. His tone had held uncharacteristic hoarseness. But where was all this going?

"You see, I'm actually on the lam too. I've kept out of sight in Central America for the past few months while I sort out some things. Some guys in The Organization would like a piece of my hide. And that's why I'm prepared to talk with you a bit before I make a final decision about what to do with you."

"Can I get dressed while we talk?" Howard ventured.

"No. You'll think better right where you are, as you are. How you react over these next few minutes will determine whether getting dressed would be a waste of your time. Dead men don't need clothes."

So, he's leaning toward killing me.

"Can I have some water?" Howard asked meekly.

"No. Again, you'll think better without water, and I don't want to create any more waste than necessary," Whitfield scoffed. "Here's the issue. Misery sometimes makes strange bedfellows. It might be possible for me to spare your life—for now at least—if you're willing to cooperate. You see, my redemption with The Organization requires me to find a way to destroy that cunt, Suzanne Simpson. Listen carefully now.

"I won't bore you with all the details, but I got shafted by that bitch. This all occurred after you bailed out of that Multima board of directors meeting in Fort Myers. She somehow destroyed every operating copy of that revolutionary software application to track hackers. The software I'm talking about was the app that helped the FBI nail Randall for his hacking misadventure. Mortimer was so excited about the potential to sell it to other companies that he moved it over to Solutions and made me president of the division. Initially, I was to market it and make Solutions bigger and more profitable. However, the app had a little security glitch that needed to be corrected, a backdoor with the potential to provide easy and undetected access to computer servers all over the world.

"A few of us decided it was better not to fix the defect. Instead, we planned to exploit it to steal a few trillion dollars from banks and other customers who bought the software from us. But to make it work, we needed to spin-off the whole division to get it out from under curious eyes within Multima. Before Gottingham could get me installed as Multima's new CEO—and in a position to do all that—John George Mortimer pulled a fast one. More precisely, that cunt Suzanne Simpson put him up to a way to shaft us.

"The Organization tried to buy Multima Solutions but couldn't raise enough cash quickly enough. To prevent Mortimer from revealing the defect and destroying the software—eliminating any chance for us to exploit it—we had to give up our ownership position in Multima. We got the Solutions division all right, but the day we signed the contract, we discovered the software app—every single copy of it—suddenly evaporated. There was nothing left but garbled code. The app was worthless."

Howard grimaced as he realized his captor's predicament. He felt no sympathy for either Mareno or Whitfield, but he understood immediately the mess they were in. The all-powerful leader of The Organization must have been mortally embarrassed, and those criminal constituents who bankrolled the initial billion-dollar investment in Multima livid. After laying out so much money, they would have expected a far higher return on their investment than a small logistics company worth only a hundred million when they first got involved. And it was probably not worth much more now.

"Things have recently changed. Mareno learned of some new developments and thought the time right to attack Multima. He got word to me about finding you because he needs my help and thinks you may be able to contribute," Whitfield continued after collecting his thoughts. "Here's the deal. We leave this ghetto in the middle of nowhere right now. We walk to your boat in the harbor and get there before light. Then, we head north toward Central America."

"I can't walk anywhere like this." Howard gestured with his cuffed hands.

"I'll adjust the restraints so you can walk. On the boat, I'll release your hands while I'm awake. At night, you'll remain handcuffed just as you are now. When we need fuel or supplies and go ashore, you'll go below deck, and I'll secure you there. If you ever try to escape, to cry out, or try any shenanigans, you're dead. And it won't be pretty.

"On the other hand, if you cooperate and help me rid Multima of that cunt Simpson, and we get full control of the entire corporation, Giancarlo says he's prepared to let bygones be bygones. You'll be forgiven."

Howard didn't respond right away. Options were limited, and he couldn't identify a single point of negotiating leverage. After a few seconds elapsed, he asked one question to test Whitfield's resolve. "What kind of assurances is Mareno prepared to give me?"

His captor instantly recognized the ploy to buy more time and wasn't having any of it.

"Decide now, Howard," he said as he stood up, calmly sweeping the chair away with one hand, and using the other to point the handgun directly into Howard's eyes.

Then, with a cold tone and impassive expression, Douglas said, "We have one hour until dawn and our hike to the boat will take almost all of that. Either you agree to my conditions and we start walking within the next thirty seconds, or I'll pull this trigger. I'll tell Mareno you tried to escape."

Howard agreed. It didn't take a genius to figure it far better to buy a little more time—and perhaps devise an escape later—than to end it all now in this tiny cottage in the middle of nowhere with the incessant barking of dogs in the background.

TWENTY-THREE

The Veranda restaurant, Fort Myers, FL
Wednesday September 26, 2018

The Veranda was one of the oldest established restaurants in Fort Myers and maintained a superb reputation for fine dining. But the characteristic Suzanne always liked best was its small garden courtyard. There, tables had greater space between them than those inside and conversations could be more private. So, James wasn't surprised when the maître d' ushered him to a large, round table set for two in a sheltered corner of the garden.

Suzanne was waiting. She rose to greet him with a warm handshake and welcoming smile when he reached the table. They chatted about banal subjects to start, and James wasn't alarmed when she introduced the subject of his retirement right after they placed their orders for food.

"Thank you for being so patient with my deliberations about your retirement request," she said. Her regret about the amount of time she had kept him waiting to deal with his request seemed genuine. "I know you've been thinking about this for some time. Did you further consider the matter after our last conversation?"

"I did," James replied. "I've thought about little else over the past few weeks. It feels right for me to retire next June. I promised John George I'd stay 'til then, but that's as long as I want to go. I find working with you exciting, and I have no doubt Multima's best days are yet to come, but I'm getting older. I don't have the same drive. And Dianne and I are still facing formidable challenges since our loss of Alistair."

Her facial expression didn't change as he shared his thoughts. It wasn't passive, nor was it animated. He guessed she'd anticipated that response, but he certainly wasn't prepared for what she said next.

"I understand your rationale, James, and I respect your preference. However, I'm going to accept your request to retire immediately rather than next June," she said slowly and forcefully with a tone slightly above a whisper.

He leaned forward to hear her comment clearly.

"I've checked with Alberto Ferer. We have the right to amend your employment contract with mutual consent. Furthermore, your age comfortably qualifies you for full pension benefits, including a full performance bonus for the current year—even if you shouldn't complete it," Suzanne explained succinctly. She waited for him to respond.

She wants me to go right now. Numb, James needed a moment to gather his thoughts to ask even a most basic question.

"Is there a particular reason you've decided to make this move right now?" he asked, a little more plaintively than he would have liked.

"No doubt you've heard the rumor I'm considering an IPO for Financial Services." She waited for him to nod before she continued. "It's true. While I haven't made a final decision that I want to recommend to the board, I'm leaning toward simplifying our business model to focus on supermarkets. It's what we know best and the sector I believe we can best penetrate for sustained growth and profits. And let's not forget, you built an outstanding company we can spin-off to realize huge returns in the short-, mid- and long-term."

James appreciated the blatant flattery. It helped soften the blow of the decision in some small measure. But it didn't answer his question.

"Thanks, Suzanne. It's good to hear you say that, but it doesn't tell me why you want me out of the way while you do your review. I might be able to help you get even more out of the IPO and further augment Multima's return on the investment."

"Of that I have no doubt," she replied without hesitation. "I have no question about your knowledge, intellect, or experience. Multima will miss them all from the moment you retire. But I think we both know that should you stay with Multima, there are unacceptable risks for the business as well."

She knew! Suzanne chose her words carefully and spoke in soft tones, but the knowing nod of her head as she peered into his eyes telegraphed her meaning as clearly as if she'd held up a sign that said, "What about Janet?"

"I think it would be best for you to announce your intention to leave Multima at the end of this month during tomorrow's board meeting. You can position your decision as the result of some recent news you've just received about a family health matter. That kind of excuse will be least disruptive to the company and most favorable to your excellent and well-deserved business legacy. I can then confirm to the board that I reluctantly accepted your decision to retire and propose the name of the person I recommend replace you," Suzanne continued, nodding firmly with each point for emphasis.

"I get it," James said with a sigh of resignation. "I appreciate what you're doing. I'll polish some comments tonight and alert Alberto that I'd like to make a statement at the beginning of the meeting. Don't worry. I'll handle it professionally."

Suzanne smiled, looked directly into his eyes, then nodded again while he gave that assurance. Did he detect just a bit of mist in her eyes as she looked away to take a sip of wine? When she set down her glass a moment later, she demonstrated her confidence that he would execute his instructions admirably. She wanted his opinion on the candidate she had in mind to replace him.

TWENTY-FOUR

Fort Myers, FL
Thursday September 27, 2018

"I met with James Fitzgerald for dinner last evening and discussed his request to retire," the CEO started her conversation with Wilma Willingsworth. "A family health matter has made it necessary for him to announce his decision to retire immediately. He'll do that at the meeting this morning. I'd like to offer you the opportunity to replace him as president at Financial Services."

The news shocked Wilma. First, James Fitzgerald was the longest serving executive at Multima Corporation. He was one of John George Mortimer's earliest recruits and closest confidants. Furthermore, he oversaw the most profitable segment of the business and was probably the most respected individual in the company now that John George was no longer active.

Could this possibly be true?

James wanted to retire at the end of the fiscal year. He talked openly about that. But whatever could have happened that he would retire with only two days' notice after thirty-eight years with the corporation? Was it his health that precipitated the decision? His wife's? Why was Suzanne sharing so little information?

Suzanne acknowledged her bewilderment right away.

"I realize this is probably a shock. Take a few minutes to process it all. I know you usually prefer to consider your options in private," she said with a sympathetic smile. "Here's the proposed compensation package. Your salary will increase by over fifty percent. The company will offer generous financial support for the transition from your current role and the move from Fort Myers to Chicago. Let's meet again in an hour. I'd like to announce your appointment immediately after James announces his departure this morning. Will an hour give you enough time?"

The package Suzanne offered was impressive. Wilma's performance-based compensation would double her current salary as Chief Financial Officer. All relocation expenses would be covered. Of course, she'd also use the Financial Services corporate jet for travel. There was only that one important catch. Suzanne needed a decision immediately.

From the tiny refrigerator under her desk, Wilma took a bottle of water and gulped it down. Water always helped her think better. Then she stood in front of the huge floor-to-ceiling bank of windows in her office overlooking the Caloosahatchee River. It was one of Wilma's favorite views and always calmed her. Then she slowly and deliberately inhaled and exhaled three times before she considered her future.

The boys were out on their own now. She put them through some of the best universities in America after the messy divorce, and they all held good responsible positions. They were now sprinkled across the nation, and she only saw them from time-to-time. Whether she remained in Fort Myers or moved to Chicago wouldn't impact any of the three in any substantive way.

She loved her current role as chief financial officer for one of America's finest large companies. Last year, Fortune magazine named her among the fifty most influential businesswomen in the nation. Rarely a month went by that she wasn't invited to speak at a conference or accept an award by women's associations that held her out as a role model for young women.

She'd frequently wondered what it would be like to run a company. Previously, there was only one fleeting opportunity—that time Howard Knight threw out her name in desperation as a potential replacement for John George Mortimer. Only then did she ever seriously think about the possibility of leading a major company.

This might be a great chance.

With Suzanne's offer, Wilma would be president of a gigantic and successful company, even if she wouldn't be the chief executive officer. Her powers would be broad, and the opportunity to influence business culture, career progression of subordinates, and the strategic direction of her business unit would present exciting new challenges. And, should Suzanne follow through on her intention to spin-off Financial Services, she might eventually find herself in the role of CEO of a huge publicly traded company.

It took only a few moments of private time before Wilma went to Suzanne and accepted the offer. They tweaked a few of the proposed conditions Wilma thought might create some unnecessary tax burden for both her and the company, but essentially their deal was done.

Suzanne wanted her to travel to Chicago immediately after the meeting. James Fitzgerald had offered to share a ride on the company jet because he was eager to start the transition. They could discuss many issues while they were flying. But first a meeting with the board of directors. Much of it was a blur for Wilma.

After James made his startling announcement right at the beginning, Suzanne delivered her prepared comments to a hushed room.

"James, it's as hard for me to accept your request to retire as it must have been for you to make such a life-altering decision. I accept your wish but do so with the greatest reluctance. I know everyone on this board of directors, and our thousands of colleagues throughout the company, hope for only the best as you enter this next phase of your life.

"That it has been necessary for you to make such a serious decision with such immediate effect is a concern for us all. But be sure our thoughts are with you as you cope with whatever changes this decision may bring. We'll talk about a more elaborate farewell celebration sometime soon, but I want to ask your fellow directors to join me in a hearty round of applause to thank you for the many valuable contributions you made to this company over a career of unwavering dedication."

The small group of fewer than ten people in the room generated loud and sustained applause for at least a minute. They all stood to show their respect while some shouted out "Good Luck" or "Enjoy it". When the applause died down, the directors took their seats again. Suzanne continued respectfully but with authority.

"While I profoundly regret it's become necessary to bid farewell to James so suddenly, I also appreciate that he generously shared his counsel with me about a possible replacement. We had a long talk about how we should handle choosing our next president of Financial Services. Since James is the only president that division has ever had, who better to know the characteristics most suited to the role?" she said with a smile that kindled more grins around the room.

"James was emphatic in our discussions. With the Financial Services group currently achieving rapid growth with the new mortgage program, we both think it's crucial for the team in Chicago to know as quickly as possible who their leader will be and what strategies that leader will extol," she continued.

"We all know James has been thinking about retiring for a while, even though we didn't expect it this soon. I was confident James had been considering possible successors for some time. When I asked him who would be the best candidate, his response was immediate and the name he mentioned was at the top of my list of candidates," Suzanne claimed. She paused long enough for the directors to see James vigorously nodding his head in agreement.

"Wilma Willingsworth," Suzanne said without fanfare. "Our current CFO has the experience and personality precisely suited to this important role. She understands the business almost as well as James and has the intellect to absorb any gaps in knowledge quickly and seamlessly. She also has the gravitas needed to impress the markets and a reputation as one of the best businesspeople in the country."

Every set of eyes in the room fixed on Wilma. Instead of her usual discomfort with the sudden and unexpected attention, she felt a sense of appreciation, perhaps even admiration. Suzanne apparently felt it as well because she moved forward decisively.

"I know this board expects to have more time to decide and consider these kinds of important shifts in our resources and structure," Suzanne signaled. "But we must decide this issue quickly. I propose to nominate Wilma Willingsworth to become the president of Financial Services according to the terms and conditions I've discussed with her and as summarized in the briefing document Sally-Ann is distributing to each of you now."

There was debate, of course. Directors treasure their independence and never want to feel railroaded into a decision by a CEO. Wilma offered to leave the room while the debate took place, but everyone assured her she was welcome to stay. Most of the discussion revolved around the urgency of the decision, but when it became clear that most directors shared Suzanne's preference for an early resolution, resistance faded quickly. There was a show-of-hands vote, and it was unanimous. Wilma Willingsworth was named the president of Multima Financial Services.

TWENTY-FIVE

On a boat about 5 miles off Taboga Island, Panama
Saturday November 3, 2018

Douglas Whitfield couldn't quite believe it. For a full month, he'd cajoled, threatened, encouraged, begged, and even physically attacked his stubborn prisoner with no success. He got Howard Knight to the Carver yacht during the night of his capture all right, and they were well off the coast of Uruguay before dawn. But all subsequent efforts to get Knight's further cooperation proved futile.

"Pull the trigger if you wish," Howard once responded to a menacing threat to kill him and throw his lifeless body overboard. The cagey bastard seemed to realize although he had everything to lose, in some bizarre way he still had negotiating leverage. Douglas wasn't convinced Knight was worth all the effort. The guy had shown his incompetence too often.

He was tempted to be rid of the bungling old curmudgeon more than once but always restrained himself with the nagging reminder of his mission. To regain his stature in The Organization—indeed to save his own life—Douglas desperately needed to find a way to steal Multima Corporation from its shareholders and destroy the career of Suzanne Simpson.

However, Knight still wouldn't cooperate with Douglas's scheme in any way—not until he had personal assurances about his future safety directly from Giancarlo Mareno and got those guarantees in a face-to-face meeting. As absurd as that might sound, it was happening. Douglas processed the bizarre circumstance as he sipped his first cold beer in a month while the others settled into a cluster around the captain's perch on Knight's yacht.

Knight had steadfastly refused to cooperate. Eventually, Douglas went ashore briefly while they passed through the Panama Canal. He called Giancarlo Mareno. Douglas expected the powerful man to authorize the bastard's elimination. With that okay, he was fully prepared to return to the boat, then just toss the bastard overboard when they were back out at sea.

Mareno shocked him. After thinking about their dilemma for only a moment or two, Giancarlo said, "OK. I'll meet him. He's key to your mission. You might know a lot about Multima's Financial Services division. But as we learned with the Multima Solutions fiasco, you don't have a deep knowledge of how the entire company works. Knight does. He may have screwed up on a couple things because of poor judgment or timing, but he knows the secrets of their corporate structure and the mind of John George Mortimer better than any of us. I'll convince Knight that helping you seize control can be his ticket to survival as well."

Over the following few days, as they wended their way through the canal, Douglas called into New York a couple more times to get updates from Mareno and instructions about their meeting.

To get there, the formidable leader of The Organization chartered a private jet which kept no records of either the flight or its passengers. Mareno arrived during the early morning hours at Ruben Cantu airport, a tiny facility near Panama's west coast. There, he walked from the private jet to a waiting helicopter without any immigration protocol and was whisked to a secluded beach on Panama's Taboga Island where Knight's Carver yacht came as close to shore as safely possible.

The huge man looked as out of place as Douglas could imagine. He wore printed shorts and a t-shirt. But he had stepped too far from shore and the incoming waves slapped against his great hulk. It appeared every square inch of his clothing was doused with water. Annoyed, he yelled at them to help him board the cursed boat.

As the yacht bobbed within reach, Mareno stepped forward and grabbed Douglas's outstretched arm to help him mount the ladder hooked over the edge of the boat. It was then Douglas realized the massive kingpin wasn't alone. Out of his initial field of vision, standing directly behind Mareno and gazing up from the water in a tiny bikini covering almost nothing, Janet Weissel smiled mischievously.

What the hell is she doing with Mareno?

Multima Financial Services had fired her. Wilma Willingsworth, the new division president, had apparently called Janet into her office in Chicago to let her know they no longer needed her services because Willingsworth didn't see any value in Six Sigma for a superbly managed company.

Janet shared that unfortunate development with Douglas, so he just wrote off the young fox as of no further of value. For weeks, he hadn't thought about her for even a moment. What possible further use would there be for the woman if she didn't serve as a mole within the business they were trying to seize? Mareno, though, apparently had something up his sleeve. After boarding, she snuggled up right beside the big guy.

Let the games begin.

TWENTY-SIX

On the Multima Supermarkets jet
Wednesday November 7, 2018

Suzanne Simpson was grateful Gordon Goodfellow had no issues with his male ego. Her president of the Supermarkets division still generously shared the corporate jet paid for entirely by his operating division. That became necessary because she honored John George Mortimer's gentle request not to buy one more jet. Of course, the aircraft owned by Multima Solutions went with that division when they sold the business off. So their fleet now numbered only two planes.

Wilma Willingsworth used the Financial Services jet and logged a lot of miles as she continued to commute between Chicago and Fort Myers once or twice a week. The newly minted division president still hadn't sold her home and moved to Chicago. Furthermore, the complex transition of her former CFO's responsibilities to a successor took longer than forecast. Suzanne valued the extra load Wilma carried and didn't consider asking her to share the second plane.

Goodfellow even now basked in the glow of his latest promotion and willingly accommodated any request Suzanne made. She guessed his malleable spirit might also have something to do with the high-level proposal he passed to her after the last meeting of the board in October. 'Confidential,' stamped in large bold letters at the top of each page, created intrigue about the document. A study of its contents quickly led to the just-completed exploratory encounter in New York.

CBA Investment Bank had discretely contacted Goodfellow to see if Multima might have an interest in buying a major supermarket competitor. When he heard the target company's name, the newly installed president of Supermarkets immediately bubbled it up to Suzanne. After she read the briefing, she couldn't believe her good fortune.

Jeffersons Stores was vulnerable. Management wasn't looking for a buyer. But the company's debt load was mounting, and CBA speculated they might have trouble renewing its financing when it became due later this year. If Multima had an appetite to buy the company, CBA had some privileged information about the capital structure and corporate cultural sensitivities.

The investment bank couldn't dangle a more appealing company to pique Suzanne's interest. Goodfellow raised a caution on the first page of his cover memo. This acquisition might be exceptionally risky and would be difficult to digest. Regardless, the potential fit with Multima Supermarkets so closely matched Suzanne's vision of where she wanted to take the company, she couldn't resist taking a preliminary look.

With over twenty-two hundred stores spread across the USA, Jeffersons outnumbered Multima locations by more than two-to-one. The competitor's annual sales of about sixty billion were almost double Multima's. And their twenty-five distribution centers served thirty-five million customers Multima currently didn't have.

If she could pull off this acquisition, Suzanne would almost triple the size of Multima's current business in one master stroke. She'd lead the largest supermarket chain in the nation, operating under a dozen different banners. It was uncanny just how closely that resembled her mental picture of how the company should look a few years down the road.

At first, Suzanne moved forward with extreme caution. She knew nothing about CBA Investment Bank, so she asked her chief legal counsel, Alberto Ferer, to investigate. He reported the bank was a boutique operation which had been around for about twenty-five years. The principals of the bank were all former senior executives of big Wall Street firms, and none appeared to have any blemishes on their careers or reputations.

She drew in Wilma Willingsworth. The only way Multima could acquire a company twice its size would be to quickly spin off Multima Financial Services. An IPO would not only generate a significant amount of cash but would also eliminate the enormous debt load that comes with owning a financial institution.

Wilma was cautiously optimistic. Financial Services was an even more dynamic business unit than she had previously realized. The management team there was superlative, and the balance sheet was strong. She had discovered no irregularities, and the only headcount adjustment necessary was the termination of Janet Weissel. They could realistically think about a spin-off sometime in the first quarter of next year.

With that stark assessment, Suzanne saw the prospects of buying Jeffersons Stores diminish rapidly. The vulnerability at Jeffersons that CBA Investment Bank proposed to exploit required action before the end of the current calendar year. A best-case scenario to complete an IPO for Financial Services was the fourth quarter of next year according to Wilma. Initially, it didn't look like they should invest time pursuing the proposal.

So, Suzanne initially dismissed the idea. But then CBA revealed another approach. The investment bank had suggestions on ways Multima might bridge the financing gap until after the disposition of the Financial Services business. Could they meet to explore some creative ways they might help Suzanne realize her objectives?

The investment bank thought it had an insight into Multima strategy because a junior partner for the west coast firm Multima previously held exploratory talks with had now joined CBA in New York. They were confident they could fit all the pieces together if Suzanne would meet with them just once. Everything would be in the strictest confidence.

CBA's ideas were surely creative. Suzanne and Gordon Goodfellow expressed only skepticism during that first session, but in the privacy of the jet, they conceded there might be a way to make it all work. Goodfellow still cautioned Suzanne about the potential pitfalls.

"I remember the challenges we had with the Price Deelite acquisition." Gordon referred to his prior corporate assignment. "When you sent me to manage that acquisition, I realized it was the toughest assignment I'd ever had. Our business cultures were very different. Company policies and procedures were not aligned. Even the values people held most important varied in many respects. I had my hands full achieving harmony and dragging that small organization into the Multima mindset. I can only imagine the challenges we'll have trying to eat an elephant twice our size. I'm not sure you and I can last long enough to ever digest them."

Suzanne respected his concerns and valued his input. He was one of her most loyal lieutenants from the time Suzanne joined Multima a decade earlier. But the opportunity still intrigued her. How often in one's career would the chance to grow a company exponentially come along? But it would require exhaustive study.

Suzanne wasn't sure how much time she'd have to undertake such an intense examination in the coming weeks. She was flying back to Fort Myers after a grueling day of discussions because it was important to spend time with John George Mortimer. There was little doubt the coming Thanksgiving holiday would be his last.

TWENTY-SEVEN

On a private jet headed to New York, NY
Friday November 30, 2018

Janet Weissel felt like she was living in some sort of surreal dream. Almost an entire year had passed since her unexpected rendezvous with Douglas Whitfield in Hawaii. Next came her training to become a Six Sigma black belt, followed by a promotion to vice president at Multima Financial Services. Then came all the media attention after her CBNN interview—before getting fired by Wilma Willingsworth. Right after that, Giancarlo Mareno himself summoned her to New York, and now this two-week trip to Panama and Costa Rica. It was all friggin' unbelievable!

Wilma Willingsworth had started the saga when she delivered that devastating news her first week on the job as division president. She walked over to Janet's small cubicle, just down the hall from James Fitzgerald's former suite and parked her fat ass in one of the two chairs for visitors.

Without any other conversation, Willingsworth told Janet they were going in a different direction. They had no need for Six Sigma, and there was no other role for Janet in the company. While she was talking, two security guards and someone from human resources hovered near her workspace. They formally escorted her out the building's front door immediately after Willingsworth delivered her message.

She didn't cry or anything like that, but she was scared. The Organization wouldn't be pleased, and Douglas Whitfield certainly wouldn't be happy either. But what could she do?

Janet drove to her apartment intending to think it all through and figure out what came next. Her mobile phone–the really private one that no one should know about—rang moments after she unlocked her apartment.

It shocked her to hear someone identify himself as Giancarlo Mareno. She almost pissed her pants. When he asked her if it was true she'd been fired from her job with Financial Services, she gasped. It had all taken place less than an hour earlier. The man's voice was just as intimidating as people claimed. But their conversation went quite well. He told her to pack up her things and gave her an address where she could ship them.

"I need your help for a while," he said. "Come see me in New York next Monday. Do you have a credit card or enough cash to manage for a few days?"

What that all-powerful leader of The Organization thought best was usually what happened. So, Janet assured him she had enough money and would meet him at the time and place instructed. Then he hung up. There was no goodbye, no looking forward to seeing her, nor any indication of what kind of help he needed. He just expected her to be there. Of course, because he was Giancarlo Mareno, she was there and waiting for him right on time.

"You're even more gorgeous than you look in your videos," he said with a leer that immediately made her uncomfortable. "I see what Douglas finds so appealing. But, don't worry, honey. You're not exactly my type if you know what I mean."

In full control of the conversation, the large, intimidating man complimented her for the work she did with the Six Sigma certification and the quality of the data she dug up for Douglas. Then he told her to prepare for a job interview the following week. CBA Investment Bank was looking for a junior financial analyst. Did she know anything about that kind of job? No, she knew nothing about financial analysis. She was a graduate in political science from Columbia.

"You've got a week to study up before the interview. I'll put you in touch with a guy who'll teach you the lingo and coach you. The job will be yours, but you'll to have to sound like you have some experience when you talk with three interviewers next week. We've got something coming up you can help us with. We need you there. Don't worry, the money and everything will still be paid, and we'll still top you up with the deposits offshore."

She went to the guy Mareno arranged for her to meet, a Business professor at Columbia it turned out. As promised, he gave her a crash course on the jargon she needed to know to sound competent.

She showed up for the interview dressed like an analyst and oozing all the charm she could muster. The interviews went well with two men and a woman, all separately. The last male insisted—if they could meet for a drink after work—he'd do everything necessary to have her hired. She had a couple drinks and then slept with him just to be sure.

Two weeks later, she expected to hear back from CBA Investment Bank, but Mareno called again. She'd start at the bank on the first of December. They'd let her know in a letter later that week. In the meantime, he wanted her to pack up a few things and join him for a trip to the tropics. Travel light. A bikini and a couple changes of underwear should be enough.

Janet met him at Teterboro Airport in New Jersey and followed him aboard a luxurious private jet. It was the most opulent she'd ever seen. Only after they were airborne did he tell her their purpose. They would meet up with Douglas Whitfield and her old liaison with The Organization, Howard Knight. With that casual comment, he went to work on his computer and didn't say anything else until they landed. She worried throughout the entire flight.

Through the grapevine, Janet heard about the huge reward for anyone who found Howard Knight and killed him or brought him to Mareno. Douglas had also revealed his relationship to Mareno. Might there be some dangerous fireworks on this trip? She was going into a situation that could be unpredictable. The Organization might do some nasty things, but she'd never planned to be anywhere near that kind of stuff.

While they waited for the helicopter after arrival in Panama City, Mareno told her about the yacht and gave her instructions.

"When we get to the boat, just act like you're wildly in love with me," he said with a menacing grin. "Then listen to everything. Remember, God gave you two ears and one mouth for a very good reason."

Surprisingly, she heard no words of greeting or harmless chit-chat when they first boarded the boat from the water. Janet dutifully played her loving and subservient role. They all shared a beer. Then Mareno abruptly sent her and Douglas below deck.

"You two can get reacquainted while Howard and I talk," he said dismissively.

So, they did. Douglas was tentative at first, confused by Janet's behavior toward Mareno.

"I've missed you," Janet said. She leaned forward, hoping a closer look down her skimpy, low-cut top might draw a reaction.

"Me too," Douglas purred after he reached inside her top to gently stroke her left nipple. "Do we have time?"

"I have no idea. It's your daddy's meeting isn't it?" Janet liked the massage on her nipple but pushed his hand away. She wouldn't make it that easy for him.

"Did he discuss what's going to happen next?" Douglas wondered. This time he reached behind her back and unhooked the top to free her breasts, then resumed stroking both nipples.

"Nothing. Just told me to bring a bikini and a change of underwear. Do you have any idea what's up?"

"Maybe. Get ready for a couple weeks of this," he said before kissing her with a deep probe of his tongue. He pulled her tightly against him and held her there. She felt his erection take form and longingly reached down to help him along.

"Douglas! Janet!" Mareno's deep voice bellowed from above. "Get your asses back up here."

She scurried to attach her top again until Mareno called out loudly. "Janet. Leave your top down there. I want to see those tits while we talk."

What a dominating asshole.

Was she embarrassed? Never. They were great breasts and no one—Giancarlo Mareno included—would ever make her feel uncomfortable about her body. Maybe that control crap was meant more as a show for Douglas.

"Howard has decided to cooperate with us," Mareno said quietly when they were all back on deck. "Douglas, you're in charge of planning as we discussed before. Howard will answer every question you have and make suggestions about things we need to consider to make it happen. He'll be like a consultant if you will.

"Janet, listen in on every conversation. Make notes if you need to. You've got two weeks to become an authority on Multima. I want you to be the broad everyone goes to for any information about any aspect of the company when you start work at CBA Investment Bank. Now get me ashore so I can get back to civilization," he muttered to end their discussion. With that charming farewell, he left.

For the first week, they discussed various Multima balance sheets while they traveled on the boat. Howard led them through all the reference notes included in the annual report until they understood every line entry. They'd motor for three or four hours, then discuss for another three or four—up to eight hours one unusually productive day.

After she learned all the assets and liabilities, Douglas used his laptop as a focal point while they dissected and analyzed the reams of data Janet had collected from her Six Sigma research. She listened intently as the men debated the relative importance of the numbers and how best to interpret them. Surprisingly, she was actually beginning to feel a bit like an analyst as they reached the harbor of Quepos, Costa Rica, midway through their second week.

When they docked in the harbor, Howard Knight, with a mischievous grin and wink, said it would probably be better if she put on a bikini top before leaving the boat. She needed to search below deck for a while after not using it for more than a week.

When they arrived at the condo Douglas had rented, they moved into a different phase and spent hours each day plotting spreadsheets to evaluate ratios and identify financial strengths and weaknesses. They structured hypothetical loans and variable interest rates to find a formula that might entice Suzanne Simpson to take their bait and make a deal for Jeffersons Stores. Both men agreed a loan was the pivotal factor to focus on.

By day they worked hard. By night she and Douglas played. There were only two bedrooms in the condo, so it all worked out conveniently for her and Douglas to share a room. The first few nights they put the room air conditioner on—with the fan speed as high as possible—to deaden the sounds of their passion. By the fourth night, they abandoned all pretense of caution and made love without restraint long into the night.

Howard never complained.

"The thump, thump, thump I hear every night is hypnotic. It helps me sleep," he joked one morning. "I've convinced myself sexual abstinence stimulates the creative side of my brain," he teased another morning after Douglas and Janet enjoyed one unusually long session. Another day, Douglas promised Howard he'd bring in a couple hookers one night after Janet left, and didn't seem to notice at all the sting of her disappointment.

How can he say such a thing when I'm standing right here?

This morning, they said their goodbyes while they waited together out by the gate. Leaving was the last thing she wanted to do, but there was no alternative. After a small red taxi stopped outside the tall iron fence that kept the undesirables out of their compound, Douglas gave her one deep passionate kiss before he wished her good luck back in New York. They'd talk a lot, he promised.

The taxi whisked her up the narrow, winding road that started in the center of Quepos and ran toward the regional hospital on the highway, a five-minute drive. At the end of the paved section, the driver turned in the direction of Dominical beach, the one with great surfing. Douglas had talked about it, but like all the other great Costa Rican tourist sights, she hadn't seen it during her two weeks in paradise.

Another five minutes after making the turn, the driver pulled off the highway into a rutted gravel driveway and cautiously advanced a few yards to a locked gate. Janet got out of the vehicle and found her way to a metal structure. It wasn't even a building, really. It had three sides and a roof, but the interior was hollow. Her eye caught a small check-in podium. Behind it stood a cute guy wearing a cap with Sansa written above its peak. He waved to her.

"Ms. Weissel?" he asked with a smile as she entered the hut. On confirmation, the young fellow motioned to a golf cart and said, "Let me give you a ride to your jet. It's ready."

It was the same crew that brought her and Mareno to Panama a few days earlier, and they respectfully welcomed her back. Less than five minutes after she was seated, the engine wound up for take-off, and the plane hurtled along the bare-ground runway with her body jolting and bouncing against the seatbelt for about a minute until they were airborne.

The view captivated her instantly. Out the left window, she watched the Pacific Ocean waves crash against the beaches on either side of the town. To her right, she looked out at green, majestic mountains. Below, miles of palm trees for as far as she could see entranced her. It was just like Douglas described, and she felt pangs of regret.

But her romantic notions didn't last long. Within minutes of departure, the angst Janet had felt since Giancarlo first described their mission returned. So much was riding on her ability to pull off this analyst job and somehow convince Suzanne Simpson to make the most critical decision of the woman's business life.

Janet's work would be entirely through intermediaries at the bank. Who knew how competent they were? She shuddered. At least two lives depended on her work and its outcome.

TWENTY-EIGHT

John George Mortimer's home, Fort Myers, FL
Friday December 21, 2018

"It's too late, Doctor Singh. I don't want to prolong the inevitable simply to gain a few days," John George first told his oncologist, although the much younger woman had long before suggested he drop the honorific 'doctor' in deference to his age and stature in the business world.

"Call me Sanjana," she reminded him. "Your comment is completely understandable. I can't offer you any guarantees, and you may be proven right. I might very well be recommending a treatment that buys only a few days in return for further painful side-effects. But are you willing to hear me out?" the petite and pleasant woman asked, instantly switching from her role as an empathetic listener to flash her usual disarming smile.

"Even at this stage you know which buttons to push," he offered, managing the barest outline of a smile. "I doubt you'll change my mind, but I'll listen."

"I won't bore you with all the details, but I've discovered a researcher in Geneva who announced incredible success with a very different approach to immunology. He just published his latest results in medical journals. During the past six months, ten patients from his control group of one hundred showed dramatic improvements. None of those patients were as far advanced as you, but the results they experienced are truly impressive. He saw weight gain, skin color improvement, pain reduction, and greater energy in all ten of these patients," she explained while apparently trying to assess his reaction.

"And the other ninety in the test group?" John George asked, allowing just a tinge of skepticism in his tone.

"The great majority of test patients showed no improvement. Tests neither accelerated nor slowed tumor growth. But there were some interesting similarities in the genealogy of the ten who showed improvement with yours. We found matches on thirty-five different gene characteristics compared to yours. I spoke with the researcher at length yesterday, and he's excited about the potential benefits his formulation might bring you. He's prepared to provide the medication at no cost and even volunteered to come to Fort Myers to oversee the initial treatments if you agree," Sanjana explained.

"I guess it would be cynical of me to suggest the great autumn weather in Fort Myers compared to those nasty storms they're having right now in Europe might also motivate him to visit us here," he replied with a benign smile.

Doctor Singh laughed cheerfully in response. "You might be right about that," she allowed, "but I think he can probably find more economical travel destinations if that's his motivation. Each of the treatments will cost his program about ten thousand dollars, and you'll need a minimum of eight over a two-month period."

"You're right. I shouldn't let myself be so cynical, but you know how disappointing it's been to watch the other promising treatments fail," John George replied in a more somber tone.

"Yes. I've shared your frustration. Every treatment showed some promise for a few days, then succumbed to cancer's attack just as quickly. I realize it's been painful for you and emotionally far worse than a roller-coaster. It's been depressing," Doctor Singh said. "Here's the thing. The treatment may be like all the others and fail, but there's a small chance it might work. If the treatment takes hold and the tumors stop growing, you might enjoy a reasonable quality of life for some time. There are almost no side-effects among test patients with gene pools similar to yours. And the results are spectacular. Patients' appearance, mood, and health are all significantly better than before they started treatments. Can we give it one more try?"

"You know I'll agree, Sanjana. I long ago decided that I'll do anything you ask. I feel a sense of purpose. I know you won't recommend it unless you think there's a chance. Even if it fails, you or your new friend in Switzerland might learn enough from my experience to advance one more step to help the next patient. When will this researcher from Geneva start poking his needles into my veins?" John George asked with his best effort to smile.

Almost unbelievably, the treatments started less than twenty-four hours later. Apparently, Doctor Singh had mentioned their conversation to Suzanne in a hurried call after he left her office. Together, they conspired to dispatch the Multima Corporation Global 5000 long-range jet to fetch the researcher in Switzerland. He arrived the following morning, met John George, and started the treatments.

Doctor Singh observed every session and used her free time during the researcher's week in Fort Myers to understand how he'd discovered the concoction his computer program predicted most promising for his new patient's specific genetic makeup. Then they waited.

John George glanced in the mirror, and a smile broadened across his face. Three weeks after the treatment started, he wasn't all the way back to his former self, but his face looked much better. The ten pounds his body had gained showed clearly in his face. He wasn't tanned because the oncologist strongly recommended avoiding direct sunlight, but his pallor was now a more ordinary shade of white.

His eyes looked more naturally blue, and they sparkled the way folks used to remark on and remember about him. His cheeks appeared much less hollow. Dimples hadn't yet returned when he smiled, but he thought his face looked fuller and more robust.

He tested how the rest of his body responded. Raising his arms slowly above his head, he stretched toward the ceiling until the tightness in his lower back reduced, and he felt confident enough to swivel his hips back and forth. Keeping his arms extended, he bent over fully until he could touch his toes. Walking outdoors the past few days had helped his body become more fluid, and the ever-present aches and pains were all manageable. Those new treatments were undoubtedly helping.

"Lana," he called out when he reached the bottom of the stairs. "Pack your bags. We're going to El Salvador."

TWENTY-NINE

A large executive home, Hoffman Estates, IL
Tuesday January 1, 2019

Just as he had for at least the past forty years, James Fitzgerald sat down at the expansive, virtually bare desk in his well-appointed home office to prepare his most important goals and objectives for the coming year. As usual, a single piece of paper sat in front of him because he always maintained he could only concentrate fully on one thing at a time. He also held a pen in his hand.

After ten minutes of staring at the blank sheet of paper and pushing his brain to function, he hadn't listed a single item. For the first year in his memory, not one compelling objective came to mind. Of course, for most of those previous years, he had specific corporate goals. Before that, he had scholastic or athletic goals. Over the years he'd achieved weight-reduction goals, exercise targets, or reading ambitions. Right now, he couldn't see himself committing to any of those quality-of-life changes.

As he stared blankly into space, Dianne walked in already fully dressed and made-up. Over one arm she carried her winter coat and looked at him unsmiling, though calm. She set an overnight bag on the floor beside the only other chair in the room, comfortably seated herself in the chair, and crossed her legs.

"There's never a good time to have this kind of conversation, and I'm a little sorry it needs to be the first day of a new year," his wife began. "But I'm going to start a new life. I'm leaving you. I'm not angry and I still have great respect for you. But our relationship is no longer working."

Dianne had finally lost her patience with his neglect. He saw the determined pursing of her lips despite her otherwise cool demeanor. He didn't know what to say, but blurted out, "You're leaving today?"

"Yes. I'm on the way to O'Hare to meet up with my friend Samantha. You don't know her, but we've become very close over the past few months. We're traveling to Martinique for a few days. When we get back next week, I'll come for my things and move them to Samantha's place downtown."

"You're moving in with this friend?" James managed to ask. She was leaving him for a woman?

"Yes. We're in love and we plan to live together, maybe even get married after our divorce is finalized." Dianne paused to let him process the shocking news, but her gaze didn't waver until he spoke again.

"Are you sure about this?" James asked. "Might it be better to just try out your new relationship for a while before making such a major decision? I know I've been less than an ideal husband lately. I'd be ready to have a trial separation or something so you can be certain this is what you want to do."

"We're sure. We're deeply in love and I've given it a lot of thought. I've already discussed it with a lawyer and we'll file all the necessary papers when we get back from Martinique."

"I accept all the blame for whatever has gone wrong with our relationship. Can we talk about it more?" He knew it was lame the moment the words left his mouth, but he couldn't stop. "Now that I'm no longer consumed with my responsibilities at Multima, maybe I can make changes to better satisfy you."

"This isn't about blame. It's about love. There is nothing more to discuss. You can stay here in the house for now, but I want you to list it for sale as soon as possible. My lawyer suggests we divide the proceeds equally. I know how much you love the cottage on Silver Lake. I'm happy for you to buy my share. Just have the property appraised by three real estate agents. We can settle the details after I file the divorce papers."

With that businesslike tone, she stood up, put on her coat, grabbed her bag, and gave him a peck on the cheek as she said goodbye. It was over.

That Dianne had left him for a woman was shocking at first. His male ego took a severe hit when she first divulged that aspect of the bad news. But it made sense. The signals had been there for several years. All those evenings out socializing with her friends. The increasing number of out-of-town girls' trips for weekends. Her apparent lack of interest or concern when they stopped making love. There was also her lack of curiosity about his nights out with Janet Weissel. Looking back, that absence of interest should have set off alarm bells.

That whole affair with Janet remained a mystery to him. He still couldn't grasp whatever had possessed him to do something so patently stupid. With all his years of experience, all the years honing his judgment, and his first-hand witnessing of the inherent dangers, he had still willingly waded into an inappropriate relationship with her. And it cost him his career. More accurately, it brought his stellar career to an early and inauspicious end.

Suzanne had handled his ousting impeccably. He truly appreciated the way she let him preserve his dignity and maintain a good reputation in the business community. But she acted decisively as well as sensitively.

From the look in her eyes when they had their little talk in that Fort Myers restaurant, he'd realized instantly there was no option but to resign.

He missed Multima Financial Services. He had never quite realized how much a part of his life that enormously successful business had become. When he woke up these days, he had no idea what he would do in the coming hours. Counterintuitively, he looked forward to winter storms so he could shovel snow or something. And he genuinely missed the daily camaraderie of those with whom he used to work and play.

The one he missed the most was John George Mortimer. The man was much more than a CEO to James. The guy hired him right out of college completely untested and without experience. Then, he helped him climb the corporate ladder one rung at a time with increasing responsibilities and influence. He remembered how John George asked his opinion on a minor financial matter the very first day he reported for work. He listened to James, really listened. And the exceptional leader usually acted on his suggestions throughout the decades James reported to him.

The last year had been tough for their relationship. Until his forced retirement, his regular management conversations were with Suzanne. His infrequent calls to John George were only brief updates on his declining health and James's best efforts to keep up the spirits of his former boss. His friend knew he was dying. But John George was willing to undergo whatever treatments the doctors recommended even if the side-effects were horrendous. He thought the knowledge the specialists were gaining from his sacrifice might make it a little easier for those with cancer who followed.

James found Wilma's invitation to join her on the Financial Services corporate jet, so he could visit with John George for a few days in October, genuinely touching. At that time, they all expected the resilient Chair to be dead by year's end. The guy had looked only days from the grave despite his best efforts to muster both strength and good humor.

The meeting itself was a little morbid. The men laughed together a few times as they shared a couple memories and reminisced about the good old days. But their time together was mainly characterized by long silences as John George preserved his energy and James tried to focus on things he thought were positive.

John George told him the oncologist would try one last Hail Mary immunotherapy treatment with a new researcher from Geneva. But his skepticism was evident. They spent most of the afternoon together before Lana tactfully reminded James her boss probably needed some rest. Their farewell was somber. Both probably assumed this to be the last personal conversation they'd ever have.

"I want to thank you, James, for everything you've done for me over our years together," John George said with a smile as he clutched James's hand and squeezed it tightly. "I could have never done it without you."

James wiped a tear from his eye at the time and found it necessary to do it again as he remembered that final admonition. "Help her James. She needs you as much as I did."

Suzanne wasn't in the room at the time, so James assumed that request was just a kind gesture from a great man saying his farewell and making it all as positive as possible. It was good to know John George appreciated his efforts. He certainly left an impression James would treasure forever. But he took it as a simple platitude.

He was surprised when Suzanne Simpson called the last working day before Christmas. In fact, her call had prompted this little exercise with the list of goals for the year. He desperately wanted to have something positive to share with her when they met because the purpose of her call was to arrange a meeting while she was in Chicago later in the month.

"I'd like your help with something if you have the time available," she said ambiguously. "But we'll need to discuss it in person."

Thirty

Multima Corporation Headquarters, Fort Myers, FL
Friday January 4, 2019

Back in her office for the first time in the new year, Suzanne drew an ominous pile of files to the edge of her desk. Determined to wade through them all before her staff arrived, she knew she should just dive in, but found shaking the leisurely pace of Latin America a challenge.

Her father's health had improved so dramatically they'd made a short trip to Central America. John George always enjoyed visiting his housekeeper's family in El Salvador, and it delighted Suzanne to hear him say, "Let's visit Lana's family again this year while we have the chance."

His tone seemed far more positive and his outlook brighter than only a couple months earlier when it appeared he had just weeks to live. His remarkable progress since the Swiss researcher started a modified immunotherapy program shocked everyone. The oncologist and researcher alike spoke in terms of improvement far more significant than initially anticipated. And John George's thinking gradually evolved to picturing his future in months, possibly even a year.

They all thoroughly enjoyed themselves with Lana's family at their humble home near San Salvador although it became necessary for them to split up for sleeping arrangements. Doctor Sanjana Singh had joined them.

"I'll only agree to his travel if I can be there to keep an eye on him," the oncologist said with a laugh when Suzanne called to check the feasibility of a trip.

Suzanne thought the oncologist joining them was a terrific idea and insisted Sanjana accompany them on the corporate jet. Lana enthusiastically scrambled to arrange enough beds with nearby family, and the situation worked out perfectly. John George practiced his Spanish for a few days while Suzanne soaked in the genial atmosphere of Christmas celebration and the joy Lana's family projected despite their modest surroundings.

Doctor Singh was also enthralled with the warm welcome she received and attended to John George like a mother hen, monitoring and recording seemingly endless data points on her laptop computer. Just before dinner each day, she'd walk a few blocks to the village Claro communication outlet where they had Wi-Fi. There, she'd transmit a digital file to the researcher in Geneva.

They had returned to Florida only the evening before, and Suzanne got an early start at her office to catch up on a week's worth of work. Despite the holidays, her assistant had organized several neatly stacked piles of documents to be reviewed and signed. On her laptop, she saw more than two hundred emails had accumulated while her technology was shut off for five days. While she waded through the tasks at hand, she was surprised to hear her phone ring and see the name Hiromi Tenaka displayed on its screen. *Japan's deputy minister of agriculture.* She picked up the call.

"I'm so glad I was able to reach you, Suzanne," he said. "I tried to call you before I left Japan, but your assistant told me you were traveling. Then I received a 'no signal available' message from your mobile number."

"Yes, Hiromi, I was away for a few days and just returned. Are you in the USA?"

"Yes, I'm in Washington. We just finished meeting with your government officials," Tenaka replied. With a nervous laugh he added, "With your current president, our prime minister wanted to be the first to meet with him this year. We never know exactly what we should expect next!"

"I understand your dilemma," Suzanne responded, her tone neutral. "Did you achieve your goals?"

"Only partially. He's a very unconventional negotiator, your president. But we've accomplished all we can at this stage. Our delegation will leave tonight for Tokyo. The reason I tried to reach you last week was to see if there might be any chance we could meet up for lunch or dinner while I'm here. I'd still like to do that if possible, but at this late date I'll understand completely if you can't." He paused, waiting for her answer.

Suzanne processed the situation, feeling no compulsion to respond immediately. When she'd first met Hiromi Tenaka almost two years ago, their meetings were completely professional, but she sensed a mutual attraction. It was somewhat disappointing never to receive another call—save that brief conversation to let him know Multima wouldn't be moving forward with his business proposal. Hiromi had accepted her decision positively, and she'd sensed he might try to communicate again after a decent lapse in time.

Admittedly, she didn't even know his marital status. So, such an expectation might have been optimistic, but why would he call out of the blue now?

"I know it's been a long time. To be candid, the past few months have been challenging for me," he said with a less-than-carefree tone. "Early last year, doctors diagnosed my wife with very severe heart problems. She had two surgeries, but they couldn't correct the problem. She died last summer. I've often thought of calling you these past few months but could never comfortably find a way to do it. When our prime minister asked me to join the delegation this time, I was determined to reach out and see what happens."

"I'm so sorry to learn of your loss, Hiromi. It must have been tough for you. How is your family coping?" Suzanne probed.

"You probably aren't aware we have no children. My wife was a career woman like you—still rather rare in Japan—so her loss really only affected her parents and me. We're all adjusting."

Suzanne wasn't sure about the situation. Sure, she'd felt some chemistry when they'd met in Japan, and she was tempted to explore the relationship more. If their initial meeting hadn't been directly related to Multima, she might well have ended up in bed with him after their private dinner. He was that charming, handsome, intelligent, and sexy! She could feel something stirring even as they spoke now.

"I appreciate you calling, Hiromi." Suzanne projected what she hoped was an appropriate amount of warmth. "As I said, this is my first day back from Central America, so the next couple days really aren't good for me. Is there any chance you could come to Fort Myers on Sunday?"

There was a pause. She knew he was probably calculating how he could juggle the logistics.

"I can get to Fort Myers okay on Saturday night or Sunday morning. My challenge is getting a flight to Tokyo to arrive no later than Tuesday morning for a scheduled meeting with my prime minister. That means we can meet for breakfast on Sunday if I leave Fort Myers about eleven."

Suzanne weighed her options. "Let's meet halfway. I'm currently planning to visit stores in the Atlanta area Monday. I could go up there late in the day Sunday and meet you for dinner. Would you be able to meet there, have dinner, then travel overnight from Atlanta to Tokyo to arrive in time for your Tuesday meeting?"

She heard clicking in the background and assumed he was checking flights. After a few more seconds, he replied that would work. They arranged the time and place they would meet in Atlanta and exchanged mutual expressions of looking forward to meeting up again.

Before returning to her stack of files, Suzanne lingered on Hiromi's call one more time. It all seemed a little curious. There had been no mention of a wife when they met in Tokyo. In fact, during that visit, he was clearly sending signals that he was interested in something more than a business relationship.

But he hadn't communicated with her for almost two years. Now, he invited her to meet up with him even though that required Hiromi to travel separately from the prime minister's delegation—presumably at some personal expense—with the added inconvenience of arriving in Japan only hours before an important meeting with his country's leader. And, all that after traveling for at least ten hours overnight.

He sure appeared interested in renewing their acquaintance.

THIRTY-ONE

A condo in Quepos, Costa Rica
Saturday January 5, 2019

It was Saturday, but Howard Knight had to check the day on his phone that morning to find out. Saturday or Monday, it really made no difference. For several weeks now, there had been nothing for him to do with his involuntary companion, Whitfield.

"Just stay quiet and out of sight," Giancarlo Mareno reportedly told Whitfield when pressed for an update on CBA Investment Bank's progress with their scheme to seize control of Multima Corporation. Howard only knew that meager morsel of information because Whitfield chose to share it. All other communication between the head of The Organization and Whitfield was kept secret. That led Howard to wonder if the whole thing was off the rails. And that was a major concern.

Truthfully, Howard had little appetite or enthusiasm for their scheme. He liked Suzanne Simpson. He always found her to be a remarkable woman. He no longer felt part of The Organization either. Although his carefully rehearsed story about Guantanamo seemed to satisfy Mareno when they met near Panama, the most favorable outcome of their meeting was an extremely long shot.

"I believe you," Mareno said that day off Panama after Howard's tearful story of his determination not to divulge any information about The Organization to his FBI interrogators. "Your fuck-up on the Multima file means you can't come back to us. But I'll let you live. I'll rescind the kill and reward offer if you properly help us with this Multima mess."

That concession alone would have guaranteed Howard's cooperation, but Mareno added a potent sweetener.

"We found Fidelia. She's living a simple life in Eastern Europe. I put the kill order for her on hold. If you help us—and we successfully get control of Multima—I'll tell you how to find her and let her live too."

The slim hope he might one day reunite with Fidelia was the only thread of motivation he had to remain patient. But even that possibility faded with more wary scrutiny. Fidelia was the most brilliant person he knew. If she'd escaped the Argentinians and was now in Europe, Mareno probably hadn't found her. The opposite was far more likely. If she sought out Mareno from her place of hiding, it didn't bode well.

Unrelenting Peril

Things went silent with Mareno almost from the time that Weissel woman started her new job at CBA Investment Bank. She was there to ferret out information related to the Multima takeover. But there was no information coming his way.

Whitfield and Mareno had even given their covert project a code name—just like the big guys. Project VEX, they named it. VEX as in to displease or aggravate. That would be an appropriate code word for the anger and annoyance both men harbored against Suzanne for the slick moves the businesswoman made to extract a billion dollars from them before destroying the very software they intended to exploit for untold wealth.

Whitfield and Knight had developed the strategy. Mareno had bought in. The woman understood her role. So why wasn't anything happening? And why the wall of silence?

"Let's just use the time to enjoy the surroundings," Whitfield said the first week in December. They booked an ATV tour for one day, then a walking tour of *Parque Nacional Manuel Antonio*. A few days later they traveled to *Playa Dominical* where they took surfing lessons. Three or four other scattered days they explored secluded beaches on either side of Quepos, but it wasn't long before they grew bored.

Whitfield suggested they try deep sea fishing the second week. He booked their tour, and early one morning an SUV picked them up and delivered them to the charming harbor downtown where Howard's boat was moored. Newly constructed, the sizable port featured modern American-style buildings with several restaurants, shops, and services. The harbor was packed with fishing boats, and the vessel their guide stopped beside was one of the largest in the fleet. Howard expected their ride would be fine.

Of course, he would have preferred they use his Carver yacht parked almost next door, but they couldn't because that Weissel woman had stolen his keys before she left. He didn't realize it until she sent a text saying she was just following orders and Giancarlo Mareno would return them as soon as their job was successfully completed.

Howard was well accustomed to the roll of the Pacific. But Douglas Whitfield did not fare as well offshore. He first complained of wooziness a few minutes after they left the inner harbor and encountered moderate chop from the incoming waves.

Although Howard found the ocean only a little bumpy, Whitfield became distressed. He refused to lie down below deck as the boat captain recommended. He wouldn't drink water as Howard suggested. So, it came as no surprise that minutes later he was heaving violently over the side of the boat as he voided his stomach.

Not once, but three times he retched and vomited until the captain inquired if he wanted to return to shore. Whitfield vigorously nodded in assent, then spent the remaining minutes of their return hanging over the side of the boat.

As a result, their touristy explorations this past month were limited to dry land despite their proximity to the beautiful ocean and some of the best fishing anywhere on earth. They started walking for exercise. Then, each afternoon they'd nap under the shade of some trees by the pool for a few hours. By no later than six o'clock, they ate dinner.

For a while, Whitfield ordered pizza every day. He demonstrated how easy it was to order from a number displayed on his telephone and have the order delivered in less than an hour, just like at home. But there was one big difference in the service. Howard was astonished when the delivery-woman came into their condo, set the pizza on a counter, then started to remove her clothes.

Whitfield was not at all surprised. He gleefully told Howard this was the same young woman who provided such excellent service to him for several months before he headed south to capture Howard in Uruguay. With a leering grin, he asked her in Spanish to hurry up and get completely undressed. It took only a few seconds because she wore nothing under the top and shorts.

As soon as she dropped her last piece of clothing and posed seductively, Douglas grabbed her hand and playfully dragged her toward the stairs and up to his room. They stayed in his room for about an hour with lots of activity and a surprising amount of squealing and laughter.

Whitfield was tightening the belt of his khaki shorts as he swaggered back down the stairs to casually proclaim, "She's all yours now."

Howard was reticent. He was no prude, but he still had fresh memories of the disaster that had followed his last imprudent escapade with a hooker: the mumps. With that painful reminder, Howard declined. Whitfield more energetically tried to encourage him to have a turn. When Howard continued to resist, Whitfield turned, climbed the stairs, and stayed with the woman for another two hours. Howard ate half the pizza while it was hot and dutifully left half for Whitfield to eat cold.

To Howard's chagrin, Whitfield ordered pizza every evening for the following three weeks, right up until Christmas when apparently even the pizza shop closed for a few days. To Howard, the entire exercise was callous and unfeeling. Whitfield apparently thought of the woman as a human sex toy. Not at all the way Howard was taught to treat women.

So, he started walking to town each afternoon just before dinner to order food from a different restaurant every day. While he sat on his yacht for two or three hours, Howard thought about his situation and occasionally chatted with other boaters. One of the boat owners nearby eventually wondered why Howard never used his boat.

"I lost the keys," Howard replied casually.

"Why don't you just order a new set?" the fellow asked in Spanish. Howard pleaded ignorance. A complete novice with boating, he had no idea how to do that. He barely knew how to drive and park the craft when he did use it. As expected, the curious boat owner offered to help.

"Just invite me aboard. I'll get your serial numbers," the fellow suggested.

Within a few minutes, the visitor had deciphered all the information necessary to order a new key and offered to see his repairman the following day to order one.

That was a week ago. Now, as Howard watched the magnificent sunset on the horizon, he realized a replacement key would arrive within the next day or two. He'd resolve it one way or another. Once he had the key, he'd make a decision.

THIRTY-TWO

New York, NY
Sunday January 6, 2019

Janet slept with the jerk once before the hiring decision just to be sure she got the job. So, she wasn't entirely surprised when the guy asked her out on another date. His name was Antoine something-or-other, and he suggested they get together for drinks the first Friday evening after she started at CBA Investment Bank. "Let's meet at my apartment for a couple, then we can slip downstairs and choose from a dozen great restaurants within a block or two," he said with a moderately charming smile.

She hesitated, assessing the situation. Into the gap of silence, he quickly added, "I'd like to celebrate our good luck that you've joined our team."

Although she suspected the reference to her business role was intended as much to remind her of his importance in the decision to hire her as any attempt at team-building, she acquiesced one more time. She didn't want any negatives impacting her ability to execute the responsibilities Mareno had assigned to her with Project VEX, their scheme to gain control of Multima.

When her taxi stopped at the address he'd given her, she took in the well-kept, attractive building in a good neighborhood. The doorman carefully assessed her as she climbed out from the back seat. His eyes locked on her legs as her short skirt revealed more of her right thigh than intended before she expertly swept her dress into position and stood straight.

He was expecting her and checked her name off a list before he showed her to the elevator and pressed the button for the eighteenth floor, the penthouse.

When Antoine answered the door, Janet immediately felt uneasy. The jerk was already high on something. She didn't smell booze or pot, but his face was slightly pink, and his eyes bulged from their sockets. When she looked closely, she could see the pupils of his eyes were more than dilated, they were huge. Tiny beads of sweat dotted his nose and forehead.

She hesitated before stepping through the open door but ultimately felt she could manage him even if he was a little high. After all, it wouldn't be the first time she needed to contend with a druggie.

He offered Janet some wine, poured a glass for himself, and turned on his considerable charm. For the next hour or so they chatted about her new job, the company, and things they enjoyed in common. The mood was pleasant, and he spoke articulately and with enthusiasm.

The only oddities in his behavior were when Antoine excused himself to "visit the little boys' room," followed by stops in the kitchen. Each time, he returned with a new glass filled almost to the brim with an amber liquid. He downed his drinks with long gulps whenever she was speaking.

When she glanced at her watch, she realized she had already been in the apartment for almost two hours. She also noticed the asshole's mood had changed. She asked if they shouldn't go to dinner before the restaurants closed. In reply, he asked her if she wouldn't prefer a line instead.

"A line?" She arched her brows slightly.

"Yeah, I've got some premium stuff, and I like to share. It'll make the rest of the night even better for both of us," he replied as his smile deteriorated into a leer.

"No, you're welcome to use whatever you want, but a little booze is all I need," Janet told him with a cheerful tone.

That seemed to satisfy him. He left the room, apparently visited "the little boys' room" again and returned with another glass of amber liquid. That made four full glasses plus whatever else he was ingesting in the bathroom. She began considering ways to escape the situation and get away from the jerk's place.

At that point, things took a turn for the worse. Instead of sitting in the comfortable chair next to the sofa where Janet was perched, the bastard planted himself right next to her and clumsily swung his arm around her neck. His arm dangled almost touching her left breast. With his drink in the other hand, he lurched sideways, tried to plant a kiss on her mouth, and missed. He also spilled about half his drink on her dress, the sofa, and the floor.

Janet jumped up, trying to shake off the foul-smelling liquid. Just as she started toward the bathroom to clean up the stain, he surprised her by tightly grabbing her wrist and violently drawing her down on the sofa with her left arm painfully pinned behind her back. With his other hand, he reached behind her head and roughly shoved her face into his crotch. She grew more alarmed when she realized he had an erection.

"That'll be your dinner, bitch," he growled as he forced her head more roughly against his jeans. At the same time, he pulled her arm upward so violently she feared he might break it. "Get your hands busy unzipping. I want your mouth around my cock pronto, or I'll yank that arm right out of its socket," he hissed. He tightened his grip and pulled her left arm even further upwards.

With her right hand, she slowly reached for his pants and unzipped them. He was wearing nothing underneath, and his now erect penis sprung from the opening. She'd experienced some violent behavior in sexual encounters before, but nothing like rape. Why was this bastard treating her so abusively?

She acceded to his demands to buy time while her mind raced with thoughts of escape.

As she stroked and tentatively kissed his foul-smelling cock, she tried to avoid retching, terrified of his reaction should she vomit. He tasted horrible, and she willed herself to think of pleasant experiences to cope with the humiliation, degradation, and pain.

He maintained his lock on her left arm as she tried to satisfy him with her right hand and mouth. Janet dared not glance up. Annoyed, he clutched her long hair roughly, forcing her head backward, forcing her to look directly into his menacing eyes. He smiled with sadistic satisfaction.

Suddenly, Janet felt another pair of strong hands grab both of her arms from behind her, locking them tightly against her lower back. She squirmed and tried to twist to look. Antoine roughly forced her mouth back onto his penis.

"Open your fucking mouth and do your work, bitch. You're going to be busy for a while."

While Janet succumbed to his command, the other pair of hands—much larger and stronger than those of Antoine—shifted his iron-like hold, wrapping one massive hand around both her wrists. He squeezed them tightly together. With his other hand, he clutched the top of her dress. One violent yank and he sheared her dress from top to bottom.

"Just like you thought, Antoine," the voice bellowed contemptuously. "Not wearing a thing under the dress. A real slut. Let me shove my cock into her ass to motivate her to blow you better," he bellowed into her ear. The smell of alcohol from his breath was overpowering.

She couldn't guess how long they continued. The pain was excruciating. Whenever she cried out, the vile sadists either penetrated even more forcefully or roughly slapped her face or breasts. After the bastards came, they held her tightly while they switched positions and pinched and prodded, demanding satisfaction anew. Semen dripped from their cocks while they repositioned, and Janet gagged as the stronger one jammed his into her mouth. He slapped her face hard and forced his slimy cock deeper down her throat.

When she was spent and no longer able to resist, they took turns using her body. For what seemed like hours, one of her captors would snort a line of cocaine or imbibe alcohol and watch while the other had his way with her. Then they switched roles, laughing and taunting her as they demanded she satisfy them in increasingly more disgusting ways. At some point, Janet lost consciousness.

When she revived, Janet found her captors hadn't been satisfied with rape. She noticed blood on her hand, then realized it was her own. Blood dripped from her face. Pain drew her gaze to streaks of blood trickling from each breast.

Looking around the room, she saw her captors had both passed out—one on the sofa snoring loudly, the other face down on the floor. In a panic, she furtively looked around for her things. Her bag sat in a corner on the other side of the spacious living area. Her dress lay in a heap between the two. Carefully, she crawled toward the torn garment, then realized it had not simply been shorn from her body. At some juncture, the deviant bastards had torn it into shreds. She had to escape and worry about her nudity later.

Janet crawled on hands and knees, making as little noise and motion as possible until she reached her purse. Scooping it up, she stood and tiptoed across the room, released the inside lock and gently opened the door.

She backed out of the apartment, watching her attackers for any sign of consciousness. Satisfied she might have a few minutes to escape, she delicately closed the door, then turned and ran toward the stairwell to her right. She couldn't take an elevator. Either another tenant or the doorman would see her. She couldn't call the police because Antoine was her co-worker and she couldn't put Giancarlo Mareno's project in jeopardy by divulging what happened.

She had no choice. Her phone showed almost one o'clock in the morning, but she called Mareno. He answered on the second ring, and Janet quickly blurted out what happened as he listened without interruption. When she finished explaining her dilemma, he asked only where she was. He would be there in twenty minutes. She should go down the stairs to the ground floor and wait in the stairwell.

Fifteen minutes later, Giancarlo Mareno opened the door to the stairwell where she huddled in the darkest corner squeezing her arms tightly around her still-bleeding naked body. Two of the largest men she had ever seen flanked him.

"Wrap yourself in this." He handed her a blanket. "What apartment are they in?"

"1802," she replied. "There are two of them—that asshole Antoine I interviewed with at CBA and another bastard. I don't know him."

With a curt nod in the direction of the elevators, Mareno dispatched his companions.

"I'll take you to my place," he said.

Giancarlo promised to make it right. First, he called a doctor as they drove toward his home that awful night. A trauma practitioner met them when they arrived and she treated Janet to stop the bleeding.

The next day, a cosmetic surgeon flew in from Naples and examined her. He outlined the treatments needed to return her appearance to its former beauty. Two separate procedures followed, all performed at his hospital where he had the technology and equipment necessary to undertake the delicate operations. There was recovery time between each procedure.

Today's flight was one more step in the long, painful process. Janet thought he probably didn't own the jet himself, but it seemed immediately available to him whenever Giancarlo Mareno asked for it. When a car and driver picked her up at her midtown Manhattan apartment at four o'clock this morning, she knew it would be impossible to change her mind from that point though she dreaded what was to come later that day.

One look in her brightly lit mirror reminded her why it was essential to follow through with the mission regardless of the pain she would surely suffer. Despite the two previous surgeries in December, her face still bore the scars of the violent attack that first week she'd started her new job. The cosmetic surgeon in Naples—considered one of the best in the nation—had corrected most of the damage. But ugly traces of the deep cuts from her attackers were still visible along with the tiny incisions her doctors made to repair the damage.

Sitting on the aircraft as the sole passenger, she instinctively patted her damaged skin to detect whether previous treatments were indeed helping her skin return to its previous flawlessly smooth appearance. With the first touch, she thought she detected a minuscule improvement. When she ran her finger back across her skin in the other direction, she ruefully had to admit not much had changed.

Her pretty face that had been such a valuable asset throughout her life seemed permanently impaired no matter how skillfully the surgeon worked. Today's treatment should finally remove the physical marks of the awful experience.

She felt flush with embarrassment as she reached for the makeup and compact mirror in her bag. It helped to apply a little more makeup, but even the expensive stuff couldn't cover the ugly lines. Janet found herself stewing about her condition often. And every time she thought about her scars, it reopened the pain her attackers inflicted on her that night and every day since. It was becoming almost an obsession. She constantly kept second-guessing her judgment and how she could have handled the circumstance differently.

As the aircraft engines slowed and the aircraft started its descent into Naples private jet airport, Janet tried to not be apprehensive. But it was hard. Her physical scar might eventually fade but other scars ran deeper and just as painfully. She was not confident those would ever fade completely. Surely, they'd never disappear while she was trapped within The Organization.

Yes, she'd return to CBA Investment Bank and do Mareno's bidding for Project VEX. But the outline of a plan to escape his control was already forming.

THIRTY-THREE

On Delta flight 7885 from Incheon, Korea toward Narita, Japan
Monday January 7, 2019

After twelve hours of travel, Hiromi Tenaka was growing tired and increasingly miserable about his current dilemma. The warm glow of his delightful reunion with Suzanne Simpson had evaporated well before his departure from Atlanta's Hartfield airport just after midnight. He slept fitfully on the flight to Incheon International Airport in Seoul despite his comfortable seat and a somewhat private compartment in the plush business class section of the sparkling new Delta Airbus A350 aircraft.

The rendezvous went spectacularly. Suzanne was absolutely radiant when she greeted him in the arrivals level of Atlanta's sprawling airport. Her dazzling smile, sparkling eyes, and glowing tan were even more beautiful than he remembered. A couple stood discretely behind her, watching his every move as Hiromi gently hugged Suzanne at the end of a formal handshake.

The man was huge—probably a former American football player. The African-American woman looked as if she spent hours each day lifting weights in a gym. Suzanne introduced them as her security detail and let Hiromi know they'd tag along for dinner.

A limousine was waiting at the curb as they left the airport, and their driver whisked them to a posh restaurant in downtown Atlanta. Surprisingly, it only took about a half hour, a fraction of the travel time to downtown Tokyo from Narita Airport, especially during rush hour.

The restaurant maître d' greeted Suzanne warmly by name and immediately escorted them to a private area at the rear. Inside the compartment, a round table was set for two with subdued lighting and absolute quiet. The security guards took a separate table a discrete distance from their conversation. Suzanne let him take the lead in their discussions.

They'd covered the small talk about their respective health, travel, and business activities in the limo, and Hiromi was uncertain how much time Suzanne would invest in their get-together, so he immediately probed for the information his minders wanted.

"I learned from the Japanese business media that you've assumed even more responsibility in Multima Corporation since we last met." He gave her his most engaging smile. "How is life going for you as a chief executive officer?"

"Usually well. I'm settled in. Our businesses are performing well, and I have a great team. You remember Gordon Goodfellow, my marketing director?" Suzanne asked, deflecting attention from herself. "I promoted him to president of Multima Supermarkets. Have you tried to contact him during your visit?"

"No." Hiromi laughed. "When you told me Multima Supermarkets would not buy the excellent proposal I made to supply fresh Japanese produce every day to Multima warehouses on the east coasts of the USA and Canada, I reluctantly accepted defeat. Other than meeting with your president and then yesterday with his secretary of agriculture, I have no other business objectives in America. I consider my call to you and dinner in this excellent restaurant as strictly personal. I'm not here to sell you anything."

Suzanne relaxed slightly as she processed his intentions, apparently relieved his interest was not commercial. She asked again about his late wife and the circumstances leading to her death. As Hiromi explained the dramatic progression of her heart disease, he felt Suzanne's empathy grow. Her sympathy seemed genuine.

"I can only imagine how difficult it must have been for you. Losing a life-partner must be one of the most difficult circumstances we face. I know divorce is hard, but even though we're separated, we can maintain some connection with our ex if we choose. Death is so final." She shuddered, her shoulders quivering visibly.

That comment opened the door for Hiromi to inquire about John George Mortimer. Even in Japan they had heard of his cancer and the dramatic announcement that he was Suzanne's father. Hiromi's efforts to disarm Suzanne's defenses and re-establish the bond they felt in Japan seemed to work. She spent several minutes describing John George's battle with cancer, its dramatic peaks and valleys.

It was clear the progression or regression of the immunotherapy treatments weighed heavily on Suzanne. Her voice broke slightly at one point in her description of how close to death they thought he was mere weeks earlier. And he felt her joy that treatments seemed more effective since a researcher from Geneva discovered some new combination of drugs.

Throughout their dinner, he could feel their bond growing stronger. She clearly enjoyed his company. Her blue eyes lit up as they shared funny stories of their respective university days in California just as they had when they last met in Japan. Her smile always seemed genuine and unrestrained, and her carefree laugh seemed heartfelt.

They talked about the food, the similarities and differences in their cultures, and even the delicate subjects of politics and religion. Hiromi was impressed with her knowledge of every subject but even more impressed with her way of thinking and willingness to consider all points of view. She seemed more interested in learning what they had in common than what issues might differentiate them.

As the evening progressed, Hiromi charmed Suzanne, flattered her in the most genuine ways he could manage, and projected interest in nurturing their relationship at every opportunity. When the woman security guard discretely interrupted their conversation some four hours later to remind them they needed to leave if they wanted to catch Hiromi's flight, he was in a quandary.

For about a half hour, she had let his hand rest tenderly over hers, smiling when he squeezed it gently from time to time. She appeared entirely comfortable with the gestures. As they prepared to leave, he politely asked if he might kiss her goodbye here in their private nook. She smiled invitingly, looked straight into his eyes, and put her arms around his neck.

As they kissed, it took only the gentlest of probes with his tongue to spread her lips for a long and passionate encounter. He adjusted his hands to her lower back, and she pressed tighter against his groin.

The sweet success in winning her affection left him miserable on the flight to Japan.

Unfortunately, that dinner was nothing but a charade, an enchanting, sexy, and enjoyable simulation, but a sham nonetheless. And, he hated himself for it as he shook his head in disgust and swallowed hard. The *Yakuza* left him little choice. If he didn't cooperate, they'd release copies of the videos and destroy his career. Of that, he had little doubt.

The *Yakuza* had become increasingly demanding. It concerned him, but he had few alternatives and no chance of escape from their clutches. It was entirely his own fault. In the months after the loss of his wife, Hiromi had suffered from depression. He continued to work and even thrived in his career, but his nights were lonely and his life away from the office was hollow.

He filled the emptiness of his nights in pachinko parlors. The bright lights and incessant sounds of the arcade machines were appealing, even though he knew organized crime owned and controlled them. The music and energy stimulated his senses. Like most Japanese people, he loved proximity to others. Unlike many Westerners who seek space to be alone and live privately, he'd learned as a child to appreciate the physical warmth and comfort of other living bodies occupying the same often cramped quarters. In pachinko parlors, this sensation—combined with alcohol and the excitement of the games—aroused his endorphins, causing him to throw caution to the wind.

Unrelenting Peril

That's what led to a library of sordid videos the *Yakuza* recorded as Hiromi gradually fell into a habit of sampling the pleasures of women the bastards kept discretely hidden in small back rooms away from the bright lights and frenzy of the parlors. The women were rewards for frequent visitors like him, especially players who wasted yen by the thousands on the criminals' machines.

"You have nothing to worry about Tenaka-san," the ominous figure told him after showing Hiromi a video of one particularly shocking session with him and the exceptionally young one who would do literally anything to please her customers. "Your personal tastes are safe with us. We appreciate your business. If you don't harm our girls, you may do as you please. However, we may need your help from time-to-time. May I trust you will show us the same courtesy of cooperation in the future?"

That was the way it started. And they were usually respectful. They never mentioned the videos again and made no requests until the night that same menacing figure summoned him to an office behind the parlor and closed the door.

"In a few weeks, you'll join our prime minister's delegation to a meeting with the American president," he said as Hiromi tried to conceal his surprise they could know that. "We want you to talk to a man in America before you go. He wants you to meet up there with a woman you know, Suzanne Simpson. You met when she visited Japan some time ago. This American needs you to get information from her."

The huge enforcer leaned forward and slipped a piece of paper to Hiromi. It had only a telephone number on it.

"Call this man as soon as possible and extend him every courtesy. Consider a request from him to be the same as a request from me," the large fellow said with a menacing grin. "Don't disappoint him. I will lose face if you come up short of his expectations, and I don't like to lose face."

When he called the number, the American never revealed his name, but his tone of voice was more terrifying than any Hiromi had ever heard. It was threatening in tenor even though he spoke softly. The American detailed the information he wanted. He emphasized Hiromi's need to charm Suzanne Simpson and establish the foundation for a long-term relationship. He underscored his expectation for Hiromi to share every detail of his conversations with the woman before returning to Japan.

Hiromi felt dreadful. He genuinely liked Suzanne and respected her significant business achievements. These people controlling his behavior seemed to have grave plans for Suzanne and now he was also entwined. Hiromi's hands trembled as he recalled the American's last words after he finished his report on their dinner conversation.

"Wait for further instructions. Keep the entire matter to yourself. My Japanese friends are watching." That's all he said before Hiromi heard an annoying buzz from their abruptly disconnected line.

THIRTY-FOUR

A penthouse suite, Hyatt Regency, Chicago
Tuesday January 8, 2019

The expense of renting a suite in the upscale hotel for a few hours was over-the-top, but Suzanne wanted to impress James Fitzgerald. She knew the man as well as he knew her. He'd immediately notice the opulence in place of her usual frugal spending habits and remember John George's frequent advice to his management team.

"People need to be reminded of their importance. The environment we choose for meetings speaks volumes about how important we think they are," her father often said.

She watched James Fitzgerald's posture straighten as he walked with her to the cluster of comfortable sofas in the living area of the suite. She caught him looking around the room in surprise, taking in the original art, the fine mahogany dining room furniture, and the magnificent chandelier that spanned at least six feet above the table. And she breathed a sigh of relief when he said, "It's certainly not the surroundings for our meeting that I expected."

"James, you realize I had no choice but to ask for your resignation," she started as they both settled into comfortable chairs at the side of the living area. "We simply could not afford to have a #MeToo moment on my watch."

"No worries, Suzanne." His shoulders slumped slightly forward again, and his eyes averted hers for a moment. "I know you had no choice. It was reckless of me to get involved with that woman, and I apologize for putting you in that position."

"How are things sorting out with Dianne?" Suzanne inquired.

James briefly recounted the latest developments in their separation, including the other woman. Suzanne listened attentively, but she'd known the details before she asked the question. Dan Ramirez, her director of corporate security, had already briefed her on the situation before she scheduled the meeting. Suzanne was pleased to note James's explanation was honest and his composure collected. She'd gone through a divorce herself and understood the challenges and emotions.

After James answered, Suzanne expressed appropriate regret about the developments before wishing them success sorting everything out. Then she veered in another direction.

"You know I didn't invite you to this swanky penthouse just to catch up on your marital status," she said with a disarming smile. "I want to offer you a job."

Puzzlement registered on James's face before he asked, "What kind of job?"

"A consultant. I'm prepared to pay you $20,000 per week until the assignment is done. I expect it will take most of this year to complete the job and I'm willing to transfer the money to an offshore account. I want no record of the payments in the US and will leave it to you how you treat the income from a tax perspective."

He'll calculate that to be about a million dollars.

"If you accept the job, you'll be responsible for all your own travel and other expenses. Those will have to come from the weekly fee. The less you spend, the more you get to keep." She smiled.

"That's a lot of money. What's it entail?" James asked.

"It involves some danger and risk to you personally. It also involves The Organization. If you choose not to accept the assignment, I'll certainly understand, but I'm prepared to reward you generously because I need your help. Multima needs your help."

For the next several minutes, she outlined the information her director of corporate security had shared with her with considerable alarm. There was substantial evidence The Organization was scheming to take another run at controlling Multima Corporation. Someone on his team in Fort Myers had learned from a friend in New York about suspicious activity at CBA Investment Bank. First, Janet Weissel—the woman who caused James's downfall—had been hired as a new employee there. However, she mysteriously disappeared after only a week on the job.

A few weeks later, authorities discovered Weissel's team leader at CBA floating in the Hudson River. At least, portions of him were found. Janet's boss and another guy had been decapitated and their torsos were found in the river. No heads had shown up yet.

What concerned Dan Ramirez most about these developments was the feverish activity around Jeffersons Stores and Multima Corporation. According to his source, the senior managers of CBA were devoting virtually all their time and considerable financial expense to dig up as much information about both companies as possible. And for some reason, those same senior managers were trying to arrange several billion dollars in standby capital. A war chest, people around their office called it.

"No reason for a war chest exists," Suzanne told James. "I've had early and confidential discussions with CBA about Multima possibly acquiring Jeffersons Stores, but I told them I'd rather spin off Multima Financial

Services and use the proceeds to pay for that purchase—if we decided to buy them, and that's a big if."

"Maybe the guys at CBA are simply hedging their bets to be sure they help you complete the deal even if the spin-off of Financial Services doesn't happen?" James offered.

"Perhaps," Suzanne replied. "Except for two crucial bits. First, the day after our preliminary meeting in New York, I called the CEO of the bank to tell him I definitely would not consider any bridge-financing arrangement. If we couldn't spin off Financial Services, I had no interest in taking on debt. There would be no offer to buy Jeffersons Stores if the Financial Services initial public offering was unsuccessful.

"Second, Venture Capital Inc. is the financial conduit the team at CBA is using to source the funds. Dan's convinced VCI and The Organization have something up their sleeve. That's where you come in."

She watched his eyes harden, lips tighten, and posture straighten before a tinge of pink gradually colored his cheeks. She had him hooked. For the next hour, she walked him through the strategy she had in mind, welcomed his questions, and frequently asked his advice on the direction she proposed. She might have been the choreographer of their conversation, but she also wanted to powerfully impart her need for his wisdom and expertise. It would be crucial to the success of her scheme.

All his signals remained positive. James gradually became more animated and engaged. His questions focused on execution. His speech pattern quickened, and his choice of words conveyed action. However, Suzanne knew the risk and personal danger his involvement posed should The Organization ever figure out his role in this conspiracy. She needed to be sure James was wholly committed.

"If I read your signals correctly, James, you're interested," she said carefully. "But, you're in retirement now. Is this a risk you would seriously consider?"

"Absolutely," James replied. "For months now, I've searched desperately for something to latch on to. This is it, without question. I realize you needed to dump me because of my involvement with the Weissel woman. I have no animosity toward you at all. On the contrary, I admire your courage and conviction to make a tough decision and execute it with grace. I've given my life to Multima and have no intention of letting such a great American corporation fall into the hands of thugs and criminals. I'm in. One hundred percent in."

It was exactly what Suzanne wanted to hear.

"Okay. Tell me where to send the twenty-thousand each week and start with the initial steps," she instructed and James relaxed. He probably assumed the meeting was about to close.

"I need to discuss a couple more issues with you. Do you have a few more minutes?"

His body tensed again, and his eye contact intensified.

"There's more than the Jeffersons Stores issue we just talked about. An old friend from college has invited me to China. Farefour Stores seems very interested in selling their Chinese operations. They threw out an attractive carrot of participation in a joint venture in Europe as part of the deal. I'm going to Shenzhen next month to check it out."

James's eyebrows arched slightly and his head tilted in curiosity before he asked, "Isn't that a little far afield?"

"Very far afield," Suzanne laughed. "But my college friend is Michelle Sauvignon, daughter of the largest shareholder in Farefour Stores. I didn't have any interest in China at first, but we've been talking off-and-on for about a year now. It gets more interesting with every conversation."

"I imagine you'll want to get some very specialized resources to help you with that," James tactfully suggested.

"Absolutely. I'd like your input on some possible names, but there's one more moving part to think about. Call it women's intuition if you like—because I have nothing concrete—but I think I may soon get an offer from Japan. And it might not be a friendly one. I met with a Japanese government official recently, someone I met during my visit there a couple years ago. He took pains to position his contact as strictly personal, but a few things didn't seem quite right, so I asked Dan Ramirez to have his corporate security folks poke around.

"Dan flashed some warning signals. It seems my contact—although he's a high-ranking official in Japan's department of agriculture—also has some bad habits. It looks like he's indebted to a *Yakuza* crime family in Tokyo. That family is rumored to own a significant chunk of Suji Corporation, one of the largest supermarket chains in Japan. Dan also suspects they may have ties to The Organization. Ramirez also wouldn't be surprised if my Japanese 'friend' started some dialog with Suji. In fact, he thinks they might try to take us over." Suzanne lowered her voice to emphasize the gravity of the situation.

"Wow," James said. "I have to let that sink in. You mean, we need to fight off these CBA bastards because they might be using Jeffersons Stores as bait to entrap us, but the real threat could be this big Japanese corporation?"

"Exactly. That's why I need you to get our scheme with Jeffersons underway immediately. But I also need to assemble a team with both

Unrelenting Peril

Chinese and Japanese-speaking resources. We may have to fight The Organization on two fronts, and that Chinese opportunity might become our best defense. Any idea where I could find the right people?"

James paused and looked upward as though seeking divine intervention, deep in thought for over a minute. Suzanne waited silently. He was processing his mental data bank at a rate of speed far quicker than most. She took a sip of the now-cold coffee to appear unhurried and relaxed.

"I think you might have the nucleus of a team already within Multima," James finally replied. "Is Wilma Willingsworth in the loop on any of this?"

"No. You're the only person I've shared this with."

"You might want to bring her into the loop because three of the people I have in mind are in the Financial Services group. If you decide to take those people, she'll be very suspicious. Plus, if this Japanese outfit, Suji, takes a run at Multima, there is no one with a better rapport among the Wall Street financial analysts and power brokers. You'll probably need her."

"Agreed." Suzanne grinned. "Now, who are those resources I need to raid Financial Services to find?"

"You need somebody with brilliant team-building skills. You've got the qualities, but you'll be far too busy to head a team. I suggest you consider Norman Whiteside. Remember how impressed I was when we acquired his small firm to be the genesis of our home mortgage program? Now that I've had a chance to work directly with him, I'm even more enthralled. He can pull a group together and have them working productively and harmoniously quicker than anyone I ever met."

"But he's running the home mortgage program for Wilma," Suzanne countered. "Wouldn't that be a great loss to her and the momentum she's built with the program?"

"It will be a loss for her, but I think we have someone who can hit the ground running. Wilma will feel little impact." James chose his words carefully. "Do you remember Natalia Tenaz, the bright young woman who handles the liaison between Financial Services and Supermarkets? She's ready. She could replace Whiteside without missing a beat."

"I see." Suzanne added a touch of skepticism to her voice. "I agree with your assessment of Norman. He could be a great fit. I need to see if Wilma shares your confidence about Natalia. What about resources with language skills?"

James responded without hesitation. "There's a senior financial analyst on Wilma's risk management team. She speaks both Mandarin and Cantonese. She can dissect a balance sheet better than almost anyone I know. And there's another woman in the funding group at Financial

Services who emigrated from Japan as a child. Perfectly bilingual. She also has extensive contacts in the Japanese banking community here."

It was precisely the kind of well-considered analysis Suzanne expected, and she continued to probe James's thoughts and knowledge for another hour before she dismissed him with heartfelt thanks, an enthusiastic handshake, and a warm hug.

After James left the suite, Suzanne sighed deeply as she absorbed the information and calculated how best she could win Wilma Willingsworth's support to give up such valuable resources and juggle her team. The tough sledding was just beginning.

THIRTY-FIVE

Nolitan Hotel near Wall Street, New York, NY
Thursday January 17, 2019

It had been several years since James needed to book a flight. More than a decade using his division's corporate jet made such flights unnecessary, even for personal trips. Senior executives had long established the need to use private aircraft for travel everywhere because of the security risks associated with public airports and scheduled airlines. The shareholders bought it.

It came as a surprise to learn travel agencies didn't book individual flights for free anymore. Even more surprising when the receptionist at one agency told him he should book his own trip online and save the fees. James gave it a whirl and selected American Airlines randomly. He knew Chicago was a hub airport for them and thought their reputation was probably okay.

After an hour, he figured it all out and reserved a first-class seat. He forgot how much time was wasted traveling with a regular airline. He left home three hours before the departure. A line-up—even for first class passengers—waited to board the flight. On arrival, he suffered another lineup to get a limousine and a one-hour ride to the Nolitan Hotel from LaGuardia Airport.

Despite the inconveniences, James's mood remained upbeat and intently focused on the meeting to come. Abe Schwartz, president of CBA Investment Bank, was scheduled to arrive at his suite. He chose the Nolitan because it was a boutique hotel near the bank's offices, but not as likely to attract the attention of the business media as some of the bigger chains. Both James and Schwartz had compelling reasons to keep this get-together out of the news.

The men had met once previously during a Multima Financial Services roadshow to promote bond purchases, but Schwartz now looked more haggard than James remembered. His eyes were bloodshot before noon and his complexion showed red blotches. Signs of a man who drank too much? His hand trembled during their formal greeting. And the poor fellow coughed several times from a cold that seemed deeply embedded in his chest. James took care to keep his hands well away from his own face as they got to the point of the meeting.

"I want your assurance that no part of this conversation is being recorded," James started with a stern expression.

"Of course not." Schwartz rose from his chair and removed his jacket. "You're welcome to check the jacket, and you can see I'm not wearing any wires. I'm just a little surprised by your call."

James waited while the man sat down again. He didn't bother to check the jacket. Frankly, he didn't know what he'd be looking for. Instead, he focused on the man's face. His relaxed expression and direct eye contact revealed his sincerity.

"It's a call I never expected to make," James said. "To be brief and candid, I've been screwed over by Suzanne Simpson and Multima Corporation. My recent retirement was forced. The woman simply has an agenda all her own, and I didn't fit into her plans. My three decades of building that empire counted for nothing, and she threw me under the bus with only a small pension and a decent bonus for 2018. I've thought about suing but decided to talk with you instead."

"Sorry to hear that, James," Abe Schwartz said with a grimace of sympathy. "But big corporations don't have hearts anymore. What triggered her decision?"

"I have no idea. Everything was going fine until she summoned me to Fort Myers for a meeting. Told me she was going to spin off or sell Multima Financial Services and wanted me out of the way. She demanded that I announce my intention to retire for family health reasons the next day at a meeting of the board of directors. I was completely railroaded."

"So, you found out we've been advising her about a possible transaction?" Schwartz explored, tentatively.

"Not from her. The bitch refused to give me any details. Wouldn't even tell me who she planned to put in my chair. I found out from Mortimer. We go back almost to the beginning, and he felt like shit when he found out what she did to me. He called me to apologize for her decision and behavior, but he's too sick now to do anything about it. Nevertheless, he's pissed about my ouster and is just as unhappy about her intention to divest Financial Services. It was actually he who suggested we make contact."

"Really? John George suggested you contact me?"

"Yeah, he wants me to work with you to accomplish three things. First, he wants to make sure Multima Corporation gets the best possible value for the divestiture if his daughter is still determined to go that route. Nobody knows more about the hidden value in that company than me.

"Second, he's desperate to ensure Financial Services doesn't fall into the wrong hands. That threat to seize control by Howard Knight and VCI two years ago really spooked him. He said you're a man of impeccable scruples who knows his way around Wall Street better than anyone he knows.

"Third, he'd like me to get my job back. I'm still good for ten or more years, and he thinks I should reap just rewards for my years of service. So, that's where I'm coming from. I'm offering to help you become an even richer man but only if any deal makes me the CEO of the new entity in whatever form it takes," James demanded with conviction.

The wily Abe Schwartz wasn't totally sold. His attempt to maintain a blank expression didn't entirely camouflage his doubt and surprise. The flattery about his reputation evoked a smile of pride, but his eyes darted sideways with failed attempts to maintain eye contact. That clearly telegraphed his discomfort. He dealt with the flattery first.

"Thank John George for the kind words the next time you speak with him. I've never met more of a gentleman in my entire business career. It's an honor and a compliment of the highest order," Schwartz replied. "I've certainly done my best to keep my reputation intact regardless of the temptations."

Then he laughed nervously. Unsure how best to proceed? Or uncomfortable making any commitment without checking with a higher power? He provided the answer quickly.

"I need to speak to potential investors about your demand to become CEO. I just recently got them comfortable with the idea of that woman Willingsworth leading the company," Schwartz said with a laugh. "But they're a conservative bunch, if you know what I mean. I can probably get them comfortable with you at the helm a lot more quickly. What else do you need before you're ready to share information?"

"A million-dollar advance on my salary as CEO. Paid into an offshore account. A cooperation agreement crafted by my attorney, making no mention of the advance on salary but with clear intentions to put me in that role—and a five-million-dollar penalty if the job fails to materialize. A standby letter of credit in that amount, redeemable within thirty days of closing should the agreement not be honored by then.

"I'll also need assurances my involvement in the deal will never be revealed, with the letter of credit redeemable immediately if there's a leak. Lastly, I have final approval on the structure of any deal with Multima. I don't intend to become the CEO of an entity saddled with untenable conditions or debt that might cripple the company in the future." James tapped the forefinger of his right hand on each of three fingers of his left hand emphatically as he outlined his demands.

Schwartz was unable to agree immediately to any of them. That would be entirely up to his backers. It also wouldn't take them long to figure out that Mortimer's goal of getting the best price for Financial Services was at odds with the rest of the demands. However, he was encouraged by Schwartz's curt nods to acknowledge each point. The man understood what the price would be for his involvement, but James had one more seed to plant.

"Obviously, my intention to get the best possible deal for the new owners of Financial Services might mean Multima can't squeeze every ounce of value out of a spin-off or IPO. I realize that. While John George is a long-time friend who suggested this course of action, the goal of getting him the best value will be secondary to the need for the new entity to succeed," James said with a rueful smile.

He wasn't surprised when Schwartz smiled knowingly, abruptly stood up, and said, "I get it. I'll talk with the interested investors. If they're not prepared to meet your demands, I'll discreetly ask around. Having you involved in the process should help us get the best possible deal for the new entity and my firm."

Intuitively, both knew the lunch James suggested when he first called to schedule the meeting was no longer appropriate. They shook hands amicably and agreed Abe Schwartz would make contact again when something developed. James could do little but wait and see if they swallowed the bait.

THIRTY-SIX

A modern condo complex, Quepos, Costa Rica
Friday January 18, 2019

The special scrambled and encrypted phone arrived in a plain brown envelope with the pizza delivery. Douglas Whitfield was so intrigued he paid little attention as the delivery woman shed her clothes just like every other time.

He read the handwritten note from Giancarlo Mareno in bewilderment and discomfort. It wasn't the content of the note that concerned him as much as the delivery. How did Mareno know about his business with the pizza restaurant? Why would he trust the owner of such an odd restaurant to deliver the device? How much more of Douglas's comings and goings was the powerful and ruthless crime boss monitoring?

The message itself was succinct.

Use only this for communication. No calls or emails on other devices. Suspect mole. Will call you Friday. Noon your time. G.

A mole inside The Organization? It was inconceivable. For more than three decades Mareno had overseen the most secretive crime syndicate in North America. Fear and Mareno's absolute control over every aspect of The Organization dissuaded any thought of disloyalty or ratting to the police. Douglas was so engrossed with the message and its implications that he left the stunning woman standing naked for several minutes.

When it registered that she was waiting for their usual romp in the bed upstairs, Douglas sent her away. Sexual release had to wait for another day. After almost two months of patience and inactivity, Douglas sensed things were about to happen. He spent several hours that night fondling the new phone as he thought through every imaginable scenario. None looked particularly appealing, but he felt cautiously ready to deal with whatever Mareno had to say.

He also decided Howard Knight shouldn't be around when he spoke with Mareno.

About a half hour before the scheduled call, Douglas set out walking toward the waterfront. The boardwalk would be quiet at lunch hour and high tide would splash waves against the breakwater making any recording of their conversation more difficult.

Precisely at noon, the new phone vibrated in his pocket. When Douglas answered, Mareno asked his usual pre-arranged security question and waited for an answer to establish he was indeed talking to Douglas. Then, in his gruff style, he cut to the purpose of his call with no greeting or small talk.

"I've left you guys cooling your heals down there because we had a snag with VEX. Your piece of ass got herself cut up. It was bad. She's been off work from CBA since the first week of December. I had to put everything on hold and spend a fortune getting her face fixed."

"What happened?"

"The little minx decided to fuck her team leader at CBA for some reason. The asshole was some kind of sadist. He and another pervert raped her, then apparently got carried away and carved her up a bit. She's okay now. Going back to work on Monday," Mareno said showing no emotion.

"Is it safe for her to go back?"

"Yeah, her former boss and his friend both had nasty accidents. We got someone else in there. She starts Monday too. But that's not why I'm calling," Mareno said with some impatience in his tone. "The president of CBA got a real interesting call last week from James Fitzgerald. You know him?"

"Of course. He was my boss at Multima Financial Services. I heard he suddenly retired last fall."

"Yeah, that's him. Apparently, that Simpson broad got wind he was screwing your favorite lay up there in Chicago and showed him the door. Seems he's not taking the firing well. Evidently, he learned about CBA's efforts to create a deal between Jeffersons Stores and Multima and contacted our friend. More interesting, the man's apparently a mercenary. Wants to secretly help CBA put it to the broad."

"Fitzgerald?" Douglas asked incredulously. "John George Mortimer's most loyal guy for thirty or more years wants to help screw over Suzanne Simpson?"

"I was skeptical, too," Mareno replied. "But our man at CBA claims Fitzgerald told him there's a secret internal agreement between the legal entities that weakens Multima Corporation financially if they spin off Financial Services. He says it would leave the parent's balance sheet decimated. Any idea what he's talking about?"

"No idea at all," Douglas admitted. "Maybe Howard Knight can help us."

"That's what I thought," Mareno agreed. "Sit him down and find out what he knows. And one more thing. Arrange a fire to destroy that boat of his. With all this delay, that little bastard might be tempted to run again. We don't want that to happen just when he might actually become useful again."

The next sound Douglas heard was a click followed by infuriating silence. As usual, Mareno had no time for the common courtesy of saying goodbye. The big man's instructions had been clear though. Interrogate Knight and burn his boat.

THIRTY-SEVEN

Mission Hills Golf Club, Shenzhen, China
Saturday January 19, 2019

With a towel draped around her neck and workout clothes damp with perspiration, Suzanne Simpson arrived from her pre-dawn one-hour run on the treadmill of the superlatively equipped fitness center in the resort complex. It was a chore to keep her nearly fifty-year-old body trim and healthy, but she maintained an almost religious adherence to the daily ritual.

She'd never dreamed of spending the third weekend of a new year in China. But there she was, drinking a cup of freshly brewed coffee and gazing out over what seemed to be the largest, most magnificent golf course in the world. There were actually eleven of them, all challenging championship terrains, plus a shorter eighteen-hole executive course.

It was dusk when she'd arrived the evening before, so this morning's peek out the window was her first opportunity to soak in the magnitude of the development and the grandeur of China's picture window to the world.

Her old college friend Michelle Sauvignon had set the wheels in motion with a call just before the Christmas break. There had been some new developments since their private conversation at the Mucky Duck in Fort Myers last year. Michelle made clear she was calling not only as president of Farefour Stores in China but also on her father's behalf. He thought it crucial to meet urgently and secretly. The best place would be Mission Hills Golf Club in China where foreign visitors were frequent, the staff was unobtrusive, and the media banned. They could come, have their important discussions, and leave with no one the wiser.

Suzanne was intrigued but busy. Before she would fly halfway around the world for a meeting, she needed to know more. Michelle was sympathetic but adamant. Her father was also a busy man. Perhaps he had retired, but he was still one of the wealthiest and most influential businessmen in all of France. He would never waste her time. What he wanted to discuss could be life-altering for Suzanne and Multima Corporation. But the window of opportunity was minuscule. They needed to meet—and hopefully act—right away.

In the end, she trusted her intuition. Michelle had been an exceptionally close and loyal friend throughout their college days, and she had been especially helpful to Suzanne and her team when they visited China on a research trip a couple years earlier. Their conversations over the past several months also showed promise. She owed her friend the courtesy of a meeting.

She apologetically informed Gordon Goodfellow at Supermarkets that she'd need to confiscate his long-range Bombardier Global 5000 company jet for a few days. He willingly complied, and Suzanne arrived with her smallest entourage ever.

She'd already spoken with Wilma Willingsworth about the resources suggested by James Fitzgerald, and her new division president immediately transferred them to the elite team Suzanne was creating. But it was too early to bring them here. Instead, she and her director of corporate security doubled her protectors. Ramirez added two Mandarin-speaking security guards so resources could watch over her movements around the clock.

Michelle met the tiny group at the private jet lounge of Hong Kong International Airport with her own security detail of four agents, a bullet-proof limousine, and two massive Cadillac SUVs. Michelle and Suzanne rode in the back of the limo. The four bodyguards divided themselves equally with Michelle's and rode in SUVs in front and behind the limousine.

It took an hour to travel from the airport to the city of Shenzhen, home of the headquarters for Farefour Stores China. Michelle wanted to give Suzanne a quick tour of the massive warehouses and offices before they continued to Mission Hills Golf Course.

The quick tour evolved into an almost three-hour visit as Suzanne became enthralled with the scope of the operation. Larger by far than any warehouse she had ever seen and populated with robots seemingly everywhere, it struck her as a masterpiece of distribution on a scale she could not have imagined.

As they rode a golf cart around the spotless facility, Suzanne peppered her host with questions, one cascading after the other as she took in the complexity and magnitude of the place. She marveled at all the movement in the warehouse. Automated lift trucks unloaded goods from an almost endless line of trucks, stacking pallets into every conceivable corner of available space. Others fed previously determined quantities of products into trailers backed up against dozens of loading docks on the opposite side of the warehouse. All were preparing for distribution of the merchandise across China. The operation was so sophisticated and massive, Suzanne couldn't think of a single facility in her company that came even close in comparison.

"It's true," Michelle said. "Most Westerners still think of China as a country populated by millions of uneducated paupers living in squalor and toiling for long hours in decrepit factories. Surely, some fit that image, but we should focus on the hundreds of millions of bright, well-educated, hard-working people who characterize modern China."

"Have you implemented this technology and scale of operation back in France?" Suzanne wondered.

"Scale, no. China has far more people than France—over twenty times the number—we can't replicate these facilities profitably at home. Even to serve the entire European market with more than three hundred and fifty million people, this would be too big. But we learn from the technical skills of our best Chinese workers.

"We often hire former government employees from the army or other services. They have technical knowledge and skills far greater than workers in the IT departments of almost any Western company. We rotate our most skillful for one-year assignments in France to help us improve technology there more quickly. Our associates love a chance to live and work abroad for a while, and we get skills we can't buy at any price at home."

"I'm impressed," Suzanne said quietly as she continued to marvel at what they saw down every aisle of the massive building.

When Suzanne exhausted her reservoir of questions, they re-assembled their convoy of vehicles and resumed travel on a modern expressway toward the city of Dongguan. Mission Hills Golf Course & Resort was about halfway along the route.

After checking into a sprawling three-bedroom suite on the top floor of the modern structure, Suzanne made her first call back home to Gordon Goodfellow, president of Multima Supermarkets. For an hour she regaled him with her highly favorable impressions of the Farefour China headquarters operation, reciting from memory observations about technology, organization of space, and the sheer scope of operations.

"Regardless what other opportunities may or may not present themselves while I'm here, I want you to embark immediately on a campaign to learn everything possible about Farefour Stores activities in China. Spare no expense and make this the single most immediate focus of the acquisition team at Supermarkets," Suzanne instructed.

THIRTY-EIGHT

Quepos, Costa Rica
Saturday January 19, 2019

The call aroused him from his sleep in the still dark hours of early morning. A panicked, Spanish-accented voice alerted Howard Knight that his boat in the Quepos port was on fire and he should come urgently, and then hung up before he could ask any questions.

At first, he thought it was a hoax. Then he realized almost no one knew this number and couldn't think of any who spoke Spanish. In fact, the only time he remembered giving out the number was to the harbormaster of the port when they arrived in Costa Rica back in November.

Neither he nor Whitfield had a car in Costa Rica. By the time he found a taxi at this hour, it would be just as quick to walk. He silently closed the door to the condo, crossed the parking lot, and opened the electronic lock on a large steel gate to leave the compound.

Walking on the left side of the paved road, Howard stayed on the smoother asphalt surface and alternated jogging and walking to reach the summit of the hill overlooking the town. Sure enough, dark smoke filtered across the town below, and the glow of flames shot into the sky as he looked toward the Pacific. The fire appeared to be in the marina.

Howard charged down the steep hillside on the street heading toward the center of town. At the bottom, he made a sharp right turn and followed a winding residential street that eventually led him to the waterfront. There was no vehicular traffic, but several people were outdoors checking out the smoke and sound of sirens. First responders might just be arriving.

As soon as Howard reached the waterfront, he bounded up the seven cement steps to the boardwalk and cringed as his fear was confirmed. The caller was right. Flames and smoke came from the exact spot where he docked his boat. Breathing heavily, but in despair, he slowed his pace. There was nothing he could do but assess the damage. If the height of the flames and density of the black, acrid smoke were any indication, there wouldn't be much left to survey.

Howard slowly trudged along the half-mile-long boardwalk and past the tiny skateboard park where the boardwalk became a worn path to the marina. It was there—just at the end—that four men jumped from behind two gigantic trees and rushed the few yards that separated them.

He had no time to react. Just as danger registered, powerful hands clamped his arms tightly against his waist, while yet another person bound both his arms and legs with strips secured tightly by Velcro snaps. Another pair of powerful hands jammed a cloth into his mouth when he tried to cry out. Someone darted toward a nearby van and unlocked it electronically with a brief flash of its lights.

Gunshots rang out—several loud bursts in just an instant—and then silence. A moment later, Howard gagged on a foul-smelling rag pressed brutally into his face and lost consciousness.

THIRTY-NINE

A comfortable home in Den-en-Chofu, Japan
Saturday January 19, 2019

After working six days a week for twenty-five years, Hiromi Tenaka was one of the bureaucrats who welcomed the Japanese government's recent mandate for leisure time and days off. He realized the government's apparent largesse was merely a ploy to encourage its citizens to spend more money, theoretically stimulating their perennially sagging economy. Still, he welcomed the treat of sleeping a little later and not rushing to the ever-crowded Tokyu-Tokyo rail line for his daily trek to the heart of Japan's largest city.

He was more than a little irritated when a voice commanded him to get up, get dressed, and get to his usual pachinko parlor immediately. It was annoying and humiliating, and he once again cursed the imperfect judgment that had caused him to become entrapped by this despicable crowd. Women probably were right when they scoffed about men thinking too often with their little heads and not enough with their big ones.

Out of options, he followed orders and arrived about an hour later in a room concealed at the rear of his favorite pachinko parlor. He was hungry and in ill-humor. When he entered the small, cluttered, and smoke-filled office, he first grimaced at the stench then coughed involuntarily as his lungs reacted to the assault on their well-being. He bowed deeply to the leader of the *Yakuza* as a required show of respect he didn't feel.

Then, he hid his shock when the other man in the room was introduced as Suji-san, chairman of the massive supermarket chain that bore his name, Suji Corporation. Hiromi bowed even more deeply. Suji-san was considered among the ten most influential people in Japan. His wealth ranked even higher. As a senior government official, Hiromi took care to maintain direct eye contact with the powerful businessman despite bending his waist past ninety degrees during his obligatory bow.

He had to camouflage his surprise once again as Suji-san curtly dismissed the *Yakuza* leader with a nod and abrupt wave of his hand.

Suji must also be involved in the Yakuza!

The oblique rumors over the years and the rare cautious speculation from occasional obscure journalists were right. One of Japan's largest supermarket chains was directly involved in organized crime.

However, he couldn't contain his astonishment when Suji-san asked—in perfect English—"Are you there my American friend?" He took care to not link a name to the voice on the speakerphone.

"Yeah, our guest has arrived, then?" asked the harsh voice Hiromi recognized from his trip to America.

"Yes, Hiromi Tenaka, our esteemed deputy minister of Agriculture is here." Suji-san blended a malicious smile with his polite tone. "Perhaps you can explain your idea and request to him."

With no other introduction, greeting, or inquiry about either health or weather, the man with the impossible-to-forget voice spoke.

"The woman is now in China. She'll be there only today, then she's scheduled to return to the USA. Call her American cell number. It's working and she's using it. Resume your love affair. Let her know you're hot to see her again and find out when she might meet you in Hawaii for a weekend. If you've done your job well, you'll tempt her sex drive. She'll tell you she's in Shenzhen, leaving for home the next day. She'll probably offer to meet you in Tokyo when they stop to refuel. You'll suggest lunch together. Say whatever you need to say, but get her there. Any questions?"

"What should I do when we meet?" Hiromi hated the meekness in his tone.

"After the appropriate lovey-dovey stuff to make sure she's swallowed the bait—hook, line, and sinker—tell her there's a great business opportunity. Tell her your prime minister secretly promised our charming president that he would allow some American investment in certain sectors. Supermarkets included. You've been charged with identifying a candidate and have learned that Suji Stores might be willing to sell. The old fellow with you there is getting ready to retire." The gruff voice and Suji-san broke into uproarious laughter. After their pause for amusement, the American resumed.

"Tell her you haven't shared that information with anyone. She'd be the first to know. Then, do whatever's necessary to arrange a meeting for her and Suji on Monday. Suji will give you his cell number and you'll call him as soon as you get her agreement. Establish a time on Monday for her to visit his headquarters. You'll meet her any time, right Suji?"

"That's right, my American friend," Suji-san concurred. "I'll make myself available any time of the day or night."

"Have your people done their homework to create a PowerPoint presentation that will bait her to make a deal?" the obnoxious voice asked.

"We're ready, my friend. We'll throw out the lowball amount we discussed."

"No more details," the voice interrupted sharply. "We'll talk off-line. Tenaka, are you clear on your mission?"

"Yes. I understand," Hiromi replied more forcefully this time than before.

"Okay, I shouldn't need to repeat the importance of this to us again, but I will. We expect you to say and do whatever is necessary to get the Simpson woman here and arrange a meeting with Suji. If you have to get your cock wet, do it. If you need to shove your filthy tongue up her ass like you're inclined to do from time-to-time, then lick away. But don't let us down," the voice boomed.

Such crude humiliation and debasement.

The voice then told him to leave the room so he could talk with Suji privately. The *Yakuza* leader sitting on a chair outside the tiny office was playing with his phone when Hiromi opened the door. His eyes brightened when they made contact before he too reminded Hiromi they were all counting on him.

The train ride back to his home in Den-en-Chofu seemed an eternity. Hiromi felt physically dirty. His stomach churned. The guilt was almost overwhelming. He felt like shit. There was just no other way to describe it. For the entire ride, he considered any other option besides calling Suzanne Simpson. No good could come of what they demanded. Briefly, the thought of jumping in front of a moving train crossed his mind.

But he could see no other alternative. He didn't have the courage to fall on his sword, and he could never cope with the certain dishonor any disclosure of the content on those videos would inevitably cause. He made the call to Suzanne as soon as he arrived home. She wasn't immediately available, so he left a message and waited.

To his relief, Suzanne returned his call within minutes. Their conversation followed the precise track the American voice had predicted. She said it must be good fortune working overtime that he should call her while she happened already to be in Asia. She was leaving China the next morning and her jet would refuel at Haneda Airport. Was that anywhere near his home?

It was almost too easy. Hiromi grimaced with disgust after he hung up and slowly set the handset on a nearby table. She'd even proposed they plan enough time to enjoy a good meal together. In fact, maybe he could reserve at that wonderful restaurant he took her to the last time they met in Japan. Her suggestion seemed to carry an alluring tone.

As he sat in his small kitchen, sipping a cup of green tea to settle his stomach, he thought again about the entire circumstance. How they first met in Japan. The delightful reunion they enjoyed in Atlanta. The warm and sensuous tone she used during their call. And, the terrible thing he was doing to set her up for a rendezvous with a kingpin in the most ruthless of criminal organizations. There had to be a way to change the trajectory.

There just had to be a way.

Forty

San José, Costa Rica
Saturday January 19, 2019

The guy was useful, but he couldn't be trusted. Douglas Whitfield made certain Giancarlo Mareno's orders were followed to the letter. After he found a vagrant and small-time thief who claimed he had the skills to burn Howard Knight's yacht in the harbor, Douglas located a safe place to hide in the underground parking lot of the marina complex. It was a tiny maintenance room in one corner with an open window facing the water. From there, Knight's boat was in his direct line of sight.

About thirty minutes before their pre-arranged time, Douglas slipped away from the condo and walked at a brisk pace through the lifeless downtown area to the marina. There he took his position. Sure enough, a massive explosion rocked the marina just before midnight.

It was a sight to behold! Better than fireworks, the flames shot thirty or forty feet in the air. Dense smoke formed in a cloud above the burning yacht as one explosion after another shattered the fiberglass shell and threw debris in all directions. Douglas was fascinated—almost mesmerized—for a few seconds. Then he saw a human form running along the dock from the boat with flames fully engulfing his clothes. Even from this distance, the blood-curdling scream of the man sent a chill of horror down his spine.

As horrible as it was, the guy actually saved him some trouble. The other reason Douglas went to the marina was to eliminate the arsonist when the deed was done. Giancarlo Mareno didn't need to tell him it was imperative the man die to avoid any possibility of him talking. The man's carelessness saved him the trouble.

Douglas left his spot in the underground parking and walked toward a rear entrance to wait for the fire trucks. He appreciated that they were slow in coming. For every minute the fire raged, the more successful his mission. If the fire trucks were ten or more minutes responding, the yacht would be destroyed entirely. Knight would no longer be able to escape by sea.

Those critical ten minutes ended just as Douglas heard the first approaching sirens. He didn't bother waiting longer. His work was done. Instead, he headed back toward the condo complex, taking a shortcut across the outdoor section of the parking garage toward the street. As he reached the boardwalk, he ducked behind a massive old tree to hide from the approaching trucks.

A frenzy of activity erupted. With the firetrucks, dozens of honking pickup trucks also approached the marina, each carrying several men. Apparently, the firefighters relied primarily on volunteers to staff their department. With much shouting and squealing of tires and brakes, the whole village seemed to arrive to battle the blaze. Amused, Douglas watched it all for a few minutes.

With the small army of firefighters down by the waterfront, Douglas checked the road. The coast appeared clear to resume his trek back to the condo. He stepped out from behind the huge tree and turned toward the boardwalk. To his amazement, Howard Knight was walking in his direction, head down and shoulders slumped forward in a posture of defeat.

Four thugs jumped out from behind two huge trees and grabbed him.

Douglas reached for his handgun, but before he could pull the weapon from his pocket, they bundled Knight into a van.

And before he could take aim and shoot, the van sped off, lurching away from the low curb with a squeal of tires. He aimed at a tire to disable it, but a sound behind him caught his attention.

"Drop your weapon!"

Without aiming, Douglas fired his gun at the approaching form. The guy cried out in surprise and returned fire.

A sharp pain pierced his left shoulder before he heard a sound.

"He's shot!"

They're American!

Douglas fired again. Two more points of pain shot through him. He lost his balance and fell sideways, landing with another crack of pain. Someone jumped on his arm with hard boots and he screamed as bones shattered. Hands grabbed him roughly and dragged him to the same van. Within moments, they unceremoniously threw him on the floor of the vehicle beside the motionless Howard Knight.

His attackers jumped into the back of the van with their victims without taking time to close the rear door. Through a haze of tears, Douglas looked from the back of the van as it careened away from the curb and sped down the street. He caught only glimpses of motion between alternating darkness and what seemed to be fog.

The van zipped past the marina entrance and along the short roadway on the south side of the port all the way to its end. There, it passed a raised barricade and screeched to a halt beside a large helicopter with its rotor already spinning.

Four captors dragged Howard from the van and hoisted him into the helicopter. The pilot tugged him into the aircraft while others pushed from below until they had him strapped him into a seat. The remaining captors carried Douglas to the helicopter and roughly hoisted him into the rear. They left him lying on the floor. Blood now covered the other men.

Where did all that blood come from?

The pain intensified, and Douglas cried out for help, but his voice was weak. Either they didn't hear him or simply ignored him, leaving him alone on the hard floor in the back of the aircraft. Knight appeared to be blissfully unaware of the hectic calls and animated voices around him as they took off.

For a few minutes, while the helicopter flew over the mountain range between Quepos and the capital of San José, Douglas continued to cry for help, his voice growing weaker by the minute. Even he couldn't hear the sounds he was making. He was groggy—in and out of consciousness—but felt the helicopter touch down. Still in a daze, he saw their captors lift Knight from his seat and lower him to the cement tarmac.

They came for him sometime later. Douglas no longer had the strength to cry out for help and barely managed to form a picture of what was happening. He saw three or four figures on the ground when they opened the door. They dragged him from the aircraft and roughly let him drop on the cement tarmac. He felt another bone give way as he landed but couldn't cry out in pain. Did they think he was dead?

As he tried to raise his head, Douglas saw one man carrying something that looked like a large leather sheet. He shifted his gaze to the left, and another form took shape. This one held a gun. It was pointed right at him.

One bright flash and everything went dark.

FORTY-ONE

Chairman's Suite, Four Seasons Hotel, Tokyo, Japan
Sunday January 20, 2019

"Time to wake up, Ms. Simpson." The female member of the security detail gently nudged Suzanne's arm for emphasis. "You asked me to wake you thirty minutes before landing so you could fix your makeup."

A morning nap was a rare occurrence, but sleep was limited during her few hours in China, and the effects of jet lag had finally caught up with her after departure. The appealing aroma of the fresh coffee another member of the team handed her helped. Within moments she was alert, in the tiny jet lavatory, and expertly touching up her hair and makeup before meeting Hiromi.

She didn't have any doubts about her decision to meet him but the strong objections of Chief of security Dan Ramirez in yesterday's call still weighed on her mind. He adamantly opposed Suzanne visiting Tokyo without Japanese-speaking security people. Did she realize how exposed and impotent her bodyguards might be when nobody spoke the language? She understood the risk, but Hiromi Tenaka would be there. Despite his purported unsavory position under the thumb of the *Yakuza*, the man was still a senior government official and Japan was a civilized country. She'd be careful, but she still intended to go forward with their hastily arranged get-together.

Ramirez relented when he realized there was no way to change her mind. She was the CEO after all. As much as she appreciated and valued his advice, the final decision would always be hers, and they both understood that. Part of his angst stemmed from news he'd received earlier that morning from his contact buried deep in a rogue unit of the FBI branch that dealt with Homeland Security. Mention of the unit immediately rekindled Suzanne's anxiety about Ramirez and some of the activities he had them involved in.

A few weeks earlier he'd explained the oddly named FBI unit. Rogue wasn't an official designation. Rather, it referred to agents assigned to any situation even remotely considered a threat to national security. Those agents could do almost anything they pleased with impunity. Ramirez liked to use the term but claimed it was never used internally.

Their recent conversation built on one they had months earlier. Then, her chief of corporate security had shared the background story about the unconventional goings-on at Guantanamo Bay surrounding Wendal Randall, Howard Knight, and the women. He gave the backstory, then revealed there was a treasure trove of incriminating information the FBI had amassed from extensive recorded interviews. Giancarlo Mareno and hundreds of his cronies around the globe were the targets.

At that time, Ramirez had explained why the director of the FBI unexpectedly pulled the plug on that extensive investigation during the period his own job was in jeopardy with the newly elected president.

Suzanne had listened, aghast. Such shenanigans simply weren't conceivable in the USA, and it shocked her that John George Mortimer had involved Multima Corporation to such an extent. Ramirez's insight eclipsed by far the meager details her father had provided to Suzanne after swearing her to secrecy.

She almost fainted when Ramirez told her the rogue unit hadn't given up. After the new president fired the FBI director, as feared, the covert resources pursuing Mareno simply went deeper into the bureau's underground. In fact, the rogues not only continued to keep Dan fully in the loop but also planted a mole inside The Organization. Suzanne hadn't thought about that conversation for weeks, but it all came back when her security chief called with startling new developments.

"Their mole learned that Mareno ordered Douglas Whitfield to destroy Howard Knight's yacht docked in Costa Rica," Ramirez started. "That order persuaded the psychologists to act. They decided the shenanigans with the boat were probably a prelude to eliminating Knight completely, likely within days."

"The psychologists?" Suzanne asked, her mouth agape.

"Yeah, the Bureau always uses behavioral specialists in these cases. Their accuracy predicting future conduct is remarkable," Dan Ramirez replied. "Anyway, they intercepted calls between Mareno and Whitfield. One giving the instructions for a fire and another confirming when it would happen."

"This rogue unit was able to get a court order to wiretap their communications?" Suzanne asked.

"Oh, I doubt it. I think they just bugged the encryption systems. Everyone buys these new encryption-equipped devices thinking they're more secure, but the Chinese and Russians have had software for years that we can plant inside the encryption software remotely. The rogue units get the software from them," Ramirez explained patiently.

"Regardless," he continued after taking a breath, "they found out when the fire was scheduled to start and decided to use the expected chaos around that incident as cover to get Knight and Whitfield out of Costa Rica."

"They planned to simply kidnap the two men?" Suzanne asked in amazement.

"More or less," Ramirez said hesitantly. "They got Knight and he's back in good health. They killed Douglas Whitfield and sent him to Cuba in a body bag."

Suzanne couldn't fully absorb this alarming news. She was speechless. Ramirez filled the gap with one more piece of information.

"It seems they launched two attacks simultaneously. They grabbed Knight without incident when he followed their bait and went to see for himself what all the commotion was about. They planned to use another team to nab Whitfield at the same time as Knight, then airlift them both out. It seems Whitfield was armed and unexpectedly shot one of the rogues in the arm as they tried to apprehend him. The rogue agent wasn't happy and reacted on impulse. He instantly returned fire with a couple bullets that finished off Whitfield. They're keeping his body in Cuba until they decide what to do with it."

That's what unnerved Ramirez and caused him to be so protective. She understood. It took her a few minutes after the call to regain her composure, and for some further time, she seriously reconsidered the wisdom of her decision. Finally, she became more convinced than before that meeting with Hiromi was a crucial element in the scheme she was crafting.

Hiromi Tenaka played his role masterfully. She admired that. When he met her in the private aircraft lounge of Haneda Airport in downtown Tokyo, he looked thrilled. His gorgeous smile beamed. His longer-than-stylish hair was just disheveled enough to be charming, and his enthusiasm was infectious.

He grasped her so tightly it almost hurt. His kiss started as a polite one, but they soon became entwined in each other's arms as his tongue probed and explored deep inside her mouth. It went on for a few pleasing seconds, almost enough to sidetrack her from the mission at hand. Slightly flustered with the intensity of his greeting, she took a moment to pat her hair into place and check her makeup with a compact mirror.

Hiromi greeted each of the security team members with warmth and ease. He asked them how they should handle transportation. He had only arranged one limousine and he couldn't find one in Tokyo that might accommodate six large passengers. They agreed to hire a taxi for the two Mandarin-speaking bodyguards. Suzanne's regular team rode in the hired car.

Once the logistics were settled, he rushed her to the waiting Lexus limousine and directed the driver to the restaurant where they had dined during Suzanne's first trip to Japan. Like on her previous visit, Suzanne was enamored by the restaurant, the food, the calming atmosphere, and the charming company. It was temptingly easy to forget this evening was no more than a charade.

But the stakes were high. So, she didn't allow herself to forget that polished acting was one of the most essential skills in any CEO's toolbox. Tonight, she'd not only display superior acting talent but also exercise enough willpower to resist temptation. She was certain Hiromi would invite her to his home and expect to make love to her. But she was determined to resist any sexual urges despite having done without for several months. She had to concede he was smooth. He didn't mention a word about Suji until they were eating dessert. And he threw out the opportunity as casually as he might inquire about her taste in chocolates.

"I really hate to bring any discussion of business into such an enjoyable social outing," Hiromi said in an off-hand manner. "But an issue came up last week I thought I should at least mention to you. If you don't have an appetite for it, there's certainly no problem. But I wouldn't want you to become upset later should you learn I was aware of an unusual opportunity and hadn't mentioned it to you."

"Sounds mysterious, Hiromi," she cooed in return. "Don't worry. Experts say a CEO is never entirely off the clock, and I know you wouldn't raise a subject if it wasn't something important."

"Thanks. It could be news of use to you," Tenaka continued. "You'll remember I accompanied our prime minister to meet with your president just before we got together in Atlanta?"

Suzanne nodded and said, "Sure, I remember. You found the crass curmudgeon rather difficult—if I remember correctly." They laughed at the understatement.

"During those meetings, our prime minister apparently promised your president better opportunities to invest in Japanese companies. One of the sectors that interested your leader was supermarkets. The American side sees an opportunity to expand food sales to Japan should one of your companies control a major supermarket chain in Japan," Hiromi explained as his manner gradually became more intense.

"That's odd," Suzanne commented. "I've heard nothing about that back home."

"We're keeping it under wraps here too, but my prime minister asked me to informally inquire about companies that might be acquired. Last week, I spoke with Mr. Suji, who is the controlling shareholder of Suji

Corporation, one of Japan's largest supermarket chains. To my surprise, he expressed some interest," Hiromi explained carefully.

"Some interest in what?" Suzanne asked.

"Apparently his health is failing. He's almost eighty years old and has no successors. He told me he would entertain serious offers to acquire part or all of his company."

"And why do you think I might find this significant?" Suzanne asked.

"Candidly, I don't know if you have any interest. But because of our friendship, I want you to know I haven't yet shared this information with anyone else—not even my prime minister. If you're giving any thought to expansion outside of the USA, this might be a wonderful company for you to consider." Hiromi moved smoothly into his selling mode.

"I really appreciate you thinking of me, Hiromi, but expansion to Japan isn't on my radar right now. Our board of directors hasn't even discussed such a possibility."

"I understand," Hiromi replied with the slightest hint of disappointment. "I'll forget all about it if you want me to. But before you make a final decision, may I add one more thought?"

Suzanne simply nodded, making no comment but conveying a willingness to listen by leaning forward and tilting her head inquisitively.

"I hope you don't mind, but I dropped your name in my conversation with Mr. Suji. He was quite impressed I knew you personally. It seems he has followed your father's career with interest and has great admiration for John George Mortimer. Mr. Suji asked me to let him know if ever you plan to be in Japan. He'd like to make your acquaintance personally. Again, I hope you'll forgive me, but I called him after our conversation yesterday. He expressed a strong desire to meet with you while you're here. He said he'd clear whatever was on his calendar for Monday if you'd take a few minutes to meet with him."

Suzanne grimaced but made no comment for at least a minute as she wanted him to think she was processing the request. When she thought her pause was long enough to be dramatic, she told him it probably wouldn't work out this time. She needed to be back in Fort Myers for Tuesday morning and didn't relish the thought of getting sleep only on a flight home. Maybe another time.

Hiromi cleverly didn't pursue the matter immediately. She liked his shrewd judgment. Instead, he switched the subject to her China trip and asked her impressions. For almost an hour, they compared notes on their respective visits to China and overwhelmingly favorable impressions of the country's economic progress and modernization efforts.

Hiromi glanced at his watch as they finished talking about the Mission Hills Golf Course. He wanted to give Mr. Suji a call before the hour was too late. The elderly man liked to turn in early but would likely be waiting for confirmation of a meeting. If Suzanne didn't want to get together, he should let Suji-san know.

At that point, she told him she'd changed her mind and gracefully acquiesced to a meeting. An immediate flicker of relief crossed Hiromi's face.

"Are you sure, Suzanne? I don't want you to feel any pressure. I'm willing to call and let him know it's not possible," he volunteered with apparent ease.

"No. I can sleep on the plane." Suzanne gave him a bright smile to reinforce her enthusiasm. "One never knows when a contact like Mr. Suji might become important. Let's make it mid-morning. I have calls I need to make back to the USA first, and I'd like to be in the air by mid-afternoon. Just be sure you tell him I'm not shopping for any new companies."

Her last comment left them both chuckling again, but Hiromi had also placed his hand on hers—just as he had during their previous rendezvous in Atlanta. She made a trip to the ladies' room while he called Suji and confirmed a meeting was set as soon as she returned to their table.

He asked if she'd like to have a nightcap somewhere. Suzanne reluctantly declined. She truly enjoyed the guy's company. However, tomorrow would start early, and she needed sleep.

"I guess that's a signal not to invite you back to my place," Hiromi tested.

"That's right," Suzanne replied with an exaggerated frown. "Let's find me a nearby hotel for the night."

"Already arranged," Hiromi said with a grin of satisfaction. "The Four Season's Hotel folks are holding the Chairman's Suite for you—just like the last time you were here."

Although the thought of once again paying more than five thousand dollars for one night's accommodation peeved her a little, the memory of that exquisite massage she had during her last visit reflexively triggered a grin. Maybe her sexual urges wouldn't be stymied after all. Hiromi initialed the bill and they left the restaurant.

Their short ride to the Four Seasons was more tranquil than she expected. Both seemed deep in thought or unsure how best to close off their evening. For her part, Suzanne was already formulating her call the next morning to James Fitzgerald. She planned to call him before dawn to be sure she had adequate time to discuss that extraordinary one-day meeting with Farefour Stores in China. For the first time, she thought the path with Michelle might eventually hold the most promise of all.

FORTY-TWO

A large executive home, Hoffman Estates, IL
Sunday January 20, 2019

James Fitzgerald saw Suzanne Simpson's name on his call display and instantly realized it was about four o'clock in the morning over in Asia. Despite the NFL playoff game just underway, he had little choice but to accept her call. He dreaded talking with her right now. He had little to report, and she'd probably be disappointed even if she concealed it well. After a ring or two of dithering, he answered.

Their initial chit-chat on the call was limited. To his relief, Suzanne didn't ask for an update on his progress with Abe Schwartz at CBA Investment Bank. Instead, she swore him to total secrecy and shared the results of her talks in China with Michelle and Jean-Louis Sauvignon of Farefour Stores.

"It was the first time I met him. I found the guy quite impressive," Suzanne began. "He must be approaching eighty now, but he walks five miles a day, works out in a gym three times a week and reads a book a week. Not bad for a retiree."

"Is he still actively involved in Farefour Stores?"

"Not officially. He passed all his formal responsibilities to their new CEO a few years ago. But he's still the single largest shareholder in the company—and a miserable one it seems," Suzanne said. This led to a ten-minute summary of the points of contention the elder Sauvignon had with his successor. James listened with increasing interest as Suzanne painted an ugly picture of an angry man willing to subvert the efforts of his current CEO to protect a family fortune he'd amassed over a lifetime.

"He swore his biggest mistake was not to maneuver Michelle into the role of CEO when he first had the chance and genuinely regretted his uncertainty about her preparedness to lead at that time," Suzanne explained to close her overview on the man's current state of mind. "But his greatest alarm centers on the current strategic direction their CEO seems determined to follow. And guess what? The new fellow wants to create a financial services division across all of Europe, as you did for Multima in the USA."

For another several minutes, Suzanne outlined her recollection of the steps the CEO had already taken to obtain banking licenses in twenty-five individual countries and lay the foundation for an expected financial empire. James not only listened intently but also grabbed a pen and notepad. He scribbled notes furiously as Suzanne walked him through the complexities of European banking which Sauvignon had described to her with distaste and scorn.

"The old man is convinced Farefour Stores doesn't have the internal firepower to properly set up and manage such a diverse and multifaceted business operation. And he's concerned the slick new guys the CEO has hired from outside the company are too reckless," Suzanne continued.

"In particular, he contrasted the bullet-proof balance sheet of Multima Financial Services with the model the new Farefour CEO is trying to build. He figures the new financial services operations will require Farefour to take on about four times the debt Multima carries to support our Financial Services unit. In his view, any misstep could cause the credit rating of Farefour to collapse and drain billions of Euros from the balance sheet. He sees that risk swallowing billions of his own fortune."

James understood instantly the gravity of the elder Sauvignon's concern. It was he who had persuaded John George Mortimer to bury a billion dollars in the Financial Services balance sheet to give his division an appealing credit risk profile for lenders and have a buffer against any mistakes or downturn. He reminded Suzanne about that stroke of genius, and she immediately grasped the implications for Farefour Stores.

"That's why he invited me to China in secret," Suzanne resumed. "The CEO is restricted by the company's charter. He can only change two directors on the board in any one year. Jean-Louis Sauvignon's cronies still dominate the board, but that balance of power will shift in 2020. Next year, Sauvignon's influence will start to dwindle because he'll no longer be able to pull strings behind the scenes."

"So, let me guess," James interjected when Suzanne paused to take a breath. "He wants you to pay a steep price to buy Farefour's operations in China. He wants you to make an offer the new CEO and his friends on the board can't refuse. He wins two ways. He simplifies management complexity by shrinking the geographic territory his people manage and raises a ton of cash to strengthen the company's balance sheet."

"That's right. You've got it exactly," Suzanne added. Was that a little admiration in her tone? "And there's actually a third win for him. Michelle Sauvignon will emerge as the superstar who created all that value and will earn a promotion to at least deputy chair of the board. He might even have enough sway to replace the current fellow with his daughter."

Suzanne asked for a moment to sip her cooling coffee, giving him a few seconds to process all the information and consider possible outcomes. This development was intriguing. His spirits rose when she carried on.

"That's why I'm calling and probably dragging you away from an NFL playoff game," she teased. "I'd like to expand the scope of your consulting assignment if you agree. I'm willing to revisit your fee and expenses if you want me to, but I need your answer immediately."

"Tell me what you're looking for, and I'll tell you right now if I'm in or not," James said with full conviction.

"I need you to continue to stoke the issues with Abe Schwartz and his folks over there at CBA Investment Bank. I doubt you've been able to advance much so far. Dan Ramirez warned me that Schwartz wouldn't dare make a decision without Giancarlo Mareno's okay. And Mareno won't give his blessing without thoroughly vetting you. Ramirez guesses he'll probably need another couple weeks.

"So, I'd like you to go to Europe and fish around. Use your contacts there to learn everything you can about all those banking licenses Farefour has accumulated and what lending activities are permitted. But I want you to rummage around without any indication Multima Stores is involved. You need to invent a plausible cover story to divert any curiosity completely," Suzanne instructed.

"I don't think that will be an issue. I've often told people that I should write a book or two after I retire and every one of them agreed. I'll position my requests for meetings and interviews as fodder for my books. Given my departure from Multima last year, I don't think it will attract any suspicion."

"Excellent idea. And if you had mentioned writing a book to me, I would have believed it instantly as well!" Suzanne exclaimed. "What about your fees and expenses? Do you want to renegotiate?"

"Not right now, Suzanne. You've been very generous. If the expenses grow too quickly, I'd appreciate the opportunity to revisit your offer. Can we leave it at that?"

She concurred, then spent another half hour reviewing the steps Wilma Willingsworth had already undertaken that morning after an earlier call. It seems Suzanne had Wilma pursuing a different channel of investigation and intrigue. Her task was probing heavyweight financial analysts in Europe about the market perceptions of Farefour Stores' overall financial health.

That Suzanne called the president of Financial Services to get that directive underway first gave James reason to pause. With both Wilma's undertaking to investigate Farefour Stores through her financial contacts in Europe and his new assignment to investigate European banking licenses, exactly where was Suzanne headed with this ostensible opportunity to buy the Chinese operations of Farefour?

FORTY-THREE

An office tower near Wall Street, New York, NY
Monday January 21, 2019

Abe Schwartz summoned Janet Weissel to his plush corner office just after nine o'clock. Her first instinct was to stop in the restroom to check her makeup.

Just to be sure the scars aren't too apparent. It was her initial interaction with her ultimate boss at CBA Investment Bank and the whole idea of meeting the guy made her uncomfortable.

She applied a little more of the liquid goop the cosmetic surgeon gave her to hide the scars where he made his latest incisions to correct damage created by the animals who attacked her. It helped. She reminded herself to check the lighting in Schwartz's office like the surgeon recommended. If she could avoid direct sunlight, the scars would be harder to detect.

Schwartz was prepared when she entered his office. The expensive Venetian blinds were half-closed, and the overhead lighting in the office was dimmed. He used desk and table lamps for light. Either someone had schooled him on the right way to handle this, or he had the smarts to research it himself. She wasn't sure which, but immediately appreciated the gesture.

"Come in Janet." He sprang from his leather chair and stepped out from behind the desk to grasp her hand with both of his. "Take a seat. I want to tell you how sorry I am about your mishap! We had no inkling of Antoine's sadistic tendencies. I'm so sorry one of our employees was so deranged he treated you that way. He deserved exactly what he got. How are you feeling?"

Janet assessed the man's nervous barrage of comments and intentionally let him stew a few seconds before she replied.

"I'm not doing very well at all, thank you. But I've been instructed to return to work and complete our assignment. So, I will. But you know exactly how it feels when we're forced to do certain things don't you, Abe?"

Schwartz's face reddened, and he reflexively ran his finger around the inside of his tightening shirt collar in obvious discomfort. Janet immediately regretted her comment. She needed this guy's support to satisfy Mareno and find her ticket to escape. So, she promptly reversed direction.

"I'm sorry, Abe. That was very unkind of me," she said contritely. Her boss continued to squirm in his large elevated chair. "I know you had nothing to do with the attack. I just feel weak and vulnerable these days. Again, I apologize. Thank you for your patience while I recovered from it all."

"I understand how you must feel. And I am truly sorry," Schwartz repeated in a more subdued tone of voice. "You're right. I too must please our mutual master. I'm not proud of that, but it's reality. And a lot of people depend on me to make sure he stays happy. Can we talk about where we go from here?"

Janet simply nodded her head and listened. For about half an hour, Abe Schwartz recounted the changes that had taken place with her team and within CBA Investment Bank. Janet asked only one or two questions of clarification as Schwartz continued his narrative. It sounded rehearsed.

Then he switched to Multima Corporation. He brought her up to date on John George Mortimer's remarkably improving health, Suzanne Simpson's recent travels, and other internal intelligence their mole inside Multima had learned. Janet became more engaged and tried to best understand his take on Suzanne's travels and what significance they might have for their scheme.

After about an hour, Abe Schwartz apparently concluded she was adequately up to date and asked if she was ready to meet with the rest of the team.

"I'd particularly like you to meet the new senior vice president we've recruited to lead the direct interface with Multima," Schwartz said before making a call. "You'll be working closely together."

Moments later, the new senior vice president arrived at Schwartz's office and was escorted in. Janet tried to mask her complete shock as the young woman approached her to shake hands. She knew her. It was the drop-dead gorgeous assistant to the president of Multima Supermarkets workers' union, Arleen Woodhaus. They met the day Janet joined a meeting with Natalia Tenaz and Suzanne Simpson to gain the union's support. She remembered the drawn-out hug of greeting from Arleen that day made her wonder if the woman might be a lesbian.

"Nice to see you again, Janet." The well-dressed young woman flashed her million-dollar smile. "It's a small world, isn't it? I'm so excited we'll be working together again."

Janet had no idea how she should respond, so she answered with a feeble, "Hey, Arleen. Yeah, it's amazing to see you again."

Her first inclination was to blurt out *does The Organization control everything?* Instead, she suppressed her growing exasperation about the formidable reach of the bad guys into every stratum of society. It was all perplexing and confusing. One route of escape Janet had briefly considered was using her new boss to extricate herself from their clutches. This avenue now appeared to be closed.

However, Janet resolved to wait and see how it played out over the next few days. There were still two other possible avenues to consider. She'd wait to see which cards this new player would use before she decided how best to take control of her fate. This new vice president might still hold one elusive key.

FORTY-FOUR

Financial Services Headquarters, Hoffman Estates, IL
Monday January 28, 2019

Wilma Willingsworth glanced at her watch and grimaced. The video link with Suzanne Simpson was scheduled to start in less than five minutes and she had scant good news to report to her boss. In anticipation, she shuffled her pile of notes and documents, then quickly sorted through them for what must have been the tenth time that morning.

From China, Suzanne had called immediately after her covert meeting with Michelle and Jean-Louis Sauvignon. With an uncharacteristic burst of optimism, she explained there might be an extraordinary opportunity to keep Financial Services under the Multima umbrella and expand into Europe at the same time.

After observing the woman as a colleague for several years, Wilma thought she knew her boss well. She considered her a cautious executive, one who examined every idea from every perspective before deciding its merits. What caused this sudden shift?

Once Suzanne was convinced of the value of an idea, she became a tireless and enthusiastic advocate until it came to fruition. But she usually showed patience and prudence as she first weighed the pros and cons. For some reason, this deal seemed to have already captivated Suzanne's attention. When the video screen turned on, Wilma outlined her less than promising news.

"There are a few complications with this one," she cautioned Suzanne. "I expect you were hoping for some positive validation out of my phone calls to Europe last week. I loathe being the bearer of bad news, but Farefour Stores has a lot of negative stuff going on."

"Tell me about it." Suzanne's tone held no trace of disappointment or concern.

"I spoke with analysts at ten commercial banks over there. All were people I've worked with before and whose judgment I trust. Every one of them told me now is not a good time to buy shares in Farefour Stores. Their concerns varied, but the most optimistic rated Farefour as a hold. Seven of the ten said they would sell shares if they held any and were recommending their clients do the same. It was hard to get any of them to say something nice about the company," Wilma explained.

"I see. What seem to be the areas of concern?"

"First, the new CEO, a German fellow named Aakker—Josef Aakker—isn't settling in very well. Farefour's board appointed him two years ago. Since then, he's alienated several directors. He encounters resistance on almost every motion he puts forward. He's had no success with the company's workers. One plan he put in place to reduce labor costs by ten percent met with strong opposition from the unions. Apparently, strikes are possible in the UK, Germany, and Italy before the end of this year.

"Seven of the twelve most senior leaders in the company have either been fired or left of their own accord. Most have landed in similar roles with competitors and carried over tons of proprietary knowledge with them. But most serious of all, Moody's is doing a review of their bond rating. Three contacts had sources who suggested a significant downgrade—a full notch or two—is probable. If that happens, their borrowing costs will soar through the roof," Wilma said. She took no pleasure from it, but with such careful enunciation, Suzanne would understand the depth of her concern.

"Let me see if I understood everything you said correctly," Suzanne replied, again with a tone that gave no indication of her feelings or reaction to the news. "CEO Aakker is on the outs with the board and his fellow leadership team. Strikes are probable in three countries. And their debt will likely be downgraded soon. Anything I missed?"

"No, you've got it," Wilma responded, taking care to reflect an equally non-committal tone. Probably better to find out which way she was leaning.

"Okay. I understand your trepidation," Suzanne resumed. "None of those issues lend much encouragement to a possible joint-venture, right?"

"It makes absolute sense for Farefour Stores to seek a willing partner, especially one with a balance sheet like ours," Wilma replied. "But any one of those developments could adversely impact our financial position should we enter into an agreement right now."

"I agree. Did you ask your analyst friends what they expect will happen with the share price should any or all of those negative factors persist?"

"Yeah, they all think the price currently reflects the market's concern about the management and board of directors issues. They think the price will neither increase nor fall on those thorny issues. But they all expect a hit to the price if there are labor disruptions in any of those countries. They suggested a fifteen percent decline with any single country, about a fifty percent decline if all three strike for more than a couple weeks. The debt downgrade would probably shave another ten percent because borrowing costs would skyrocket," Wilma explained.

For the next few minutes, the women continued to talk about what Wilma gleaned from her research. Suzanne asked more questions about the labor issues, Farefour's financial position, and other bits Wilma was able to share. Though Wilma was always impressed with Suzanne's ability to process and digest information, she was more fascinated than usual when Suzanne issued new instructions.

"Let's set aside any thoughts of a joint venture. We're both on the same page there," Suzanne said. "But I'm also revisiting the wisdom of splitting Financial Services from Multima. Your arguments about the intrinsic strategic value to the company are strong ones. I still want us to grow by doing an acquisition or two, but I'm wondering if we can't raise some cash to do that another way."

"If you want to do it quickly, we could sell off some receivables from either the credit card or mortgage divisions or both. I could probably find investors who would buy them from us for cash and we continue to manage the receivables for a fee. We might be able to raise up to ten billion fairly quickly with securitization of our loan receivables."

"Look into it," Suzanne said. "When can you have something ready for the board to consider?"

FORTY-FIVE

A plush penthouse apartment, Miami, FL
Friday February 1, 2019

A few moments after the private jet took off from San José International Airport in Costa Rica, Howard thought he knew who snatched him from the boardwalk in Quepos, Costa Rica. It didn't take rocket science to conclude his captors were with the FBI, not The Organization.

Douglas Whitfield was dead. They'd already told him it was Whitfield when he asked who was inside that body bag they threw into the underbelly of the jet before they took off from the capital. The aircraft carried no markings. The exterior color was a dull brown, and the interior had eight seats in an equally neutral beige with virtually no luxury appointments.

If Douglas Whitfield was indeed close to Giancarlo Mareno, there was little chance the powerful man would have eliminated him like that. They were supposed to be working together on VEX after all.

They must be taking me back to Guantanamo.

"No, you're headed to Miami," one of his guards replied when Howard asked where they were headed for a second time. "But that's all I'll confirm for you. They'll deal with you when we arrive. In the meantime, if you want to talk about the Dolphins, I'm all in. You want to talk about anything else, we have nothing to say."

So, the flight from San José to Miami was a quiet one. About two hours out, they offered him a bottle of water and a cold sandwich. Howard had little appetite but managed to consume about half the sandwich made from some meat he was unable to identify by taste, covered with a shriveled morsel of lettuce, with a yellow tomato adding no detectable flavor.

It was still dark when they arrived at an airport south of Miami. Homestead maybe. Once they landed and taxied to an area beside a dark office building, they led him down the steps and across the tarmac to a large, black Chevrolet SUV. Another person waited in the rear seat. He introduced himself in an entirely different manner.

"Hello, Howard," he said with a welcoming smile as he enthusiastically grasped and shook his hand. "I'm Steve and I'll be your minder. Relax. You're in no danger, and we'll transport you to some nice accommodations for the next little while. That's all I can tell you, though. So don't ask me any questions about your status. Are you a football fan?"

When Howard shook his head, the fellow switched subjects and found they had common ground talking about food and wine. He did a commendable job of conversing with his prisoner in a tone that was friendly and cheerful throughout the half-hour drive. But each time Howard tried to ask a question about who they were and why they had captured him, the guy simply switched the conversation back to food or wine.

In Miami, they stopped in front of a high-rise apartment tower on Brickell Key, just off US Highway 1 at the start of Miami's downtown core. The sky brightened with dawn as they hustled him into an elevator immediately inside the front doors apart from the others. A security guard sat in the lobby, but he didn't look up or indicate interest as Steve guided Howard into an elevator, its doors held open by yet another new face.

This time there was no conversation as the elevator sped to the top floor, a penthouse, Howard assumed, again apprehensive. The notoriously stingy FBI was unlikely to have a penthouse apartment in such an exclusive area of town. Before he had time to become wholly alarmed, the elevator glided to a stop, and the doors opened with another press of a button by the new guard. An FBI agent? Perhaps. But he wasn't sure.

Inside, Howard was astounded to see luxury everywhere he looked. The suite covered the entire top of the building, easily more than four thousand square feet, with floor-to-ceiling windows on all sides. He looked around a huge living area with three sofas and three La-Z-Boy chairs, and a mahogany dining table large enough to comfortably seat a dozen people. Beyond the dining area, a huge modern kitchen with exotic appliances, grills, and multiple matching granite counters caught his eye.

Then Howard took in the view outside. It was spectacular. The sun was just appearing on the horizon to the east and the effect was gorgeous. It was exhilarating. Howard's spirits soared despite his worry about his captors or their plans for him. Things might not be so rosy in a few minutes, but if it all ended now, it couldn't have been with a more magnificent view.

Remarkably, the world didn't end. Instead, Steve asked, "Would you care for a glass of wine?"

As an inducement, he opened the door to a wine cabinet that held at least a hundred bottles maintained at an ideal temperature. A good idea under the circumstances—even if it was a little odd to imbibe before breakfast.

Howard selected a pricey Beaujolais. His captor opened the bottle and served him an oversized glass filled to the brim. A few minutes later, the man asked what Howard would like cooked for breakfast, then prepared everything he ordered and served it at the huge dining room table. There was no other conversation while he ate the food and drank the wine prepared by the still semi-anonymous guard known only as Steve.

Finished eating, Howard decided to wander about the apartment and explore his surroundings. He peeked into all three bedrooms. Two were evidently occupied. Clothes hung in the closets of each and the adjoining bathrooms had toiletries and shaving supplies on the counters. A third bedroom appeared unoccupied.

As Howard sauntered out of the third bedroom, he noticed the entrance doors to the elevator they'd used earlier. Cautiously listening for sounds, Howard deduced his captor was still washing dishes in the kitchen, so he pushed a button on the wall to see what might happen.

Instantly, he screamed in horror as an alarm sounded and a violent shock shot through his body, causing his arm to recoil from the button with such force he lost his balance and tumbled awkwardly to the floor. The guard breathlessly dashed into the room with a weapon drawn and pointed it menacingly at Howard's face.

"Make no further attempt to escape," Steve warned. "I'll adjust the voltage to kill you next time. On the other hand, you won't be harmed and will be treated very well if you stay away from that button. It's your choice."

The guard kept his word. Every night, Howard was locked in his room. The rest of the time, he could wander about the apartment, watch TV, listen to music, read current books from an extensive library, or work out on fitness equipment he found in a fourth room. Steve slept on the other side of the apartment suite.

Every day, it was the same routine. The guard would release an electronic lock on Howard's bedroom door each morning about seven. When he came out of the room, the man would ask what he'd like for breakfast, then prepare and serve it. The same applied for lunches and dinners.

Steve never introduced himself more formally and seldom spoke except to ask Howard his meal preferences. The sole exception was a daily phone call to order food and supplies, then a brief and hushed conversation with whoever delivered the order an hour or two later. When Howard tried to start a conversation or ask a question about anything, the man would merely shake his head.

Until today. Howard heard the usual buzz of someone wanting to come up the private elevator much earlier than the habitual ring after an order for supplies. Steve checked a message on his phone screen before he keyed a code into the alarm device. A few moments later the door opened, and Howard held his breath in anticipation. When he recognized the tall man stepping from the elevator, his knees became weak and he trembled.

"You know who I am," the cultured gentleman said with a surprisingly quiet and refined voice. "There will be no formal introductions. I'm sorry it's necessary to keep you in captivity but trust you've enjoyed your surroundings and our hospitality while you acclimate again to the United States of America."

"Sure, good food, great books. Too bad I'm just a rat in your gilded cage. I'd like to know why you're holding me here in a cell that can kill me if I push the wrong button."

"I'm sorry that's been necessary too. How long it will be necessary depends entirely on our conversation this morning. Let's sit down and chat," the gentleman offered, pointing to the leather sofa and chair to his left.

"Here's the situation," started the man who once served as a highly respected director of the FBI. "My special investigation is entering its final stages. I've read transcripts of all the conversations you had with the FBI when you were incarcerated in Guantanamo two years ago. You provided an impressive amount of information. It's truly a shame the director of the FBI was unable to move forward with indictments at that time. But things are different now, and they'll soon be able to act."

The gentleman stared into Howard's eyes intently as he pronounced those last words slowly—and with understated emphasis—before he paused.

"I know all about the deal you made with the FBI. I fully understand your reluctance to testify against Giancarlo Mareno and the leadership of The Organization. But we need you to reconsider and help us. Granted, you're here against your will. But we've tried to give you a taste of the quality of life you lacked these past two years while you were in hiding. You can have it all again if you cooperate with us. We can arrange for you to live safely in the lap of luxury just as you are right now. The only difference? You'll be a free man, living in another country, with a new identity and the full protection of the United States of America."

Howard had to ponder what the gentleman implied. He felt no obligation to respond immediately and took his time to think about the man's comments. The gentleman sat quietly, looking at Howard but demonstrating patience with an understanding smile.

"It's tempting," Howard said after a minute or two. "Really tempting. Over the past two years, I've lost my dignity, the only woman I ever loved, and my freedom. But I think that special woman in my life had it right. There is no escape from Giancarlo Mareno. Even if the FBI is successful in a court of law, Mareno has incredible reach everywhere in the world. I think I'll be better off just moving around. It delays the inevitable a little longer."

"I understand how you feel." The gentleman shrugged and maintained his smile. "But there's more hope than you think. The love of your life, as you call her, isn't dead. She was never returned to the Argentinian Gestapo. She cooperated with authorities in Europe and provided a trove of information.

Working with a special team inside Interpol, the FBI are preparing now to act. We expect at least two hundred arrests in over fifty countries. The combined efforts of the FBI, Interpol, and other law enforcement agencies around the world will undertake the greatest counter-attack against organized crime the world has ever seen. But you're one of our missing links. We need you and your testimony to help seal the deal."

The refined gentleman stayed for more than an hour as he listened to Howard's concerns and countered each with patient, thoughtful, and reasoned responses. In the end, the two could not reach an agreement, but the gentleman asked Howard to think about it for a few days. Then he turned to the guard and softly instructed him to deactivate the internal electric alarm system while Howard considered his options.

FORTY-SIX

An office in Chiyoda-ku, Tokyo, Japan
Monday February 4, 2019

It wasn't the prime minister himself who called but someone in his office. Regardless, Hiromi Tenaka loathed what he'd just agreed to do and was desperately trying to think of a way out.

After arranging a meeting between Suzanne Simpson and Suji-san a few weeks earlier, Hiromi thought he had honored his obligation to the *Yakuza*. Even though no one had officially notified him, it was the impression the manager of the pachinko parlor left him with when he agreed to arrange that meeting. Naïvely perhaps, he expected they would destroy the incriminating videos.

He had done everything they asked. Well, almost everything. He arranged for Suzanne to meet with Suji-san on impossibly short notice when she stopped in Japan. He accompanied her to the meeting at Suji Corporation headquarters. He even sat through the entire two-hour presentation Suji-san made to Suzanne. It took twice as long because every comment the chairman made in Japanese needed to be translated into English. Hiromi even helped the translator from time-to-time just to accelerate the process.

Suzanne listened politely to the presentation from Suji-san, but her manner and comments were quite clear. While Suji Corporation was an impressive company with enormous potential, she didn't think Multima Corporation would consider this offer to explore a link-up between the two companies.

The cultures of the organizations were very different, but they were almost the same size. Multima would need to borrow enormous sums of money to finance an acquisition. She wouldn't try to persuade her board to devote precious resources to exploration of a merger or acquisition with so little probability of making a deal.

Suji-san had seemed satisfied with her position. He showed no irritation or disappointment with his body language. He beseeched her to think about the idea and consider floating it with her board when she deemed appropriate. He smiled graciously and bowed respectfully as they parted.

It seemed Hiromi had done everything right except get Suzanne Simpson into bed. He certainly tried the night before the meeting with Suji but to no avail. He couldn't remember a time he had been more charming, and he used every tool of persuasion he had learned in all those management development courses. In the end, she was always polite, always calm, but also steadfastly firm. No. She would not go back to his place. She wanted a few hours of sleep before her flight to America.

After the meeting with Suji Corporation, he gave it one last try. That time she was a little curt but equally emphatic. Nothing would happen between them during this visit, she finally rebuked as they chatted on the way to Haneda Airport to meet her company jet. He was glad her security detail had traveled in separate cars so they didn't see his humiliation at her continued rejection.

Still, after all those efforts and the good things he'd accomplished for them, the people in the *Yakuza* had the temerity to again use him to conspire with Suji Corporation. The whole thing wasn't just distasteful, it was probably illegal. These criminals certainly had some grander vision than simply attracting a buyer for the Japanese supermarket chain.

Now, they came back to him with this further demand to set up another rendezvous in Hawaii. He had no choice. The bastard in the prime minister's office brought up the cursed videos immediately after Hiromi showed the slightest hesitation. It all felt like a noose tightening around his neck.

He grappled for a solution that could satisfy their demands but also let him save face with Suzanne. He might persuade her to meet him in Hawaii for a weekend. She gave him all the right signals before they said goodbye and their chemistry still seemed strong. Even her goodbye kiss was as passionate as the one he stole in Atlanta. It should just be a matter of fitting a weekend into her schedule.

But he found the other part of their demand repulsive. Suji-san would also travel to Hawaii at the same time as Suzanne and Hiromi. They wanted Hiromi to surreptitiously facilitate a meeting between the two again. This time, they wanted the meeting to take place in the hotel suite of the Japanese business tycoon. Apparently, he was prepared to make her an offer she couldn't refuse.

That people associated with the *Yakuza* would be so keenly interested in selling this Japanese company to Suzanne was a grave concern. Even more disconcerting was the involvement of the prime minister's office in the proposed business transaction. And how did all this fit with the US president's demand to allow takeovers of Japanese supermarkets?

FORTY-SEVEN

Multima Corporation Headquarters, Fort Myers, FL
Tuesday February 5, 2019

"You need to bring me up to date on Douglas Whitfield's death before we start," Suzanne told her corporate security chief as they began their morning conversation hours before most staff would arrive.

"Yeah, I learned a little more since we spoke when you were in Asia," Dan Ramirez explained. "The rogue unit of the FBI was in a real quandary about what to do with Whitfield's body when they returned to Miami. Killing him wasn't part of their original plan, and they probably should've just left his remains in Costa Rica for authorities there to deal with. Regardless, they needed a solution. So, they shipped him to Barbados."

"Barbados?" Suzanne queried with an arched eyebrow.

"Whitfield had dual Barbadian-American citizenship. He was born there, and his mother still lives in Bridgetown. She was the only known family. So, the FBI guys worked discretely through police channels to ship the body back there."

"Does that relate in any way to your request for this meeting? Your message said you'd like to talk about Mareno and The Organization."

"It does. We knew Whitfield was part of The Organization. We knew that when you scammed VCI out of their shares of Multima. What we didn't know was that Giancarlo Mareno—The Organization's head honcho—was his father. We only discovered that when the body got back to Barbados and his mother went ballistic. It seems her grief was so great she went around the bend. Got on a plane to New York and confronted Mareno in public. She screamed about him being a murderer and physically attacked him."

"A woman from Barbados confronted and attacked Mareno?"

"Yeah, she had no chance against the huge brute. He subdued her within a second or two. She'd maintained a relationship with Mareno since before Whitfield was born but had always insisted on living in Barbados to avoid being near his criminal activities in the US. Whitfield's death caused some sort of a mental breakdown."

"Wow. This is almost surreal," Suzanne replied. "How did you learn all this?"

"The mole planted inside The Organization by that rogue unit of the FBI was close enough to see and hear it all. They also found out The Organization is plotting a serious attack on Multima Corporation to exact revenge for what they perceive as your swindling them on the Multima Solutions deal. It seems they expected to get ownership of that fancy software Mortimer gave Solutions—the one with a defect. They found some other use for it to harvest millions, maybe billions of dollars. When you scuttled that, Mareno lost face badly with his partners in The Organization. So, Whitfield was hiding out in Costa Rica to quarterback this mysterious attack on Multima to redeem both Mareno and Whitfield with the unhappy factions."

"That's a mouthful you just shared there, Dan. Is all this info coming from this mole the FBI has planted inside The Organization?" Suzanne shook her head in disbelief.

"Most of it," the security chief resumed. "The part about Mareno losing face as a perceived motivation for his planned attack on Multima came from Howard Knight. The rogue unit has him squirreled away somewhere in the US, and Knight's cooperating with them again."

"Dan, this worries me," Suzanne said, leaning toward him for emphasis. "Is there no end to this mess? These people gained ownership of a successful technology company with brilliant people and unlimited potential. They really feel short-changed?"

"That's the story from Knight," Ramirez replied.

"And your involvement with this rogue unit of the FBI terrifies me too," she added. "It seems the FBI feels an obligation to keep you informed. Is it normal for them to share information like this with former members?"

"No," Ramirez replied sharply. "I think they just feel an obligation to see that John George Mortimer gets good value for his ten million dollars."

Suzanne blanched at this reference to her father. She had no notion John George had initiated the rogue unit's actions or paid the people there to do their work. She merely said, "Explain."

Ramirez controlled the narrative as Suzanne listened intently and without interruption. John George had specifically asked Ramirez to operate outside normal channels and laws. Multima paid ten million dollars to the FBI as a 'donation' for security research. Part of that amount ultimately was used to make a deal with Wendal Randall—a captive of the FBI at the time. Randall was the first to accept the FBI's offer of witness protection before he helped them locate Knight in Argentina.

After all that, Ramirez gave her a high-level overview of more new information obtained from interviews with Howard Knight since his recapture. It took more time than she expected and revealed more complications. Was she finally getting real insight into the morass her father had created?

"How do we ever get out of this, Dan?" she asked.

"I don't see any alternative but continuing to cooperate with the rogue unit of the FBI. They're on a path to indict Giancarlo Mareno and hundreds of his cronies in the US and around the world. Until they successfully arrest those people—and put them away—we should expect the threats, schemes, and attacks to continue," he concluded in the detached, matter-of-fact manner used by police around the globe.

Suzanne remained uneasy with the entire circumstance. The physical danger they could manage. They would fend off threats to Multima to the best of their ability and probably prevail. But what if this entire swamp of underworld activity—and Multima's role in it—should become public? Would it ever be possible to explain the illegal payments, the denial of basic American legal rights, and perhaps even the death of an American citizen? Would the company's image as a stellar corporate citizen become forever tarnished? She had no immediate answers. There were just too many moving parts with too few apparent solutions.

"As usual, I'll follow your advice, Dan," Suzanne concluded. "It looks like our options are limited, and you seem to be well plugged in. That should help us defend against their attacks. Let's continue to stay close on this. And let's lose any paper trail. No more emails. Call my mobile, the new one with the scrambler software you got for me. And one more thing: let's agree Multima will not put any more money into this project under any pretense.

"Now, I need to shift subjects. In two weeks, I'm off to Hawaii for a personal vacation for a few days. I'll be meeting Hiromi Tenaka, my friend from Japan. Is there any special preparation we need for that trip?"

FORTY-EIGHT

Multima Corporation Headquarters, Fort Myers, FL
Tuesday February 5, 2019

James Fitzgerald passed Dan Ramirez in the long corridor leading to Suzanne Simpson's expansive office suite. They greeted briefly before James entered the office and warmly hugged his former colleague and CEO. When the door closed, and their small talk was out of the way, Suzanne started right in with her purpose for getting together.

"Naturally, we'll need to keep this between us for the moment," Suzanne said with a conspiratorial smile. "I really appreciate you recommending those resources from the Financial Services team for my special task force. Wilma cooperated fully, and I brought her into the loop on everything. She's the only person besides me you should talk with. You were right about Norman Whiteside. He's a fantastic team builder. His people churned out some great analysis already. But I want them to shift gears, and I'd like you more involved with the task force directly."

"I'll consider it, but I must confess, I'm a bit confused here," James admitted. "When we met in Chicago to discuss the consulting assignment, you asked me to infiltrate CBA Investment Bank and keep you informed of developments there. Then you asked me to gather as much information about European banking licenses as possible under the pretext I'm writing a book. Today, you invite me to headquarters. You must already realize that word of my visit here will get back to CBA. They might even know I'm here before I leave the office. What's going on?"

"Right on all counts," Suzanne replied. "I've been unfair to you by shifting course so frequently. First, don't worry about CBA. I've already planted the story around the office that you're visiting today to discuss a settlement. I've strategically let a couple people know you asked for one last meeting to discuss your perception of unfair severance related to your retirement before you take formal legal action. The people at CBA may already know that as we speak, but I think your cover for the visit is valid.

"The summary you sent me about European banking licenses is outstanding," she continued without a pause. "You delivered everything I expected. If I understood your conclusions, Farefour Stores actually did everything right with their licenses except in Poland and Norway?"

"Yes. They have all the proper licenses to do business with credit cards and home mortgages in every EU country except those two," Howard confirmed.

"Other than that, you think Farefour Stores could create a financial services division like ours?" Suzanne clarified.

"From a licensing perspective, yes. From a practical perspective, no. Surprisingly, at least a half-dozen of my sources over there voluntarily offered information to me about Farefour without prompting. Some of the financial heavyweights are concerned about Farefour's ability to pull it off."

"I've heard the same," Suzanne replied. "There's concern about management stability, board support, and balance sheet depth. Is that what you heard?"

"Exactly. There's a verifiable schism between the new CEO and both his board of directors and management team. Speculation is the new fellow will be forced to cool his heels with any diversification into financial services until he has full control of the board. That could take a couple years according to some."

"You might have a little built-in bias, but what do you think about the business viability of the idea?" Suzanne asked.

"You're right. I think there is a strong probability of success with the right balance sheet and management team. Credit card growth in Europe lags America by far. Demand is strong and growing. Housing prices in most European countries are rising quicker than in the US, and lenders there are still very conservative. I have no doubt our business model could be emulated there with similar success."

"That's what I thought, too," Suzanne said with a broadening smile. "That's why I asked you to come in today and why I'd like you to discretely coach the task force working from their secret office in Chicago."

For the rest of their one-hour meeting, Suzanne did most of the talking as she shared her latest ideas. When she finished, James Fitzgerald felt proud to tell her he was in—all in.

Forty-Nine

Sheraton Kauai Resort, Island of Kauai, Hawaii
Saturday February 16, 2019

Hiromi's unease grew from the time Suji-san's limousine picked him up from his home and drove him to the airport. He expected to be the only passenger and hid his shock when he found Suji-san seated in the rear seat of the luxury Lexus. His discomfort increased as they talked on the way to Narita.

"For the next few days, do not refer to me as Suji-san," the business tycoon said with a sinister grin, showing his discolored teeth and gold fillings as he leaned toward his guest. "My name is now Suzuki-san."

The chairman of Suji Corporation opened a passport to show his new identity, then passed a similar one to Hiromi. "Your new name is Takahashi." Both false names were as common in Japan as Smith or Jones in America. Of course, the whole idea of using fake passports shocked Hiromi and compounded his unease.

"Leave your real passport with my driver to avoid any suspicions with security or anyone else who might discover it. He'll have it for you when he picks us up from the return flight. Your credit cards, too. Here's more cash than you'll possibly need. You can keep whatever is left over," the executive said with a rather demeaning thrust of his hand stuffed with American dollars.

There was no more conversation on route to the airport. The powerful businessman also said little while they checked in, passed through security, cleared exit immigration, and sat comfortably in the first-class lounge of Japan Airlines for about an hour. Their flight to Honolulu was uneventful and the connections smooth. All but the passports and identity change seemed normal to Hiromi until they reached the hotel.

Suji summoned him to a spacious suite on the top floor of the resort and instructed Hiromi to sit down. He reviewed the strategy they had agreed upon. Charm the beautiful Suzanne Simpson to the extent she would agree to an unplanned meeting with Suji the next morning. At that meeting, Hiromi would act as a translator while the chairman tried again to persuade the woman to win the support of her board of directors to buy his company. Once more, the powerful businessman assured Hiromi he'd make Suzanne an offer she couldn't refuse. Uncomfortable with the whole circumstance, Hiromi agreed to do his best.

"But your best might not be enough, Takahashi-san," the businessman replied with a refined tone, eyebrows arched, and his smile menacing. "You will not only accomplish the goal but also exceed it. We're going to raise the stakes. You will not only seduce the woman but also get a photo of your magnificent penis lodged comfortably in her mouth."

Hiromi recoiled at the suggestion and didn't hide his distaste. "Suji-san ... I mean Suzuki-san ... I could never do that to a woman—especially a lady I hold in high esteem." His voice quivered.

"Take your high esteem and shove it up your ass," the chairman spat, now more threatening and vulgar. "I want the woman ready to agree when we hold our little discussion on Sunday morning. You'll do exactly what I said. You'll put this powder in her drink, drag her up to your room, strip her, rape her, and take a photo with your cock deep inside her petulant little mouth."

"I can't do that," Hiromi whispered. This man obviously wanted to debase and destroy Hiromi but now intended the same for Suzanne Simpson.

"You will do it, you groveling worm," the chairman scorned. "Agree to it, or I make one call and some disgusting photos with your face in places it should never be will arrive on your minister's phone. This is not a negotiation. It's an order."

His mission had tormented him ever since they first demanded he set up the get-together with Suzanne in Hawaii. He hated being used in such a crude and obvious way but had few options. That would end with his return to Japan in a couple days. Suji-san specifically promised to destroy the incriminating videos if Hiromi did everything they asked.

He ordered flowers and a bottle of chilled champagne for delivery to her room before she arrived. Such gifts charmed American women, and it was now crucial for Suzanne to respond to his allures. There was far more riding on his success.

The breathtaking beauty and lush surroundings of the posh resort didn't impress him, but Hiromi spent several hours walking, thinking, and desperately looking for a way out. He found none. His despair grew.

When Suzanne arrived with her security detail, only the huge man and the African-American woman were with her. Unlike in Japan, they apparently were satisfied no special language skills or cultural sensitivities were required for Hawaii.

Suzanne again looked radiant. He loved that English word because it not only described her extraordinary beauty but also evoked her joy and outlook. She was delighted to see him again, just as he would feel if his current quagmire hadn't sucked him in. But he took care to convey none of his anxiety to her scrutinizing eyes.

They embraced warmly and enjoyed a long and sensual kiss of welcome before she suggested the security detail leave them alone while they walked around the property. They strolled for an hour—talking, holding hands, and laughing warmly at each other's jokes. Clearly, Suzanne enjoyed his company and responded to his charm.

They had salads and iced tea for lunch while they planned their two days together. After a short chat about several touristy alternatives, Suzanne suggested they take a helicopter ride. Hiromi agreed immediately. They made the arrangements, took a shuttle bus to the airfield, and enjoyed a ride of more than two hours at a price Suzanne negotiated with the pilot before departure. The security detail joined them on their trip but stayed in the rear seats with no interruption to the pleasure Suzanne and Hiromi shared up front with the pilot.

She pointed to spectacular volcanoes, lakes, and scenery below. They touched each other often and shared looks of appreciation, happiness, and contentment as the helicopter tour thrilled them again and again. Hiromi performed his task well.

"I'm so glad you suggested we meet here in Hawaii, Suzanne said as they finished the ride. "I love the island and the resort you picked is my favorite. You seem to know exactly how to win my heart."

Back at the hotel, they changed into swimsuits and waded in the pool or lounged around its perimeter for a couple hours before they went to their respective rooms to shower and change for dinner. Laughing, Suzanne pretended to scold him for taking an adjoining room and playfully threatened to move a heavy piece of furniture in front of the joining door.

They parted with more sensuous kisses and exploratory touches. She moved away though when he touched the skin just above her left breast for the first time.

"Later," she said suggestively before she unlocked her door and swept in, closing and locking the door firmly behind her.

Dinner was delicious. Suzanne ordered for both, returning the courtesy Hiromi had shown in Tokyo almost three years earlier. She ordered a California white wine that tasted like an award-winning vintage. Their appetizer was a shared bowl of giant shrimp, tasty with a slightly spicy sauce. The beef tenderloin was even more flavorful than Kobe beef from Japan and just as tender. The fresh fruit dessert featured ripe Hawaiian pineapples and was the perfect light and sweet combination to finish a meal.

They took another walk around the property. The lights on the trees, shrubs, and flowers created a new sense of magic. Hiromi pulled her more tightly to him and they sauntered with their arms around each other's backs, marveling at the moon, appreciating the sounds of the evening, and talking more softly and tenderly. He felt her unspoken love.

After they went back inside the resort, Hiromi suggested a nightcap in the spacious lounge that included a string quartet playing soft tunes. Suzanne agreed, and they ordered another bottle of wine. Their conversation evolved from flirtatious to amorous. Hiromi received signals that all was on track and felt both joy and horror at the same time. But he made sure his facial expressions reflected only serene happiness.

When she needed to visit the ladies' room, Hiromi carefully scrutinized the lounge to see if anyone was watching. Suzanne had dismissed her security detail, and they were nowhere in sight. He paid particular attention to another Japanese man sitting a few tables away, also with a light-skinned American-looking woman. They seemed engrossed in their own conversation. And the few other patrons all appeared focused on their own little worlds.

Hiromi discretely took the small envelope from his pocket, shifted its contents to one end, and deftly poured it all into Suzanne's glass of white wine in one motion. He stared at the glass as he watched the tiny crystals dissolve slowly and blend transparently with the amber liquid until there was no evidence of the powder apparent in the glass.

A few minutes after Suzanne returned to the table, she took a sip. She didn't notice anything, but Hiromi felt knots in his stomach. It took full concentration to maintain his smile and deliver a light-hearted comment about their day. She took another sip after telling him how much she enjoyed everything they did together and this one was almost a gulp. Suji-san told him to move quickly after Suzanne took a couple sips of the wine.

"Let's get some fresh air again." Hiromi rose from the table without waiting for a response. He reached out and playfully tugged Suzanne upright. In the same motion, he slipped his arm around her back. With the other hand, he left a hundred-dollar note on the table.

By the time they reached the lobby, Suzanne already showed signs of fatigue.

"Wow, I can't believe how tired I feel all of a sudden. Let's go upstairs instead." She stifled a yawn.

As the elevator doors opened, Suzanne's head dropped gently against his shoulder, and her body became heavier. By the time the elevator doors opened at their floor, Suzanne was no longer conscious. Hiromi kept her upright. Within a few more steps, her weight became a struggle. He dragged her the forty or fifty feet to the door of her suite. Beads of sweat dripped from his brow as he breathed more deeply, still trying to maintain a casual walking pace.

At her door, Hiromi tried to balance her body with one hand while he searched in her bag for the key with his other. Unsuccessful after a minute or two, he decided instead to take her into his room. That key was easy to access and there would be less chance of discovery by another guest.

Just as the door to his room sprung open, Hiromi heard the elevator doors open and glanced backward. As he turned, two huge hands powerfully gripped his upper arms and pulled back on them violently.

He shrieked in agony from the vicious snap of each shoulder dislocating or breaking. The pain was excruciating. They threw him to the floor and Hiromi tried to reach toward his injuries but couldn't move either arm. He managed to raise his head just enough to see someone had snatched the drugged body of Suzanne Simpson. They were dragging her away.

Someone removed his money and passport from his pockets before strong hands dragged him by his feet through an open door. Tears distorted his vision. Someone lifted his head from the floor and wrapped an arm tightly around his neck. With one violent wrench, everything ended.

FIFTY

A tiny apartment, New York, NY
Saturday February 16, 2019

The day before marked three full weeks Janet Weissel had been back at her job with CBA Investment Bank. As she relaxed and watched the tiny television she had shipped from Chicago with the rest of her things, she started her second glass of the cheap wine she'd picked up earlier that afternoon. It was time to think more about how that job was going. More accurately, it was time to think about how it was not going anywhere at all.

She couldn't recall a time in her life that was more boring. Every morning, she sought some menial task just to stay awake. Her new boss—Arleen, the gorgeous woman who used to work with Multima's union—had spoken to her exactly three times. Each time, the bitch had created some mindless assignment a high school junior could complete within minutes and told her to take her time preparing it. It was just for background color.

Janet's initial hope that the familiar face who became her boss might be able to help advance her personal goal to escape the clutches of The Organization fell flat. She'd failed to establish any kind of rapport with the woman, and her suspicion the bitch might go both ways and respond to sexual advances also proved wrong. She only needed to watch how the woman chatted up the young studs around the office. They practically drooled from her attention, and the woman likely satisfied sexual urges with compliant male interns or junior analysts.

Since her first day back on the job and her welcome meeting with Abe Schwartz, Janet hadn't even seen the man. His massive private office was located on another floor of the building, and he seldom visited the lower-level peons. Regardless, there had been no memo of instructions, no email, no voice mail. Nothing.

Of course, it had also been impossible to connect with Giancarlo Mareno. Few called the powerful leader of The Organization. If he wanted to speak with you, he called. Such a lapse in communication was a little disconcerting to her. After his sympathy, support, and almost daily calls following the vicious knife attack, the current communications void was worrisome. The last time she'd heard from the big man he also told her Douglas Whitfield would soon be in touch to coordinate next steps in the deal they wanted to engineer between Multima Corporation and Jeffersons Stores.

After all, that was the only purpose of her job at CBA. So why was Douglas Whitfield incommunicado? Was he following some alternate instructions from Mareno? Had Knight caused a new complication? Was there a new twist between Jeffersons Stores and Multima they didn't want to reveal?

To pass the time, she flicked off the comedy rerun and grabbed her iPad instead. A quick Google search of news related to both companies produced only stories picked up from mundane media releases or the occasional story about an analyst's updates. She read them all and found nothing new or of interest.

Janet rechecked her messages, looked at her social media feeds for a few minutes, and found nothing that piqued her interest. On a lark, she decided to do a Google search for Douglas Whitfield. She hadn't done one since the first time she'd met him in Fort Myers almost three years earlier and wondered what she might find now.

She was stunned to see the first listing was a *Barbados Today* story with the headline "Barbadian Born Businessman Laid to Rest." She read the complete story as tears trickled from the corners of her eyes. There was no doubt. The article referred to the same Douglas Whitfield. His listed mother's name was exactly as she remembered it from her first research. But the story made no sense.

Died of gunshot wounds. Body mysteriously delivered to police by unknown persons. No knowledge of man's whereabouts since 2017. Mother distraught and seeking answers. None of the information in the article seemed right. She'd seen him in Costa Rica only a few months earlier. They'd made passionate love together every day in Quepos.

With another glass of wine, Janet processed the shocking news more clearly, and the tears dried. Of course, his whereabouts were unknown to the world at large because New York newspapers had published speculation that Douglas had probably met the same end as his murdered friend Earnest Gottingham. Who could know how he was killed? Did Howard Knight somehow overtake him and use his own gun to kill Douglas? Did Mareno have anything to do with it?

Regardless, Janet felt hurt and anger—lots of anger. With unbridled fury, she stripped off the clothes she wore, slapped makeup on her face, sprayed perfume on her body, slipped on the sexiest short dress she owned, and strapped on her highest heels. She'd deal with her grief the only way she knew how.

FIFTY-ONE

A high-rise office tower, Shenzhen, China
Sunday February 17, 2019

Two days before, Wilma had joined a conference call with Suzanne Simpson while she set out her objectives to Michelle Sauvignon and asked for the get-together in China. The casual and relaxed way Suzanne outlined her ideas to her close college-days friend impressed Wilma. Almost immediate interest from the leader of Farefour Stores China surprised her too.

Their entire conversation took a scant fifteen minutes and the bond of confidence between the two seemed extraordinarily strong.

"Gordon Goodfellow will just tag along," Suzanne summed up at the end of their call. "I was so captivated with your operations there in China I'd like my Supermarkets president to have a glimpse at what's possible. As we already agreed, James Fitzgerald will lead our delegation and discuss the overarching details with you. Wilma will focus on ideas related to Multima Financial Services. They'll bring me up-to-date when they get back. If you need me, I'll be in Hawaii on a brief vacation, but don't hesitate to call. I'll have my phone with me."

Wilma Willingsworth had to shake her head a few times after that call. First, she rarely traveled outside the United States. When she did travel, Canada and the Caribbean were the only locations she explored. For this trip, the recently appointed president of Multima Financial Services found it necessary to dash home and locate her passport before she could agree to Suzanne's request.

Fortunately, the passport was still valid for another year, so Wilma told her CEO she'd get the required visa and take an overnight flight to China for the meeting with Michelle Sauvignon. Then she spent several hours on the internet learning what she could about China and the sprawling new city she was to visit. The information was astounding. A fishing village until the Chinese leader Deng opened China's borders to foreign interests at the end of the last century, the famous business center near Hong Kong was now larger than virtually every city in the US, with over twelve million inhabitants.

Shenzhen was also the home of Farefour Stores headquarters in China, the same building Suzanne had visited only weeks earlier. Immediately after their arrival, Wilma and her companions completed the same eye-popping

Unrelenting Peril

tour that so impressed the CEO of Multima. They were all amazed as their host casually demonstrated the environment, functions, robotization, and logistics capabilities of the enormous warehouse.

Once the meeting started, James Fitzgerald led off for the Multima team. His PowerPoint presentation was masterful. He visually painted a picture of how their respective organizations looked today and how they might evolve should both companies work together.

His presentation graphics were effective, showing where the companies could come together for mutual benefit and identifying which segments were problematic. James's mastery of the details was mesmerizing.

Wilma had always held her predecessor in high regard. But his command of the situation during the discussions with Michelle rose beyond any presentation Wilma could remember. He used all the right words: cooperation, synergies, collaboration, interactions, savings, growth, profits. He used them often with sincerity and respect. She particularly liked the way he portrayed an admiration for both companies and their respective strengths. His soft-spoken delivery was soothing and reassuring. He checked all the boxes for a textbook successful negotiation.

Wilma thought Michelle appeared comfortable with the direction of their talks. She made point-form notes. She asked questions that showed not only interest but also active analysis of the information. Her facial expression was primarily neutral, but occasionally tiny creases in her brow betrayed discomfort. James noticed the signals. Each time, he probed more deeply to ascertain the real concern and addressed it.

When it was Wilma's turn to describe the financial aspects, Michelle again showed an active interest and absorbed the numbers easily. She asked good questions to clarify and was even prepared with some equally attractive alternative structures. Everyone seemed pleased with the financial outline and their general progress.

Something changed. Over the past couple hours, Michelle's answers became more superficial, perhaps masking underlying concerns. Despite Fitzgerald's considerable skill and Wilma's patient financial review, they finally came to a point where Michelle Sauvignon thought it best to have a conversation with Suzanne in Hawaii. They glanced at their watches and saw it was about ten o'clock Saturday evening in Hawaii.

"Maybe not the most convenient time to reach a CEO on a vacation," Michelle said with a relaxed laugh and a casual wave to suggest her old friend would forgive them if the time of the call proved inopportune. They all listened to the phone ring from the speaker on the boardroom table. It rang at least a dozen times before defaulting to voicemail where Michelle left a message asking Suzanne to call them as soon as possible.

James Fitzgerald took another run at solving the impasse when it became apparent Suzanne wasn't immediately available. Michelle Sauvignon again engaged patiently and politely, but she withheld agreement to their proposal. She insisted that she needed to connect with Suzanne.

As the clock advanced toward the dinner hour in China, there was still no call from Suzanne. Reluctant to abandon their discussions without agreement, James Fitzgerald suggested they take a break, freshen up, have a late dinner about nine o'clock, and try Suzanne in the wee hours of Sunday morning in Hawaii. Surely, with Suzanne's well-known penchant for returning phone messages quickly, they could connect with her by then.

They all agreed. As they relaxed in their hotel rooms, Wilma tried Suzanne's cell phone another three times without success. The group reconvened for dinner and enjoyed a feast until almost midnight. The mood was light, the food extraordinary, and James Fitzgerald returned to their meeting purpose often throughout the meal. But it was all to no avail. Michelle refused to divulge the sticking point until she spoke with Suzanne.

Wilma couldn't identify at precisely what point their talks veered off track, but they had undoubtedly reached an impasse. They decided to spend the night and hope for a call from Suzanne. About noon the next day, the Multima team thought it odd Suzanne Simpson hadn't returned their messages for a dozen hours but concluded their work in China was done.

After all that energy, time, and expense, they'd fly back to the US without either an agreement or a precise idea which direction their discussions should take next. It was going to be a quiet and unsatisfying flight.

FIFTY-TWO

An office tower near Wall Street, New York, NY
Monday February 18, 2019

Douglas Whitfield's death affected Janet more intensely than she expected. Her intention to drown her sorrows by partying like there was no tomorrow the night she received the news turned out to be a dud. Four glasses of some concoction whose name she no longer remembered dulled her senses only marginally. The pain remained real and intense.

A dozen or more usually acceptable males had hit on her over a few hours in the club. She would normally have let any one of them satisfy her needs. But in the end, she went home alone.

There, without warning, she burst into tears that gushed for what seemed like hours. She screamed out several times as grief overcame her, and she abandoned any effort to suppress the pain. The guy was a jerk. There was no doubt about that, but she loved Douglas like no one else. She had always believed something more satisfying and permanent would eventually develop in their relationship. This loss sucked. She couldn't imagine feeling more alone.

That weekend Janet slept long hours. When she was awake, she ate and drank little. She lacked the energy or will to exercise, leave the apartment, or perform any of the small tasks she might do on a typical weekend. Douglas's death haunted her thoughts.

She actually thought Giancarlo Mareno might call. If Whitfield was indeed his son, wouldn't it be normal for him to let her know personally he'd been killed? Would he not also feel a need to share some grief? Was it possible he didn't even sense the depth of her love for Douglas Whitfield? No. The man must lack the most fundamental human feelings. He was a machine, and his callous disregard of her during this tragedy intensified her resolve to find a way out.

But first, duty called. She needed to find a way to finish this business with CBA Investment Bank and their escapade to gain control of Multima Corporation. Reluctantly, she returned to the offices of CBA Investment Bank just as Mareno demanded.

Without warning, there was a sudden deluge. Just before nine, Abe Schwartz circulated an email to nearly half the company, demanding that everyone meet in the conference room on the third floor at nine-thirty sharp. Arleen, the bitch Janet reported to, sent another email about ten minutes later, telling everyone to bring their laptops to the meeting and—if they hadn't done so already—download the Microsoft Project app because they'd all need it for the meeting. Schwartz's orders.

Just as people got up from their desks to comply with those instructions, an email from some administrative assistant notified everyone the meeting would be delayed until ten o'clock. Then, Arleen sent another email with an attachment for everyone to read. It was a news clip from the *Wall Street Journal* about Jeffersons Stores and the expected resignation of their CEO later that morning. Before Janet could finish reading the entire speculative article, Schwartz sent another email advising the ten o'clock time would no longer work. Plan now for eleven.

Someone in a nearby workstation suggested they organize an office pool to guess what time this mysterious meeting would actually start. They hadn't finished laughing when the bitch sent yet another email, including links to three other wire service articles about the malaise at Jeffersons Stores. One suggested the board would be creating a committee to study strategic options.

Janet glanced up at a television monitor on the wall always set to CBNN—the commercial business news network they all checked from time to time for breaking business developments, stock prices, and currency trends. A banner floating across the screen in bright red graphics screamed *Lender Calls Jeffersons Stores Loans for February End.*

Janet looked at the calendar. The end of February was only ten days away. Somebody was clearly putting Jeffersons Stores in an extremely difficult position. Her fingers sped across the keyboard of her laptop to find out who that lender might be. Not surprisingly, the principal lender was CBA Investment Bank. Her employer was demanding repayment, before February 28, of all 3.27 billion dollars owing under an operating loan.

What the hell is going on?

Suddenly, a message from the bitch came by email. They needed to get to Schwartz's office pronto. Bring laptops.

Upstairs, chaos reigned. A dozen or more people milled around the perimeter of the large office talking in small groups. In one corner, Abe Schwartz had a mobile phone pressed to his ear and was loudly defending his position to another party who seemed to interrupt him every minute or two. His suit jacket lay crumpled on the arm of his elevated leather chair. His shirt sleeves were rolled up almost to his elbows. Perspiration beads dotted his brow despite the winter setting on the office thermostat. Actually, the office felt chilly.

An administrative aid scurried around the room handing out files with individual names on them and encouraged people to help themselves to coffee before they took a seat. In another corner, a vice president of something-or-other had shoehorned Arleen into a discussion that was so intense his burly stature blocked her view of the room and left little avenue for escape. Although Arleen stared at something on the floor, she appeared to listen intently. Every few minutes, she nodded either acknowledging or agreeing with everything the hefty vice president was telling her.

Outside the office, a crew from CBNN arrived and were loudly setting up lights, cameras, and assorted technical equipment necessary for some sort of interview. Another administrative person scurried about like an overgrown mouse as she tried to maintain some semblance of order. The television crew generally ignored her pleas and protests.

Janet took in all the confusion with curiosity and bemusement. Abe Schwartz had taken extraordinary action quickly. This was not the somber environment of a bank that treasured its reputation for careful analysis, prudent decision-making, and meticulous organization. What had influenced Schwartz to make such a dramatic announcement with seemingly little advance notice?

CBNN's presence was another curious situation. If Schwartz had just delivered the ultimatum to Jeffersons Stores, how did CBNN hear about the story so quickly? And how did they get an interview crew to the office in such a short time? Things were so chaotic Schwartz apparently forgot he called the meeting. He punched more numbers into his phone an instant after he said goodbye to the first caller. As he waited for the call to connect, he hurried from his office, seeking either refuge or privacy.

The heavily built vice president who had been talking at Arleen must have decided his message was adequately received and understood. Once finished, he spun on his heel, glared menacingly at the television crew outside the glass walls, and marched from the room without a word or gesture to anyone else in the room.

Arleen looked shell-shocked. She seemed to tremble as Janet discretely glanced across the room. Her beautiful complexion was gone. In its place, large red blotches covered her face and bare arms. She looked defeated and ready to burst into tears. The woman clutched her chest with both hands and breathed deeply, her eyes closed. Was she having some sort of medical emergency?

Apparently not. Arleen slowly opened her eyes and looked skyward for a moment as though she was asking for guidance from above. The second she noticed Janet looking her way, her million-dollar smile returned to its usual place with its usual charming intensity. The woman took a final deep breath and charged across the room toward Janet.

She wrapped her arm around Janet's shoulder and physically turned her to face the door.

"Let's go. There won't be a meeting here after all," she said. "We'll go to my office and I'll fill you in on all the details. But the main message is that by Friday we must develop and deliver to Suzanne Simpson a definitive proposal for Multima Corporation to buy Jeffersons Stores with a loan provided by CBA Investment Bank. That's the easy part. The other part of our mission may be a little more challenging. They insist it must be an offer that Multima Corporation can't refuse."

A definitive offer to buy a company they had not yet thoroughly analyzed? Within five days? A financing proposal for a loan of at least five billion dollars for a borrower they still didn't understand and hadn't worked on in over two months? Further, if they gave Suzanne Simpson the offer on Friday, she and the Multima team would have only six days—including a weekend—to make a decision that would double the size of the company in one stroke and involve more risks than Janet could even begin to imagine.

FIFTY-THREE

*A private medical clinic, Kauai, Hawaii
Monday February 18, 2019*

When Suzanne woke from sleep in the wee hours of Sunday morning in Hawaii, she was disoriented. She recognized her security detail but none of the others in the room. They spoke to her, but their voices only sputtered disjointed words. She couldn't understand what they said or why such a large group of people gathered around her.

Through partially opened eyes, she discerned two people in uniforms like those of law enforcement. The others were casually dressed or wearing brightly colored outfits. Maybe nurses, Suzanne realized as she focused on medical equipment and the sterile environment around her. The first time she stirred was brief. Despite trying to force her eyelids to remain open, she drowsily fell back to sleep.

When she roused a second time, she was struck by bitter nausea. Two women immediately guided her to a toilet. She disgorged everything in her stomach quickly but still felt drowsy and dizzy. Both nurses gripped her elbows for support when she wavered momentarily returning from the bathroom. After more sleep, her mind was clearer when she woke up for the third time. Her female bodyguard sat in a chair near the bed, reading a magazine.

"What happened?" Suzanne asked.

"Your Japanese friend slipped what they think is Rohypnol in your drink when you went to the ladies' room."

The date rape drug.

"No," she gasped. Horror and incredulity laced her voice.

Her friend, a man she trusted and was attracted to, had roofied her? Why? She hadn't shut him down. Impatience? It made no sense.

"You're wrong. He wouldn't." She swallowed around a lump in her throat, terrified of the implications. Had he raped her? She did a cursory body scan, starting with her vagina. No pain. No stinging or chafing sensations. Her terror eased, but only slightly.

"He got you to the entrance to his room but was intercepted by some unknown Japanese assailants. They were carrying you down the corridor towards the elevator when we all arrived on the scene. We freed you, hopefully with no injuries?" the African-American guard asked.

"I'm feeling fine. Just drowsy. What time is it?"

"The drug was very potent. For a while, they even considered whether they'd need to give you an antidote. You're sure you're not hurt?" the woman asked again.

"No, I'm fine but I'm a little embarrassed to make such an elementary mistake. I haven't worried much about getting drugged on dates since I was in college. It's not common in our crowd," Suzanne said. "You don't think anything happened ..."

"No." The female bodyguard replied emphatically. "There was no time. From the moment you left the lounge until we recovered you, no more than three minutes had elapsed. Nothing happened. Mr. Tenaka was not so lucky. He died before we arrived. It was definitely you they wanted."

"Died?" Suzanne questioned with alarm as she struggled to a sitting position on the bed. "What happened?"

"We think the bad guys were part of the Japanese organized crime world, the *Yakuza*. The best we can figure, they used Tenaka to woo you to Hawaii so they could seize you for some other purpose. Neither guy is talking, but they both have part of their fingers missing. It's called *yubitsume*, a practice common in the criminal underworld in Tokyo. It looks like they no longer needed Tenaka and killed him when they tried to snatch you."

The male bodyguard joined them, and Suzanne peppered both with questions about the incident until she was sure she understood everything. Then she asked the doctors a dozen more questions about their observations related to the drug, precautions she needed to take, and how the drugging might impact her travel back to the mainland.

The doctors patiently answered her questions while they poked and prodded around her throat and nose, gazed into her mouth, and checked reactions from her eyes with a few tests. They recommended she stay in the clinic one more night. She could leave Monday morning if everything still looked good. In the meantime, would Suzanne like to move to a more comfortable suite with a telephone and internet connection?

Alone, a sense of dismay enveloped Suzanne. She felt no compulsion to weep. It wasn't love she felt for Hiromi, but it was something greater than affection. Despite his flaws, she'd adored his company and regretted there would never be a chance for anything more to develop. She supposed their relationship probably was doomed from the beginning, but she still felt profound sadness. Death was so final, and it pained her that Hiromi's was so violent. But it was what it was.

Comfortably settled into a suite so luxurious she didn't want to know how much it cost, Suzanne was grateful for a call from John George.

Once he inquired about her condition and state of mind, he switched to his role of father.

"It's important to put yourself first for the next little while. Don't worry at all about the company. It will manage itself without you for a few days," he said with conviction.

"I know. I'll follow your advice and don't worry, I'm fine and I'll be home soon."

"Take your time. I did a little Google research about drugging in these types of cases. It seems the dosages these people slip into drinks are often much higher than needed to achieve their purpose. Those seeking to make mischief often seem to err on giving too large a dose to be sure the drug has its intended effect," he cautioned.

"I'll relax for a day, John George. And don't worry, I won't make any important decisions," she said with a laugh.

Later, Dan Ramirez also called. She chatted with him and brought the security guards into their conversation. Suzanne emphasized her gratitude for Dan's advice and the team's great work to keep her safe. She thought Dan might want to talk longer. She sensed he might have something more sensitive to share. But after a pause of a second or two, he formally shut down their conversation with his usual brief goodbye.

The remainder of her Sunday in Hawaii she did yoga, read part of a book her security detail bought for her, and tried to eat. Despite her best efforts, Suzanne had trouble keeping food down. After every meal or snack, nausea returned almost immediately. And she remained drowsier than she would like.

When the corporate jet left for Fort Myers, with a refueling stop in San Diego, Suzanne was determined to push herself to full recovery during the eight-hours flying time. For the first couple hours, she read and responded to email. After a cup of good Hawaiian coffee, she switched to the paper files jammed into her briefcase. Then she read a stack of articles her staff had clipped from publications they thought would be of interest as she traveled.

Dan Ramirez called again, causing her to tense up.

"You might not have heard. CBA Investment Bank publicly announced they're calling the loans they have with Jeffersons Stores. The market is panicking. Jeffersons' shares have dropped thirty percent on the New York exchange today. Normally I wouldn't phone you with that kind of news, but this might also relate to another call I got. The rogue unit's plant inside The Organization reported in today too. This Friday, CBA Investment Bank will supposedly present you a loan offer to back your purchase of Jeffersons Stores. An offer you can't refuse."

Suzanne spent another half hour talking with her chief of corporate security. She drilled down on the message they received to parse every word and discuss the possible implications for Multima. What did the phrase "can't refuse" imply? Would the offer come with a subtle threat or another bomb attack on a Multima store to weaken Suzanne's resolve? Were extra security measures needed? What action should they take in the few days before this supposed offer arrived from CBA Investment Bank? She was exhausted after the call.

Without setting down her phone, Suzanne pressed a speed dial number for James Fitzgerald. Her highly paid consultant was in the air with Wilma Willingsworth, so she asked him to switch on the speaker and all could conference openly.

"Tell me all about your meeting with Michelle Sauvignon in China," Suzanne said as soon as they were both on the line.

"We tried to reach you while we were with Michelle but couldn't connect with you. Is everything all right?" Wilma wanted to know.

"I'm sorry. I didn't get your messages," Suzanne replied.

Why didn't I see an alert on my phone?

Unwilling to discuss her misfortune in Hawaii, she ignored Wilma's question. "Was there a snag?"

"A snag would be a good way to describe it," James answered. "Michelle's body language was positive as we painted a picture of our intentions. She asked a lot of clarifying questions that clearly demonstrated interest. And she didn't push back on any specific issue. Strangest thing though. She refused to accept or reject the idea until she spoke with you personally. She just wouldn't budge."

"How did you leave it with her?"

"Our departure was very positive," Wilma answered. "Michelle was really apologetic about insisting she connect with you before moving forward. As James said, I think she's keenly interested. And call it intuition, but I sensed that it was just as important for her to speak to her father as it was to talk with you. During dinner, she mentioned that her father must have his phone off while he's traveling. I'm guessing that she'd tried to reach him as well at some point in our sessions."

"I expect that's the case," Suzanne replied. "They're very close. Should I try to call her, or might it be better to let her stew a couple days?"

"I'd recommend you try sooner rather than later. Without her support, the entire scheme becomes exponentially more difficult to pull off," James said.

"I agree," Wilma added quickly. "It's clear you guys have a special bond. I think she'll show her hand to you even if she doesn't have a green light from Jean-Louis Sauvignon. James is right. We can do it without her, but the deal becomes a lot easier to seal if she's with us."

"OK, I'll call her today and let you know. In the meantime, let's discuss next steps to be sure we're all on the same page."

For the next hour, the three executives dissected James Fitzgerald's plans again. They confirmed the timing. They reviewed individual responsibilities and follow-up. They double and triple checked the sequence of events. When all were satisfied, Suzanne made one final request before signing off.

"Wilma, if you can manage without your jet for a few days, I think it better for James to take it and set up shop in Paris until we're done," Suzanne suggested with little room for discussion. None was required.

As soon as she finished the call with James and Wilma, Suzanne pressed another speed dial number to call Norman Whiteside. Her leader of the new special task force to deal with this unfolding drama was with his team in Chicago. At Suzanne's prompting, he pressed the speaker button on his phone so everyone could participate.

"It's going to be a hectic week, folks," Suzanne started with a tone as lighthearted as she could manage. "We'll need to shift gears and pick up the pace of our research. First, let's set aside everything you've been working on related to Suji Corporation. We won't be pursuing anything with them. Don't think of your work as wasted; we never know what might happen in the future, but I have no intention of proceeding further at this stage."

Suzanne paused, just in case any of the participants on the call wanted to clarify her instructions to abandon a project to which they'd just devoted several weeks of effort. No one did, so she took another sip of her coffee and continued.

"It looks like things might heat up with Jeffersons Stores. Nothing concrete yet, but there's a chance we'll see something before the end of the week. Norman, deploy your resources as you see fit, but here's what I'd like before Friday. Let's get our hands on a copy of the loan agreements Jeffersons have with CBA Investment Bank. They should be in the SEC filing. If there's not enough detail there to see all the undertakings and events of default, call Dan Ramirez in corporate security. He might be able to get a copy. Work with Albert Ferer in legal to analyze the implications of anything unusual."

"You want the document CBA relied upon to call their loans last week, right?" Norman Whiteside clarified.

"Yes, exactly. We need to understand what made it so difficult for Jeffersons to comply, giving CBA an excuse to call the loans. Then, I'd like to see detailed cash flow projections for Jeffersons over the next two years—the most detailed you can build from publicly available information. Get someone to drill down on every analyst report available. I think they have fourteen or fifteen following the company. We're looking at any hint of negative comment. Have someone pose as a private investor to contact every analyst who made a negative comment and get background for their negatives. Then, check each analyst's latest views on every issue he or she raised. Find out as well if they had any new concerns before the loan was called," Suzanne instructed.

"You're looking for all the dirt we can find, right?" Whiteside wanted to confirm.

"Precisely," Suzanne said. "I'd like to make this duckling look as ugly as possible. Have a team model our numbers, too. Get your folks together with the Supermarkets' finance resources at headquarters and update our own cash flow projections. Develop a model where we assume all Jeffersons debt at its current level."

For another few minutes, Suzanne continued to identify in granular detail all the information about Jeffersons Stores they needed to amass and get to her no later than Friday noon. When she finished, the team recapped their understanding. Suzanne could detect excitement mounting in their voices as they processed and articulated the enormity of their task and its significance to the company.

Satisfied her information needs were clearly understood and achievable by Friday morning, Suzanne dismissed the team and made one more call with the press of a speed dial button.

"Good afternoon, Michelle," she chirped when the ringing stopped. "I understand you'd like to chat."

FIFTY-FOUR

A plush penthouse apartment, Miami, FL
Wednesday February 20, 2019

Howard Knight had lived in the luxurious penthouse apartment for about a month. It was confining though. He hadn't been outside the suite the entire time and his patience was wearing thin. He tried to keep active, but he'd added a bit of a paunch with the great food his minder prepared combined with far less physical activity than usual.

He worked out for about an hour every morning but found it boring. He walked around inside the suite to have something to do every hour or two but spent the rest of his waking hours watching television or answering questions for the FBI. The chief interrogator— "Owen. That's all you need to know"—claimed things were simmering with The Organization file. The political climate was changing.

"Our guys upstairs think our chances of getting indictments have improved measurably. By at least fifty percent," he said one day. Owen rode up the elevator to the suite every morning punctually at nine o'clock. Howard's minder would greet the well-dressed young man, then leave for errands while Owen grilled Howard with questions for about three hours. At noon, his minder would ring the buzzer, and Owen would release the lock before he packed up his briefcase to leave. It was the same routine every day.

Howard first found the questions annoying. Most of them were the same questions they'd asked him and recorded when he was incarcerated in Guantanamo over a year earlier. One day Owen finally explained why.

"Every afternoon, when I leave here, I go back to the office and analyze your responses to my questions. I've got an app that checks both versions for discrepancies. We can detect any minor variances. When it's time to testify, we'll know precisely which questions you're able to answer with no variances. We'll focus on those in court. It'll be more difficult for the defense attorneys to trip you up with minor details. Some trials are lost because of a tiny contradiction that destroys the credibility of a witness."

Answering the questions again was monotonous, but Howard's recall was almost total. Even Owen marveled at the consistency. He claimed to have never seen such a clear memory. And all this was important even if a little unpleasant. After all, this was to secure his release, another new identity, and a more stable future.

On the negative side, neither his interrogator nor Howard's minder knew when the indictments would start.

"It all depends on the guys upstairs," Owen always said with a shrug. His minder never even gave him that much. He limited his response to an identical shrug.

They must learn that at Quantico.

This morning, there was finally a new development. The tall, refined gentleman who'd once led the FBI—but didn't introduce himself during his first visit—returned.

"Do you know a woman named Janet Weissel?" the man politely inquired after the brief pleasantries were out of the way. Howard only nodded in acknowledgment and waited for the visitor to explain.

"We've been led to believe you know her very well, is that correct?"

"Yes," Howard replied. "She reported to me when I was part of The Organization. Extremely bright. Columbia grad. Completely amoral."

"What do you mean 'amoral'?" the gentleman inquired.

"She came from a bad family. They threw her out when University became too expensive for their comfort. Janet worked her way through college as a call girl. Don't know from personal experience, but word was that she was nothing short of phenomenal in bed. Ran her own private business. Videotaped everything. Made even more money by blackmail. No moral compass at all, so she was perfect for our needs." Howard grinned.

"What did The Organization have her doing at Multima?"

"While I was a director at Multima, we planted her on the communications team," Howard explained. "Her main job was to report back bits of information to me. If we needed something from a file, she'd get it and send it over to me. She slept with a couple directors on the board and a few financial analysts on Wall Street to keep them pliable."

"Can you give me an example?"

"As I told you, she videotaped all her Johns, even if she was fucking them for us. If we needed a guy on the board to support a particular corporate direction and that director was reluctant to support us, a gentle reminder of the videos usually brought him around. Same with the analysts. If we needed a report skewed in a certain direction, analysts would usually see the wisdom of changing their recommendation or investment rating on Multima Corporation. We didn't do it often but planned for the days when leverage might be needed."

"Was that her only role at Multima?"

"While I was there," Howard replied. "Later, I heard from Douglas Whitfield that Multima management shuffled her off to some obscure marketing job in Chicago. But that was after I left the board."

"Do you have any idea what she's doing now?"

"Not entirely," Howard lied. "Before he died, I heard from Whitfield that she might be back in New York, but I can't be sure."

The tall gentleman shifted uncomfortably in his chair as he weighed the response. Howard sensed the man wasn't quite buying what he was selling, but Janet was really a victim of all the crap in The Organization. Maybe Howard had become comfortable incriminating the leaders of the criminal outfit, but he saw no benefit to throwing foot soldiers under the bus as well.

The gentleman from the FBI pulled out his telephone and clicked his thumbs on its keyboard a few times until he found what he was looking for.

"How does Abe Schwartz fit into all this?" the gentleman asked, his tone more assertive.

It was Howard's turn to pause and think carefully before answering. He assessed what the FBI might know. Right from the beginning, they made it clear his answers to questions had to be truthful. If they caught him in a lie, the whole protection deal could be scuttled. Schwartz might be a victim too, but Howard wasn't prepared to jeopardize his own survival by protecting the man.

"Now that you mention Abe Schwartz's name, you remind me where you might find Janet," Howard said with his most neutral expression.

The gentleman cocked his head to one side inquisitively and waited for Howard. For about an hour, Howard explained Abe Schwartz's unfortunate gambling addiction and the way The Organization exploited his compulsion to risk large sums of money until they ultimately controlled every major decision his company made. He explained how The Organization laundered billions of dollars through CBA Investment Bank to infiltrate—and then effectively control—dozens of legitimate businesses.

Howard answered the gentleman's questions about the methods used by The Organization to increase their influence and control over both CBA and borrowers from the investment bank. He was astonished by how quickly the tall gentleman absorbed the information and asked follow-up questions that showed a keen understanding of business, business law, and loan documentation. When Howard finished his explanation, the famous visitor asked what he promised would be his final question.

"If you were advising Giancarlo Mareno the best way to gain control of Multima Corporation, what would you tell him?"

By that point, Howard was not surprised by the question. A person known to be as astute, analytical, and brilliant as the man facing him had no doubt connected most of the dots between Janet Weissel, Abe Schwartz, and Giancarlo Mareno.

His deal for protection required him to answer all questions truthfully, but this one called for an opinion rather than facts about The Organization's activities. Any answer required some speculation. Howard deduced the critical link they needed to create. With the best poker face he could manage, Howard replied, "I'd tell him to forget about it, let it go. The company just isn't worth the trouble."

The gentleman wasn't entirely satisfied with his answer and appeared tempted to challenge—or at least follow up—but apparently remembered and respected his promise to make it his last question. As the man looked directly at Howard and thanked him for his information, he rose from his chair and gathered up his phone and notes.

Howard decided to try once more. If anyone knew, it would be the tall gentleman.

"Do you have any idea when the FBI will issue indictments and get this show underway?" he asked with just the hint of a grin.

The gentleman displayed a patient and kind expression for a moment. Then he shrugged and walked away.

FIFTY-FIVE

An office tower near Wall Street, New York, NY
Friday February 22, 2019

Abe Schwartz was clearly feeling more pressure than he could comfortably handle. Throughout the entire six days since they started the crazy assignment, Janet Weissel couldn't remember seeing him without beads of perspiration on his brow, his shirt sleeves rolled up to his elbows, his tie askew, and his manner agitated.

He called Arleen every half hour demanding some new study or a copy of a document or a new spreadsheet that changed all the assumptions to some new scenario. Janet found it difficult to discern any logical pattern to his demands or any method to the apparent madness.

She had to hand it to her boss though. Arleen didn't seem fazed by it at all. After the first two days of the chaos, she started popping down the corridor to Janet's cubicle.

"It's easier to explain his demands to you in person," Arleen offered with a sympathetic smile and nervous laugh. "He's under a lot of pressure with this one. We'll just have to tolerate his moods and the additional stress he creates, handling it all as best we can."

Easy for you to say. Janet returned a tight smile before changing course for the umpteenth time that day. The primary challenge seemed to be finding a way to profitably manage the loan CBA Investment Bank wanted to make to Multima Corporation. That loan dominated every conversation and was the focal point of all the confusion.

Apparently, Abe Schwartz felt their offer needed to be much lower than CBA Investment Bank's usual prime rate. Multima wouldn't be interested otherwise. But CBA's costs of borrowing and servicing the debt were just too high to make a profit with anything lower than prime.

Whoever Schwartz was borrowing from wasn't prepared to lower their expectations. Regardless of the rate Abe offered to Multima, the undisclosed party still wanted its regular rate of return. CBA would just have to find a way to reduce its cost of servicing the loan.

Janet had little doubt the mysterious person was Giancarlo Mareno himself. This deal was too important for the head of The Organization to delegate to some lieutenant. If she knew Mareno, the huge man would be sitting in a comfortable chair somewhere, his massive hands making the phone held to his ear look like a child's toy, while he worked his resources around the globe at all hours of the day and night.

The powerful man's calls to Abe Schwartz likely represented only a small percentage of his conversations, so Mareno's manner was probably already gruffer and more intimidating than usual. For some weird reason, she even felt a little sorry for the harried bank president.

In contrast, Arleen thrived on the atmosphere. She still spent a lot of time with the young analysts, but she talked with them about the Multima deal rather than flirtatiously fishing for a good lay. Janet grudgingly came to admire the intricate details the woman wove into their proposal as it took shape. She really seemed to understand the stuff.

The past thirty-odd hours had been the worst. Thursday morning, Janet arrived at the office as usual about eight o'clock. Arleen Woodhaus was already there meeting with Abe Schwartz in his office. A receptionist instructed Janet to get her tiny ass up to the president's office immediately. The ordinarily cheerful and charming woman showed none of her usual good humor as she rolled her eyes and made chopping motions with her hands to emphasize the importance of her message.

As Janet entered the sprawling office, Abe Schwartz was lecturing Arleen about the proper presentation of a document as crucial as a loan offer to Multima Corporation. Did she realize the entire future of their bank rested on this deal?

Finally, the terms of the proposal to be delivered by noon the next day were deemed adequate. Schwartz had satisfied the funders of the loan and found a way for CBA Investment Bank to eke out a meager profit. There was no quarrel there. All the angst related to how they planned to summarize and present the deal.

"We need every slide of the PowerPoint to jump off the screen," Abe emphasized. "We'll have to get Suzanne Simpson's attention so powerfully she's forced to take the proposal to her board of directors. She's already going to be a little pissed we're just giving her six days to study, negotiate, and accept the deal."

They spent the rest of the morning trying to develop an initial slide to present the deal as compellingly as Abe had demanded. Right after a quick lunch at her desk, Arleen called again from the president's office.

"We need to make more changes. Come upstairs again, right away." Arleen hung up without waiting for a response.

Someone in finance found an error in the costing formulas. The deal would no longer make a satisfactory profit for CBA Investment Bank. Janet and Arleen needed to get with the finance team and review the profit-and-loss projection again, line by line.

That exercise took them well into the night. One of the participants even fell asleep as Arleen was asking a question, but they eventually found ways to trim expenses without increasing risk to the bank.

After midnight, Janet was packing her bag to leave when Arleen buzzed her. There was another problem. Abe Schwartz was on his way back to the office and wanted them to stay. The funder of the loan wanted them to reduce the rate further to make it even more difficult for Suzanne Simpson to reject the deal out of hand. They had to rework everything to reflect an annual loan rate one full percent lower.

The sun rose as Janet and a couple analysts from the finance team finally hit the send button on her computer and delivered the reworked proposal to Arleen. She would discuss it with Abe as soon as both arrived at the office. No one should leave yet.

Janet learned there was a shower in Abe Schwartz's office and a secretary told her it would be okay to freshen up there. Cleaner and somewhat refreshed, she was just leaving the private bathroom when the president dashed into his office, still talking with someone on his phone as he trudged across to his desk.

Noticing Janet, he motioned for her to sit down in one of the chairs facing his desk. He looked even more haggard than usual. His clothes were so rumpled she wondered if he had slept in them, if he had slept at all. He paced nervously behind his desk as he listened to the other party. His eyes looked somber. His shoulders slumped as though completely defeated. His hand holding the headset trembled as he continued to apologize profusely for his misunderstanding. He took full ownership for the mistake and assured the person everything would still be ready for delivery at precisely noon.

When he finished the call, he didn't sit down. Instead, he turned his back to Janet, held both hands to his face for a moment, took an audibly deep breath, and hung his head for a second or two before he turned to face her. His eyes were distant, no sign of life beyond the pupils. In a tone barely above a whisper, he finally spoke.

"We can't wait for Arleen to get in. I'll need you to tweak the proposal again. The funder wants another quarter percent, twenty-five basis points. The lending rate to Multima can't increase. Talk with the guys in finance and get them to rework the spreadsheets to see how much we'll lose on the deal. Get that done quickly and call me with the bottom line number. When Arleen arrives, come back up here. I want us all to do one last review of the spreadsheets and presentation before we email the offer at noon."

Dismissed, Janet followed the instructions. It took only a few minutes for a financial analyst to recalculate the numbers. He inserted the lower rate to reflect a reduction of one-quarter of one percent and watched the

Excel spreadsheet spit out the new results. All color drained from his face as he pointed to the bottom line of the spreadsheet, to the huge number highlighted in red.

It was a negative twelve point five million dollars for every year of the loan! Over the term of the loan proposed to Multima, CBA Investment Bank would lose a staggering sixty-million dollars! How could they possibly survive that kind of deal?

To her amazement, when she called Abe Schwartz with the dire news, there was no immediate explosion of disbelief, anger, or frustration. He simply repeated the amount of the loss to verify his understanding, then reiterated his instruction to come back to his office with Arleen as soon as she arrived.

It was only a few minutes until Arleen popped in with a cheery "Good morning." They immediately took the stairs to Abe Schwartz's office. As they opened the door from the stairwell to the elegant lobby just outside the president's office, they heard a loud, piercing shriek.

Both women rushed into the office and took in the scene. An administrative assistant stood beside Abe Schwartz's desk screaming continuously despite her hands covering her mouth. Blood and gore spattered the desk, the ceiling, and all around the office. Schwartz's lifeless body was slumped forward on his desk with much of his brain missing.

Arleen rushed forward, whipped a phone from a pocket of her suit, and snapped a picture of the scene and a piece of paper on the desk. Then she calmly wrapped her arms around the screaming assistant and led her from the room. In shock, Janet tried to move away from the doorway but stood transfixed by the grotesque site before she vomited on the floor.

Arleen took charge. She seated both Janet and the assistant on sofas in the lobby, then called 9-1-1. She also made a few other calls Janet couldn't hear clearly as she sat traumatized, unable to absorb the horror of the scene. When the police and emergency workers arrived, they agreed Janet and the assistant could wait in Arleen's office where they would be more comfortable and away from the scene.

Arleen seemed to be upstairs for a lot of the morning while police were investigating the apparent suicide. Detectives came to retrieve Janet and the administrative assistant separately. One team took the assistant down the hallway. The other team interviewed Janet right there in Arleen's office.

It actually took longer than Janet expected. She thought they'd just ask her to describe what she saw when she went upstairs to discover Abe Schwartz's body. Instead, they wanted to know all about her career with CBA Investment Bank. When did she start working there? What was her job? How did she interact with Schwartz? Why was she in the office with him earlier? Why did she need to use his shower? What was his state of mind that morning? Who was he talking to on the phone? What did she hear?

Janet had trouble thinking clearly. She was exhausted. Her brain was foggy. Words failed to form easily. She stopped sentences mid-stream, forgetting the point she'd intended to make. Her hands trembled for a long time, and she inexplicably broke into tears more than once.

It seemed their flood of questions had no limit. Before she realized it, Janet had spent over two hours with the detectives, answering questions carefully and honestly. She tried to understand in which direction the detectives headed with their line of questioning.

Of course, she avoided any reference to Giancarlo Mareno, especially when she denied knowledge about who Abe Schwartz might have been speaking to before he instructed her to change the loan proposal for Multima Corporation.

Throughout the interview, Janet felt nauseated. She told the detectives, and they granted her brief breaks to drink water and compose herself during the especially gory parts they wanted her to describe. They never pressed her unreasonably for more details but cleverly circled back and framed their questions differently if they suspected she might have more to offer. Janet was impressed with their skill and compassion. She'd never thought of detectives as real human beings before.

When they released her, Arleen recommended she go home for the day, offered to call a cab, and escorted her down the elevator. It was a short three-floor ride, but Arleen used those few moments to silence Janet with a finger to her lips and tuck into her bag a tiny piece of paper. With a final hug as Janet left the elevator, Arleen whispered, "Read it now."

In the rear of the cab, Janet plucked the note from her bag and read the message. *Meet me here. 15 minutes.*

She read out the address to the driver.

FIFTY-SIX

Multima Corporation Headquarters, Fort Myers, FL
Friday February 22, 2019

"NYC police are on their way to a reported suicide in the president's office at CBA Investment Bank. The body is apparently Abe Schwartz, but they haven't made a positive ID," Dan Ramirez told Suzanne in his usual curt tone.

"What?" she gasped, stunned at the dramatic news. She took a deep breath and regained her composure before she cautiously replied, "How are we learning this news?"

"We have a way to monitor the NYC internal communications systems with keywords. Schwartz's name came up and my people checked it out. It's a fact. Plus, my guys from the rogue unit of the FBI were also aware within minutes of the 9-1-1 call. They have a source inside CBA Investment Bank, someone who actually saw the corpse."

"This is truly shocking." Suzanne switched her handset to its speaker, so Wilma Willingsworth could also hear the conversation. "Wilma and I were just reviewing our strategy for handling the loan offer you expected them to deliver today. How awful!"

"This will devastate his wife," Wilma added. "I've met her and she's the sweetest lady you can imagine. She and Abe were one of Manhattan's great love stories."

"I don't want to sound cynical, but I still expect there will be an offer related to Jeffersons Stores coming soon," Ramirez offered. "You folks probably know the circumstance better than I do. Schwartz may have been the sole owner of CBA, but my people think The Organization still has others inside and probably won't take long to recover."

"That's hard to imagine," Wilma ventured. "If I remember correctly, Abe had no children—certainly none involved in the business. And, I doubt he had much of a succession plan. Abe was really a one-man show when it came to decisions. He had a reasonable number of subordinates on his management team, but they all seemed to simply follow Abe's instructions."

"James Fitzgerald is meeting with Jean-Louis Sauvignon in France right now," Suzanne said, changing the subject. "How does this new development impact our discussions over there?"

"From a security perspective," Ramirez said, "I don't see any imminent danger. If you go ahead with the deal, CBA Investment Bank or someone else might still make you an offer related to Jeffersons Stores. It probably won't happen today, but I'll be surprised if you don't see something develop soon. I guess we see what happens on the 28th when the full loan payment Schwartz demanded comes due. We know Jeffersons can't pay it. What we don't know is how CBA will act on the default."

"If your information about the backer of the loan is right, and if The Organization is really funding the bank, will it really make any difference with the Jeffersons loan? If the money is ultimately owed to the underworld, won't they still expect to collect it?" Suzanne asked.

"Yeah, the money will still be owing to The Organization, but CBA might revoke the demand and give Jeffersons more time to pay," Wilma replied. "They could easily negotiate an extension. Like you say, a management team is in place at CBA."

"Yes, they might just take orders from a new grande capo. Maybe Giancarlo Mareno will give the marching orders himself," Ramirez interjected. "The Organization might see this as an opportunity to force our hand—expecting we might accept an even less favorable deal rather than watch CBA throw Jeffersons into bankruptcy, severely debasing the franchise."

There were a few moments of silence while the trio thought through the significance of what each had just said. Suzanne straightened in her chair and cleared her throat.

"Either way, I guess that means we should still expect to see an offer from CBA delivered one way or another. If we move forward in Europe, do we leave ourselves vulnerable?" Suzanne asked.

"I have to leave the grand strategizing to you people," Ramirez answered. "What you're doing in Europe is well outside my scope of expertise and probably way beyond my pay grade."

Suzanne suppressed a smile as she realized the chief probably didn't know he earned far more than Wilma and more than her own salary before she became CEO. John George Mortimer's obsession with security rewarded the man generously in the cost-conscious Multima corporate structure. Regardless, he was right. The business leaders on the team needed to assess the strategy, not the security experts.

Dismissing Ramirez with her usual thanks for informing her so quickly after the sad event, she hung up and devoted her full attention to Wilma.

"I think we need to get the entire team on the line, don't you?" Suzanne suggested.

"Agreed. I can get the acquisition folks up in Chicago on a video link. Would your assistant be able to get James hooked in?"

"Yeah. Sally-Ann will find a good excuse to interrupt James in the meetings. He'll have to invent some reason to push the pause button over there without arousing suspicion or concern with Sauvignon. While you and Sally-Ann cover those bases, I'll bring Gordon Goodfellow into the conversation. He's not in the loop on the details yet, but I'll swear him to secrecy and bring him up to date with what's going on," Suzanne advised.

Wilma Willingsworth nodded enthusiastically. Then, her forehead furrowed with a new concern.

"It's certainly your call," she said, "but I wonder if we didn't exclude Dan from our conversation a little too early. Might there be a chance we need him to use his less than orthodox sources for information or assistance at some point? Would it help if he had a first-hand understanding of the entire situation?"

"You're right, of course." Suzanne reached across the desk to gently touch the back of Wilma's hand. "I should have thought of that. Thanks for the good catch. I'll call him first, eat some humble pie, and get him in here."

They had to act quickly. It was already almost four o'clock in Avignon. James Fitzgerald would be finishing his discussions with Jean-Louis Sauvignon within a couple hours if everything went according to plan. If any changes were necessary, they needed to make them within the next few minutes.

Tomorrow morning Sauvignon would launch his part of their scheme.

FIFTY-SEVEN

A comfortable home with a pool, Avignon, France
Saturday February 23, 2019

James Fitzgerald cringed involuntarily when he saw the incoming video notification from Suzanne Simpson. He sensed there was a problem before he touched the screen to accept the call. As soon as the CEO shared the news of Abe Schwartz's suicide, his angst increased. He maintained a neutral expression and camouflaged his discomfort from the Sauvignons sitting across the table from him in the spacious living room.

However, Michelle detected that James might need privacy for a few moments and graciously suggested she and her father retire to the backyard to sit by the pool, leaving their guest some space for his conversation. James, too, expected the conversation would be a short one and was amazed when Suzanne opened the group discussion expressing her inclination to move forward with both schemes unless there were compelling risks she hadn't identified.

James bided his time—he was just a consultant after all. He switched his phone to video and listened while Wilma speculated about the probability of Mareno moving forward with the loan and acquisition proposal in the short term. Even The Organization would probably need a few weeks to replace Schwartz. CBA Investment Bank managed billions of dollars. First, they'd likely need to find and install a high-profile CEO the markets could trust.

Gordon Goodfellow once again counseled caution. He reminded the group how challenging their small acquisition of Price-Deelite a couple years earlier had been. That deal was a fraction of the complexity of the one contemplated with Farefour Stores. If it also became necessary to deal quickly with a possible Jeffersons Stores integration, it could strain the management resources at Multima.

Dan Ramirez pointed out the FBI's current psychological profile of Giancarlo Mareno suggested they were dealing with an extremely conservative personality, someone who made decisions slowly and deliberately, a man averse to risk and who took few chances. He also hinted that his former colleagues might be more advanced in their investigations of The Organization than many people realized.

Without interruption, Suzanne listened to input from each of her subordinates in Fort Myers and those linked in from Chicago. She telegraphed her keen interest in hearing their views and opinions with body language. After a few minutes, she asked James for his thoughts.

"Let me frame my biases for everyone," he said. "You all know I'm working here in France as a paid consultant. I'll also remind the group that I'm still a major shareholder. I've kept all my shares in the company, so I speak not only as a consultant but as an investor."

"I'm very mindful you still hold about five percent of the outstanding shares," Suzanne interjected calmly, probably to underscore the importance of his holding.

"There's also a question of my legacy with the corporation—how I'll be remembered for years to come—that enters my thought process," he continued with his usual deliberation. "We should focus our attention on the prospective deal with Farefour, not Jeffersons. Not because I'm here in France deeply involved in negotiations, but rather because this relationship—if we can pull it off—is a generational deal.

"An opportunity like this comes along only once or twice in a career," James continued. "A deal with Jeffersons or some other company of their ilk is fairly common and may become even more widespread as the supermarket business in America consolidates further. You analysts have had a better opportunity than I to look at the financial health of the companies, but would it be fair to say Farefour is the stronger company financially, and by quite a wide margin?"

There was a short silence on the call as everyone considered his argument. Suzanne prompted Norman Whiteside to comment.

"James is quite right," the leader of the new team focused on acquisitions said. "Farefour has a stronger balance sheet, far greater geographical reach, and huge potential for growth if they can replicate the financial services business in Europe to the same extent we've developed ours in America. If we had to make a choice between the two, my vote would definitely go to the Farefour scheme."

The debate continued for almost an hour as each participant voiced the pros and cons of the respective opportunities. James was a little uncomfortable with the long time the Sauvignons were cooling their heels outdoors by the pool, but he knew Suzanne needed to let the video conference serve its purpose.

She wants to build a consensus. They should move forward with the Farefour scheme regardless of what might arise with The Organization or with Jeffersons Stores.

They achieved that consensus as their conference reached the one-hour mark. With a grin of embarrassment, James invited the Sauvignons back inside and let them know about Abe Schwartz's untimely death. He didn't share any other details from the call, and the Sauvignons discretely didn't probe into the interruption any further. In fact, the pace of their discussions quickened when they resumed.

There was hesitation about the timing for each of the steps they considered. Both Sauvignons raised a dozen or more questions of clarification as they homed in on the deal. However, within just a couple more hours, the three had shaken hands on a deal that would rock the global supermarkets business—if they could pull it off.

As James now patiently waited for the Sauvignons to do their work, he continued to study the volumes of data related to the banking licenses Farefour had put in place across Europe. Even though it was a Saturday, he was able to reach recently developed contacts as necessary to clarify questions, still using the guise of a book he was planning to write. By day's end, he felt increasingly confident about their ability to make it work.

After he finished fifty laps of the pool and was drying off with a towel, his cell phone rang. It was Michelle Sauvignon and her message was succinct.

"My father has the support he needs. Tomorrow morning they'll announce a special meeting of the board to discuss the future of CEO Josef Aakker. By tomorrow evening, Farefour Stores will have a new business leader."

FIFTY-EIGHT

New York, NY
Friday February 22, 2019

It was a modest German restaurant with about twenty tables. When Janet arrived, the host asked her name, then guided her to a small private room at the rear of the restaurant. The area even had a separate door. When the maître d' closed it, Janet heard only the sounds of relaxing orchestral music playing softly until he returned with a cup of green tea and advised that Ms. Woodhaus was on her way and should arrive any minute.

When she arrived, Arleen offered no formal greeting. No smile. No encouragement.

"If you continue along the current path, what you saw today will be you," she said grimly even before she removed her coat and sat down. "Whether you do yourself in like Schwartz, or someone else does it because you crossed them, what you saw today is what you'll eventually face if you stay with The Organization."

Janet was aghast. This woman, who had been such a kind and caring person only a few hours earlier, now presented herself with the tenderness of a rock. Deep furrows in her brow marred her beautiful face, and her lips pursed in determination. Her eyes shot daggers of accusation. Janet stayed silent.

"You're a beautiful young woman," Arleen resumed. "You're exceptionally bright. I have no doubt most men drool just being around you, never mind getting a taste of you in bed. You might even get a thrill hanging out with powerful animals like Giancarlo Mareno. But today you got a glimpse of how life evolves with his kind. It never ends well. I'm here to give you a chance to escape from it."

"There is no escape," Janet replied in resignation. "I've thought it through from every angle. Giancarlo holds all the cards. I have none."

"Inside The Organization that's entirely correct," the woman replied tersely. "You have to get away from The Organization. We can help you do it."

Arleen then drastically changed her tone and manner. Suddenly, the reassuring smile returned. Her pearl-white teeth sparkled, and her eyes softened almost hypnotically as she explained her role. She was a special FBI agent on assignment at CBA. Her work with the bank ended that day as it would no longer be safe for her to return to the office. She would disappear later that night for another assignment in some other part of the world.

Janet had one chance to seize the opportunity. If she agreed to cooperate, Arleen would get her into the FBI witness protection program. She explained how Janet would need to go into hiding until an indictment and trials could take place. There was no way to know how long that would take.

The FBI was closing in on Mareno and his friends, but only the director would decide when indictments would start. Trials could take years. Once the trials were out of the way, Janet would be given a new appearance with more cosmetic surgery.

She'd assume a different identity with all necessary documentation. She'd be relocated permanently to a secret place, perhaps even a friendly country like Canada. No one, including the FBI, would know until the last days before it all took place. In a fresh location, they would find Janet a satisfying job for which she was qualified, and she could start anew. She had no time to think about it. Janet needed to decide before Arleen left the restaurant. There would be no further negotiations.

Although Arleen explained everything in a friendly and reassuring tone, Janet was terrified. It all seemed grimly final. Testifying wouldn't be that hard. After the incidents with Douglas Whitfield, the knife attack on her face, and the gory death of Abe Schwartz, Janet would've liked nothing better than to see Mareno served justice.

All she had to do was tell the truth about her roles at Multima Corporation in Fort Myers and Chicago and recount her visit to Costa Rica, describing all their talks about seizing control of Multima. Then, she'd be expected to tell about her involvement in CBA Investment Bank. She would need to explain how she got the job, about the knife attack, and Mareno's help with cosmetic surgery to repair the damage. She could do all those things without difficulty.

As she thought it through, the offer became increasingly appealing. In less than an hour, she had clarified issues like the protection, income, location, and lifestyle she'd be able to expect in the new life. Janet agreed to do it.

Within fifteen minutes of her decision, Arleen gave her a hug at the front door of the restaurant and bundled her into a waiting unmarked car that sped toward the private airport in Teterboro, New Jersey. That was the only information her driver gave her as he focused intently on the still-heavy Manhattan traffic.

At Teterboro Airport, the car slowed but didn't stop. Instead, a guard waved them onto the tarmac where they eventually stopped beside a gray, unmarked private jet. A pilot waited on the ground and guided Janet up the stairway, drawing it up the instant Janet stepped inside the aircraft.

She was the only passenger, so the pilot instructed her to take any seat she liked. He didn't know where they were headed yet, but they'd be in the air for three to five hours. When he received confirmation of their destination, he'd come back and give her a better estimate of their travel time. In the meantime, she should enjoy the complimentary snacks and sodas.

About two hours into the flight, the pilot came back to say they were headed to Miami.

"They already sent us in a southwesterly direction from New Jersey, so we just have to double back toward the southeast. We'll need a little more than an hour," he explained in the typically reassuring tone of a pilot.

They landed at an airport south of Miami, a former national guard base, her escort on the ground explained as she helped Janet with the last step off the aircraft.

They headed downtown. A few minutes after they passed Coconut Grove, the woman turned into a towering condominium complex facing the water. She led Janet to one side of the main lobby, away from the bank of elevators. There, she called a number and Janet heard an audible click before concealed elevator doors opened. The woman motioned for Janet to enter but stayed outside the elevator as the doors closed.

The elevator doors opened again only a few seconds later. Janet took in a palatial suite—better than any of the hundreds of hotels she had visited. Through the living room, she looked out on a magnificent view of the harbor, with lights sparkling in the moonlight, and the bay reflecting magical patterns in the water.

Then, she noticed the gorgeous hunk standing just off to the side of the elevator.

"I'm Steve. I'll be watching you for a while. Would you care for a glass of wine?" he asked with only a hint of a smile. Before she could answer, another face appeared in the corridor and Janet almost fainted.

Howard Knight!

Before either could say anything, Janet rushed across the space between them to wrap her arms around him and hold him more tightly than she'd ever held a man while fully clothed. She sobbed uncontrollably. Her whole body shuddered, and she couldn't speak when she tried. The words refused to come out.

"Don't worry, Janet," Knight whispered as he returned her embrace. "We'll be okay now." Then, his arm still around her comfortingly, he led her to the wine cellar Steve guarded and pointed to a good vintage red wine. At ease in the deluxe La-Z-Boy chairs, they both drank well into the night as Janet sadly recounted the horror of her day at CBA Investment Bank and the whirlwind aftermath.

Then, the interviews began. Within minutes of her devouring the breakfast Steve prepared for them, he released an electronic lock and a man and a woman stepped into the apartment. They were from the FBI they said without offering even first names. They wore torn jeans and stained t-shirts. He had a couple days' growth of beard while she looked like her last visit to a hair stylist might have been several months earlier.

"We'll be taking your statements," the woman said simply. "Our first session should only last three or four hours. It's Sunday after all."

Ten hours later, the pair left the apartment as Steve announced dinner would be ready in just a few minutes. Would she like a glass of wine?

No kidding I'd like a glass of wine.

FIFTY-NINE

On a Multima private jet headed to Fort Myers, FL
Monday February 25, 2019

Wilma Willingsworth savored a few hours of relative relaxation as she cruised toward southwest Florida. Her day had been more taxing than most, and the days to follow suggested more of the same.

The *Wall Street Journal* article caught her eye almost by accident. She didn't read that iconic business newspaper as often as she had before it changed ownership about a decade earlier, but this day, she'd stopped at a Multima supermarket to pick up a copy. She knew the *Journal* had an excellent European bureau and was curious how their correspondents were handling the story about Farefour Stores.

Jean-Louis Sauvignon had acted with the haste James Fitzgerald predicted after their meeting. Using his influence, Sauvignon demanded an emergency meeting of the board of directors to resolve his long-simmering feud with its CEO Josef Aakker.

That secret meeting was held at Sauvignon's chateau in the south of France and Aakker wasn't invited. The *Journal* reported that was the main reason their business took an entire day to settle. According to sources, directors appointed by the CEO—and loyal to him—were livid such a momentous discussion could take place without giving Aakker an opportunity to defend himself.

The normally staid and formal group of elite French businessmen almost came to blows as voices were raised in anger, threats were made, and procedural delays were invoked at every stage of the nasty get-together. The Journal's source claimed it was by only a one-vote margin, but Sauvignon's iron will and potent influence over those directors loyal to him prevailed.

However, according to the *Journal*'s source, the dissenting faction of directors exacted a small concession from Sauvignon. Aakker would be fired as CEO with immediate effect, but Michelle Sauvignon would be appointed to the role only on an interim basis. The unhappy directors forced the dominant shareholder to concede they'd search for a permanent CEO. His daughter was just one of the candidates under consideration to hold the position permanently.

"That may be true," Suzanne said when she called to talk about the latest developments in Europe. "However, I spoke with James a few minutes ago. Businesses are closed for the day over there, but they'll issue a media release first thing tomorrow morning. Sauvignon was able to engineer the second stage of our plan. He mended relationships with the dissenting directors overnight and convened another meeting at his chateau today.

"It took a while, but the wily old guy eventually won," Suzanne continued. "They're preparing a media release for you to approve as we speak. The joint venture between Farefour Stores and Multima Financial Services will be announced immediately after you sign off on the press release. Congratulations on your new business unit!"

"I guess those congrats really depend on how successfully James can leverage our balance sheet to get loans and sell bonds," Wilma responded with a nervous laugh. "We need him to find that ten billion in commitments he promised before we can hope to achieve any critical mass with the joint venture."

"He seemed confident he could deliver, but the tough slogging starts now. He'll need a few days," Suzanne replied.

Is there an edge of concern in her voice? Wilma waited for Suzanne to continue.

"You're calling the American banks with subsidiaries in Europe to get their cooperation. Is that right, Wilma?"

Wilma had already talked with three of those banks before the call and had verbal undertakings for more than three billion. Each promised to make their commitments formal the day after the joint venture deal with Farefour Stores was announced. To this point, the lenders loved Multima's strategy. They thought it was a real winner.

Patiently, Wilma continued her call with Suzanne for several more minutes, rechecking responsibilities and sharing observations about any tweaking that might become necessary in the coming days. Wilma loved the way Suzanne listened to her comments and advice and almost always immediately grasped the significance of the message she wanted to convey. John George Mortimer had not always comprehended the nuances as quickly. That was the reason she was eager to point out the other tiny article she'd noticed on page four of the business section in the *Journal*.

"Jeffersons Stores to Renegotiate Loans with CBA" had caught Wilma's eye. The article didn't provide much more detail—only that the CFO of CBA Investment Bank had issued a media release advising the markets that CBA had agreed to renegotiate its outstanding loans with Jeffersons.

This announcement was a bit odd. First, it was rare to see companies or banks announce an intention to renegotiate a loan. Instead, they usually issued a press release after the deal had been made. Second, banks disliked renegotiating terms of a loan for which they had already demanded full repayment and dreaded drawing attention to a willingness to do so even more. Third, to appear in the *Journal* on a Monday morning, the media release must have been prepared and delivered to the newspaper sometime on the weekend. Someone had worked overtime to get their message out to early Monday readers.

"Right," Suzanne acknowledged when Wilma pointed out the article and her unease. She seemed to think about it for a moment.

"We certainly know Abe Schwartz didn't make the announcement," Wilma said with a nervous laugh she immediately regretted. "Someone at CBA felt compelled to announce they were renegotiating the Jeffersons loans even before Abe's funeral. I think we should dig into this a bit."

Wilma knew Suzanne had her hands full with the Farefour deal in Europe and that it occupied almost all her available time. This obscure article might be nothing at all, so Wilma was reluctant to push too hard. However, given the strange timing, she wanted her CEO to be alert.

"Thanks for bubbling up your concern on this one," Suzanne finally concluded. "Let's not take any chances. Let's get the acquisition team to see what they can uncover today. I'll also ask Dan Ramirez to see if his corporate security people can ferret anything out. To be prudent—and make sure we don't have any communication gaps—how about you and the team fly down tonight? Let's set up a war room here until we can gauge accurately where all of this is going."

As a consequence, Wilma and Suzanne's elite team were now in transit with everyone uncertain where this saga was headed next.

SIXTY

A plush penthouse apartment, Miami, FL
Tuesday February 26, 2019

"Are you folks smoking something illicit down there?" the angry director of the FBI thundered loud enough to cause the speakerphone on the dining room table to vibrate for a second. Then, with a tone of sarcasm or scorn—Howard couldn't tell precisely which—he added, "Isn't there already enough obsession on cable news about collusion?"

Howard Knight was shocked to be included in their teleconference. He also had the impression several other people were already on the line when their minder Steve announced they should join the conversation. There was total silence though. Not even a hint of breathing or background noise was evident for several long seconds.

"Get the woman out of there today," the FBI director spat out, his anger unabated. "We're not supposed to be running a goddamned singles resort. Our witnesses shouldn't even be talking to each other let alone copulating like rabbits in the lap of luxury. Make it happen and make it happen today. The last thing I want to see is a fuckup when we're so close."

After sputtering out the command, the FBI director didn't say goodbye. He just left an irritating dial tone in his wake. It was he who had initiated the call. Howard, Janet, and Steve all looked at each other with expressions of bewilderment.

He's right. Howard found himself agreeing. He and Janet Weissel really shouldn't have enjoyed a good romp in bed like that. He still wasn't sure exactly how it had happened.

Janet had worked another eight hours or more with her interrogators in the living area. He hadn't paid much attention to their sessions because he really had little interest in what she told them. His only concern was the info he provided and would need to testify about in court if they ever got around to indicting someone in The Organization. He spent the day working out on the fitness equipment, watching television in his room, and reading *The Missing President*, a novel Steve thought he might enjoy and bought while running errands.

After the investigators left, Steve prepared dinner for them as usual. Then, he cleaned up the kitchen before he retired for the night to his private room, probably to watch television.

While Janet and Howard watched some forgettable movie on Netflix, she suddenly said, "I liked it when you put your arms around me yesterday. It was really comforting and thoughtful." Then she stood up from her La-Z-Boy chair, walked over, and sat next to him on the sofa. "I could use another hug," she almost whispered in a soft, husky tone.

Howard put his arm around her and drew her in a little more closely for a moment, then shifted his arm to rest it on the top of the sofa back behind her head. Janet didn't move away. Instead, she wiggled in a little more tightly and leaned her head against his shoulder. They watched the movie that way for a while.

At some point, he started stroking her shoulder repetitively. She didn't seem to mind, so he continued touching her. Soon, Janet began caressing his left arm, the one resting in his lap. When he looked down, she slowly turned her head upward. Without thinking, he leaned forward to give her a gentle kiss on the cheek. She shifted her face, so he planted the kiss right on her lips. To his amazement, her lips parted delicately, and her sensuous tongue teased his mouth open.

It had been months since he'd been with anyone and nature took over. Their kisses and playful motions with their tongues soon became more heated, passionate even. Within moments, they were tugging at each other's clothes and removed enough that Howard suggested they go to his room before Steve discovered them.

They made love with reckless abandon the first time, then more lovingly and tenderly the second. Howard remembered falling asleep with his arms wrapped loosely around her and was still in that position when Steve knocked at the door to announce the investigators had arrived for Janet's next session. Was she in his room?

The interrogators stepped out of the special elevator before the couple had fully dressed, and the male agent came to the door of Howard's room after Steve revealed his discovery. The bastard was probably hoping to get a peek at naked prisoners.

The female agent made a call to report the sexual activity between the witnesses, and it wasn't long before the FBI director was on the phone yelling in anger. Moments after the grating dial tone ended the FBI director's tirade, the female interrogator ominously gripped Janet's elbow and led her to gather up a few possessions before they escorted her from the apartment.

SIXTY-ONE

MPH Hospital, Fort Myers, FL
Tuesday February 26, 2019

John George Mortimer was increasingly amazed at how well his body was responding to the new immunotherapy treatment the Swiss researcher had concocted and his oncologist dispensed. He looked better. He felt better. The cursed MRI images showed the cancerous tumors still ominously there but no longer growing. There was still hope.

His health had improved enough for him to revert to a favorite habit of relaxing on the screened lanai at the back of his stately home overlooking the Caloosahatchee River. He found it relaxing to sit there, enjoying a glass of wine and admiring the spectacular sunsets.

His housekeeper, Lana, continued to stay at the house despite his improved mobility and spirits. She claimed it was too much trouble to move all her things back home again. She'd rather keep the current living arrangement for a while. She still worried about his health and fretted should anything happen in her absence, so he left it for her to decide.

The thoughtful woman who had served him for so many years started joining him on the lanai after she finished her work in the kitchen. John George enjoyed her company. Lana spoke Spanish with him to keep his language skills primed, and he loved to listen to stories of her time growing up in El Salvador.

She also helped to offset his peculiar feelings about not having more time with his own daughter. He often thought about the years he'd missed while Suzanne was growing up and occasionally wondered how his life might have changed had her mother ever made contact to let him know about her birth. It wasn't a feeling of remorse or anything similar. Rather, it was a tinge of regret for what could have been.

Suzanne remained immersed in the Europe project. He admired her ambition to hatch such a creative idea and mastermind the strategies. They were growing the business in ways he'd never considered. But it also meant she carried an awesome burden of responsibility. She took huge risks. But she also realized people depended on her making the right decisions at the right time. It was a burden he too had felt and still did.

He knew Suzanne spent long hours in her office, maybe up to twenty hours some days. She didn't want to disturb him while he might be resting, but he knew she also needed time to unwind quickly and refresh for the next hectic day. So, he was content to do his own unwinding with a glass of red wine and Lana's excellent company.

Because his health had been improving, he became unsettled when he couldn't immediately find a Spanish word. He hesitated, thought about it again, finally found the word, and then realized his speech seemed a little slurred when he used it. He tried again. Same muffled result. Lana leaped from her chair and turned to face him.

"Stand up, John George," she commanded in a tone he didn't recognize. "Please, stand up, right now," she repeated when he was slow to respond.

Reacting to her request, he reached to set his glass of wine on the small table between them. Something happened. Either he missed the table, or he tipped the glass. He wasn't sure which, but a half glass of red wine suddenly splashed across the floor in front of him.

"Never mind the wine. Stand up now," Lana repeated with more urgency.

When John George used his left arm to push his body away from the chair and lift his frame, the arm felt numb. There was no tingling. No pain. It was just an unexplained numbness in his upper arm.

"Raise your arms above your head," Lana commanded again as she stared at him intently.

Both arms felt heavy. He lifted his hands to about the level of his chest, then needed to rest and try again. He still found it hard to form words. He thought he told Lana that he'd be okay but wasn't entirely sure he said it clearly.

"Sit down again, John George," Lana said as she dashed from the room. He slumped back into the chair. When she returned, talking animatedly with someone on the phone, he heard her say his address and ask them to respond urgently.

"I think it's a stroke," she emphasized. "His speech is slurred. He has some difficulty with his left arm, and his mouth is drooping unusually on the left side."

There was a pause while Lana listened to the other person on the call.

"Yes, I told you his name. It's John George Mortimer, the chairman of Multima Corporation. You need to have the ambulance take him immediately to MPH Hospital. They know him there. They're treating him for cancer. I'll contact his oncologist and alert her as well, but please hurry."

SIXTY-TWO

Fort Myers, FL
Wednesday February 27, 2019

The way things were going in Suzanne's world, bringing that elite team from Chicago to create a war room outside her office was fortuitous timing. They were already working at optimum productivity. The first day they arrived, Wilma and the team concentrated on helping James Fitzgerald in Europe. To make their joint venture scheme work, they needed to raise at least ten billion euros, leveraging the combined financial resources of Farefour Stores and Multima Corporation.

They were well on their way to the desired target until all hell broke loose.

First, there was the strange announcement after the stock markets closed Monday. Gordon Goodfellow called to let Suzanne know he'd just watched a breaking story on Fox Business News. Jeffersons Stores planned to start negotiations with Multima Corporation to explore a possible merger of the two companies.

What's going on?

She summoned the vice president of corporate communications to her office and asked Edward Hadley what he could tell her about the story.

"We just became aware too," he explained. "One of my team handed me the story from a Reuters news feed two minutes ago. She checked and learned a formal media release was sent out over the CEO's signature a minute or two after the markets closed at four o'clock. Here's a copy."

They both took a few moments to read the release in silence. It appeared legitimate. The release carried the Jeffersons Stores corporate logo. The CEO's name and its spelling seemed correct. The background info about both companies looked right. Everything looked real except one thing: no one in Multima's leadership had spoken with anyone from Jeffersons. Suzanne was bewildered.

Edward Hadley had his people make a few discrete calls. They learned someone in the office of the CEO at Jeffersons had indeed instructed their communications team to draft the release. There was apparently no CEO signature on file, but their source revealed an executive assistant had approved the announcement. The Multima team couldn't reach the CEO to ask about it. As a result, everyone went home that night confused and wary.

Tuesday morning, things became even more chaotic.

James Fitzgerald called her at three in the morning in a panic. He had already received eight calls of alarm from contacts at European banks. What was happening at Multima? Why were they not made aware such a major merger was on the horizon? How could they honor their loan or bond commitment when Multima was contemplating such a material change to its structure and financial position?

Suzanne was in the uncomfortable position of explaining that she didn't know what was going on. She assured James there had been no dialogue with Jeffersons or any intent to discuss a merger. She'd get Edward Hadley working on damage control immediately and asked James to do his best to calm fears and allay concerns.

Hadley met her at the office before four in the morning and three of his communications experts showed up minutes later.

"We need to get our message out quickly," Edward affirmed. "The New York business networks are building their morning features now. If we don't get the word out, American viewers will hear the false narrative hundreds of times today. Any attempt to counter it later will be in vain."

Within minutes, one of the communications experts was sitting in Suzanne's office drafting a media release on a laptop perched on her lap. She read it back to Hadley and Suzanne for enhancements and touch-ups on the spot. When they were satisfied, she cued up a printer, produced a paper copy and had them quickly sign it before she dashed out to feed the wire services.

"We've got to do more than issue a release," Edward urged. "We need to get you a network interview this morning. I recommend we contact Liara Furtamo. I know she blindsided you during that interview about the hacking incident that time you were in Hong Kong and word of John George Mortimer's cancer got out. But she still has the largest viewing audience. She loves an exclusive breaking news story, and with your communication skills we might be able to nip this thing in the bud."

"Okay," Suzanne replied to buy a little more time. "What time slot do you think she might do it live?"

"I'll shoot for the eight o'clock hour before the markets open. I think she'll agree."

"All right, I'll get Wilma and her people out of bed and in here to man the phones when the American media start to make inquiries. Team up your communications experts with a task force member so the message is consistent, concise, and correct. If the lenders here get nervous, those who James Fitzgerald is trying to hold steady will become apoplectic," Suzanne instructed with a wry smile.

Within minutes, she had roused Wilma from her slumber and exacted a promise to be at the headquarters before seven. She called Sally-Ann at home and asked her to get a makeup specialist in before seven as well. She'd need a lot of help this morning. Suzanne had appeared in dozens of interviews and knew how essential it was to project just the right image for the television cameras. With a good percentage of the viewing audience, her looks were more important than her message. Unfortunately, that was the modern reality.

"Multima Corporation is focused exclusively on our new joint venture with Farefour Stores in France," Suzanne replied to Liara Furtamo's first on-air question. They were live, and Suzanne was careful to flash her most sparkling smile and use an emphatic tone. "Farefour is a wonderful company which has already done a lot of the necessary legwork. We'll bring our long-established expertise with consumer lending and sage financial knowledge under Wilma Willingsworth's leadership."

"But, if that's the case, why would Jeffersons Stores put out a release that suggests otherwise?" Liara responded with a mischievous smile.

"I can't speak for Jeffersons Stores. Candidly, I haven't yet been able to reach their CEO to ask him about it," Suzanne answered, arching her brows and tightening her lips for an instant. "What I can tell you is this: Should Jeffersons Stores truly want to explore a relationship, this is something we are not prepared to consider for the remainder of this year. We intend to remain laser-focused on our European financial services expansion."

"There's another rumor circulating out there," Liara began, slowing her pace of delivery for dramatic effect. "Rumor has it that James Fitzgerald was sniffing around CBA Investment Bank a few weeks ago. It's no secret he's less than enthralled with you since he 'retired' from Multima. Does he have any role in all of this?"

Suzanne felt alarm. Liara Furtamo had surprised her before, but she'd learned from that experience. This time, she showed no expression of shock despite her surprise the woman had that information. She successfully held her smile. She should have anticipated this twist but decided to just tell the most plausible story she could invent on the spot.

"James Fitzgerald retired from Multima last year," she began. *Create some distance in time.* "When it became clear we would move forward with the Farefour joint venture project, I hired James to help us identify and establish funding resources for the new business in Europe and here at home. He may well have had contact with CBA Investment Bank as part of that exercise. He's doing a wonderful job bringing onside a good number of strong, well-established financial institutions on both sides of the Atlantic. I want to personally assure all those financial partners we remain totally committed to our European expansion."

Liara Furtamo took a moment to decide if she should pursue that line of questioning. Apparently, Suzanne's response satisfied the journalist. She changed her tack almost completely.

"A couple years ago, we were the first to report that John George Mortimer was being treated for cancer," Liara Furtamo stated.

Still unable to resist an opportunity to pat herself on the back.

"How is your father's health? Is he still acting as chairman?"

"Yes, he's still very much our Chairman and I value the active role he continues to play," Suzanne said with conviction. "Cancer is a very challenging disease. He has good days and others that are more difficult. But we all love having him around and don't expect him to retire anytime soon."

The interview continued for a few more minutes, giving Suzanne two more chances to work into the conversation her exclusive interest in—and focus on—the joint venture with Farefour Stores. As she removed the tiny microphone from the collar of her suit jacket, Suzanne thought the mission should be accomplished. Within the next few hours, the picture with funders would become clearer.

She didn't expect a call from the CEO of Jeffersons Stores, but Sally-Ann left a note on her desk saying he had tried to reach her during the interview. Could Suzanne return his call as soon as possible?

"I think this could be a wonderful opportunity for both of us," David Jones, the CEO of Jeffersons Stores, said after their opening pleasantries. "It's a shame what happened with Abe Schwartz, but I must say, the new management team seems much more accommodating."

"I would say so," Suzanne replied without enthusiasm. "Calling your loan one week and increasing it exponentially the next seems a bit odd, doesn't it?"

"I understand your skepticism. I was a little shocked, too. But they said it was all a mistake. Probably Abe Schwartz was a little unbalanced mentally when he made the demand and then shot himself," the CEO added, trying to lend credibility to his outrageous assertion.

"David, I'll be candid with you. I have great respect for Jeffersons. Although we've never met, I'm sure you're a gentleman and a highly capable CEO. I don't know if you saw the interview I gave CBNN or not. Regardless, I said Multima Corporation is fully focused on the cooperation agreement we already announced with Farefour Stores in France. We have no appetite to explore a merger or any other relationship with you right now. We need to stay focused on that joint venture."

Jones was reluctant to accept her position. They volleyed back and forth politely for a few more minutes before Suzanne lost patience with his refusal to accept her decision.

"David, I don't want to sound impolite, but I also want to be clear," she said. "I'm not prepared to take this to the board, and I'm not going to dedicate resources to exploring any relationship at this stage. I won't close the door entirely. If you'd like to touch base again, about this time next year, I'll think about it then."

"I also don't want to sound impolite," Jeffersons' CEO replied, raising his voice just slightly. "However, if you're unwilling to discuss our interest with your board, I may be forced to make an unsolicited offer."

"Forced?" Suzanne asked.

"Yes, forced in the sense that you leave me little alternative," he said quickly.

"If you decide to go that route, be sure I will use every tool at my disposal to resist your overtures," Suzanne declared. "I warn you that any unwelcome interest will cost both our companies unnecessary expense and time, but Multima will not waiver. I know our shareholders, and I know our board. I have their full support on this issue and have no doubt I'll maintain it."

Their call ended moments later with little pretense of cooperation or amity. Within an hour, Suzanne was locked in discussions with Alberto Ferer, her chief legal counsel, to plot their defense. They soon drew Wilma Willingsworth into the discussions, then they linked in James Fitzgerald who was now in Paris.

"You were great on the CBNN interview," James said. "Within minutes of your appearance, I started to get calls back from the funders. Your confidence and clarity really assured them. We had every single firm back onside by the close of business over here."

"Thanks, James. Good to hear," Suzanne countered. "But I think you'll need to batten down the hatches. Things are about to get rough again."

They brought Fitzgerald up to date on the unsolicited Jeffersons overture and threat of an offer directly to shareholders and the board. For more than an hour, they recapped all the legal mechanisms they could use to defend the company. They talked about shareholder communication strategies and explored other ideas to minimize the damage.

In the end, the executive team decided the best available option was the secret plan they already had discussed. They'd just have to accelerate it dramatically. Then they talked about the most suitable way to communicate their intended new direction with Farefour Stores. Everyone agreed. The optimal method was for Suzanne to leverage her special relationship with Michelle Sauvignon. Nothing was possible without the support of Jean-Louis Sauvignon, and no one knew better how to manage her father than Michelle.

Suzanne and her closest advisors reached that conclusion just minutes before Lana called to alert her about John George's suspected stroke. It was already about three o'clock in the morning in France when the disaster with her father struck. It was far too early to call Michelle anyway, so Suzanne rushed to MPH Hospital and met Lana there only minutes after her father had been whisked into the emergency room.

Several stressful hours passed before Suzanne was able to consult with John George's medical team. They were treating him with drugs to counter the stroke. There appeared to be improvement, but the neurologist needed more time.

After midnight, a nurse escorted Suzanne into the curtained area where they were treating John George. He was awake.

I'm Doctor Wu. I'm the on-call neurologist who treated your father. He had a stroke, but the prognosis looks quite positive."

The doctor turned to John George and said, "You owe your housekeeper a big thank you. She saved your life. EMS got you here quickly, and we were able to limit the damage. You'll have some speech and mobility issues initially, but we'll get you some help to regain most of your capabilities. You'll just have to be patient."

"Doctor Wu thinks our immunotherapy treatments may have triggered the stroke." Doctor Sanjana Singh, the oncologist took over. She too looked at John George and softly said. "We'll be taking a pause with treatments until we determine which component caused the negative reaction. I'll work with the researcher in Geneva to try to get you back on some modified version as soon as Doctor Wu thinks it's safe."

"You gave us all a scare, John George," Suzanne whispered as she stepped forward, planted a kiss on his forehead, and touched his shoulders with both hands. "Don't try to talk now. You need to rest. Your speech will improve soon. We'll talk all you want then. I need to get back to the office, but Lana is here. She'll keep me updated and I'll drop in and out when I can. Please know I'll be thinking about you all the time. By the way, relax. Everything is all right back at the company. I'll bring you up to date later."

From the emergency room, she settled into the rear seat of the limousine. As soon as the door closed, she reached for her phone and hit the speed dial for her office. As Suzanne waited for the call to connect, her female security resource arched her brows and motioned for her to apply fresh lipstick, reminding her of an earlier request not to let her back into the office until she fixed herself up.

Fumbling with her bag and makeup kit, Suzanne pressed the speaker button and set down the phone on the small working table in front of her.

The security team would hear the conversation, but she was now accustomed to their continuous presence. Every person on the team had been meticulously scrutinized. Alberto Ferer also required them to sign documents promising never to divulge details of overheard conversations under any conditions. They could be trusted.

Her executive assistant, patched the call through to the conference facility they now referred to as their war room. From there, Wilma would connect with Michelle and Jean-Louis Sauvignon for a call James Fitzgerald had been arranging while Suzanne was at the hospital.

With no sleep, the stress of John George's health crisis, and the next call all on her mind, she reapplied her makeup while her security guard balanced the mirror of her compact. Ultimately, their efforts were in vain. Two large tears escaped despite her valiant efforts to contain them. They slowly trickled down her cheeks, streaking the freshly applied makeup.

It was a good thing she had no TV interviews scheduled today. At least her upcoming call with Michelle Sauvignon wasn't a video link. Her friend wouldn't see Suzanne's strain, dejection, and sadness. Somehow, she'd find a way to get it all together before Michelle came on the line. She had to persuade her friend to make the most important decision of her life. And she needed that decision to be the right one.

SIXTY-THREE

A beach house southwest of Miami, FL
Wednesday February 27, 2019

Janet Weissel was damned if she'd let them treat her like that. If they were going to deal with her like a friggin' child, she'd just act like one. It was bad enough the FBI director disrespected her so rudely on that call a couple days earlier. After the call, the FBI agents didn't even politely ask her to move. Instead, they forcibly wrenched her arms behind her back and shoved her toward the elevator. She only had time to grab her bag and a toothbrush.

They stuffed her into the back seat of a car waiting outside the building with no explanation of where they were going. Every time she asked one of her minders what was going on, the woman agent growled to shut up or wait and see. They'd be there soon.

They turned off the highway to the Florida Keys. Shortly after, the car stopped at an out-of-the-way beach house hidden from the road by rows of palms short and tall. The female agent grabbed her arm again, and none too gently dragged her, half walking and half stumbling, over the soft sand toward the house. Inside, she nudged Janet to a bedroom, pushed her inside, and then slammed the door before locking it. They left her that way for a few hours while they discussed something of apparent importance outside in the driveway.

Another car arrived with more people. She didn't know how many. But someone soon came and unlocked the door. At least four people entered the room carrying restraints which they applied to her wrists and feet. She could only move her feet a few inches at a time when they finished with her. Her wrists were also firmly locked. When she asked for water, one of the agents told her to open her mouth and they poured some water in. They did it again a couple more times until she'd had enough.

Janet was so angry she was trembling. The bastards had asked her to help them. They'd promised her safety in their witness protection program. They'd interviewed her for hours on end.

"Why are you treating me like a captive animal?" she demanded to know.

"Can't you figure it out, you slut?" The female agent jutted her chin only inches away from Janet's. "You and your horny accomplice have put this whole exercise in jeopardy. The FBI director is rethinking our entire plan. Those bastards in The Organization may very well get off scot-free, just because you assholes had to have a welcome-home fuck before we completed the interrogation. Do you realize just how many thousands of hours have been devoted to this mission? Do you know how many people put their lives at stake so you could get a cheap orgasm with an old has-been like Knight?"

"Well, you can fucking well forget my cooperation if you're going to treat me like this!" Janet yelled. "I haven't broken any laws. And it was your friggin' colleague in New York who persuaded me to become a stool and help you bastards. Until you start to treat me properly, you can fucking well take your questions and shove them up your ass!"

A good-looking male agent arrived a few minutes into their tirade and led the female agent away from the room, leaving Janet screaming to herself for some minutes. When she stopped, someone new entered the room. To her amazement, it was Arleen Woodhaus—the source of all her current troubles—sporting a stern expression.

"This is very serious," Arleen said calmly as she moved forward to release the cuffs from Janet's wrist. "We're in the final stages. We need to finish your interviews today. If you don't cooperate, I can't guarantee you the deal. The FBI director has calmed down somewhat, but you must tell us everything you know before the end of today. If not, he's willing to release you and let The Organization have its way with you. We don't want to see that do we?"

Janet continued to vent for several minutes anyway. Arleen listened patiently. She didn't interrupt. She didn't argue. Instead, she stood with her arms crossed comfortably across her chest, head tilted to the side and her expression neutral.

When Janet finished some minutes later, Arleen repeated the urgency.

"I can't change what happened at the apartment, and I know this treatment humiliates you. But think about the big picture, Janet. If you don't share what you know, we can't move forward. If we can't get Giancarlo Mareno behind bars, this madness will continue. You might survive for some time because you're an intelligent woman with an indomitable spirit. But there is little doubt you'll eventually look just like Abe Schwartz that morning we found him. The only question is who will pull the trigger? Will it be you? Or Giancarlo Mareno? Or one of his brutal executioners? Think about it."

With that admonition, Arleen turned and left the room. Janet was left to ponder the woman's arguments. She didn't have many options left.

Tears welled in her eyes. She found it difficult to control her thought patterns and logic temporarily failed her. Her brain was muddled and the room felt like it was closing in on her. But she refused to cry and finally mustered enough clarity to weigh the slim alternatives.

Abe Schwartz's gruesome suicide still haunted her day and night. The loss of Douglas Whitfield left a painful gap she couldn't explain. She must have loved him despite the miserable way he treated and used her. Giancarlo Mareno was indeed an animal. Except for his kindness after she was raped, his tone was demeaning and controlling. She had no doubt he could order her death easily and without hesitation.

And what should she feel about her one-night romp with Howard Knight? What could attract her to a guy old enough to be her father? Was it merely a case of two people who needed some affection to satisfy base sexual desires? Or was there something more there? He had held her in his arms more tenderly than any man she could remember. When he spoke, he was always respectful, calm, and steady. When she talked to him, he listened. And although it was brief, their sex was very, very good.

She took only a few more minutes to decide. Janet went to the door of the bedroom and tried the door handle. It turned. Meekly, she opened the door and stood still while she looked around a living room she had seen for only seconds before they bustled her into the bedroom.

Arleen sat alone on a tall chair beside a granite countertop tucked into a kitchen nook. She was alone. All was quiet except for the hum of an air conditioner. Eventually, Arleen looked up from her phone when she realized Janet was standing in the open doorway, but she said nothing.

"I'll cooperate," Janet said evenly. "But there's a big 'if.' If you return me to the apartment in Miami with Howard Knight and let us stay there together until this is all over, I'll give you the evidence you need. If not, release me now and I'll take my chances."

"You know I can't make that promise," Arleen replied coolly but not unequivocally. "The director of the FBI made the decision to separate you. He's not a man to change his mind easily."

"Too bad. It's up to you to change his mind." Janet stood rigidly upright to emphasize her determination. "The director of the FBI's reaction is wrong. Only people in the FBI know that Howard and I were staying in that apartment. What we might or might not do in that apartment is not the business of the director or anyone else. And if you can't keep secret our whereabouts and living arrangements, how can we trust your vaunted witness protection program?"

Arleen made no reply. Her face remained neutral, but Janet could tell she was thinking about the argument. Janet waited for the woman to process her demand fully before she went on.

"Until now, during the interrogation by your colleagues, I've simply answered questions. I've answered them fully and truthfully just as we agreed," Janet explained. "Get your director to reverse his command and let Howard and I live together in the apartment until you move us into the witness protection program. Once you do that, I'll provide you with some new information—something none of you know about."

"Tell me about it." Arleen's expression softened.

"Before you came to the office on the morning Abe Schwartz died, he discussed the deal with me. He had me reduce the financing cost for Multima with CBA Investment Bank absorbing all the lost revenue. He also instructed me to get the analysts to re-cost the loan. When I got the information from the analyst, I lied. I told him Abe Schwartz wanted a USB thumb drive file of the entire deal, including all the funding details. He made me a copy. I put it in a very secure place. It describes—in every detail—the exact sources of CBA's funding."

Arleen rushed across the room so quickly Janet was initially unsettled. The woman wrapped her arms around her and squeezed tightly.

"The missing piece!" Arleen said joyfully. "Let me talk with the director. We'll find a way to get him comfortable."

SIXTY-FOUR

Multima Corporation Headquarters, Fort Myers, FL
Thursday February 28, 2019

The conference call with Michelle Sauvignon and her father became far more stressful than Suzanne had expected. In the car, she managed to apply enough makeup to get herself presentable but was chagrined to see a video link set up when she entered the meeting room next to her office.

They insisted, Sally-Ann mouthed to her with a shrug of resignation when she saw Suzanne's expression.

Jean-Louis and Michelle were already patiently waiting in comfortable chairs in what was probably a den in one of their palatial homes. James Fitzgerald was seated at a work desk in his hotel suite in Paris. Wilma Willingsworth, Dan Ramirez, and the task force under Norman Whiteside were all grouped around the large mahogany table in the conference room.

Suzanne tried to get the pleasantries out of the way quickly so they could get down to business, but her long-time friend immediately noticed something was amiss.

"Is everything okay?" Michelle wanted to know after the usual inquiries about the weather were out of the way.

Suzanne hesitated for a moment to assess her options. Her professional inclination was just to say yes and make some flippant remark about a miserable night's sleep. But she quickly remembered the enormity of the request she was about to make. She'd be asking Jean-Louis and Michelle Sauvignon to make a life-altering decision. She owed them total honesty. Any fudging of the truth now might come back to haunt her if they later found out the real situation.

"It's been a long night," she said. "John George had a health incident at home last night and needed to be hospitalized urgently. I spent several hours with him, and it looks like he's going to be all right, but they're still doing tests. It gave us quite a scare though."

Jean-Louis's face immediately showed concern and empathy. The dreaded realization of an older person that the conversation might be about him in other circumstances? It looked like he wanted to probe more deeply, but discretion won out. He simply asked Suzanne to relay his heartfelt wishes for a quick and complete recovery.

"Let's get right to the purpose of this call," Suzanne suggested more forcefully than she intended. "All the reports I've been receiving from James and Wilma indicate the joint venture is off to an excellent start. Is that perception a correct one from your perspective?"

Michelle and her father both nodded enthusiastically as Michelle replied, "Yes, your team has been fantastic. Confidence shown by the lending community so far has been overwhelming. Your TV interview the other day was really impressive, and I'm getting nicely settled in with our management team. They're accepting me in my new role and everything appears harmonious. I can't thank you enough for quickly putting to rest the ugly rumor about a possible relationship with Jeffersons Stores. That really had my team worried."

"I wish I could tell you the rumor was dead, but I can't," Suzanne said "Unfortunately, although we have no interest whatsoever in a relationship with Jeffersons, it seems they're not deterred. I expect to see an unsolicited offer to buy us. I don't know exactly when, and we're prepared to fight it of course, but we think the most effective deterrent is to move forward more quickly with the longer-term plan we've talked about."

"Move forward?" Michelle arched her brows with an exaggerated expression of curiosity.

"Yes, here we have a special term for our defense. You've probably heard of it—a 'poison pill.' We need to move forward with our previous philosophical discussions right now rather than next year as we anticipated."

"No! No! No!" Jean-Louis Sauvignon protested. "It is impossible! The timing is all wrong. Michelle has only been in her new role a few days. She's had inadequate time to bond with her management team. The board of directors hasn't yet become comfortable with her abilities. Our lenders will again get spooked. It will all fall apart!"

Suzanne had expected resistance but was taken aback when she measured the intensity of the old man's furor. She elected just to let his message sink in with the group and see if he chose to vent further. He didn't. Instead, Michelle intervened with a calm voice of reason.

"Let's not be too hasty with our conclusions," Michelle said without looking at her father. "Of course, this new idea comes to us as quite a surprise. We need some time to get our heads around it. Let's look at it this way: If we don't follow Suzanne's suggestion and Jeffersons Stores makes an unfriendly offer as they threatened, we'll have exactly the turmoil we fear anyway. Lenders may think Suzanne lied to them and the shareholders during her TV interview. How would we control that damage?"

Suzanne looked directly at the video camera lens but caught several nods of agreement from her colleagues around the table. Jean-Louis would see that as well. With admiration for the skill of her old friend's handling of her father's outburst, Suzanne tossed her an oblique thank you and offered the father a face-saving gesture.

"That's our fear," Suzanne said with conviction. "We agree with all the risks Jean-Louis identified. He's absolutely correct in his assessment. But we talked about it extensively here and couldn't identify a better alternative. I'm willing to listen if you have any suggestions."

Jean-Louis Sauvignon noticeably relaxed. His shoulders slumped from an earlier aggressive posture to one more akin to resignation. It looked like he got it. They were all in an impossible bind. There was little alternative if he was to realize his dream.

"When do you expect to receive the offer?" he asked.

"Their CEO wasn't precise, but Alberto Ferer—our chief legal counsel—thinks it will take a week or two for them to get together a package they can send to shareholders. He's confident they won't make any announcement to the media without everything ready to go out."

"You're asking a lot, Suzanne," Jean-Louis said after a silence of almost a minute. "We have to get the board onside and do exactly the same preparation Jeffersons Stores will be doing. We too will need to have a package ready to go to our shareholders for them to accept such an important decision. I see the wisdom of your strategy now, but I'm not sure I can deliver enough support from the board of directors. Several are still upset about our ousting of Aakker."

"Would it help if Suzanne flew over to join your meeting?" Wilma asked, glancing at Suzanne in apology for throwing out the unexpected suggestion.

"That's a great idea," Michelle replied instantly. "Let's make the board of directors so much a part of the process they feel like they're making the deal, not simply approving it. Let's have Suzanne make the sale."

She turned from the camera to face her father as she made the statement, and her tone projected not only endorsement of the idea but also eagerness for it. Jean-Louis again took about a minute to calculate the odds and consider the negatives. When he replied, his tone was measured and even.

"Is there any possibility John George could join us?" he asked. "That would also help immensely."

"No, that's not possible." Suzanne's voice broke. A tear escaped from her eye and she made no effort to hide it as it trickled down her cheek. "No, that won't be possible, Jean-Louis. It will be entirely up to us."

The video conference remained silent for a few moments. No one seemed entirely sure where to go next. Suzanne took a tissue from her bag and wiped away the wayward tear. Composed, she took control of the discussion again.

"If everyone agrees, I'll fly over tonight with the team. We can massage the final details tomorrow. I'll meet with your board on Saturday," she offered. "We need to have board agreement by Sunday. To head this thing off, I need to announce the decision before the stock markets open Monday morning."

Jean-Louis gave his assent with a simple nod.

Just as they'd planned, James Fitzgerald took over the conversation. He proposed they all meet Friday in Iceland to be away from the scrutiny of business media in both America and France. He'd reserve a meeting room in the Reykjavik airport for noon. Assuming they finalized the outline of the deal Friday, they could invite the board of directors to Provence for a meeting on Saturday. Perhaps Jean-Louis would like to invite everyone to his home near Avignon.

Suzanne permitted her thoughts to drift away from the dialogue. The mention of John George had triggered strong emotions she hadn't expected and found difficult to suppress. She made a mental note to check with the neurologist before she left. Would it be too much for John George to let him know what they were planning? Or, would it be better just to let him know the outcome when she returned Monday? After all, she was about to take the biggest gamble possible with his corporation.

SIXTY-FIVE

Aboard a Multima jet
Saturday March 2, 2019

Wilma Willingsworth recalled clearly that first time she met Suzanne just after John George Mortimer had bought the Canadian supermarket chain she led and elevated her to the role of president at Multima Supermarkets.

At first, Wilma wondered if it was Suzanne's beauty-queen appearance that explained her spectacular rise to the summit of leadership in the supermarket world. Or did she really have the know-how to manage successfully? Within moments of meeting, she realized Suzanne was the real deal. Her intellect, memory, and attention to detail had impressed Wilma.

An introvert herself, Wilma was amazed by Suzanne's people skills and the younger woman's ability to convert the most awkward circumstances into positive and rewarding outcomes. She also admired her recognition of her limits and weaknesses. Finance was clearly not Suzanne's strongest asset.

Surely, she knew far more about the subject than most, but she wisely realized that when it came to finance, she was no match for Wilma. Rather than try to compete in matters of finance, Suzanne had always treated Wilma as a resource. She sought her opinion, then listened and usually acted on her advice. That's why Wilma thought of herself as a sort of mentor to the woman who had become her boss.

Lately, Wilma had been particularly gratified to see the extent to which Suzanne engaged her in the overall management of the company. She was still the president of Multima Financial Services and that remained her number one priority. But, when Suzanne needed to poach some of her best resources to form the task force under Norman Whiteside, instead of moving them all to Fort Myers, she left them under Wilma's watchful eye in Chicago.

Effectively, this kept Wilma in the loop on developments, even if Norman Whiteside technically reported to Suzanne. That positioning meant Wilma was entirely up to speed on all the issues when things started to percolate with Farefour Stores and the whole Jeffersons mess. Even with such a head start, getting ready for a meeting with the board of directors of Farefour involved a much steeper preparation curve than she expected. Suzanne effectively gave the team one day to ready an entire acquisition.

Unrelenting Peril

Yes, they called it a merger. But there was no doubt that Suzanne intended to make Multima Corporation the largest and most diversified supermarket chain in the world after Walmart. And she intended to do it while her father was still in a hospital recovering from a debilitating stroke. The woman seemed to know how to manage stress.

Suzanne hadn't slept the night before her crucial video conference with the Sauvignons. Wilma noticed that right away despite the freshly applied makeup. Suzanne's step was just a tad slower and she had less energy. Strain showed when a few tears escaped during the call. No doubt she would have preferred to shed them more privately.

Regardless, the CEO remained in her chair at the head of the conference room table all morning, took a break to visit John George at the hospital when the team broke for lunch, then rejoined them for the entire afternoon session, visiting John George again when they broke for dinner. In fact, she was with the team—involved in every aspect of the transaction structure—until Alberto Ferer pronounced the offer ready just after midnight.

They all went to either their homes or hotels for quick showers and fresh clothes before they met up at Page Field for a departure at one o'clock in the morning. Then they all collapsed in their seats to sleep for a few hours. The flight to Reykjavik was a little more than eight hours, so they used the Supermarkets Global 5000 jet that had more range.

They arrived with just enough time for a hot breakfast in the airport before they all marched upstairs to the conference room James Fitzgerald had arranged. James and the Sauvignons had already flown over on another private jet. They, and their small executive team, all looked fresh and relaxed when Suzanne started the meeting.

"Let's start with a page-by-page review of the offer," Suzanne said with a cheerful smile once they'd dispensed with greetings. "I've asked our chief legal counsel, Alberto Ferer, to build the offer around the conversations we had in China. Naturally, there were some tax and regulatory issues to consider, so I'll ask him to lead the discussions and address any questions or concerns that may arise."

Wilma was an observer of the proceedings for the next two hours as Ferer explained the proposed actions, welcomed discussion about any comments the Sauvignons might have, then listened to any concerns. At the end of his section, they had identified a dozen issues to solve. With a lawyer from Farefour, Alberto broke away as the larger group's attention shifted to the financial details.

Suzanne had assigned that responsibility to Wilma, and for almost two hours she walked through the economic components of the deal, noting and addressing issues as she went. After the finance part of the deal was reviewed by the whole group, Wilma broke away with the CFO of Farefour Stores to devise solutions that would be acceptable to both parties while Suzanne walked the Sauvignons through all the human resource issues including the management structure and reporting channels she envisaged.

The process continued that way—rotating narrowly focused discussion about individual business components—until Jean-Louis Sauvignon pronounced the deal satisfactory. He would recommend it to the board of directors of Farefour Stores the next day.

After their meeting, James negotiated use of the showers in the first-class lounge and suggested everyone might want to refresh before they headed out at midnight. Sleep would again be limited to naps on the corporate jets as the respective teams headed toward the south of France for the meeting of their lifetimes.

They'd have only one chance to convince the board of Farefour Stores that a merger was the best choice for both companies. Increasingly, both management teams were coming to believe it was the only choice. That conviction intensified when Dan Ramirez received a late-night secret call from one of his contacts in the rogue unit of the FBI. They all agreed their deal unquestionably needed to be done and announced before the markets opened Monday morning.

As Wilma Willingsworth fastened her seat belt for take-off, she thought about the irony and permitted herself a tiny smile. They should all buckle-up for the ride of their lives the next morning. It would be tough for any of them to sleep.

SIXTY-SIX

A palatial chateau, Avignon, France
Saturday March 2, 2019

James Fitzgerald was pleased with the welcome the group of over twenty participants received when they arrived at the massive chateau near Avignon in France's region of Provence. Everything was as he expected. After all, he had spent three hours on the flight to Iceland discussing the minutiae of preparations with Jean-Louis and Michelle Sauvignon. Every detail needed to be as close to perfect as possible to set an appropriate atmosphere for the high-powered business elite who were the board of directors of Farefour Stores.

The staff had neatly prepared the chateau's twenty-four bedrooms. When visitors started to arrive, it was too early to know whether anyone would actually sleep in them that night. That would depend entirely on the success of the negotiations, but Jean-Louis also wanted the participants to have private space available throughout the day.

All rooms were equipped with secure Wi-Fi. All were comfortable, welcoming spaces where directors could slip away from formal discussions to freshen up or talk privately with other parties. Although the directors had already been sworn to secrecy, Jean-Louis understood several directors had other masters to whom they must answer. The one representing France's largest bank surely could not make such a momentous decision without consulting at least the chair or CEO of his bank.

Exotic aromas of a deluxe breakfast tempted guests as they arrived. Gradually, they made their way to a huge dining room decorated with some of France's most beautiful oil paintings and furnished with meticulously restored antique furniture that may have once been used by royalty.

Michelle Sauvignon had notified her directors they were meeting to discuss an important business relationship with Multima Corporation, and her team had worked around the clock with Edward Hadley's communications team. Before dawn on Saturday, the directors all received emails including elaborate information packages about Multima, its management team, and detailed descriptions of its separate business divisions to study as they traveled to Avignon that morning.

Most were curious to meet their American visitors and used the minutes before their meal to circulate, introduce themselves and get to know Suzanne and her team better. That Suzanne grew up in Quebec and spoke French perfectly—albeit with a Quebecois accent—gave her an advantage. However, the elite board members all spoke English acceptably well and mingled easily with the other Multima executives.

James found it striking how quickly men and women succumbed to Suzanne's considerable charms. Her social skills were legendary and her ability to connect instantly with people was evident as she worked the room—meeting, touching, and talking briefly with each of the people she would soon need to persuade. One particular Farefour director caught James's attention and triggered some unexplained unease.

"Oh my God!" Suzanne shook hands uncertainly with Mathieu Dubois, the board representative for France's largest bank. "I read my briefing document but didn't realize it was you. What has it been, thirty years?" Jean-Louis Sauvignon immediately conferred on Dubois the honor of sitting next to Suzanne.

Jean-Louis spoke first when everyone was seated around the long, stately table adorned with mountains of food. He planned to speak in French as they'd agreed, but he first politely acknowledged his American visitors.

"Welcome to my humble abode." He bowed deeply to Suzanne and then to the rest of the group while everyone laughed at his gross exaggeration. "I am honored you have agreed to attend our important meeting, especially those of you who come from America. I beg your understanding for the reasons I'll address the room in French, but you are aware of the importance of these matters my colleagues will need to consider. I'll keep my remarks short for everyone's benefit."

His audience laughed again, probably to humor him. The old man also knew how to work the room expertly. He took a long look around the room, making eye contact with each of the directors before he started his comments in French.

"The food is getting cold, so I'll be brief. I know several of you made significant changes to your personal plans to be here. I truly appreciate you making such accommodations for an old man," he said with a crooked grin. "Before we eat, I want to explain the purpose of our discussion. I will ask you to listen carefully to a proposal Suzanne Simpson and her team will make.

"She'll provide all the details, but in simple terms, Multima is proposing to merge its business with Farefour Stores to create the second largest supermarket enterprise in the world. Such a proposal will require your careful consideration. Multima's team and your management group are prepared to spend as much time as you need today, and tomorrow if necessary. But we must vote on the proposal no later than midnight Sunday as other events are set to unfold early next week. If we choose to seize the opportunity, we must announce it early Monday morning. If you decide not to accept the offer, Multima must know our decision and chart a different course," the powerful leader stated emphatically.

Suzanne appeared to listen intently, but her disarming smile had faded and she looked uncomfortable for some reason.

"So, let's enjoy a good meal," Jean-Louis continued. "Let's get to know one another better, and consider the questions and concerns we'll ask Madame Simpson to address during her presentation. Suzanne, would you like to make any comments before we eat?"

"Only three quick points, Jean-Louis," she said in French. "First, I echo my profound gratitude for this opportunity to meet each of you to discuss our idea. Second, we'll do everything we can to be sure your investment of time in this meeting is also an excellent investment decision for Farefour Stores. Third, I realize it is almost a sin to force hungry people to listen to me talking while the aromas of a delicious meal beckon. *Bon appetit!*"

The group visibly relaxed as they shared a burst of laughter and repeated to each other the traditional French wish for enjoyment of a good meal. Almost immediately, hands reached across the table to pick up bowls of cooked foods, fresh fruits, and cereals while servers poured refreshments.

James was also relieved to see Suzanne's composure return as she appeared to engage in active conversation with her assigned seating companion. Conversations continued throughout the meal. James heard questions about the American economy, Multima's competitors, company policies and procedures, and some deeper inquiries to test Multima's values and business outlook.

Jean-Louis's strategy was off to a good start and he took pains not to rush the group off to a meeting room. In fact, breakfast took almost three hours as conversation continued and servers refreshed small, delicate cups with strong coffee.

Curiously, Suzanne and Mathieu Dubois left the table twice for brief conversations outside the room.

SIXTY-SEVEN

A palatial chateau near Avignon, France
Saturday March 2, 2019

Suzanne used a trip to the *toilette* as an excuse. She suspected Mathieu Dubois might seize that opportunity to squeeze in a brief private conversation in the corridor, well away from the ears of Jean-Louis Sauvignon and the others. So, she used the few moments of privacy in the bathroom to get her head around this unusual encounter.

She knew Dubois from her days at Stanford. With his now full beard and graying hair, she didn't recognize him from the briefing documents she'd studied flying over from Iceland. But as soon as she saw his charming, mischievous smile, she immediately identified him and made the connection.

His biography didn't mention Stanford of course. He flunked out during the first year after excessive partying and inadequate scholastic focus.

Instead, his resume highlighted his graduation from *Université Paris Panthéon-Sorbonne*. Apparently, he had enough money and family influence to attend the most prestigious university in France and graduate from the education hub of the country's business and governing class.

They hadn't been particularly close, but he was a member of the tiny Stanford francophone community. They socialized a bit their freshmen year. To be honest, their relationship was a little more than socializing. She slept with him a few times. They weren't an item, and they didn't have sex regularly. She was only nineteen at the time, adventurous, and it was the eighties, after all. She hadn't seen or heard from him since.

It was important to assess where he fit in the puzzle and whether she should treat him as a potential ally in the battle to come.

"What a delightful surprise to meet up again this way," Suzanne said with feigned enthusiasm as she came out of the *toilette* to see him leaning against the wall opposite smoking a cigarette.

"I'm surprised you recognized me. I surely show far more wear and tear on this body than you do. It's amazing. You look almost the same as you did thirty-five years ago—maybe even more beautiful if that were possible," he said with unabashed flattery.

"Oh, how I wish that could be even remotely true," Suzanne replied with a carefree laugh. "It might be time to change the prescription on those stylish eyeglasses you're wearing."

Mathieu took another draw on his cigarette, blowing the smoke he exhaled well away from her.

"It looks like you're going to make a monumental pitch when we finish breakfast," he said. "You know you're going to have an uphill battle, right?"

"Why do you think that?"

"The board is very divided these days. Jean-Louis didn't make any friends with his sabotage of Josef Aakker. Even his allies thought it rather crude how he dumped Aakker overboard to create a job for his daughter. She might be capable, but Josef was one of us."

"Do you think the board will judge an exciting new business opportunity based on what may have happened in the past?" Suzanne took care to avoid a confrontational tone.

"Maybe. We French are proud people. Our friends are very important to us and our memories are very long," Mathieu replied with a touch of menace surfacing. "You'll probably need some help to get done whatever you're proposing to us today."

"Can I count on our friendship for your support when it comes time to vote?" Suzanne asked directly.

"Maybe. Let's plan to have a drink after the formal session ends." Mathieu flashed his charming smile again. "Our bank values its relationship with Farefour Stores. We do the banking activities for all the stores in France. We'd really like to expand that relationship to all their stores across Europe. Maybe, we could chat about that sometime later?"

"Sure." Suzanne forced herself to match his charm with her own smile before returning to the dining room to rejoin the group.

SIXTY-EIGHT

A palatial chateau near Avignon, France
Saturday March 2, 2019

Finally, Jean-Louis invited everyone to the ballroom. James was amazed to find an ornately decorated room the size of some hotel meeting facilities with rows of crystal chandeliers and a huge oak table in the center of the room. A massive screen had been installed at one end and large comfortable chairs ringed the table with name cards indicating where each attendee would sit.

Suzanne strode to the end of the table and took her phone from a leather bag. Within seconds, the screen illuminated a PowerPoint presentation ready for delivery. The text was all in French. James only learned later that Suzanne had instructed Edward Hadley not only to prepare a presentation based on their agreement in Iceland only a dozen hours earlier but also to work with his communication specialists in their Canadian operations to have every slide translated to French.

The presentation was uploaded to Suzanne's phone only moments before they moved away from the breakfast table. She hadn't seen either a final English or French version of her slides before she started.

She delivered a performance many could never equal with days of preparation. Speaking entirely in French, Suzanne walked the group through the rationale for their proposal. She generously praised Farefour Stores management for their achievements. Their global reach. Their phenomenal technology in China. And their prudent foresight to prepare for diversification into financial services. She touched all the bases.

Then she segued into the benefits Multima could bring to a combined relationship. She highlighted their strength in financial services, and James felt a little embarrassed when she praised his efforts, although he could actually only understand his name. Suzanne also talked about Wilma Willingsworth and her accomplishments in the financial arena. The audience showed respect by their nods, broad smiles, or thumbs-up gestures of appreciation.

Using PowerPoint slides as her guide, Suzanne wended her way through their pitch for almost an hour, pausing to patiently answer any questions posed. At last, she got to the deal structure.

Looking at the English version of the slide on his own telephone, James noticed she planned to follow the path he first suggested to pique their interest and gradually reveal the specifics. She started with a comparison of the companies, emphasizing their similarities. Total sales were about the same. The number of employees was similar. Management structures were only slightly different. Even bottom-line profits were remarkably consistent. Suzanne didn't emphasize it in her tone, but the graphics reinforced that Multima was marginally bigger, more efficient, and more profitable.

Then Suzanne walked them through the new organization structure they had agreed upon in Iceland. Multima executives would dominate the company organization chart, but there would be no reductions in headcount at either the executive or store levels. Instead, surplus human resources would be redeployed into a rapid expansion of the newly created Farefour Financial Services across Europe, generating an additional revenue stream for the new entity.

Her presentation constructed the argument that Multima would be the surviving entity. Farefour Stores would keep its name and organization for the markets outside North America. The company would continue to trade on the Paris stock exchange. Michelle Sauvignon would continue to serve as CEO of Farefour's global operations. Even the directors would keep their jobs while Multima added a couple more to oversee its interests. But in the final analysis, Multima would hold fifty-five percent of the voting shares. Farefour investors would hold forty-five percent.

At that point, things derailed. James noticed an immediate cooling of interest. Eyes previously fixed on Suzanne darted around the room as though gauging how their colleagues were reacting to the suggestion. Suzanne noticed it right away.

She set down her phone and asked if there were any concerns with that component of the proposal. There were. She was bombarded by expressions of dissatisfaction. James couldn't understand the words, but he could feel the intensity. Suzanne had touched a sensitive nerve. This proud French corporation was to become subordinate to a slightly larger American entity with virtually no experience outside its domestic market. It was the one powerful point of resistance Jean-Louis had feared.

During their meetings in Iceland, Jean-Louis had warned that French patriotism was deeply ingrained in their culture. Likely, only he would be able to deal with it adequately. Suzanne promptly suggested they all take a short break before they discussed this vital concern.

SIXTY-NINE

A palatial chateau near Avignon, France
Saturday March 2, 2019

Jean-Louis Sauvignon couldn't stem the tide of objections to the proposed corporate structure. He not only agreed to the break Suzanne suggested but also told her they should take lunch before they resumed. Suzanne immediately accepted his suggestion.

With Suzanne's encouragement, the Multima and Farefour executive teams talked informally with individual directors about the parts of the proposal they liked. Some took walks in the cool outdoors. Others huddled around the large conference table in small groups. A few adjourned to the dining room to chat while they waited for food.

During lunch, Suzanne summoned the two management teams to the room assigned to her. They all stood in a semi-circle around her bed because there was no place to sit. She asked for feedback from the individual conversations. It became clear there was a slim majority of directors who strongly opposed the 'takeover' of Farefour Stores by an American company. On the other hand, almost all the directors liked the potential for success with such a merger. They agreed Jean-Louis and Michelle should take the lead for the session after lunch.

The afternoon was not productive. For more than three hours, several directors who strongly opposed the proposal dominated the discussion with theatrics and disparaging arguments. Jean-Louis tolerated the dissent and patiently tried to reason with the objectors, but logic couldn't overcome arguments grounded in emotion. Suzanne let the directors vent and left Jean-Louis in charge with his patience and calm reasoning.

They took another break for dinner. Jean-Louis thought a couple glasses of wine with a good meal might help a few directors to shift their views. While Suzanne doubted the likelihood of that happening, she understood the sanctity of eating to the French psyche. Hungry, there would be no chance of an agreement. With a glass of wine, the probability might grow marginally.

After dinner, Suzanne took the lead in the meeting room again. She used an old method she'd developed years earlier to try to influence the thought process. They all agreed to switch the discussion to English, and one of the serving staff found an easel with sheets of paper on it. Then she enlisted Michelle Sauvignon and James Fitzgerald to help her with the exercise.

"Let's have a little fun," Suzanne said. "I'd like to prepare a list of all the things about our proposal that you like. I'm going to name a component, James or Michelle will write it on our sheet of paper up here, along with the comments you share. When we think we've adequately discussed the subject, we'll vote on how to categorize it. Given the pros and cons, do we agree it's a reason to do the deal or a reason not to move forward? Once we vote, we'll tape the sheet of paper up for everyone to see. The wall behind me will show the reasons to do the deal. Over there will be reasons not to move forward."

The board members all laughed or cleared throats nervously at the suggestion. They'd probably all participated in these brainstorming exercises as students or in the early days of their careers, but not in the past twenty or more years. Possibly in polite deference, they followed her instructions. Within an hour, one wall was plastered with sheets of paper, the other almost bare.

"I think our pattern is clear," Suzanne summarized cheerfully well before the room might become annoyed. "We all agree there are far more reasons for the merger than against it. I also think we can sort out most of the points of contention. But I can't change the facts. We are an American corporation. Some of you are extremely proud of your French heritage. Let's think about it overnight. Respectfully, I ask you to seriously consider what is most important—a great opportunity for our respective shareholders or the country in which our new entity is headquartered."

Some directors moved to a sitting room where they enjoyed another drink or two, smoked cigars, and chatted. Others retired to their rooms where James supposed some would call their financial masters for marching orders while others would probably concentrate on a good night's sleep in preparation for the morning session.

For Suzanne and the team from Multima, it was an entirely different order of business. They convened in Suzanne's room, huddled around the bed, perched on chairs they brought from other rooms or sat cross-legged on the floor. She outlined the direction she wanted them to pursue. Then she asked James to spearhead the effort while she had another meeting.

SEVENTY

A palatial chateau near Avignon, France
Saturday March 2, 2019

Time was running out and Suzanne was no longer confident they could carry the day. Emotions and passion seemed just too strong. Regardless, she remained determined to win over the needed number of directors.

She would start with Mathieu Dubois, the board representative from France's largest bank. Suzanne's security detail kept a watchful eye down the hallway as she slipped into his room.

He appeared relaxed and had already shed his jacket and opened several buttons on his shirt. He had the window to his room open, but the smell of smoke was still overpowering, and he lit another cigarette as soon as Suzanne sat in the only chair.

"Thanks for coming," he said. "Would you like a glass of wine?"

"No thanks. I'd like to stay focused on your request to get together," Suzanne said formally to dissuade any ideas about other intentions. "How do you think it looks for our proposal?"

"It's a great proposal. You did a fantastic job presenting it. But it won't sell," he said without humor or sympathy. "You've underestimated French pride. We love our institutions and Farefour Stores is one of those we love best. You'll have to make your case a lot more compelling."

"How can we do that from your perspective?" Suzanne asked, choosing her words with care.

"I spoke with my chairman at the bank. He feels the only way we could support your proposal would be for you to give us something dramatic. Something we could use to show an expansion of French influence while we become subjugated to an American corporation."

"You're talking about the banking relationship?" Suzanne ventured.

"Yeah. If we could get all Farefour's banking activities on the continent, we could help Multima sell the positives of our relationship and point to things like our expanded French banking influence into other parts of Europe as reasons to support the deal." His smile appeared forced.

"I don't do business that way, Mathieu. You'll need to earn the banking relationship. That means you'll need to persuade Michelle and her team that your bank represents the best value proposition for the services you provide," Suzanne said.

She watched his manner change. The smile disappeared. He rose from the edge of the bed and casually walked across the room. There, he slowly picked up his phone from the night table beside his bed.

He pressed a couple keys and scrolled down until he found what he was looking for. Then, he faced Suzanne and held the phone at Suzanne's eye level to display a photograph.

It took a second or two to register but the photograph was her. Completely nude, nineteen years old and fully engaged in sex. She remembered the photographs. He swore he had deleted them, but this shot clearly showed her astride Mathieu's erect penis, which was deep inside her. Of course, his face didn't appear in the picture. No one would ever know it was him.

"How could you?" she spat out with a mixture of outrage and embarrassment. "You told me you deleted them all!"

She instinctively reached for the phone, but he swung away from her grasp, his expression taunting.

"No, getting angry and trying to delete it now won't help. Other copies exist, anyway. And don't scream out for your security goons. If they manhandle me, I'll just get this photo in circulation more quickly."

Panic, fear, and outrage flooded through Suzanne all at the same time. But she quickly regained perspective. He was right. Should she involve her security team, she would lose two ways. He probably would circulate the embarrassing photo, and she would certainly lose his vote on the merger proposal. There was little alternative. She'd have to negotiate.

SEVENTY-ONE

A plush penthouse apartment, Miami, FL
Saturday March 2, 2019

Janet shook Howard knight from his sleep with urgency amid the loud knocking. His watch showed the time was just past two o'clock in the morning. The insistent thumping continued.

"Open the door!"

Howard didn't bother to put on any clothes. If it was that urgent, they'd just have to cope with the sight of his naked and slightly paunchy body.

Steve waited outside the room. They hadn't seen their former minder since the telephone dust-up with the director of the FBI who subsequently ordered Steve re-assigned for his incompetence.

"Get dressed. Both of you," the agent instructed. "We have to move you to another location immediately. Shit's going down. We're leaving in five minutes. Don't pack anything."

Howard didn't know what to make of the order. He hesitated, trying to gather his wits about him, still drowsy.

"What do you mean we have to move to another location?"

"Just get dressed. We'll explain everything in the car. You too, Janet Weissel. I know you're in there," he shouted. "We need you at the elevator in five minutes. Like the Nike commercial says, just do it!"

They complied. What else could they do? Janet pulled on the clothes she'd worn the night before. Howard took time to get fresh underwear, socks, shorts, and a t-shirt.

They quickly brushed their teeth and snuck a quick kiss before opening the door to find three other agents in the room with Steve. All male. All big. And all heavily armed. Instead of a discrete bulge from an inside pocket of their jackets, these FBI agents looked more like a tactical squad from a local police department. And, just like the agents in Guantanamo, their fingers were coiled and ready.

One grabbed Howard by the elbow and started toward the elevator. Another seized Janet's arm and restrained her from following him. It took both agents' hands to subdue her as she protested.

"It's already been approved for us to stay together. The director signed off. He knows we're here together," she hollered trying to pry herself away from his iron-fisted grip. "Howard, tell them. This is all a mistake!"

Steve told her to calm down. "We have to transport you separately. We know all about the deal, but we're losing valuable time. Our orders are to transport you in two separate vehicles. You'll be humping each other again soon enough."

The elevator opened. Steve entered with Howard and a guard who restrained his arms for the descent. At the base of the elevator, there was another pair of heavily armed agents wearing night-vision goggles and scanning the area around the elevator in nervous spurts. They shoved Howard's head downward and pushed him roughly into the vehicle before Steve jumped into the front seat. Another agent rushed around the car and into the back with Howard. The driver pressed the accelerator to the floor, and they left the building with tires squealing.

As usual, his captors refused to answer questions. When he made a polite inquiry as to what was going on, Steve said, "You'll get answers to all your questions soon. Let us concentrate on the mission. My ass is on the line to get you there alive."

Surprise now turned to fear. What could possibly be going on that had these FBI agents in such a state of alarm? What could make it necessary to relocate them? Why was a move so urgent? The emotional roller coaster continued.

The previous couple days had improved measurably with emotional highs. He had been delighted when Arleen Woodhaus escorted Janet back to the plush Miami apartment. He had been even more thrilled when she rushed from the agent's side and wrapped her arms tightly around him and gave him what was probably the most passionate kiss he'd ever experienced.

Arleen eventually had to pry them apart. She had asked him politely to stay in his room for a few hours. They needed to interrogate Janet again. It had to be private. He needed to put on the television in his room, set the volume up louder than usual, and stay there until they completed the interrogation. Would he first like to get something to eat or drink?

It was longer than a few hours. In fact, Howard wasn't sure what time they started and ended, but other agents brought him pizza once and wine or cold drinks three different times.

Janet refused to tell him much about the interrogation or why it took so long, but she did say the FBI agents were almost giddy with the information she'd shared. And the Woodhaus woman apparently helped Janet a lot. They left her with the impression they were now anxious to move forward with the indictments quickly.

"It won't be long now," Arleen said to Janet as she hugged her goodbye. *So, what had changed?*

The car soon screeched to a stop at the harbor. All the agents opened their doors at the same moment, and Steve reached around the rear door to grasp Howard's elbow again. They ran down the board path from street level to the docks surrounding the harbored boats—all of them far bigger than the Carver yacht the FBI had provided him last year. An agent fired up one of the boat's diesel engines while Steve shepherded Howard below deck into a sleeping area.

About five minutes later, they led Janet down the hatch to the same sleeping quarters. The yacht was backing away from the dock before her feet touched the floor of the boat. They locked themselves in an embrace of desperation as soon as she reached the bed.

An hour later, Steve returned to chat.

"We'll be at sea for a few days. There's a major operation about to start. The director isn't taking any chances. Until they get the indictments and have the people behind bars, he doesn't want you anywhere close to accessible. See that helicopter up there? It, or another like it, will hover over us for the next two days. It's annoying, but they'll take out any vessel that tries to approach before it gets closer than two miles."

Naturally, Steve refused to answer any further questions. They'd get all the information they wanted in good time. *Que sera sera*. If his time was up, there couldn't be a better way to go. He wrapped his right arm around Janet's shoulder, tilted her head gently upward and started a long kiss, his tongue caressing the inside of her luscious lips.

SEVENTY-TWO

A chateau in the south of France
Saturday March 2, 2019

It didn't get any easier. The unpleasant encounter with Mathieu Dubois was just the start of an arduous night. As soon as Suzanne returned to join the group in her room, she found widespread discord. James and the rest of the team had argued with Alberto Ferer the entire time she was away. The chief legal counsel had dozens of reasons why her latest idea couldn't work. All his arguments were reasonable, his objections sound, his concerns genuine.

Suzanne restored order and focus quickly. She reminded them of the magnitude of their challenge and appealed to their desire to accomplish the ultimate goal. There was little to be gained by holding fast to intractable positions. They needed to find a solution for every one of Alberto's concerns. One-by-one Suzanne set out to tackle the obstacles and arguments.

The team stood or sat almost shoulder to shoulder in the tiny room, gathered around her bed, with someone's phone perched on a pillow in the middle. Apparently, even the wealthiest French citizens considered a bedroom to be used only for activities in bed and saw little need for empty space beyond it.

Although it was still cool outside, the room was hot, stuffy, and uncomfortable with so many occupants working under stress. Even after they opened the windows, Suzanne noticed beads of sweat around James Fitzgerald's brow. Her own hands often felt clammy. When they needed to have side conversations, Suzanne and her team had to whisper to avoid disrupting the flow and impeding progress.

Wilma was a great ally in the process with Alberto. She realized immediately where Suzanne was going with her questions, probes, and arguments and used her legendary knowledge of the stock markets and government relations to keep Alberto focused on the essential issues. Gradually Wilma wore them down with a judicious question here, an appeal for flexibility there, or an equally reasonable counterpoint when needed.

James had been lukewarm initially, and Suzanne wondered if that might be a reluctance to play too significant a role in a decision well beyond the scope of a consultant. But he warmed to the direction she pursued and ultimately posed the two questions that seemed to most noticeably influence Alberto's judgment.

"In the final analysis, does it really matter where the corporation is headquartered?" he asked. "Every jurisdiction will listen to any concerns we have about regulations, won't they? If we relocate and we're unhappy about the impact of certain laws or procedures there, is it conceivable they won't address our concerns?"

Suzanne noted the subtle use of 'we' and 'our.' Although James was technically a consultant, he spoke and acted like the ultimate insider and team member. Alberto contemplated the questions and weighed the intensity of James's passion. Eventually, he started to come around.

Alberto linked in four subordinates from his legal team and ordered them to stop whatever they were doing that Saturday evening to research securities regulations for the stock markets in France, the USA, and Canada. They all kept the speakers on their phones muted while they did their research so they could be back in the conversation at any time.

About three in the morning, Suzanne decided they should bring Michelle Sauvignon into the fray. Without her unqualified support, the new idea would be a non-starter. She agreed to join them and within minutes met Suzanne in the corridor outside the highly active bedroom freshly made up and wearing a new outfit.

Suzanne confided to her about Mathieu Dubois's malicious threat. Michelle was visibly shocked and admitted she didn't know how to react. She'd never trusted the guy, had never slept with him, and was surprised to learn he and Suzanne had been involved. Suzanne explained his demands and their negotiations while Michelle listened, her eyes downward and her shoulders slumped. She agreed to discretely share the information with her father while leaving out as much graphic detail as she could.

Suzanne carried on with the group conclusions as they wandered up and down the hallway talking in a tone just above a whisper. Michelle needed only a few moments to grasp the benefits of their new plan and was thrilled with the direction. She wanted to get her team involved because she wasn't yet familiar with French banking and stock market regulations. After all, she'd spent most of her past few years in China.

Another half-dozen people crammed into Suzanne's tiny room over the next hour or so, and the Multima team brought them up to speed on the discussions and the direction they were pursuing. After all the necessary information had been shared and absorbed, Suzanne recapped their intentions and watched each participant's body language intently for any signs of resistance.

There were a few questions—all of a technical nature and all reasonable concerns about reasonable issues. Suzanne was gratified to see emotion was not driving their thought processes and suggested they break into groups by function to get both teams working on other straggling challenges.

Michelle, James, Wilma, Alberto, and Farefour's chief legal counsel stayed in the room when the teams divided off by function and left for other rooms. With a glance at her watch, Suzanne realized that it was already about nine in the evening on the east coast of Canada and the USA. It was time to bring in one last important decision-maker.

Alberto Ferer used the sophisticated telephone system in Multima's headquarters to link in the prime minister of Canada. He was apparently enjoying a late dinner with his family in a Montreal restaurant when his staff reached him. It took almost a half hour to link his cellphone through a secure line in Ottawa.

Suzanne explained their idea as the dynamic young prime minister listened without interruption. She knew his reputation for quickly grasping complex subjects, retaining even the minutest details. So, she spoke concisely and rapidly, respecting every moment of his valuable time.

"I'm delighted to learn this information," he proclaimed when Suzanne was finished. "Yes, you can count on the Government of Canada. When I made the offer to John George last September, I had the full support of my cabinet. Nothing has changed. When would you like to make the announcement?"

"I'll present the idea to the board of Farefour Stores in about three hours," Suzanne replied. "If they agree, I'll need to formalize the approval with my board, but I don't expect any issues and hope to announce the decision before the stock markets open in New York Monday morning."

"Okay. Work with my people when you have the decision. Of course, I won't be there for the announcement, but my office will prepare a formal statement. Good luck with your meetings." With that cheerful farewell, the politician known for his sunny ways left the call to rejoin his family.

Michelle roused Jean-Louis Sauvignon about six in the morning. While Suzanne showered, her team worked with the Farefour management folks to put the finishing touches on the latest PowerPoint she would use to sway the reluctant board.

By seven that morning, Michelle, Suzanne, and Jean-Louis sat in the huge dining room drinking strong black coffee and munching on flaky croissants. The patriarch was quiet and projected an air of sadness when Suzanne arrived. He didn't speak until he took three or four sips of coffee and polished off a croissant.

"I am terribly sorry, Suzanne." His voice was barely audible. "I never meant for it to become this personal or so vulgar."

He looked only seconds away from tears. Suzanne reached out and patted the back of his hand, but she said nothing and tried to look composed. Michelle carried on.

"We both feel horrible and if you want to abort our plans, we'll understand." She gave Suzanne a meaningful look.

"No. I'd like us to carry on. Maybe one day I'll have to wake up to my picture splattered on Instagram or Facebook and feel the humiliation of lewd comments, but our project is too important to abandon. Let me tell you how we propose to break the impasse."

As she spoke a tiny smile formed on Jean-Louis's creased face, affirming Suzanne's suspicion that he liked her idea. He raised objections, of course. He asked pointed and well-informed questions, but as they worked through the issues and concerns, his tone became more positive, his eyes more alive, and his enthusiasm quite evident. In the end, he solemnly promised to do his best.

With Jean-Louis' support secured, Suzanne had one other urgent call to make. Lana was at John George's side in the hospital and responded when her cell phone rang. Yes, her father was progressing nicely, but he still had some difficulty forming words. The doctors assured him it would get better with time and treatments. She offered to wake him so they could speak.

A few moments later, Lana returned to the line. Suzanne supposed that rousing him from a possibly drug-induced sleep had not been as easy as expected.

John George was groggy when he answered but seemed coherent when Suzanne asked simple questions about how he was feeling. It was difficult to understand the precise words he used, but the message seemed one of positive hope. Satisfied his comprehension was adequate, Suzanne gave him a two-minute overview of what she planned to do. He listened without interruption or comment. When she asked what he thought about it, his response was simple and relatively clear.

"Good job. I agree."

When the entire group got together at eight o'clock for breakfast, they numbered twenty-four around the huge oak table in the ornate ballroom. Suzanne made her way to the massive screen as everyone settled in with coffee and more croissants.

She pressed a button on her phone to project the graphic one of Hadley's communication people had created just before the meeting started. Suzanne took a moment to admire both the graphic and the message she was also seeing for the first time. It showed the logos of both corporations as caricatures. Both logos were turned vertically on the screen instead of horizontally and appeared to have their respective 'arms' around each other in a symbolic embrace.

"Ladies and gentlemen, let's see if we can make that graphic a reality," Suzanne said in French with what she hoped was her most dazzling smile and welcoming tone.

"Our management teams have been busy the past few hours. We listened to the concerns you expressed yesterday. We thought carefully about ways we might accommodate those concerns while we work to create the second largest supermarket company in the world, with highly profitable financial services in both North America and Europe.

"We think our solution is a good one. It's a concept that will not entirely satisfy any of us, but it's a solution that can work. I'll explain the idea fully, then we'll spend as much time today as we need answering questions and discussing the proposal. As always, if you have better ideas to suggest, the management teams and I will welcome them and give them full consideration.

"But we ask you to reach a conclusion today. As soon as possible, but no later than midnight, we must insist you vote on our proposal. We passionately hope you'll decide in the affirmative, but we'll accept your decision either way," Suzanne emphasized. She took care to stretch her arms wide, make her smile bright and her eyes sparkling to underscore her warmth and welcome.

She took about thirty minutes to review the deal. Edward Hadley had reminded her every director would have forgotten some detail about the deal from the previous day. Some may have forgotten as much as eighty percent of the small specifics. So, she took time to walk them through the proposed structures and financial implications, careful to keep her pace deliberate and pausing often to invite questions or concerns.

Though it pained her to do it, she engaged Mathieu Dubois as politely, patiently, and warmly as the other participants. She made eye contact directly and tried to respond to his annoying questions and dubious objections as naturally as possible. Inside, she seethed.

As she approached the last slide, she became more encouraged. Most directors' body signals seemed more positive. They apparently liked much of the proposed deal and were guardedly waiting for her solution to break the impasse on the emotional issue that divided them. She didn't make them wait longer than necessary.

"We now propose to make the headquarters for the newly created entity in Montreal, Canada," she said avoiding any drama. "It makes sense. Even with the American tax reforms last year, the tax rate in Canada is marginally lower. Further, I spoke with the prime minister of Canada early this morning. His government is prepared to subsidize our tax rate further if we decide to headquarter in Montreal. Of course, I don't need to remind any of you that France's taxes are far higher than they are in both Canada and the United States.

"Neither the president of France nor our current American president will welcome the news if you decide to accept our proposal, but we're confident we can eventually placate both leaders and their governments. Business operations will remain headquartered where they are. Only my small group currently based in Fort Myers will move. Frankly, I expect to have the most vociferous complaints about a move from my staff. They probably won't like leaving sunny southwest Florida to relocate to sometimes frigid Montreal," she added with a tension-reducing chuckle.

The directors joined her in laughter. A couple even called out jests about how different the climates really were. It was a good reaction, and Suzanne paused to let the room relax more.

"I want to conclude by saying that I think this proposal is a great one for both companies. It's a deal we can all be proud of and one we can defend to our shareholders. I'm eager to get started tomorrow morning to bring two great organizations together to make one fabulous new company that will be admired around the world," she said in summary.

The applause started with Jean-Louis and spread around the room. No one cheered or whistled, but the clapping of hands was polite and lasted for about a minute. Not quite as long as Suzanne would have liked, but enough to let her know her modified proposal satisfied more than a few of the directors.

Jean-Louis moved to the head of the table as Suzanne dimmed the screen. He had no PowerPoint or other prepared materials. For an hour, he spoke from his heart with a mixture of fact, emotion, and passion. As he spoke, he walked around the table, looking at some directors directly as he addressed a difficult point. Other times, he'd reach out to put an arm around a director or give another shoulder a gentle squeeze. He talked about his first days as founder of the company and the support he'd received from the board throughout his tenure with the company.

He skillfully shifted from the past to the future and reminded everyone that Amazon was the competitor they needed to bulk up to compete with. He drew a picture of how chaotic the disrupting American superpower could make their business in the future. He passionately made a case for financial services as the ultimate differentiator from such a competitive threat. He ended with strong words of personal support for Suzanne and the Multima team.

"They are precisely the kind of partner we need."

He certainly delivered his best, as promised. When he finished, Michelle Sauvignon took over the discussions as they had agreed she would. The entire Multima executive team stayed utterly silent. Patiently, she worked her way around the table, encouraging every director to voice an opinion and share his or her concerns. It took almost two hours with a couple coffee breaks interspersed.

Every time there was a concern, it was Michelle who handled the response. She skillfully framed her replies in the context that she provided an answer based upon the issues as she understood them. She never once asked Suzanne to answer directly, nor did she draw upon her father. Clearly, she had decided to make this a conversation between her and her board of directors. The board appreciated her tactic.

By noon, objections became more muted. The passion had reduced. There were no signs of unusual tension or open indications of anger. At one point, she simply acknowledged the directors probably all had people they'd like to consult and proposed a two-hour break. They'd all reconvene for lunch at two. With their concurrence, she'd like to hold a vote. With nodding heads of agreement, they dispersed.

Jean-Louis Sauvignon personally greeted each director at the door as they returned from their break. It caused a line-up to get into the room, but the directors understood intuitively that they should have a word with him before the vote. His conversations were brief, but he was apparently conducting a personal survey of what direction the vote would take. He warmly thanked each director with a handshake and paternal pat on their shoulder to reflect his appreciation of their position.

Michelle asked for a consensus to vote on the proposal before lunch was served and nods again welcomed her suggestions. Michelle had two of the household staff pass around the proposal outlined in detail. It was twelve single-spaced sheets of paper for each director by the time the legal people had summarized every component of the deal. She gave the directors a further few moments to study it.

When she called for a show of hands from those who supported the deal, all directors but two raised their hands in approval. One of the dissenting directors was Mathieu Dubois.

SEVENTY-THREE

Paris, France
Sunday March 3, 2019

Within minutes of the vote, the group in France settled down to an elaborate luncheon served to perfection. For several hours, the directors washed down the food with bottles of the finest wines from Jean-Louis's cellar. Their lunch would extend for hours, and a few would stay the night because they enjoyed themselves too much.

Suzanne and the two management teams took their leave at the earliest opportunity. Private jets whisked them back to Paris. There, waiting limousines delivered them to Farefour headquarters. Their urgent mission: prepare for a dramatic announcement for the following morning. Within minutes of arrival, the office was a hive of furious activity.

Respectfully, Suzanne waited until four in the afternoon—Paris time—before her team started assembling a quorum of Multima directors in the United States to approve the deal. That still meant she had to roust the Bank of The America's CEO from his bed at five in the morning on the west coast of the United States.

They'd started preparing the announcement materials well before Suzanne confirmed the support of her board, and it was fortuitous they'd jumped the gun. It took almost twelve hours to finalize documentation for signing, prepare media releases in several languages, and extend invitations to influential French politicians to attend the announcement. There were dozens of details that needed the involvement of both teams and occasionally the intervention of Suzanne or Michelle to resolve issues quickly and amicably.

By midnight Sunday, they were ready. Suzanne and Michelle slept for a few hours at her place nearby. The management teams stayed at the Paris Hilton right beside the Eiffel Tower where they'd announce the merger to dozens of invited guests and the world's business media. All were grateful for the opportunity to enjoy a reasonably good rest. For Suzanne, it was her first full night's sleep in four days. That she'd survived through all the stress and fatigue amazed even her.

Everything went according to plan with the announcement. Jean-Louis thought it better he not attend, so he stayed in Avignon. With aplomb, Michelle and Suzanne carried out all the necessary media rituals and mingled with the dignitaries. Government leaders reacted with polite congratulations, and the media seemed jubilant about such a major story to start their week. Champagne flowed freely. Free food was devoured. Both Suzanne and Michelle circulated for an hour after the announcement, shaking hands, posing for selfies, and accepting congratulations.

By two o'clock, they were in a limousine on their way to the airport and the parked Bombardier Global 5000 jet. On the tarmac, they said goodbye, and both shed a tear or two. Their hugs were genuine and long. The mammoth achievement they pulled off would have been impossible without the unfailing support of her best friend from college. Even back then, they felt destined to do something genuinely remarkable together. But this deal was only possible because her friend was willing to take a subordinate role.

They decided they'd maintain a stalemate with Dubois. They wouldn't antagonize him by immediately canceling Farefour's relationship with his bank. But should photos of Suzanne ever surface, Michelle would cancel their agreement instantly. That would probably hold him in check.

Regardless, Michelle would have a much more significant role in running the new merged company than her title would suggest. Suzanne expected they'd have conversations at least weekly on a wide range of subjects affecting the company. Her friend's intellect was outstanding, her creativity unlimited, and her judgment sound. Eventually, they'd need to create an entirely new position for her.

On the plane, Suzanne's first inclination was to sleep but her team wanted to party. They broke out a case of champagne leftover from the announcement, and for the first two hours of the flight, joyous pandemonium ruled as they released weeks of pent-up tension. Champagne fueled their laughter, squeals of delight, hugs, and repeated congratulations.

The stock market in Paris reacted positively to the announcement. Shares in Farefour Stores soared almost twenty percent from the opening bell. Suzanne was equally eager to see how the New York market would react, so she pulled out her phone as they flew over Ireland. Multima Corporation shares were flat shortly after the opening. Not bad. Often a company making an acquisition saw its share value drop a few percent immediately after an announcement. Multima prices holding steady was a win.

Two other stories on her feed caught her attention and set her thoughts racing. "Dozens Arrested in Pre-dawn Raid" screamed a headline from the *New York Times*. A combined task force of FBI, New York State police, and New York City police had raided dozens of homes at four o'clock that morning in a coordinated effort that saw arrests of at least eighty people—many of them well-known business people from Wall Street and other prominent addresses in Manhattan. The Dow Jones Industrial Average was down almost fifteen percent as a result.

The arrests and indictments were part of a nationwide operation that had captured more than two hundred people associated with a criminal element known as The Organization. Among those in custody were politicians, judges, state government officials, and one individual identified as Giancarlo Mareno, reportedly the leader of the outfit. In an unusual step, the department of justice was requesting no bail for any of those indicted for a minimum of thirty days. Authorities expected to present evidence to grand juries powerful enough to deny bail until trial in most cases.

Suzanne's initial inclination was to raise her arms in a joyous squeal of delight, but she knew this was just the first step in the process. Dan Ramirez had warned her arrests would only be the beginning. She'd be patient.

Another story two squares down on her feed was equally captivating.

"Japanese Food Giant Buys Jeffersons Stores." The headline had no exclamation marks and type less bold than the story about Mareno's arrest, but it was even more intriguing. What had happened in the five days since the CEO of Jeffersons threatened her with an unwelcome takeover offer? The hunter was now the prey?

It became clearer. The picture of a broadly grinning Japanese executive was unsettling. Suji-san—the chairman of Suji Corporation—was pictured with David Jones of Jeffersons Stores at their Tokyo headquarters. The picture said it all with one telling detail. Both men faced each other, bowing in respect as most executives would at such a signing ceremony, but David Jones was bent over so fully his head was below his waist as he tried to look up at Suji-san who had barely tilted his head downward.

There could be no doubt about the dominant partner in that particular 'merger of equals' as The Times categorized it. Suzanne's unease grew as she read the story.

"This is just the first acquisition of many to come in America," Suji-san reportedly crowed to the assembled media. He intended to become the owner of the largest supermarket chain in America within ten years.

With a sigh, Suzanne made an entry in her phone calendar. Her first meeting the next day would need to be with corporate security.

ACKNOWLEDGEMENTS

My novels are truly a collaborative effort. The process starts with an outstanding team of editors who provide input and suggestions. I value their input more than words alone can adequately express. Kim McDougall, Paula Hurwicz, Mariana Abeid-McDougall, and Val Tobin all helped me to polish the story with critical editing and proofreading that improved my work beyond measure. All remaining shortcomings are entirely mine.

Next, I asked a few select people to read early drafts and give me critical feedback on content and specific industry knowledge. Heather & Dan Lightfoot, Andre Morin, Cathy & Dalton McGugan, and Cheryl Harrison all read early versions. Their incisive feedback and comments were of immense value.

Tracy Kagan (our daughter), and Murray Pollard (friend and former colleague) provided valuable insight about their personal experiences with breast cancer and inspired me to create more awareness about this insidious disease.

Castelane performed admirably. Special thanks to Kim McDougall for her patience, outstanding cover design and eye-catching book layout. Most important, I truly appreciate her pulling it all together with unmatched professionalism and continuous good cheer!

To my family and friends around the globe, thank you for providing a lifetime of support and encouragement. You're the ones who instilled my confidence that anything is possible with enough patience, determination, and perseverance.

FOLLOW GARY D. MCGUGAN

Facebook
https://www.facebook.com/gary.d.mcgugan.books/

Twitter
@GaryDMcGugan

Gary D. McGugan Website
https://www.garydmcguganbooks.com/

Instagram
Authorgarydmcgugan